Genevieve Lyons was born and educated in Dublin, where she began her successful career as an actress. She became one of Ireland's leading ladies, and was one of the founders of the Dublin Globe Theatre. Ms Lyons gave up her acting career to bring up her daughter Michele and has also spent time teaching drama and writing original plays for schoolchildren.

Ms Lyon's sixth novel, THE PALUCCI VENDETTA, is published by Macdonald, and she is currently working on her seventh, SUMMER AT DRANMORE, to be published by Macdonald Futura.

D0596914

Also by Genevieve Lyons from Futura:

GENEVIEVE LYONS

Zara

Futura

A Futura Book

First published in Great Britain in 1990 by
Macdonald & Co (Publishers) Ltd
London & Sydney

This edition published by Futura Publications in 1991.

ISBN 0 7088 4983 0

Printed and bound in Great Britain by
BPCC Hazell Books
Aylesbury, Bucks, England
Member of BPCC Ltd.

Futura Publications
A Division of
Macdonald & Co (Publishers) Ltd
165 Great Dover Street
London SE1 4YA

A member of Maxwell Macmillan Publishing Corporation

This book is for three wonderful friends:
Patsi, David O'B. T, and Peter Kurth,
with thanks

Prologue

This is Zara's story. I heard it from her own lips, listening attentively to her in the long summer twilight as the smell of roses filled her room, or through the dark autumn evenings while a bird sang its heart out in the tree beneath her window. And in the winter, which saw the end of her story, we hugged the fire as she disclosed to me, speaking as if in a dream, a world exotic and remote. This telling of her story started as a trickle and turned into a flood as our friendship grew. Until that last terrible night when I was sole witness to the final curtain.

Witness and party to a crime. Or was it a crime? You can be the judge of that. At all events, remorse does not bother me and I feel no guilt. I would do the same today given the same circumstances.

At first I did not credit much of the tale she told. It was too bizarre, too strange. Yet she told it with conviction, never contradicting herself, never faltering, each small piece adding to the jigsaw until at the end it all fell into place.

When I went to live at Oakwood Court in the fifties, I was trying to become a writer. I was, as I recall, and probably am still a listener by nature, a spectator, an observer. I am inclined to keep a low profile and people tend to overlook my presence. Thus, I was aware of Mrs Armitidge long before she was aware of me. The sight of her disappearing into her apartment, the distinctive scent of her perfume on the stairs, were soon noted by me.

7

Her apartment was underneath mine. I noticed her visitors – men, swarthy, Mediterranean types, middle-aged but somehow glamorous, their coats worn draped over their shoulders, their hands often bearing rings.

They came in a steady flow to her apartment, two or three a week. At first my fertile imagination leapt to the most obvious conclusion. And then I met her and that notion was swiftly banished.

How to describe her? It is difficult without resorting to cliché. She was then, I verified later, in her fifties. She was not pretty, but she was certainly beautiful. It was not an obvious film-star beauty; rather she caught and held the attention. She had mystery, she was intriguing.

Slim as a reed, always in black or sometimes wine-coloured velvet, she was literally a dark lady. Dark hair framed a tiny heart-shaped face dominated by enormous eyes. It was the eyes that were most arresting, that compelled you to look twice. They were curiously velvety, like a butterfly's wing, and their expressing was achingly sad. It was this sweet sadness that gave you the feeling you absolutely had to help her.

When she first fixed me with those eyes she was standing in her open doorway waving goodbye to one of the male visitors. I stood stockstill at the foot of the stairs, watching as if hypnotised.

"How do you do?" she asked in her deep, heavily accented voice, and held out her right hand. In her left was a tortoiseshell cigarette holder which held a black cigarette which she puffed continuously. I shook the proffered hand awkwardly.

"My name is Zara," she said, "Mrs Armitidge."

"I'm Janine and I live upstairs." I sounded out of breath and felt clumsy, pumping the tiny hand which resembled a child's but for its adult boniness.

"I know." She smiled. Her face lit up and sadness vanished from her eyes, like sun after rain. "Please come and have tea with me," she said.

"Now?"

She shrugged. "Of course. Or tomorrow. Or the next day. I'm always here." It was an opportunity not to be missed. I am nothing if not curious and this woman was obviously exceptional. Everything about her riveted my attention.

"Now," I said nervously, "if that's all right?" She bowed graciously and ushered me in.

The room I found myself in was comfortable but oddly impersonal. The furniture did not seem to me to fit with the personality of the woman. It was heavy and the colours sombre. My interest was caught by the icons on the walls. She saw me looking at one of them particularly. I gazed at the beautiful face of the Virgin, the cool expressionless eyes and etiolated nose giving the face an intrinsic purity which was highlighted by the gold of the icon. Beneath it on a little shelf was a tiny crystal glass containing a red rose.

"You chose the best," she said. "That one is by Andrea Rublov. They could be picked up for a song in Paris in the twenties. Russian emigrées traded them for bread. That one is priceless."

I listened. It was what I did best. I had found out in that first visit one thing. That she was Russian, a White Russian.

I wondered about the picture in an ornate silver frame of a dashing, wickedly handsome man in an RAF uniform. His buccaneer grin so drew my attention that twice I did not hear what she said and had to ask her to repeat herself. It annoyed her slightly.

We had tea. She made it herself at the table beside her chair using a large exquisitely wrought samovar. She served the tea with lemon.

I took to dropping in to see her often after that. She liked my company, she said, and loved to reminisce. We became quite close although there was something about her that forbade real intimacy.

Our friendship developed and little by little she began to

9

talk about her past, drawing back the curtains on a life that astounded me. I accepted it all. She was so obviously no liar. The details matched every time, for she often repeated herself. The better I knew her the more I realised that her adventures had formed her. She was passionate, melancholy, gallant and fatalistic. The world she came from was a world where murder, intrigue and death had a viable place. It was a world foreign to me but one with which I became familiar as I grew to know her. It was a world which fascinated me and I was more and more intrigued by it as she led me into the dark labyrinth of her past.

PART I
Russia

Chapter One

As a child Zara lived mostly in apartments in the Alexander Palace in St Petersburg and the Summer Palace at Tsarskoye Selo, some fifteen miles south of St Petersburg. Her family had besides a house on the banks of the River Neva and a hunting lodge far north of Pesochny, shrouded in dense forest.

She had known the glory of St Petersburg but she remembered only the dark side. Yet the city was a place of light and the palaces, Rastrelli's elegant creations, golden and beautiful. Peter the Great, who had made it his capital, insisted all the houses should have gardens, and Catherine the Great asked that the residences should be painted different colours. They delighted the eye, those elegant stone houses painted pistachio green, powder pink, sky blue, primrose and *eau-de-nil*. They were cool pale colours against the Northern sky and the Neva, flowing past, carrying on its pale grey bosom snow-floes from the frozen Lake Ladoga.

Memory, said Zara, played strange tricks. She had returned to Leningrad, as it was now, her heart a stone within her. She had discovered a city of pale, clear light and delicate beauty, but in her memory it was always cold and dark. Or at least in her nightmares.

She had gone back to the Alexander Palace where she had once lived. It was now a museum and she an ordinary tourist. She had wandered through the golden rooms and

13

recognised none. They were hung with paintings and had that unlived-in air common to such institutions. She remembered voices and in her mind's eye saw tangled limbs, amber-lit on silken sheets. She shivered at the memory.

She had always been afraid of her step-mother, a woman of dark temperament, tempestuous anger. She had once heard her father say: "You are a disgrace, Anya. If you are not careful I'll pack you off to the Convent at Smolny."

Her step-mother had laughed. "You would not dare!"

Anya was a violent woman who often struck the small Zaroushka, as she was always called then. Zaroushka barely minded. Anya's blows were at least a manifestation of feeling and the small girl often felt lost and isolated in the bewildering world which surrounded her. In the circles she inhabited children were seen as unwelcome interruptions, little incursions into the unfolding drama of grown-up life. It was a world of violence, glimpsed through half-open doors or semi-drawn velvet curtains. Down echoing corridors Zaroushka heard angry voices raised to curse; screams in the night. All her memories were cloaked in terror. Only Maminka was warm and large and comforting, Maminka who had nursed her and bathed her in infancy and was the only predictable and permanent factor in her life.

Zara's mother had died in childbed and the baby, a boy, an heir, died too. Her father, Prince Alexei Alexandrovich Vashinskov, had married again. His second wife Anya, half-Polish and half-Russian, a princess with glittering connections, stormed into Zara's life when she was three years old. Maminka said privately that she was evil and had put Zaroushka's father under her siren spell.

"For no mortal woman could behave so," Maminka sighed, "or change a man so drastically."

The Prince, once a benign and jovial giant who came to kiss Zaroushka goodnight, and who always chuckled and allowed her to play with his watch and chain, for a time had become an angry preoccupied critic who could not bear her near him. The memories she brought back of his first wife were too painful for him to bear, he said. He was nervy and jumpy and often absented himself from home or the apartments in the Alexander or Summer Palaces. He could not easily put up with Princess Anya's flagrant infidelities, and so he ran away.

As she grew older, Zaroushka realised that her step-mother took lovers. She was a voracious man-eater. The Prince was too proud to allow the taint of divorce to blemish the family name. Besides, Princess Anya had become great friends with the Tsarina. They were distantly related and Alexandra was an hysterical, foolish woman who could not keep a level head and was an appalling judge of character. At least that was Maminka's opinion.

Prince Alexei wanted to send Anya away, to the convent at Smolny or even better back to her family in Poland but he was frustrated in this desire by the Tsarina's devotion to her. Princess Anya would have caused an unholy fuss if her husband even hinted at such an eventuality. Everyone knew how tenacious Her Imperial Majesty could be when her friends were threatened; the whole Court had tried to get rid of the monk, and look what had happened. The evil man was still there, and the people who had tried to bring about his downfall all banished. So Anya took her lovers and the Prince remained, for the most part, away from home.

There was no reassurance in Zaroushka's life. She lived in palaces too large to fathom, constantly losing her way in dimly lit, echoing corridors. The only comforting place she remembered living was the hunting lodge, Danya Bolovna. The dense forests which surrounded it were magical in the snow, and it was the place where she always saw her father. Away from the evidence of his wife's adultery, Prince Alexei was again a relaxed and loving father. She prized her visits to him there, despite the dangers that must be run. And there were wolves. You could hear them howling at night when the wind blew in the right direction. Anya never went there. She found it too isolated. She liked crowds and parties, balls and entertainment.

Once when the small Zaroushka was bound for the lodge, wolves had chased their troika.

It was night. The train had been late. The sky encrusted with stars was a deep cobalt blue. Zara was wrapped in Maminka's shawl, her face pressed to the large soft bosom. Her face was cold, the rest of her warm against the vast body of the servant. She had been content, up later than usual, knowing she would soon see her papa.

Out of the night they had come, howling, tearing along beside the troika. They had circled the vehicle and Maminka had screamed and lost her head. She had stood and that was a stupid thing to do in a troika. Piotr had kept his, thank God. He had beaten off the wolves with the whip in one hand whilst he shot at them with the gun in the other.

For the small Zara it was the first of many fearful memories. She could smell Maminka's fear-sweat and feel her heart thudding beneath her cheek as she shrank lower and lower beneath the sheepskins that covered them. She could see the thick white snow stretching into the horizon and the gaping bloody hole in one wolf's throat, the stinking intestines of another, the spattered brains of a third. She could see their slavering jaws and cruel teeth, hear their howls and whining, feel their hot breath on her cheek. She had shivered and shaken in fear, too afraid to cry.

But Piotr won in the end. He was a big man and very brave. He said they had been saved by the skin of their teeth.

"If there had been one more, just one, we would all be bloody corpses now, lying there with the carcasses of their brothers in the snow," he said with relish.

"Hush!" cried Maminka. "The child."

She covered Zaroushka's ears with her hands and pulled her fur hat closer over her head and they all three stared at the bodies of the slaughtered wolves and at the snow drenched with blood. Then Piotr cracked his whip and they hurried onwards through the night.

The Prince was waiting for them. He stood in the entrance hall in front of the fire, smoking his pipe, a sure sign that he felt relaxed.

"Papa, Papa," cried Zara, flinging herself into his arms.

"Hold on, *devachka*. Tell me what the matter is?"

He scooped her up into his arms and held her close. The fabric of his jacket was rough against her face but she felt so safe, so protected in the circle of his arms. As the terror left her she was swept away on a tide of tears.

"What is it, *golubchick*? Tell Papa."

"The wolves … the wolves …" was all she could get out.

Maminka, carrying in the basket containing Zaroushka's clothes, had to explain their adventure. The Prince listened attentively: Maminka was prone to exaggeration. Zaroushka was grateful for the retelling. She snuggled up to him, glad of the closeness, and when Maminka was finished wallowed in his comforting. He said she was his brave little girl, his *devachka*, and fed her Turkish Delight. He praised Piotr for his bravery and presence of mind and gave him a rouble and a pair of boots. To Maminka he gave a beautiful new shawl from Nevsky Prospekt. She nearly died of joy.

For a few days after that Zaroushka was in seventh heaven. She sat in front of her father on his Arab stallion and rode through the snow, her face rimmed in fur and cheeks red from the sharpness of the air. Sitting there like a queen, she did not worry about wolves.

They rode across a grey and white landscape, the tall naked trees standing sentinel in serried ranks, black lines against the ice-blue sky. They rode through the forest. The ground was uncluttered for the trees were densely interwoven overhead, like the aisle in St Basil's Cathedral. Zaroushka loved these rides with the wind whistling, a wild and lonely sound, and snow blanketing the earth, and laughcd and waved when she saw the black silhouettes of fellow-travellers in the swirling white world. If they saw the Prince on his horse with his little passenger, they returned her wave and she felt warm inside.

Over the door at Danya Bolovna there was a bronze double-headed eagle. One head represented God and the other Civil Life, her father said. It was the symbol of the Russian Monarchy. The effigy frightened Zara but when they returned from their rides and Maminka brought them the *tête à tête* teaset, gold-plated on a tray of mica, she forgot her fear for she would have tea with Papa. It was a two person teaset, meant to be shared with a loved one. The "selfish" teaset had a prettier design but it was only for one.

"You'll never forget how old you are, Zaroushka," said her father one day. "You are the same age as the century. Let me see … it is the year 1909 which means you are nine years old, *golubchick*." He chucked his darling under her chin and Zara felt cocooned in the warm circle of his love.

The rooms at Danya Bolovna were candle-lit, yet she always remembered it as being bright there. It was the high-ceilinged rooms at the palace that dwelt in perpetual shadow. Her father told Piotr, "The wolves are out tonight – lock up the animals". She was not afraid for her father was there so how could anything hurt her? He promised he would shoot a bear and she cried and begged him not to.

One night she saw caravans in the snow outside. Brightly dressed women were moving over the sparkling white surface. The gypsies came to the kitchen that night and the Prince asked them up to the big hall to dance and tell fortunes. Zaroushka had never seen anything like the gaudy clothes they wore. Yellow and red, bright blue and cerise, their skirts glittered with little mirrors sewn into the centre of embroidered flowers. The mirror circles drew piercing shafts of light from the candle flames and shot them back like torches.

The gypsies' eyes were black and impudent. They wore bracelets on their ankles that jangled when they danced. Zaroushka sat on her papa's knee while the gypsy girls formed a circle in front of the log fire and stamped their bare feet on the stone flags of the floor, shaking their tambourines. Papa laughed at their songs. The men wore animal skins over their shoulders and smelled ripe and oniony. Maminka brought slivovitz for the gypsies and hot chocolate for Zaroushka.

But the following day *she* arrived. Anya was in a worse temper than usual, having been forced to flee Petersburg. Servants' gossip had it that she had lost her latest love, the son of Prince Boris Valenski. Prince Boris, a powerful man in his own right and not dependent on Royal favours, had arrived unheralded at the love nest and seized the youth, naked as a baby, plucking him from Anya's arms. He had threatened the Princess that he would shoot them both if he ever found his son alone with her again. Anya was humiliated, and now she took out her rage on everyone in Danya Bolovna.

That night Maminka snored on her mattress at the bottom of Zaroushka's bed. Zaroushka thought she would suffocate. The room was sealed against the cold and strongly smelled of Maminka's sweat. Normally Zaroushka did not mind, in fact she liked the warm body-smell, it reassured her when she was scared.

This night, however, she was physically revolted by the smell of her servant. She knew it was because of her step-mothers unexpected appearance at Danya Bolovna. Her arrival had disturbed the even tenor of her tranquil days with her father and set her at sixes and sevens.

Zaroushka opened the window. Danya Bolovna was built of wood, an old chalet with a balcony running around the upper storey. A cold blast of wind greeted her and she drew in her breath sharply. The air smelled of pines and was sweet in her nostrils. The world below was blanketed in snow that shimmered under the stars. The stillness soothed her troubled spirit.

Her peace was shattered almost immediately by the crash of breaking glass. She jumped back from a spray of flying shards as the window from a room further down the balcony shattered. It was her father's room.

Zaroushka could hear loud voices: Anya's and the Prince's. She crept along the balcony, trying to keep her bare feet out of the bitterly cold snow. She could not see anything, only hear the angry voices.

"Why do you always lie to me? Have you ever told me the truth? Do you know what the truth is?" It was her father's voice.

"I lie because there is nothing more. Don't you see? I'm empty, drained of everything but boredom." Anya's voice was cold with anger as she continued: "It's your fault. You'll never understand. You are too ... honourable." Zaroushka could hear the hiss in her voice. "Always the 'right thing'. God, it drives me mad!"

"You'll be the ruin of us, Anya." The Prince's voice was despairing.

Anya laughed, that cold tinkling sound that made Zaroushka shiver. "Ruin? But that is my aim, you stupid man! I hate you, don't you know that?"

Zaroushka trembled. She would have liked to kill her step-mother. How could she say such horrible things to Papa?

"But why, Anya? I have never understood why. I have never harmed you. What have I ever done that you should hate me so?"

"You have never satisfied me, you fool! Half of St Petersburg has plundered my body and yet you do *nothing*. You run away. I despise you, do you hear?"

Zaroushka did not understand what they were talking about. She simply recognised the anger, the hatred, in their voices. She jumped now as she heard her father cry out in anger and frustration. "Well, my lady, I'll plunder you tonight. Slut! Slut!"

Zaroushka thought he was crying there was such pain mixed with the anger in his voice. She heard a table crash and something break. She raised herself on tiptoe and looked into the room. She saw her father leaning over Anya on the bed. Her step-mother's dress was torn and she was struggling and her father seemed to be shaking her, jumping on top of her. Zaroushka hoped he was killing her. She would have liked that better than anything else.

She heard another noise and turning her head saw Minimka half in and half out of the window further down the balcony. She was struggling and seemed to be stuck. Her broad face was angry and she vehemently beckoned Zaroushka to return to her.

The child tried to obey but she found it difficult to move. Anya's screams of protest had turned into something else: animal cries that frightened and repelled her. But she was so cold, her bare feet so numb, that though she tried to escape those horrible sounds from her father's room she found she could not compel her body to obey her. Maminka, propelled by anxiety for her charge out in the freezing night and what the Prince would say if he ever found out, succeeded at last in squeezing her bulk through the window. She waddled down the balcony and, grabbing Zaroushka's arm, dragged her back to her room. She pushed the girl in through the window.

"Unlock the door in the corridor that leads out here," she ordered. "At once, unless you want me to die out here in the snow."

Zaroushka could not feel her feet but she managed somehow to unlatch the door and let Maminka in. The old soul took Zaroushka to the kitchen and put her in water so hot that she wept. She scolded her charge roundly, keeping up a monologue of complaints until Zaroushka was warmly tucked up in her bed again.

21

And still she could not sleep. She kept hearing the voices of her father and step-mother raised in anger which had changed to ... what?

The next morning the Prince left for Petersburg and Zaroushka was ill and had to stay in her bed for a week. Hot and feverish one moment and chilled to the bone the next, with her father's absence her fear of the wolves returned.

Whenever she closed her eyes the image of their red eyes and their pointed fangs, the obscenity of their broken bleeding bodies in the snow printed themselves across the dark interior of her eyelids and her nights were filled with terror.

"You will be the ruin of us Anya." Zaroushka could hear her father say.

His words echoed in her head along with the answering peal of silvery laughter.

When her fever was over they returned to Petersburg. Princess Anya was bored away from the capital. She had forgotten the boy in a week and longed to recommence her hectic life there. So the servants packed their bags, and they went to the Alexander Palace. Since her experience in the snow Zaroushka observed her step-mother with new eyes. She knew now that the Princess hated her papa and was determined to keep watch on her.

What she saw frightened and fascinated her.

It was because they dwelt in the Palaces that she saw some of the things she did. The huge buildings were badly laid out, the bathrooms situated at a distance from the bedrooms, and Zaroushka was always sick with dread that at night she would have to relieve herself. As a consequence rarely a night passed without her having to get up and pad, in her nightdress like a wraith, down the echoing corridors. The sights she saw disturbed her dreams and troubled her.

The visions came back to her in her waking hours and she found it difficult to look people in the eye.

Once she saw her step-mother bathed in golden light from

dim lamps, her amber hair unbound, naked body pearly white, shadowed with dark hair. Breasts like globes bounced as she moved over someone prone and white-fleshed beneath her. She shouted through red lips, "Ride, ride, ride!" and struck with her fists, not seeming to mind the red hair that caught between her fingers was her own as she hit the face that lay half-turned to the light and tore her own hair out by the roots. She cried out and arched her back as if someone had shot her shoulder blades then dropped, inert, on to the white body beneath her.

Zaroushka nearly cried out when she saw a slim red trickle of blood run down the cheek of the man lying there on the red brocade of the *chaise-longue*. She saw it was Andreas Lemcov, a young Officer in the 8th Brigade of Guards. For a long time she paused, shivering in her nightgown, too fascinated and repelled to move from the golden scene splashed with blood.

Zaroushka forgot her full bladder and hurried back to bed.

She shook Maminka who was in her usual place fast asleep at the foot of her bed.

"Maminka, Maminka."

Zaroushka described as best she could what she had seen happen on the scarlet couch. The old woman laughed.

"Aye. Aye child. They were only ..." she used a rude word Zaroushka did not understand but had heard her father rebuke Piotr for using. "It was passion," Maminka continued seeing her look of incomprehension, "Love. The way of the beasts of the field and a man with a woman. In season. Except that your mother is always in season. She is a cat on heat at all times of the year." And she laughed a coarse laugh that Zaroushka did not like.

"Do not call her that," she cried.

"What? A cat on heat? Well, she deserves it." Maminka looked stubborn.

"No, no. My mother. Do not call her my mother. She is

23

not." Zaroushka's face was red at the insult and she was near tears.

"Ah, hush, hush, *golubchick*." Maminka cradled the child in her arms and soothed her with crooning sounds and chatter. "Ah Zaroushka you have had a shock. It is not good for a *devachka* to see the things you see. You are only nine years old after all and still a child. Aye, aye, aye." Lulled by the monologue and the warm closeness of Maminka, Zaroushka fell into a troubled sleep.

Their rooms were, in her memory, always dark and high-ceilinged. Fires burned in the grates, fires that cast leaping shadows on the walls and hissed and crackled in the dark. The logs cried out in pain and protest as they burnt. Maminka said that the living wood whimpered when you set it on fire and Zaroushka often shrank against the wall at night listening in horror to the logs crying in pain. She preferred the stoves.

She kept imagining she had seen the worst her stepmother could do only to be surprised and shocked all over again, for Anya's single-minded pursuit of pleasure left her oblivious to the usual promptings of discretion.

On another occasion firelight painted a scene from hell, or what Zaroushka imagined hell looked like. This time she found herself standing trembling in the arched entrance to a room full of flickering ruby shadows. The patterns of crimson and gold leaped and shimmered across the beautiful tiger-face of the Princess Anya. She stood in a golden robe, stiff-embroidered in amber and scarlet thread, which fell from neck to ankle. It was wide open, revealing her long sleek legs, the hard flat stomach, the out-thrusting breasts, the dark mass of groin and the pinpoint of silvered hollows in belly and throat.

She had a whip in her hand. It looked to Zaroushka like her father's walking stick with a long snake attached, a curling, live snake that wound its length about the body of the young man who cowered before her, naked and trembling. Along the creamy surface of his skin the coil of horse-hair had left a pattern of blood, a surreal design that seemed almost a decoration. Anya's lips were drawn back over her teeth and she seemed to her step-daughter a devil in a flame-filled inferno.

The girl gave a cry of horror and the whip paused in its snake-dance around the pale body and fell, losing momentum, lifeless to the floor. Zaroushka took her eyes from it only to meet the golden eyes of her step-mother who was looking at her with a wild stare that terrified Zaroushka half to death. The child put her hands across her mouth to stop herself from screaming. In two strides the Princess was across the room. She hit Zaroushka across one cheek with the palm of her hand and across the other with the back of it. Then she pulled a velvet curtain across the archway and shut the scene from Zaroushka's sight.

She stood there, quite still, not making a sound, not crying. She heard the whistle of the whip once more, singing through the air, then she left and went back to Maminka.

The old woman was waiting for her. The child frightened her, she was so pale and still.

"And what have you seen this time? For you've seen something I'll be bound by the look on your face," the old nurse asked her. She put her arms around Zaroushka and found the child was shaking like a leaf. "My God you have the palsy. Sit. Sit here, tell your old servant everything. From now on you'll have a pot in the room, under the bed. I do not care what the Prince or the Princess thinks or what they command. You'll have a pot and not go wandering around the place seeing scandalous sights and having nightmares."

Zaroushka told her what she had seen and her nurse made no effort to explain to the little Princess for truth to tell she did not understand it herself.

"Aye, we should have had her with us the night of the wolves," she said, "She would have torn their throats out and drunk their blood. Ach!" She shook her old grey head and added, "Well, Drushenka tells me that the witch is pregnant. She says she got into that state in Danya Bolovna, but I would not like to hazard a guess who the father really is. I don't think either God or the devil knows that. But my fine lady will not be able to carry on any more, I think."

But she did. Her belly swelled, its hard surface little by litle becoming distended, and still to the scandal of the Court Anya went her turbulent wilful way, unheeding, uncaring. And still the Tsarina refused to listen to the gossip about her friend.

Zaroushka liked the idea of having a little half-brother or sister.

"The witch will not want it, I am certain," she said to Maminka. They always called her 'the witch' when they were alone.

"I can care for the baby, like you care for me. I will be its Mama. It will be lovely, someone all my own."

For she had no one other than Maminka. Her father was not in Petersburg or Tsarskoye Selo. Precocious, she haunted the corridors, constantly being shooed out of sight by footmen or maids, always solitary. Governesses came and went with monotonous regularity. For the most part they were French and hated the climate, and the boredom of the Russian Imperial Court. In a very short time they found the Princess's behaviour intolerable, broadminded though they were in the main. The bizarre atmosphere around her was disturbing. The governesses went back to Paris with little recollection of their quiet charge, glad to reach civilization again, and with the totally erroneous idea that the Princess Vashinskova was a typical Russian.

"There goes another one," Maminka would say, "sure that the Russians are devil-ridden because of the witch. Ay, ay!"

Sasha was born, a beautiful child. Zaroushka was not allowed to see him at first. She found out that she had been wrong about the witch for Anya worshipped her son and kept him near her as much as she could. And Zaroushka, when she saw her little brother, instantly became his slave. All her pent-up loving-kindness was poured out now that she had something to look forward to, a focus in the hitherto aimless sea of her life. The fact that her step-mother's maid Drushenka was old and tired and often lacked energy enough for the baby made it possible for Zaroushka to make herself indespensible. She spent hours playing with the tiny child, her heart filled to bursting point with a love she had never believed herself capable of. She'd always believed she loved her Papa, but saw that it was more like adoration for he was so remote and often, like now, she did not see him for months. But here was her baby brother, sweetsmelling, fresh and soft, needing constant attention and returning her love in a hundred ways. Why, he smiled now when he saw her, a special smile for her alone.

Her father these days was busy with the 'dangerous political situation', Maminka said. In Moscow there was rioting in the streets, and there were conspiracies and secret meetings. The government was worried and the Prince had informally been requested to stay there and keep an eye on the situation. Besides, he liked to keep far away from his wife. But he came to see Zaroushka occasionally and those were good times. She sat on his knee and played with his watch as if she were still six years old. He would sigh and ask if she were happy. The conversation was always the same.

"Yes, Papa. Lonely, though, Sasha is adorable but he is so little. And Mam'selle has gone home and I have no one to talk to. I would so like a friend."

"Well, we must see about that. You shall go to your cousins in Moscow this summer. It is difficult, you understand. Your step-mother has to be at Court. The Tsarina will not make a move without that mad monk and Anya. What taste, God help us! But, my child, we'll get you another governess and soon you shall visit your cousins."

Zaroushka swiftly realised these were empty promises. It was not Papa's fault. She was such a small part of his life, she knew. He was up to his neck in saving Russia from the new and disturbing elements that threatened her sovereignty and therefore her stability.

He said to her one day, "When it comes it will be the end of the world as we know it."

She was not sure what 'it' was, but felt sure that it must be better than life as she lived it now.

Sasha grew strong and sturdy and played heedlessly around the grown-ups. He was never scolded as Zaroushka inevitably was. Doubts had been cast on his paternity. Nothing was publicly said; Anya's position at Court made that impolitic. If you wanted to find favour there you were obliged to cultivate her friendship. Zaroushka remembered the darkness of the night at Danya Bolovna and her father's voice: 'Well, my lady, I'll plunder you tonight'. She kept her own counsel.

Now twelve years old she was tall for her age, dark-haired, dark-eyed and thin as a starving cat, Maminka said.

Sasha at two was round as a butter-ball, blond as a buttercup, blue-eyed and spikey-lashed. He dimpled everywhere: his cheeks, his knees, his chin, his elbows. His laughter comforted the lonely girl, his plump clinging arms unlocked the floodgates of her love and her heart opened to her chubby little brother. For the first time in her meagre existence she knew unconditional love and the exchange of real affection.

Maminka had always been there for her but the nurse was a little stupid, a little coarse. She was an earthy woman, a peasant, and it was on a primitive basis that Zaroushka loved her. She needed Maminka for warmth and physical content. Maminka provided food and hugs, she bathed Zaroushka at night in the tin tub behind the Chinese screen and comforted her when she had nightmares. But she often frightened the little girl with her scary tales and horror stories. For her the world was very simple. She saw things in two shades: black or white. Things were either good or bad. You sinned, you were banished from God's favour; you were good and you went to Heaven, or were happy here on earth. Zaroushka knew this was not true. Her father was a good and honourable man yet anyone could see how he suffered.

Sasha, though, was the sun. He was light and laughter. He was sweet smells and tranquility. Even Anya when she was near him was benign. She lost her brittle edge and became soft. Zaroushka was surprised at her step-mother for up 'til then she shared Maminka's opinion of her as a totally evil woman. Watching her lean over Sasha and play with him, her face clear of guile, her love for her son visible for all, Zaroushka did not see the woman she had always hated.

And so the year passed: Zaroushka and Sasha playing together while Anya plundered the Tsar's soldiers for younger and younger lovers, while the Prince planned strategy and preached conciliation as the storms gathered ominously over Russia.

Chapter Two

It was one brisk spring morning that Maminka came rushing to Zaroushka to tell her the Princess wanted to see her. Zaroushka got a great fright for Anya never sent for her step-daughter. Indeed, communication between them of any sort seemed to be the last thing she desired.

"Oh, don't make me go, Maminka. I'm frightened of her. She's a witch, you know she is." Zaroushka was almost in tears.

"Be a big brave girl and get along with you. She'll not eat you. She couldn't face your papa else. And do hurry. You don't want to aggravate her."

Maminka shooed the girl out of the room.

"Come with me, Maminka, do." Zaroushka tiptoed back into the room, wide-eyed with apprehension. "Besides, I don't know where to find her. I'll get lost."

Maminka saw the logic of this. "Oh, all right." She eased her vast bulk out of her chair, scratched under her arm and sighed. Her old feet were weary and she had hoped for a rest.

"Come along. Oh, you are a nuisance," she scolded but Zaroushka did not mind because she knew the old servant loved her.

They hurried down vast corridors lined with mirrors that sent their reflections bouncing back at them. Zaroushka's heart thudded in her breast from fear. She could not think why she had been summoned. Perhaps she had offended

31

without knowing? Like Maminka said you could sin against God and not even know. What could it be? Oh, what could it be?

At last Maminka opened a door. She pushed Zaroushka into a high-ceilinged room with tall windows that looked out over the Neva.

Her step-mother stood at one of the windows, her back to the door. She did not turn around but said, "Thank you. You may go Maminka."

The old woman went and Zaroushka was left trembling, clutching her handkerchief, praying she would have courage to bear whatever it was.

The minutes ticked by. As usual when nervous Zaroushka wanted to go to the lavatory but she dared not ask.

At last the Princess turned. Her face was pale. She wore a long crimson velvet gown trimmed with sable. She stared at the little girl before her. Zaroushka visibly flinched.

"You hate me, don't you?"

It was not a question but a statement. Zaroushka said nothing. Looking at the Princess Anya she realized for the first time how beautiful she was. She twisted the handkerchief she held between her fingers.

Anya removed her gaze from the child. "I don't blame you. I have done nothing to make you love me." She stared off into space for a moment. "I never seek to be liked, then I'm disappointed when no one cares for me." She shrugged. "Ah, well, I think I'm set on a road to self-destruction."

She paused, plucking aimlessly at the fur on her sleeve. "People don't understand," she said, as if to herself," I *do* things others only dream of. They are jealous of me because I have the courage and because I don't care for their opinion. I am not ashamed, you see, and I should be. It's all Boris's fault. If only ... if only ..."

To Zaroushka's horror it looked as if she were about to cry, but Anya glanced about the room and pulled herself together. Her gaze lit on Zaroushka and for a moment she seemed not

32

to know who she was. Then recognition dawned.

"Ah, Zaroushka. I had forgotten you for a moment. Come here, my dear." She sat down on a high-backed gilt chair and beckoned. The girl approached her timidly. She had never been this close to her step-mother before. She could see the matt white skin and a tiny scar above her top lip.

Anya took the child by the chin and looked into her eyes. "What a wild frightened creature you are. I have a lot to answer for, *n'est ce pas*? Ah me, I'll burn in hell for you."

She laughed, her cold tinkling laugh, but for the first time Zaroushka caught the despair, the sharp edge of hysteria. Anya glanced sharply at her step-daughter.

"You look at me exactly as your Papa does; eyes frightened and questioning. We cannot communicate, your father and I. We tear each other to pieces. And he always wants to know what I am thinking. That is very boring." She glanced into the girl's solemn eyes. "Still, what would you know about such things? I am sorry, my dear. You have been unfortunate. Through no fault of your own you are caught between two opposing forces. Poor little Zaroushka." She sighed then her voice changed, "Your Papa wants you in Moscow. You are to stay with the Rostovs. You and Maminka are to get the train tomorrow. Piotr will take you to the station."

Zaroushka felt her heart leap for joy: Papa, Moscow, tomorrow! It was the most wonderful news, but even at her tender age she had too much self-control to let her step-mother see her delight. The Rostovs were her cousins, Princess Sonya her Papa's sister. She did not know them very well. She had been told each spring that this year she would visit them but until now the proposed trip had never materialised. Now she was to go at last and she could not believe her luck. She wanted to shout and sing but she sat calm and still, waiting to be dismissed.

They set out next morning; Maminka with the large basket that held Zaroushka's clothes and a small one containing a picnic for their journey. Black horses stamping in the snow, the footman trying not to meet her eye. Had he been Anya's lover? she wondered. He was very good looking.

Zaroushka was excited, trying to remember her Aunt Sonya and her Uncle Vassily. The last time she had seen them had been at her mother's funeral when she was three.

Maminka kept up a constant litany of nervous complaint. She hated being uprooted, separated from her cronies. She regarded Moscow as a den of iniquity and the forthcoming visit with trepidation. They both slept on the train, the steady rhythm of the wheels and the swaying carriages lulling them to sleep. The plush upholstery irritated Zaroushka's cheek and when she woke one side of her face was bright red.

The journey was very long. They had left in the early morning and arrived in Moscow in the late evening. Prince Vashinskov was waiting in the station. The lamps were glowing yellow in the steam from the train which filled the place with gloomy clouds that every so often obscured Zaroushka's vision. There stood her father, tall, bearded, his eyes anxiously searching the crowd. In the bustle and fuss of the station she saw nothing but her dearest Papa. Servants hurried here and there, retrieving luggage; mothers and nannies herded children together and porters bustled about. A sausage seller cried his wares down the platform and a boy was running up and down the length of the train, papers for sale tucked under his arm, crying out the headlines. Zaroushka saw none of it, heard none of it, but ran to the Prince and was enveloped in his arms.

"Papa, Papa!" Near to tears she hugged and kissed him, clinging to him for dear life. Her intensity frightened him.

"There, there. Zaroushka, my darling, easy now, easy. I thought I would surprise you. I've come to take you to the Rostovs. They said they would send a coach, but I thought I would like to meet you in person after your long journey."

"Oh, Papa, darling. Darling Papa," was all she could say.

He bundled her and Maminka into the Rostovs' coach and they jolted through the amber lights of Moscow.

The Rostovs' house was a large mansion with many windows, painted lime green outside with white shutters and a classical portico. It was set back from the Volkhonka Prospekt. The street was fronted by a pretty garden and was very near the Grand Kremlin Palace and the Moskva river.

They had finished dinner and were waiting in the hall which was light and bright, and full of the warmth of welcome and fresh flowers. It was semi-circular, floored with jade-green marble and decorated with Doric columns of the same. Zaroushka thought it beautiful.

Uncle Vassily Rostov was a small, tubby man, full of puppyish *bonhomie*. He frisked about his young niece, urging hot chocolate, bon-bons, fruit and nuts to be administered to her at once. His wife, Princess Sonya Rostova, Prince Alexei's sister, stood head and shoulders above her husband and had a narrow, elegant face and body. She was quiet and controlled in her movements and had large dark eyes of great depth and beauty which Prince Vassily swore were reproduced in Zaroushka.

"You are so pretty, my dear, but so thin. Why, there's nothing of you. Skin and bone. We must plump you up in Moscow."

"I look after her well. I take care of my young mistress beautifully, I promise I do," Maminka piped up from the back. Tired from her long journey, feeling completely disorientated, she was hurt at the implied criticism. Vassily was mortified and at once full of apology.

"I'm sure you do, Maminka. 'pon my soul, I'd swear to it," he anxiously placated her.

"We must get you to bed, my dear," Sonya said, looking at Zaroushka sympathetically. "You must be tired after your long journey. How was it, Maminka?"

"Tolerable, Highness, tolerable." Maminka had heard Prince Alexei say that many a time on his return from

35

Moscow and she tried it out now, very pleased with herself for the way it sounded. A look of mild surprise flitted across the Princess's face, then her attention was caught by the simultaneous arrival of a tall young man and a pretty young girl of Zaroushka's own age.

"Ah, but you must meet your cousins, Dmitri and Nina. This is Zara, called Zaroushka. I hope you will make her stay a happy one."

Prince Vassily, hopping from one foot to the other, said, "You and Nina must become great friends, Zaroushka. Great friends."

"How are things in Petersburg?" the Princess inquired politely. Suddenly an air of awkwardness seemed to fall over the little gathering. Even Zaroushka's father seemed ill at ease, and Prince Vassily appeared overcome with embarrassment.

"Very good," Zaroushka told the Princess and the unease was dispelled in a burst of activity. Maminka was drawn away by one of the Rostovs' servants, Prince Alexei kissed his daughter goodnight and she felt suddenly exhausted.

She saw Prince Alexei go off with his brother-in-law.

"We'll be at the English club," Vassily said to his wife and went to kiss her mouth, but she turned her head and his lips brushed her cheek instead.

After a snack of hot chocolate and pancakes in the library, Nina pulled her cousin upstairs.

"Mama asked Vashenka to turn my old nursery into a room for you," she said to Zaroushka, her face flushed with excitement. "She did it beautifully, don't you think? It means you are right beside me. My bedroom is here, see? And yours is just there. Its got a connecting door so we can pop in and out and chat with each other all the time." Her plump face was full of goodwill and she squeezed her cousin's arm. But Zaroushka's face had become pale and drawn with fatigue. "Ah, but you are tired, cousin. I forget. I'm just so happy to have you here. Forgive me. I'll send

Maminka to you. She'll help you to bed." She hugged the drooping girl who could barely respond to such a show of affection. It made her feel weepy.

At the door Nina turned and said, 'We'll go riding tomorrow. Oh, I'm so glad you've come. We'll be great friends, Zaroushka. You'll see."

A sob caught in her throat. She felt a wave of happiness and gratitude so immense it nearly swamped her. No one had ever said this kind of thing to her before. She was not used to the language of family affection and the love her cousin offered overwhelmed her. She smiled a little tremulously at Nina and nodded.

"Thank you," she said. "Thank you very much."

The next morning Zaroushka was awakened by someone bouncing on her bed and shaking her gently. She had slept heavily and late and her return to consciousness was delightful. Her cousin sat beside her, her rosy face beaming with affection. She had brought a cup of tea which she left on Zaroushka's side-table. She looked down at her cousin, dimples chasing each other in her cheeks.

"Wake up, sleepy-head, we're going riding."

"What a lovely awakening," Zaroushka murmured. Nina looked perplexed. She was a pretty, vivacious girl with a soft round face and wide china-blue eyes. Her hair was heavy and fair, centre-parted and tied in a large satin bow at the nape of her neck. She was wearing a smart riding habit.

"Why do you say that?" she asked.

Nina's whole life had been spent in the bosom of a family who adored her and whom she adored and she took it all for granted. What was to Zaroushka a wonderful and rare occurrence was an everyday affair to her cousin.

Zaroushka sat up, suddenly energetic.

"Oh, never mind," she said. She did not want gloomy thoughts to spoil her joy. "I'll tell you another time. Let me drink my tea and I'll be ready in a minute."

She was as good as her word. Nina, she found, was a superb horsewoman. She went to the riding school for young ladies opposite the Grand Kremlin Palace. There she learned dressage and was one of their top pupils. Zaroushka was astonished at the expertise Nina showed in keeping her beautiful mare under complete and effortless control. It seemed quite easy but Zaroushka knew that appearances could be misleading and Nina was actually extremely skilful in her handling of the horse.

Zaroushka was enchanted by everything in Moscow. She could see it was not nearly as pretty as Petersburg but it was not the sights that endeared the place to her so much as the Rostovs. She had not known such a happy family life existed and to be part of it changed the face of every building, lent magic to everything she did and filled her heart with content. There was such a warm atmosphere in her uncle's house, a feeling that the family members lived together, slept close under the same roof, ate together around the same table, argued and laughed and fought, ran in and out of each other's rooms, careered down bright corridors, played and were, above all, part of a happy whole.

Not that the house was small or cramped; far from it. It had a ballroom, three reception rooms, a beautiful dining-room, a library and music room as well as kitchens and the bedrooms. It was just that Zaroushka was used to long corridors where the only human being she might bump into was a dignified footman or a frightened maid, and rooms in which two people were lost, vast chambers that needed crowds to seem even remotely full.

This was freedom, she thought, this was happiness. She found herself in the bosom of a family and thought nothing could be better.

Her Aunt Sonya remained the calm unruffled centre around which family life revolved. Uncle Vassily seemed to follow his children's lead and always deferred to her. To Zaroushka's surprise her aunt, so warm and affectionate with her children and niece, was just a tiny bit cool with her husband. Zaroushka who was very sensitive to the undercurrents in relationships and was by nature an observer, felt she could not be wrong about this, but neither could she understand it. A remote look came over her aunt's face when Vassily demonstrated his love in an impulsive hug or a kiss. She drew back slightly. Yet on other occasions her love and concern for him were patently obvious and manifest in a hundred ways. It was a mystery, thought Zaroushka. She did not understand her elders and, content for once, decided not to try.

Nina was full of life and laughter. She was heedlessly happy. To her each day was a new and wonderful present to be unwrapped in happy expectation, lived to the full, and in the evening regretfully relinquished.

Her brother Dmitri was passionately interested in politics and constantly argued about current affairs with anyone who would listen to him.

"He must stop saying such inflammatory things," Sonya said.

"Don't worry, my dear. He's only a child," Vassily replied, laughing. Dmitri was eighteen and seemed very grown-up to the fourteen-year-old Zaroushka. He was like his mother and also bore a passing resemblance to his little cousin in everything but height. Although Nina was young, already she was showing signs of later curvaceousness and would probably take after her father. But Dmitri was tall with crisp brown hair and the huge Vashinskov eyes. He had the same expression, intense and soulful, as Zaroushka, Prince Alexei and Sonya.

Zaroushka settled into her new life immediately. She felt she had been tightly wrapped or bandaged, like a mummy, and now someone had pulled a string and the binding had fallen away and she was free. She could relax, laugh, cry, be silly, be like other people.

As well as riding in the forest outside Moscow with Nina

and the grooms and Dmitri, they went visiting, something quite new and exciting for Zaroushka. They also went roller-skating and ice skating. And sometimes they went on picnics. It was a wonderful new life that she was precipitated into and Zaroushka's only worry was that she would not know how to behave; that she would do something wrong. She had never been trained, except by Maminka who knew nothing of polite society. She need not have worried. Her own inherent good taste and sharp observant eyes prevented her from making any gaffes.

"Did you know my mother, Aunt Sonya?" she asked one day at tea.

Dmitri was lounging on the sofa reading a newspaper, his long legs sprawled out before him. Nina was sitting on the floor by her mother leaning her face against Sonya's knee. She yawned every now and then for she was tired from her riding.

"Indeed I did, Zaroushka."

"What was she like?" She could not keep the anxiety out of her voice. Her aunt looked at her sympathetically.

"She was very lovely. A gentle sweet creature, very like yourself, my dear."

"It's just that Papa never speaks of her. Only Maminka remembers. And Maminka is not very …"

"Eloquent?" Sonya smiled at her niece. "Yes, I understand. Well, my dear, whenever you want to speak of your mama just come to me and we will talk." She glanced at the door as Vassily entered, his reading glasses perched on the end of his nose. "Come and join us for tea. We were speaking of Zaroushka's mother."

"She was lovely. A beautiful child, my dear. We all adored her." He patted Zaroushka's head as he passed her, glanced at his wife then sat down. Nina rose and hurried to his side.

"Papa, please may we stay up for the ball? Oh, do say yes, *please*." She had put on her most coaxing manner. Vassily could refuse his daughter nothing, so he looked over at Sonya.

"Ask your mother, dear child."

"A party? Here?" Zaroushka breathed.

At the Alexander Palace or in their homes she was never allowed to mix with the adults or participate in the *soirées* and grand balls her step-mother attended. As her father stayed away from his wife as much as possible, and as Princess Anya was permanently at the side of the Tsarina, their entertainments and parties were of a very different style to the evening of dancing and refreshments that the Rostovs shared with their friends.

Nina got her way and preparations began. Her aunt insisted on ordering Zaroushka a grown-up dress from Nevski Prospekt and when she put it on for the party, all at once she believed in Maminka's God. He did bring joy to good people. The Rostovs were good so their home was full of happiness which rubbed off on all who came in contact with them. She felt that Maminka's God held her safely that evening, and indeed all through her visit to Moscow. He blessed her as Maminka promised He would because she was good. But it was easy to be good when you were happy, so easy.

Zaroushka looked at herself in the long bevel-edged mirror. Though she was thin and was not blessed with Nina's curves, the dress suited her and she realised that she looked very pretty. She wore an embroidered and beaded white chiffon sheath over a fine satin shift. Little pearls hung from the elbow-length sleeves and from the bodice and just-above-the-ankle hem. Princess Sonya had given her a choker of seed pearls with one large pendant pearl that nestled in the hollow of her throat, and quite lovely pearl earrings that dangled almost to her shoulders. She was not old enough to put up her thick dark waist-length hair so she and Nina wore their tresses centre-parted and tied behind with satin bows.

41

Nina came in while she stood admiring her reflection in the mirror. "Oh, Zaroushka, you do look pretty," she said, and came and stood with her arm around her cousin's waist.

"It's all thanks to your mother," Zaroushka said. "No one ever thinks about my clothes at home. Or anything else for that matter." She turned and hugged Nina. "Oh, you'll never know how happy you are making me." She turned back to the mirror again and wrinkled her nose. "Are you sure I'm pretty? I'd much rather look like you, have blonde hair and something here." She covered her flat chest with her hands. Nina giggled.

"No, you are perfect. You look all innocent and sweet." She sat on the bed looking at her dark and fragile cousin. "What's it like at the Palace?"

"Lonely," Zaroushka said immediately then sighed deeply. "Oh, so lonely. I have absolutely no one to talk to except Maminka, and I'll always be a baby to her. No one pays the least attention to me. I think I could die and none of them would notice. Papa is away so much and when he is there he is always busy. Or quarrelling. And my step-mother ... Oh, Nina, I hate her! I hate her so much." Tears had come to her eyes.

Nina pulled her cousin on to the bed beside her. "I understand, Zaroushka. Really I do."

Zaroushka shook her head. "No. Dearest Nina you couldn't, you are incapable of understanding hate. You are too nice. You live here, surrounded by your loving family. There is always a warm and cosy atmosphere and your mother and father are sympathetic and kind. My step-mother is heartless and cruel ..."

"I *know*, Zaroushka," Nina interrupted.

"How could you?"

"You see ..." Nina hesitated. "Well, the Princess caused my mother, and Dmitri and me, and poor dear Papa a lot of pain."

Zaroushka looked at her, surprised and apprehensive. An

awful dread had crept into her mind and she caught her breath as Nina continued: "Didn't you ever wonder why we never saw you? My mother is your papa's sister after all."

Zaroushka shook her head. "I didn't think about it. My life is so strange, I don't know whether families normally see each other or not. Why didn't we? See each other, I mean?" The dread became a certainty and a cold fear clutched her heart. She loved these people so very much that the idea of her family causing them pain was abhorrent to her. Even here Anya was going to reach out and spoil things for her and all this happiness would be snatched away.

Nina looked at her cousin, a troubled expression on her face. "Are you sure you do not love ... you do not like your step-mother?"

Zaroushka's eyes opened wide and she gasped, "If you knew! If only you knew ... Of course not. I told you, I hate her."

"Well, I don't know whether I should tell you or not."

"Oh, Nina, you can't leave me up in the air like this. I'll not rest until I know."

"Well, it was some years ago. Mama has not forgiven Papa yet."

Zaroushka's throat was dry as dust. She swallowed, waiting for Nina to continue.

"Your step-mother, my Aunt Anya, 'borrowed' my papa and had an affair with him. That is her word: 'borrowed'. She said to Mama, 'I borrowed Vassily on my visit to Moscow, I hope you do not mind. You may have him back now.' And she laughed at Mama, a cold little laugh."

Zaroushka nodded. She knew that laugh.

"I heard her through the drawing room door," Nina continued, "and Mama crying. She cried for weeks. Dmitri wanted to kill Aunt Anya when I told him. No one blamed Papa except Mama. We all know dearest Papa is the kindest sweetest most amiable man in the world, but any fool could see he was no match for Aunt Anya. But Mama said he had shattered her trust in him. She simply could not feel the same way about him ever again."

Nina was surprised to see her cousin in tears.

"Oh, Nina, how could she? Oh, how awful! I'm sorry, so sorry."

"Darling Zaroushka, it isn't your fault."

But Zaroushka felt it was. Somehow she felt guilty. Guilty that she had anything to do with the Princess Anya, that she was in any way connected with the perpetrator of such wanton cruelty. It seemed inconceivable to Zaroushka that anyone could be cruel enough to do such a thing to this warm and loving family. She was aghast that such malice existed but knowing her step-mother not really surprised.

She wondered how her aunt had felt about her coming to Moscow. Ordering the curtains, the lovely coverlet for the bed, the flowered china lamps and the dainty dressing-table, all chosen so carefully, so sensitively. Had she had to swallow hatred of someone associated with the woman who had spoiled her life?

But even as she thought it she knew it had not been like that. Her aunt was a good woman. She was not vindictive.

Nina realised what she was thinking. "My darling, darling cousin, you are your father's daughter. My mother loves her brother and you have no connection in her mind with that … that …"

"Witch," Zaroushka said, "we call her that, Maminka and I. The witch."

"My mother never blamed you. How could she? But you see she was afraid, when you were younger, that if she asked you here – then that woman –"

"Witch," said Zaroushka.

"That witch," Nina repeated, and the two girls giggled a little. Then Nina's face became serious again. "My mother was afraid that Princess Anya might come with you and she could not have borne that. She never wants to set eyes on her again. That is why we never go to Petersburg. Your papa understands. Do you?'

"Of course," Zaroushka said emphatically. "I'm only amazed that your mother can bear to have me here at all. She has been so generous and kind to me."

"But she loves you, Zaroushka, we all do. As long as that woman ..."

"The witch," Zaroushka cried, laughing, relieved and a little hysterical.

"The witch," Nina said, laughing with her. At that moment Princess Sonya entered and found the girls helpless with mirth on Zaroushka's bed.

"Oh my goodness, what gaiety already! Don't you both look beautiful? Here, let me look at you properly."

Her thin expressive face was lit by a smile. She wore black velvet with diamonds at her throat and ears and Zaroushka thought she looked very lovely. She checked the girls, tucking in an errant curl here and straightening a ribbon there, until she was satisfied.

"There now, perfect," she said. "Come along with me, girls. Are you all right, Zaroushka?" she asked, glancing into the large anxious eyes so like her own.

"Yes. Oh, yes thank you, Aunt," Zaroushka said hastily.

I'd kill the witch if I were Aunt Sonya, she thought, and take pleasure in it. I'd kill her slowly. That's the difference between us. Aunt Sonya would never entertain such thoughts whereas I believe I would do it. I'm capable of it.

The thought frightened her and she shook her head. She wanted tonight to be perfect. She wanted her aunt to know how much she appreciated such hospitality.

'Aunt Sonya," she said, gently laying her gloved hand on her aunt's arm, "thank you. Thank you for everything. You have been so kind to me."

A quick smile softened the Princess's face and she bent over and kissed Zaroushka's cheek.

"It's a pleasure, my dear. You are a credit to your father."

Zaroushka's heart overflowed with joy.

45

Downstairs the house had been decked with flowers. The green marble hall was full of fashionable people fashionably dressed. There was an orchestra playing in the ballroom and couples had already started to dance.

Princess Sonya brought the girls to a group of young people who were drinking lemonade and chattering like magpies in a corner of the ballroom. They greeted Nina with squeals of delight. Zaroushka could think of nothing to say, however. She found Nina's friends a bit of a trial and was a little jealous of her cousin's ability to chatter and joke with everyone. They all knew each other whereas she was an outsider. They were extremely polite and did their best to include her in the conversation but it was uphill work.

Then Zaroushka saw her father enter the ballroom and her heart lifted as it always did when she saw him. She excused herself and crossed the room eagerly. He was so tall, so distinguished, she thought. He stood glancing around the room as if he was looking for someone. He said something to the man beside him, a remarkable-looking man as tall as he.

Zaroushka had no time to look further at the stranger. She flung herself into the Prince's arms.

"Papa, Papa, you're here! Oh, I'm so happy."

"There you are, dearest child. I was searching for you. But I'd never have known you. How grown-up you look! How pretty. Ah, my little one," he pinched her cheek, "how quickly time is passing."

He turned to the tall man beside him. "Baron, this is my daughter. Zaroushka, may I present the Baron Klaus Hoffen von Eldrich?"

She smiled prettily and bobbed to the man with her father. He was very striking. His hair was raven black, almost blue, as were his brows and the trim little moustache he sported. His eyes were dark as night and held something in their depths that frightened Zaroushka a little. Two deep clefts ran from nose to mouth, a mouth that was smiling yet curiously humourless. He bent stiffly, clicking his heels to acknowledge her curtsey.

'Princess. Alexei, I will see you later perhaps.' And with a nod to each of them he left the ballroom.

Prince Alexei looked at his daughter and smiled, "May I have this dance?"

"Oh yes, Papa, please," she breathed. He took her arm gravely and led her forward and they joined the dancers on the floor. Her father held her lightly but firmly. Zaroushka had never danced with him before and thought to herself that she had never been so happy. She held the lace skirt of her dress up on a ribbon round her finger. She could feel her face glow with excitement, pride and love. As they whirled about together the pearls and crystals pattered against the backs of her hands and her cheeks and she could feel the jewels move in the hollow of her throat. This was what it was to be grown-up. Moving to the music, confident of your partner, happy to be in his arms, delighted to be led, feeling safe there and joyously aware of your body clothed in soft materials, obeying you and your partner. Oh, it was so sweet, so sweet.

"And how do you like it here in Moscow?" Prince Alexei asked her, smiling at her flushed face as he waltzed her around and around until she was light-headed.

"I love it, Papa. Oh, I love it," she cried eagerly. "Aunt Sonya is so kind to me and Uncle Vassily ..." She thought of what Nina had told her about her uncle and her step-mother and wondered for the first time if her father knew. She realized too that she could not ask him.

"... is a darling. Nina and I are great friends and Dmitri is – like a dear kind brother. Thank you for bringing me here, Papa. Moscow is wonderful."

He looked down at her glowing face as they danced. His look was quizzical and understanding.

"You need to be with a proper family," he said, almost to himself. "I only wish ..." He did not finish the sentence and

47

she could see that she had lost his attention. His mind had wandered elsewhere.

When the waltz had ended, much to her disappointment for she could have danced with him all night, he delivered her back to Nina and her friends. She did not mind their chatter now. The fact that she did not know the people they spoke of did not bother her any more. She sparkled, she laughed, she joined in, she was on a pink cloud. One of the boys danced with her, then another. They were impressed with the fact that Prince Alexei was her father and that she lived sometimes with the Tsar and the Tsarina. Between dances she gossiped with Nina and the boys brought her lemonade and ices. Nina told her who people were and they were laughing together when she felt someone tap her on the shoulder. She looked around and her heart missed a beat when she saw it was the Baron.

"Princess Zaroushka, will you do me the honour of dancing with me?"

She was not at all sure she wanted to dance with this man.

"How popular you are, cousin," said Nina, laughing, and Zaroushka was troubled by her feeling of reluctance. After all the Baron was a friend of her father's. She did not know how to say no, so gave in with good grace.

He was a stiffer dancer than the Prince and more measured and formal in his dancing than the boys. He held himself very straight, as if he had a poker down his back, she thought, and almost giggled.

He held her very gingerly, almost as if he did not want to have more contact with her than was necessary. Yet he looked at her so oddly. His coal-black eyes burned into hers but he touched her back with only the tip of one finger and let her hand rest lightly in the palm of his open gloved hand. His body was rigid as they moved in strict tempo to the music.

"Are you enjoying yourself?" he asked politely.

Zaroushka, still trying to accustom herself to the phenomenon of this strange man, was thrown for a moment.

"I beg your pardon?" she said stupidly.

"Enjoying yourself?" he repeated patiently.

She nodded her head, feeling gauche and young for the first time that evening.

"Oh yes. Very much." She did not know what else to say and felt acutely embarrassed at her inadequacy. Then she said, "Are you visiting Moscow too?"

Again the strange humourless one-sided smile. "I suppose I am in a way," he said, and she felt foolish again. "But," he continued flatly, "not for long, I think. War is coming to Europe. I am German. It will be difficult working out where my sympathies and best interests lie."

She did not know what he was talking about and was glad when he was silent for a while. Then he spoke again, glancing down at her. "You have your father's looks."

Zaroushka did not know whether this was a compliment or not, so she said nothing. He looked over her head again. "I know your step-mother. She is a remarkable woman," he said, then lapsed into silence again.

When the dance was over he gave a tiny stiff bow and left her. She turned to find Dmitri at her elbow.

"I see the Baron is enamoured of you, little cousin."

She shivered. "I do hope not. Tell me, who is he?"

Dmitri took her arm. "Let me get you a lemonade first."

He steered her to a window embrasure in the green marble hall, and having seated her and pulled a small table near her so that she could deposit her fan and dance-card on it, left her for a moment.

If she turned her head to the right she could just see into the ballroom where couples whirled around and around; she could glimpse the flashes of the women's jewels, the bright colours of their dresses, the mirrors full of light; hear the muted roar of their conversation and the tinkle of their laughter under the music of the orchestra. If she turned her head to her left she could see through the window to the stars above and the drenching moonlight in a night of deep

49

velvet blue. She could see the pools of orange that the lamps threw on the paved courtyard and beyond that the gardens, full of lurking shadows. She thought of those white palaces where she had spent most of her life 'til now, those fairy tale buildings with golden rooms that were cold and intimidating. She felt a flood of relief that she was not at Court but in this warm embracing place, and wished she could remain suspended in this moment of time forever.

Dmitri returned with champagne, not lemonade and sat beside her.

"If you don't tell, neither shall I," he said, grinning at her. "Fourteen is *nearly* grown-up and I think you are older than your age so a little champagne won't hurt you."

She sipped it gratefully for she was very thirsty after the dance. She did not tell him that she was quite used to wine. Her step-mother had never seen any reason to forbid what was, in the Palace, the most common beverage.

"It is so beautiful, your house," she said to her cousin, trying to convey her delight in the place. "It's so light. I love it."

"It was rebuilt after Borodino, so it's quite a new building. I'm glad you like it, Zaroushka."

"Tell me about the Baron. He is a friend of Papa's?"

"I don't know. I don't know who your father's friends are. His real friends. Politically speaking he has some very strange bed-fellows." He paused, frowning. "He is a wonderful man, your father."

"I know." Love for her father glowed in her eyes, but Dmitri shook his head, his face serious.

"No, Zaroushka, I don't just mean as a father, as my uncle. I mean that he is one of the few men in Russia who understands what is going to happen, what must eventually happen. He is working to try and soften the blow."

"What do you mean? What is going to happen?"

He did not brush her off with a generalisation. She was honoured because he treated her like a grown-up and dignified her question with a serious answer. Truth to tell, Dmitri rarely found a sympathetic audience. Those in agreement with him thought that he was too young and too privileged to participate in political discussion, and those who were not in agreement with him did not want to hear what he had to say and called him a traitor to his class.

"You see, Zaroushka, long ago Peter the Great tried to modernise Russia, tried to drag her out of medieval closed-mindedness and stagnation. They all fought him – boyars, clergy, his aunt Sophia and his idiot brother. It's the same today. The rulers in Russia always resist change. They stagnate. It's fear, I suppose."

He looked at her seriously, his handsome face creased into earnest lines. "We, the aristocracy in Russia, are rooted in the past. All over Europe storm clouds are gathering and yet our leaders refuse to look outward, refuse to acknowledge that we will be involved. They refuse to bring Russia into the twentieth century. Your father knows this. He is one of the few to face facts."

"But, Dmitri, what have we to do with the rest of Europe?"

"Spoken like a true Russian princess, Zaroushka! No, don't be hurt." He was quickly conciliatory when he saw her expression, crest-fallen like a child who has been chastised. "It is not your fault. We are not educated to question, to reason. The Tsar is related to half the crowned heads of Europe. We speak French as much as we speak Russian. Our cuisine is French. We prize European culture above our own – and we do it, Zaroushka, at our peril.

"We, the aristocracy, feel we owe an allegiance to Europe. But not the Russian people. If there is a war in Europe – and your father says it will have started before this year is over – then the Tsar's relatives will insist he takes sides, becomes involved. The Russian people will not like that. They will be called upon to fight for something they have no knowledge of. Feeling is already running high."

51

"What do you mean, Dmitri?" This was all completely new and fascinating to her. She listened with avid attention, afraid to miss anything, worried that she would not grasp every detail. She wanted desperately to understand.

"Well, in this country the ordinary people are discontented. There is a stirring in the land. People are asking questions. Why do we labour so that only a few can have everything? Why are we poor and hard-worked when the privileged few idle their days away in luxury, doing nothing? Why am I near to starvation when they feast at tables groaning with enough food to feed my family for months? A twilight has been reached. The monarchy is despotic as any absolute monarchy is. They mean well, they do not think they are harming anyone, but their sheer lack of awareness is criminal.

"The incestuous nature of our powerful group, the aristocracy, is causing a deep national discontent. Instead of listening to the rumbles, moving towards the people, trying to find a solution – instead of sensing their malcontent, trying to find ways to even things up a little – we are drawing closer together with our own kind and further and further away from them, the people, the backbone of Russia. We are pretending that nothing is happening.

"We are a tight-knit clique who draws strength from outmoded notions of birth and position. We are an exclusive clan that blinkers its eyes to what is really happening here and in the rest of the world. We are merrily dancing towards our own funeral. The rumble of discontent is all around us and we are too busy with all this."

He gestured to the whirling figures in the ballroom and to the laden tables where people were eating in the dining room off the hall. From the library came the rattle of dice.

"It's exactly like the King of France and his silly queen. They were deaf to the trumpet calls of doom that blew so loudly in their ears. It is sounding now throughout this land and we also are too deaf to hear it."

"I never knew all this. Never thought. It's all new to me. I'm overwhelmed." Zaroushka's mind was buzzing with ideas. She couldn't cope with all the thoughts and questions Dmitri had put into her head.

"But don't you think that the people will do anything for their 'Little Father'?" she asked.

"It's true they love the Tsar, but he must begin to listen to them. They hate your step-mother's friend, the Tsarina. In any events, it's getting too late to …"

He never finished the sentence for just then a stone came hurtling through the window with a crash and a tinkle of glass, missing Zaroushka's cheek by inches. They jumped to their feet, startled and confused.

"What on earth?" Dmitri cried, turning to the window, but he and Zaroushka were unceremoniously pulled back by the Baron. Seconds later another stone came crashing in after the first. Stones and rocks now came flying into the lighted house and glass flew everywhere. There were frightened screams from the female guests.

The Baron Klaus Hoffen von Eldrich hurried over to Prince Vassily who had come from the library to see what was happening.

"My God, what on earth is going on?" the plump Prince cried in dismay, staring at the stones and rocks and broken glass that littered the hall.

"Send for the soldiers, quickly. For God's sake, hurry," the Baron cried, running to him. "Out the back way for the soldiers," he shouted to a footman who was dithering about, one moment trying ineffectually to clear the glass, the next ducking to avoid the flying missiles.

Prince Alexei came running into the hall. His face flooded with relief when he saw Zaroushka unharmed.

"Thank God! Someone said you were hit. Are you all right?"

"Yes, Papa, yes. What is it?"

"It's all right. The soldiers are outside," someone called,

and the screaming stopped.

Everyone crowded into the hall and moved towards the windows to see what was happening. Outside a small crowd of peasants and students were, in their turn, screaming as mounted soldiers, bayonets fixed, converged on them from both ends of the street.

"They're killing them!" Zaroushka cried, appalled. "The soldiers are killing them."

"Serves them right. Blackguards!" someone said.

"No, Papa. Stop them. Oh, please, stop them."

The Prince drew her away from the window.

"It's no more than justice," a woman in a velvet dress shouted.

Prince Alexei stood with his arm around his daughter. "No," he said quietly. "Don't call it that."

His words were heard.

"Are you then a Bolshevik or a Menshevik Prince Alexei? Eh? Do you betray your class, your country and your sovereign?"

The man who asked the question was a large florid-faced person who was mopping his brow with his handkerchief. Others near him nodded in agreement.

"No, I am not, Vosto. I am a realist. Look at it this way. We are few. They are many. We must listen to them before it is too late."

"Listen to animals? You must be jesting, Prince." The coterie around the large man murmured in assent.

The Prince was angry too, Zaroushka could tell. His hand tightened on her shoulder-blade. She felt him take a deep breath.

"It is statements like that, my dear sir, that are at the root of all our problems. A closed mind achieves nothing."

"But they are trying to destroy us, that rabble," the woman in the velvet dress cried. The Prince took his arm from around his daughter and bowed to the assembled company.

"When will you realise that it should never be 'them' and 'us'? Excuse me, I must take my leave. I must see what caused this trouble. Do please return to your pleasure as if nothing had happened."   Prince Vassily shook his head in great distress. "Oh dear, oh dear," he murmured.

"Papa, you must not go out there! It's dangerous." Zaroushka followed her father to the door and tried to restrain him but he took her arm from his and said gently to her, "No. I shall be all right, dear."

No one said anything as he went out of the front door but as soon as it had been closed behind him a buzz of conversation broke out. The man called Vosco cried out over the murmur: "Who are the Prince's real friends? That is what I would like to know. What can he think when he leaves us for them?"

Zaroushka felt tears spring to her eyes.

"Didn't you hear him?" Dmitri cried. "There should be no 'us' and 'them'. Oh, it's no use!'

Vassily waved his hand for silence, "I apologise for what happened," he said, his face flushed in distress, "but I would ask you to remember that Prince Alexei Alexandrovich is my friend and brother-in-law." His wife came and stood beside him, laying a hand on his arm. "Under my roof I will not tolerate any utterances against him," he finished more firmly. 'If anyone feels they can no longer accept my hospitality, the footman will bring round their carriage at once."

There was a low murmuring among the guests but no one spoke out.

Dmitri turned to Zaroushka. "He has no friends, your father. Neither the peasants nor the aristocracy trust him. Not even the students."

"Why Dmitri?"

"Because he simply will not take sides."

Vassily was running about ordering brandy to be served to those who were shocked and urging people to calm themselves, though, someone remarked, he would do well to take his own advice.

"Father is agitated because he feels he is somehow to blame," Dmitri said. "He seems to think unpleasant things are always his fault."

It was the Princess who smoothed the atmosphere, recreated calm. She sent a message to the orchestra to play something gentle and romantic, she had all the footmen circulate with champagne and brandy, she had the maids remove all the glass and closed the velvet curtains, shutting out the imperfect world.

She moved people about, breaking up groups who were being alarmist or inflammatory and asking the chief agitators to reassure this lady or that. Soon the party was on an even keel again, merry and lighthearted as if there had been no violent interruption.

But for Zaroushka there was no going back. She had crossed a boundary. She had learned things tonight and was eager for more knowledge.

"What did that man mean? About Bolshev ... whatever?" she asked Dmitri.

By now he was a little bored instructing his young cousin. He wanted to escape and find out more about the evenings startling events from those who would know the facts. But his mother passed by just then.

As if she knew his innermost thoughts she smiled at him. "How nice of you, Dmitri, to look after your cousin so well. It is kind of you," she said, and he was obliged to stay on at Zaroushka's side at least for a while.

This time he took her away from the windows and sat with her at the back of the ballroom. The place had been cleared for a special troop of dancers from Georgia to perform. The dancing, the leaps, the bright and colourful costumes, the shouting and the exuberant virility took her breath away. For a while they were both silent. This too was Russia. Zaroushka's face glowed and she clapped her hands together

56

in delight. others joined in and soon everyone there forgot the disturbance had ever happened, forgot their differences and whooped and clapped and yelled encouragement at the dancers and each other. An air of unity encompassed them, one and all.

Zaroushka looked about the room, her eyes picking out her Uncle Vassily, rosy-cheeked, slapping his knees, sweating profusely and laughing in childish glee. She could see her Aunt Sonya standing a little apart, cool and beautiful as if she had just stepped newly groomed from her room. She was talking to a servant, her watchful eyes darting about the huge chandeliered room, trying to see and forestall her guests' needs. There was Nina, surrounded by her young suitors, flirting with them in what she, at fifteen, thought was a daring and provocative manner but was in reality innocent and unsophisticated. And here at Zaroushka's side the handsome idealistic face of Dmitri, duty-bound to stay with her for she too had understood her aunt's message. She looked at them with an overwhelming surge of love and affection.

"Oh, dear God, let it never stop. Never and never, Amen," she prayed, and as her prayer finished so did the dancers. To loud applause they left the room. Once more the orchestra began to play and couples drifted here and there and the footmen crossed the floor with trays of drinks. Zaroushka turned to Dmitri.

"I don't want to hold you here," she said. "Please, if you want …"

"Oh no Zaroushka." He looked embarrassed, then recovered and said, "Your question … what Vosco meant. He was being insulting to your papa. He is a stupid man and you must pay no attention to him." Dmitri sighed. "There are, unfortunately, a lot like him."

"But what did they mean … those names?"

"They are two groups. They want roughly the same things but they are growing further and further apart. The

57

Mensheviks hold that the rights of the individual are sacred. They fight for reform of government and more education. The Bolsheviks are a breakaway group and are led by the exile Lenin. They want a social revolution, not just here in Russia but internationally. Lenin believes the war between nations should become a war between classes."

"Oh, Dmitri, I'm getting lost. It's all so complicated."

"Well, dear cousin, why not leave it for this evening? It has been a hectic night and you must be bewildered by everything that has happened."

Zaroushka smiled. "It has been a lovely night. Except for …"

She thought of the soldiers and the people running, screaming. Truth to tell she was tired and her mind was teeming. She needed time to sort out all that had happened and all she had learned.

"Only one thing more, Dmitri, then I'll let you go. I know you are dying to escape. No, don't protest, I don't blame you a bit. You have been wonderful to me this evening. Thank you."

Dmitri blushed. He thought his little cousin very sweet and lovely and felt protective towards her.

"What do you want to know?"

A comical expression of puzzlement crossed her face. "I've forgotten," she wailed. He laughed and kissed her cheek. "Never mind. It will come back to you tomorrow," he replied. "Oh look, there's Nina and Mama."

"I'm sending you girls up to bed,' the Princess said as she arrived at Zaroushka's side, Nina in tow. "It's way past your bedtime and a lot has happened. You are probably more tired than you realise."

Nina protested vehemently but Zaroushka was glad to go. As she mounted the stairs she glanced around for one last look. She saw Dmitri sneak out of the house and smiled to herself. He was probably going to try to find her father. It made her feel good that he admired her papa so much. The orchestra was playing a lively tune now and she could hear whoops and see flashes of colour as couples danced past the open ballroom doors. Two officers in the Imperial Army were talking in the hall. One threw back his head and laughed while the other slapped his thigh. The footmen moved around serving drinks. Vassily was trotting after Sonya as she moved, tall and stately, among her guests, exchanging a word here and a smile there. Two young men were flirting with a voluptuous blonde woman who was teasing them both. She slapped one of them on the knuckles but he obviously enjoyed it.

Zaroushka was about to look away from all the activity in the hall when a shadow detached itself from the darkness of the embrasure where she and Dmitri had sat a while ago. She saw it was the Baron. He had been sitting there so motionless that she had not noticed his presence. When he stood, he turned and looked up at her. She felt the piercing black eyes boring into her. She remained there a moment pinned by his unrelenting gaze. Then she shivered and hurried up the stairs to Nina.

Chapter Three

The following months passed in a whirl. June slipped into July and July into August. So much happened yet events slid into each other smoothly. Nina's governess, Mademoiselle Valérie, gave them lessons. She was shocked at Zaroushka's ignorance.

"*Mon Dieu*, you know nothing, nothing," she said. She pursed her lips and shook her head. She was horrified at Zaroushka's lack of literary knowledge. The girl had read nothing at all and found it difficult to decipher the simplest words.

The governess told the Princess who shrugged and said, "There are extenuating circumstances, Mam'selle. Do not agitate her. Let her enjoy herself."

The governess pursed her lips. She had never heard of such a thing. Enjoy her lessons! What was the world coming to?

"Poor little girl," the Princess mused as she poured the tea.

"She will be going back to her old life soon enough."

But Zaroushka was not totally ignorant. She loved and understood the opera and ballet and they went to both in the Bolshoi Theatre. They also visited the circus. She went with her cousins to picnics and parties, she played tennis and croquet, and Nina and herself were asked to the races. Life was packed with enjoyable events.

But she saw, too, crowds in the streets queueing for

bread. The sight made her thoughtful. The events of the night of the ball and her conversation with Dmitri had opened her eyes and now she saw things that she had been oblivious to before. She began to notice individuals and groups on the periphery of her world. She had taken servants, the populace, the workers, for granted. She had not detached them from the landscape as living entities before. Now she suddenly found herself aware of that vast multitude of people and she was shocked by what she saw.

Poverty was rampant, misery everywhere. Dmitri told her that less than one in three people could read and write, that they lived in medieval squalor, and the worst thing of all in his estimation was that no one in a position of authority would listen to their complaints.

"The intellegentsia are angry. The students have meetings and tempers become overheated. That's what happened the other night at our party. There had been a meeting and on the way home the crowd passed our house, they saw the lights and heard the music. They could see the people dancing. They saw opulence, richness abounding. What one woman, any woman there, was wearing would feed a poor family for a year. No wonder they were angry." He spread his hands then sighed. "How awfully callous we must seem to them. In any event it was too much for them. Someone threw a stone. Another followed. All their pent-up anger and frustration was unleashed."

They were in an open carriage on their way to a picnic. Nina and Zaroushka sat on either side of him almost covering him with their white lawn skirts. They had ribbons at their waists and hair. Dmitri wore his flannels, a linen jacket and a straw boater. Prince Rostov and his wife were in a carriage in front of them, and behind them followed the brothers Vladimir and Yuri Kutuzov, friends of the Prince. They were a jolly pair, intent on enjoyment, happy to appreciate good food, wine and company. Last of all was the servants' dray.

It was a sunny, bright day. A sweet breeze blew, lifting their hair from their necks and playing mischievous games with their hats. Nina held hers on with her hand as the broad brim blew back from her face instead of shading it. Her brother was still deep in conversation with Zaroushka.

"Oh, Dmitri, I wish you'd stop all that political nonsense," she cried. "You are so serious. I'm sure Zaroushka does not want to hear such boring stuff."

"But she asks me," he protested, "I didn't bring it up. She did."

"That's right, Nina. It's so interesting and I never knew any of it before. Dmitri is terribly knowledgeable."

"Oh well, if you really *want* him to be boring, don't let me stop you. Oh, bother! My hat will be torn from my head, see if it's not."

The horses clopped down the broad boulevards towards the Vorobyovy Hills for a picnic on the banks of the river. There was a jetty there they could swim from, and boats. On the way Dmitri pointed out places of interest, but even he, in spite of his ideals, had become used to the gaunt faces in the crowd. It was those faces Zaroushka was becoming aware of, the despairing expressions that etched themselves on her mind.

Soon they had left the city and their conversation became light and desultory. Nina and Zaroushka giggled together and though it was the most natural thing in the world for her cousin, for Zaroushka it was something rare and precious; to giggle at nothing, to be light-hearted, to chuckle over inconsequential things with a dear friend, was for her a wonderful experience.

The girls sat about on the green banks of the river while the servants laid out the feast. Birds sang overhead and a flight of cranes winged their way across the pale sun. Zaroushka and Nina reclined on cushions, their backs against a stout willow.

The smell of grass, the fragrance of the hedgerows, the

singing of the birds overhead, all gave Zaroushka a heady feeling of contentment. Deep within her was an ache so bitter-sweet it hurt. It sprang from the feeling that this was not really her world. She must hold happiness tenderly for it was transient and might disappear.

Dear God, never let me forget how I feel now, she prayed.

Nina's head had drooped onto Zaroushka's shoulder and her long golden lashes brushed her softly flushed cheeks. Her white lawn skirts had floated above her legs and her little cream kid boots stuck out, one pointing one way, one the other. Zaroushka smiled to herself at the sight of them. She did not disturb her cousin but nor did she allow her own drooping eyelids to close. She did not want to waste a moment of this day.

The men were around the corner. They had stripped and were swimming naked as new-born babes. Through the trees she could catch glimpses of their heads bobbing about in the water and hear the loud cries and shouts and splashing coming from behind the promontory as they jumped into the river. Later Nina and herself would change into striped costumes in the tent the servants had erected on the other side of the copse and they would paddle in the shallow near the jetty.

She looked up into the fragile blue of the sky and saw the black shadows of a flight of wild duck gracefully move across the face of the primrose-yellow sun. How beautiful life was when you were with people you loved. She glanced at the relaxed and sleeping face of her cousin.

The curve of her cheek, the curls that clung to her forehead, the rosy mouth half-open, touched her heart. She wanted to take Nina in her arms and hold her there and kiss the pearly damp forehead in passionate gratitude.

She looked across to where her Aunt Sonya was instructing the servants, her head tilted to one side, her elegant neck encased in lace swanlike as she oversaw the arrangement of food, flowers and cutlery on the damask cloth. She wanted to bury her face in her aunt's lap and whisper to her over and over like a prayer, 'I love you. I love you. I love you so.'

She thought of Dmitri's handsome earnest face, the movement of his long slim hands and the expression in his eyes as he explained some political nicety to her. He was never impatient with her or, she thought ruefully, if he was he never showed it. She wanted to kiss him too. And Uncle Vassily, round as a porpoise, his doggy eyes begging for affection. She wanted to pat him and hug him and tell him he was a good man, and the evil lay not in him but in her step-mother, the witch back in St Petersburg.

Nina awoke suddenly, on an instant. She suggested that after lunch they go for a row up the river and Zaroushka languidly agreed. Aunt Sonya called them to lunch, and the girls cried to the men: "Lunch! Lunch!" Their calls echoed around the banks, sending the birds fluttering away in alarm.

The men returned, laughing, casually dressed in shirt-sleeves but with their boaters firmly on their heads for shade. The Kutuzovs hung shyly back, waiting to be placed. How nice they were, Zaroushka thought, happily fitting in and trying to please. She felt full of the milk of human kindness on this most beautiful of days. "I could love anyone today," she said to Nina who giggled.

They ate, brushing away bluebottles and bees, consuming herrings *à la Russe*, salmon and sturgeon with salad, jellied pike-perch, *studen* (which was a meat jelly) and caviare on buttered rye bread or *blinis*. They drank Massandra wine from the Crimea or lemonade for the young people.

"I wish you could marry Dmitri and come and live with us forever," Nina said to her cousin.

"Nina, don't be tactless," her mother admonished her. "Poor Zaroushka and Dmitri will be embarrassed."

But Dmitri had not heard.

"We cannot go on indefinitely importing everything," he

was saying earnestly to his father who had undone his waistcoat and the top button of his trousers preparatory to slipping his hat over his eyes for an after-lunch nap. He was not really listening.

"We have to go into production for ourselves. The world is passing us by."

"Is it, m'boy?" Vassily asked, patting his stomach with a contented smile. "Well, maybe that's not a bad thing, eh?"

"Oh, why won't any of you see? I know you are happy, Papa, here, on this beautiful day, but it will not last. We are living on quicksand."

"I'm afraid Dmitri is becoming more and more of a renegade," Aunt Sonya said to the Kutozovs. "Ever since Yevgeny Lemcov was sent to Siberia ..."

The Kutuzovs bounced to their feet, worried that they might be drawn into an argument.

"We're going fishing," Vladimir said. "If you'll excuse us?"

"If you'll excuse us?" Yuri echoed, and Sonya smiled and nodded.

"Who was sent to Siberia?" Zaroushka asked Dmitri.

"My tutor," Dmitri replied. "He was a Menshevik. He and his fiancée were sent away.'

"Tutors shouldn't have fiancées," Sonya said firmly.

"It was a disgrace, Mother. I stopped believing in God after that."

He sounded angry and there were tears in his eyes.

"I am not going to quarrel with you, Dmitri, so don't imagine I am," Sonya said serenely. "Be an angel and get some ice."

Dmitri stood up quickly and went to where the servants were clearing up.

"He was very fond of Yevgeny Lemcov," Nina said softly. "It was a shock."

"Whatever happens one should believe in God," Sonya said gently. "Otherwise what would one do?"

"I *have* to." Zaroushka thought of Anya.

Nina looked up, surprised, then glanced at her mother who was studying Zaroushka.

"What do you mean?"

Zaroushka chose her words carefully.

"I am surrounded by evil. Oh, I don't mean that everything in Petersburg or in the Palace is bad, of course not. But I, personally, have wickedness all about me. If you believe in evil, then you must also believe in good." She paused, wrinkled her brow then continued, "The Church I do not like so much." Sonya's hand flew to her mouth. "But God is good. He must be. So He will save me. I *have* to believe in Him or I'd be lost."

Dmitri came hurrying back carrying a large silver flask. He seemed quite recovered.

"Father is asleep," he said.

"It's quite unnecessary to tell us that Dmitri. We can hear for ourselves."

Vassily lay on his back, eyes covered, gently snoring.

The girls had a paddle. They shrieked when Dmitri splashed water at them, and when they had dressed climbed into a rowing-boat and sat arm-in-arm while he rowed them downstream at a leisurely pace. Maminka stood on the bank keeping a weather eye on Zaroushka. She did not hold with bathing and certainly not with going out in boats and courting disaster.

"People should stay on dry land, where they were meant to be," she murmured grouchily to herself as she watched the little bark round the bend in the river and disappear out of sight.

There were ducks on the river and they saw a pair of black swans near the bank under a willow tree. The river was lined with slim ranks of silver birch, pearl grey, delicately leaved. When they looked over the side of the boat they could see fish in the clear green depths.

They waved to Vladimir and Yuri who sat side by side

motionless on the bank, their lines in the sparkling river. They let the boat drift and no one said anything at all.

It was late when they reached home. Zaroushka was tired and happy. Sonya said she would send a little light supper to the girls on a tray, which she did. Their talk was intermittent. Zaroushka felt drowned in a golden lassitude as if all her nerves were coated in honey. She kissed Nina and that night for the first time she did not lie stiff and straight in her bed. She lay down and her body curled like a cat's in a warm, relaxed ball, and she slept soundly, dreamlessly, until morning.

When she came down for breakfast her father was waiting for her. She ran into his arms, hugging him, happy to see him, to smell his dear familiar smell and feel his beard tickle her when he kissed her. Life seemed perfect. She could not think of anything more she wanted.

"I've come to take you home to St Petersburg, dear child," he said. She felt her stomach lurch followed by the sickest feeling she had ever known. But she said nothing. He was her father. He knew how happy she was here and he would not send her back to the witch unless it had to be.

There was a chorus of protests from the Rostovs but Prince Alexei remained adamant.

"We cannot impose on my brother-in-law's hospitality any more, my dear. Enough is enough. Dearest sister, you know that we are grateful but duty calls."

Duty? What duty? Was he just using words? Zaroushka did not know. What she did know was that it was all over. The lovely time had come to an end. She swallowed her feelings, showed her father a clear and smiling face, while all the time her heart felt cold and dead.

So she returned to the Alexander Palace and, inevitably, the snow came. The days of warmth and sunshine were over. The swollen freshets foamed down the mountainside and turned to ice. The land was mantled in a crust of shimmering silver. Skaters on the iced ponds breathed clouds of vapour. The dark grey twilight of snowy nights was long and magical, a time to wonder and hold your breath. When Zaroushka flew like a bird across the frozen surface of the lake she could feel for a moment the sadness leave her and hope, faint hope, return; if it had happened once it could happen again.

The marble statues in the grounds of the palace were covered for the winter so that they would not crack in the below zero temperature. They looked like ghosts to her in their white drapery – wraiths trembling in the grey mists of eternal dusk.

She always felt cold. Sometimes at night she awakened chilled to the marrow. Lying in her too-large bed in the dark she would shiver in fear and wonder if there was any escape.

Her step-mother's heavy malaise and restless discontent steeped the atmosphere with unease. She found herself resenting the fact that her father had brought her back here, and for the first time her staunch devotion to him foundered. She knew he was a man who obeyed the rules and was forced to live with someone who recognised none. But it did not make it any easier for his daughter that he expected her to remain with the Princess Anya when he was so often away.

The Tsarina's anxiety was mounting day by day. As the Tsarevich relapsed soon after each false return to health, her high-strung nervous tension, her dependence on the monk or indeed any crackpot peddlar of miracles, pervaded the Imperial Russian Court and engendered an atmosphere both jumpy and mistrustful.

For Zaroushka there seemed no ultimate escape from the dark days, no hope of emergence into the sun.

Court life was the goal she was supposed to dream of, Maminka told her, yet the thought of attaining it gave her nightmares. Marriage was another goal she was encouraged to look forward to but the mere thought frightened her. She had only to think of the example of Princess Anya and her father, or indeed the Tsar and Tsarina, to see the hell which grown-ups could make of life. Even the Rostovs had shown her an Uncle Vassily labouring under a burden of guilt and an Aunt Sonya unable to forgive the wound he had inflicted. Marriage did not seem an attractive proposition for the young and lonely girl. It seemed to offer no reassurance, only enormous danger.

Nor did the Church bring her any comfort with its promises of hellfire and damnation if she were not good. The hirsute priests smelled of stale sweat and rotten teeth. The overpowering mixture of their body odour, the incense and the hypnotic chanting gave her a headache and made her feel faint. There was a green-fleshed Christ dying on the cross in the great Byzantine icon over the altar that frightened her, and the vestments the priests wore, embroidered in pearls and gold thread, the sable circle around their heads and the velvets studded with brilliant stones, made her feel sick. She thought of Moscow and the starving faces and was disgusted.

After her return from Moscow the palace seemed larger and more oppressive than ever before. Her step-mother barely greeted her, hardly seemed to realise that she had been away. But Sasha leaped about in ecstasy at her reappearance. He had grown in her absence and his rapture at seeing her compensated her somewhat for the feelings of isolation.

The journeys down the echoing, endless corridors recommenced; the hours spent waiting around for meals, for a governess to arrive, for the music teacher to come. Being hustled out of one room because someone important was arriving and out of another because the servants needed to prepare it for a State function. She was never sure whether she was supposed to be where she was. She was permanently expecting dismissal or at least interruption by nervous footmen. It encouraged her sense of insecurity.

The Princess Anya was scandalising everyone again and

Maminka, tut-tutting said, "Piotr told me, this time it's twins. The Mayakovs, both of them, devils they are! She has them both. At the same time." Maminka nodded. She looked odd at the moment for she had toothache and was nursing herself with a poultice of milk and linseed oil on her face. It did not interfere with her gossiping. "And the priest's been sent away to Lensk. There was a scandal. Ay, ay, ay!"

One nice thing happened. The Tsarina insisted that Zaroushka had lessons from Herr Dortmuller, a fat little piano-teacher from Saltzburg whom she found instantly sympathetic.

He was extremely ugly with the bald skull and fine skin of a baby. His infant's mouth was small, daintily outlined with the soft hair that dusted his upper lip and grew in a tuft on his chin. He looked, Zaroushka thought, like the picture of a Chinese mandarin she had seen in a book once. But he was the kindest man and he grew fond of the lonely girl.

He taught the royal children and the Tsarina thought it a good idea and a generous gesture to have him give lessons to her friend's small step-daughter. She had made the gesture carelessly not realising what solace it brought the teenage girl. Herr Dortmuller instilled in Zaroushka a lasting love of music and a smattering of German. They often conversed together in that language and spent many hours playing the beautiful old piano in the music-room.

The older her step-daughter grew the more the Princess Anya avoided contact with Zaroushka. Seeing this, and not wishing to antagonise the powerful princess, others followed suit. It was from Herr Dortmuller Zaroushka learned that war had broken out in Europe.

He said it had been raging for some time but she had heard nothing. She felt stupid not knowing and asked Nina in a letter to get Dmitri to explain, but Nina did not mention the subject in her reply.

Zaroushka also asked her father but he evaded her

questions. All he would say was, "This is a very unpopular war in Russia. There is so much unrest here now that what they do in Europe seems irrelevant to the ordinary Russian people."

"They are fighting nevertheless, Papa. Piotr says ..."

"Piotr only quotes propaganda," her father interrupted. "He is a good servant of the Emperor, and the Emperor thinks we should be at war."

He told her that the Rostovs had gone away. She cried that night. They had not said goodbye. Her father said they had left in a hurry. There had been riots in Moscow. They decided they had to get out. Zaroushka felt as if an invisible support had been removed. Since her visit to them they had become the hope she clung to. She thought of them as loved ones she could trust, to whom she could turn if things became unbearable. To find that they had gone left her feeling bereft and totally alone.

She became a good pianist. Herr Dortmuller was proud of her. But eventually he too left. Anti-German feeling ran high in Russia, increasing as the war dragged on. Zaroushka could not understand the cruel things her fellow countrymen said to Herr Dortmuller. As if, she said indignantly, the war was his fault.

"We are not all like those people," she told him.

He had come to the palace with a cut eye. A crowd had set upon him outside his lodgings and someone threw a stone. They called him 'Hun' and spat upon him. The gash was deep and the peace-loving musician was deeply distressed.

"I had to run, Zaroushka. Run! My poor little legs were not made for running." He held them out before him. They were fat and short and trembled from the unusual exertion. "Only that I was coming here, to the Palace, I would be dead, I think."

"How can people be like that?" she asked. "They don't know you. They know nothing about you except that you are German."

"It is enough." He shrugged. "People like to have someone to hate. It makes them feel good, feel righteous. 'We' are good. 'They' are bad. 'We' group together and vent our resentments, our disappointments, our frustrations, on 'them' for 'they' are bad and therefore we are justified. We can then give reign to our basest instincts and kill and rape and pillage and –" he shrugged again – "persecute harmless people like me. We do not blame ourselves for our vile acts for, after all, we have only destroyed what is bad. 'They' cease to be children and pregnant women and piano-players like me who love all peoples and want only a peaceful life filled with music."

"It's not fair," Zaroushka said to him. Then frowned and added, "It's what Father said. Something about the fact that there should never be a 'them' and 'us'."

Herr Dortmuller nodded his too-large head. "He is a wise man, your father."

Shortly afterwards he stopped coming to the palace. She waited in the music room for him at the time he was next due but he did not arrive. She waited and the shadows lengthened in the blue room and the moonlight fell through the window in a cold and radiant shimmer. Then she heard with a heavy heart that he too had left Russia. She missed him dreadfully. She practised the piano endlessly as if by that action she could keep her friend near. She had in any event little else to do. After Herr Dortmuller left she still continued for hours at a time, rehearsing her scales, pieces of music she loved, but little by little he slipped away until she could hardly remember what he looked like, and that was the greatest heartache of all.

Her father did not come. She had no idea where he was. Sometimes she heard people talking about him.

"The Prince is doing wonderful work," someone said after his name was mentioned. Someone else said, "It is a pity that Prince Alexei is such an idealist."

"Your father is a remarkable man," Princess Sophia told

her in the lilac salon when she was taking tea with the Grand Duchesses.

She was asked to do this once in a blue moon and disliked it as much as they did. They never knew what to say to her or she to them. Her step-mother disliked her being there at all. The Tsarina hardly seemed aware of her presence once she had graciously greeted her. Polite and inconsequential conversation flitted about the room, a strain to them all.

Zaroushka was used to silence. She liked it. The Grand Duchesses were not and did not. She was not skilled in the art of conversation like them and was lost when anyone tried to involve her in light chatter. Feeling clumsy, she looked stubborn and hostile so no one warmed to her. She felt their indifference and was aware how awkward she must seem, how untutored in social graces. She wondered if her father knew how lonely she was.

More and more the Princess Anya avoided her. Zaroushka was a young lady now and she had the youth the Princess coveted. Anya's hectic life was beginning to tell on her. She was terrified of getting old. Once when they were having lunch in their rooms in the palace – the Tsarina was indisposed and the Princess was forced to eat where the servants served – she looked across the table at her step-daughter, her eyes glittering. Zaroushka always tried to avoid eye-to-eye contact with Anya for her step-mother's feverish gaze unnerved her.

"How pretty you have grown," she said, and Zaroushka coughed.

Her step-mother's attention had made her swallow her food the wrong way. She blushed to the roots of her hair and Maminka slapped her back but still she coughed.

"Here, drink some wine. That will fix it." Anya handed her the glass and Zaroushka obeyed. "We must find some young friends for you," she continued. "I really must introduce you into Society. But not yet. Not quite yet."

When she had gone, Maminka said to Zaroushka. "She

doesn't want you around. Think of it, at all the balls and parties. Your bloom, your youth. The witch would hate it." She smiled tenderly at her charge and touched her cheek with a withered and horny hand. "You know, Zaroushka, you have the bloom of a peach on your cheek. You will be a man-killer with those eyes."

"Oh, don't say that please, Maminka," Zaroushka begged. That was the last thing she wanted to be. Success with the opposite sex – the mere thought alarmed her. Men frightened her. Except for her father, Uncle Vassily and Dmitri.

After that lunch she aided her step-mother by avoiding her and became adept at never drawing attention to herself.

The days when she would happen upon her step-mother engaged in extra-marital romps seemed to be over. Perhaps because she knew better now than to look. If she came upon anything that remotely smacked of a sexual encounter she fled the vicinity as fast as she could.

Until one night ... Zaroushka was forced to leave her warm bed and make the long cold journey to the nearest bathroom. Shivering, she drew on slippers and an ivory knitted shawl over her long white nightdress. On her way back she saw the double-doors at the end of a mirrored corridor open and light spill out into the hall. Trapped, she retreated into the window embrasure where there was a padded seat. There were heavy velvet curtains looped back from the glass. Zaroushka cowered behind the folds on the side nearest the door, the better to conceal herself. If she had crouched in the other corner she would have been instantly in view of anyone coming down the corridor. Her heart was beating so loudly she was sure that in the silence it would be heard.

There was a long pause, then she heard the click of heels on the marble floor. Her step-mother's voice said something to a man. Whoever it was he answered with a loud laugh.

"Yes, my dear Princess. Yes, you are quite right," he said

clearly. The voice was accented and Zaroushka recognised it at once as belonging to her father's friend the Baron Klaus Hoffen von Eldrich.

She shrank even further into the shadows, pulling her feet in under the hem of her nightdress. She heard her step-mother say, "Well, my dear Baron, why should we not fiddle while Rome burns? It is so much more amusing than weeping, *n'est ce pas*?" Then the staccato tapping of her heels retreated into the distance.

There was a silence in which Zaroushka felt the presence of someone, waiting, listening, a silence filled with expectation. She remained quite still her temples throbbing, not daring to breathe. She had not heard the Baron's footsteps.

Suddenly the curtain was pushed abruptly back and she was revealed, shivering in her corner. She looked at him, startled and fearful. He had taken her by surprise and she realised that he must have walked down the long Samarkand carpet that ran from door to door so she would not hear him coming towards her.

She met his black eyes with as much defiance as she could muster, but did not speak. He towered over her, looking down at her, a faintly amused expression in his eyes.

"Why, child, what are you doing here? Listeners, you know, rarely hear anything good. Why do you hide?"

She did not answer, just stared back at him. He wore his evening clothes and she could smell the faintly acrid smoke of his cigarettes. It made her cough.

"Your mother and I dined together," he said lightly.

"Not my mother. My step-mother. She is my step-mother."

Zaroushka bit her lip, furious that she had been stung into a retort.

"Ah, the child *can* speak. Very well then, your step-mother and I dined together tonight."

She turned her head away and sat, her hands folded in her

76

lap, as if her being there was the most natural thing in the world.

"Has your father made arrangements for you in case of ... er, trouble?" the Baron asked after a pause.

"Trouble? What do you mean?" she asked, puzzled.

He shook his head, "Oh, nothing. Now, let me see ... where are you housed in the Palace?"

She did not respond to his query by as much as a flicker. He scrutinised her face for a time, still with that amused expression in his eyes. Then he laughed. It was not a pleasant sound.

"It will not be too difficult to find out," he said. "Don't worry, I only want you to be safe."

He leaned forward so that his face was near hers and again she could smell the stale tobacco on his breath. She hated his nearness but was too nervous to run away.

"Listen, if anything happens ... Some of us can see it coming. Others are blind. Your father can see it, but he plays for time. He is gambling with the one commodity that will destroy him." He tilted up her chin with a long finger. "But, *leibling*, if you are frightened, if anything happens, remember I am your friend. I will help."

She said nothing and realized that he was a little drunk. All she wanted was to get away from this terrible overpowering man.

He took his hand away and laughed again. "You don't know what the deuce I'm talking about," he said, "I know it is difficult to believe now but remember my words, I will help. You and your brother. When you need me, just call."

She looked up at him, enormous eyes expressionless. He stared back at her for a long slow moment then abruptly left her.

For days after Zaroushka puzzled over the conversation. At night in her dreams she could see his face. It both fascinated and repelled her.

Then she forgot him.

That summer they spent in the Alexander Palace and Zaroushka was happier than she had been since her return from the Rostovs. Princess Anya, although indifferent to her step-daughter's education, was very particular about her son's. So busy was the little boy kept that his sister had seen little of him. But now, during the summer break, a new freedom prevailed and Zaroushka was able to enjoy the company of her little half-brother.

Sasha had taken to insisting she stay by his side and being included in all his activities reduced her sense of isolation. She sheltered behind his popularity, enjoying his sparkling company. Sure of being loved, blessed with a sunny disposition and an impulsive need to give his love, Sasha was a very good influence on his half-sister. The ice around her heart thawed in the warmth of his affection. She would look at his trusting face turned to her, feel the confidence with which he snuggled up to her or clasped her hand, and her love for him spilled over.

That summer she was happy. Sasha appropriated the beautiful palace as if he were the Tsar himself. He was as popular as Zaroushka was unpopular. The Grand Duchesses doted on him and only the Empress resented his vitality and glowing health which she compared unfavourably with the ailments of her young son, the Tsarevitch Alexis.

The heir was a source of continual worry to the Tsarina and nowadays the terrible monk was constantly in attendance. He had always alarmed Zaroushka who thought of him as a tall black wraith with the power in his countenance to mesmerise, perhaps to drive you mad. Yet the gentle Empress relied on him, turned to him in her anxiety. Zaroushka kept out of his way in her usual self-protective manner.

It was out in the grounds with Sasha that she found most happiness that summer. There were endless grottoes and pavilions to frolic about in, granite terraces to run up and down, trees to climb and bowers and gardens to play

78

hide-and-seek in. There were poplars, alders, aspens, willows and birch trees. Endless fountains played. They loved to hold their hands beneath the dazzling diamond-spray and splash each other, shrieking with delight.

"It's lovely here. Don't go away again, Zaroushka. I miss you when you are gone. I wish you could always stay." Sasha sighed as they sat, backs against the cool pink marble, and looked over the rolling velvet parkland where the deer grazed.

"Oh, I don't, Sasha! I wish we could live at home, just us. Like a real family. Even the Emperor and Empress are together more than we are."

"I like being with the Tsar and Tsarina. I like living in a palace," Sasha said stoutly. "Anyhow, I'm always with Mama. And Papa sees me often. It's only you who wants to leave Zaroushka."

She sighed. "Yes, it's only me. I'm the outsider." She smiled wryly.

"Sorry, Zaroushka, I didn't mean to hurt you." He was immediately contrite, his warm affectionate nature troubled lest he had upset his sister. He hated to upset anyone. "It's just that …" He hesitated. "Well, I wish that you and Mama would …"

Zaroushka shook her head. "We'll never get along, Sasha. She is not my mother and she simply does not like me."

"Oh dear, I'm sure she does. If you tried you could win her over. She is very easy to coax whereas you can be very prickly, Zaroushka. Oh, how I wish we could all stay together and love one another and live happily ever after."

She laughed. "Sasha, that's for fairy tales," she said.

He frowned and stuck out his lower lip. "Well, I don't see why not. You could learn to love Mother. Father could stay with us all the time. Who could be unhappy here?" He spread his hands and looked around at the beauty of the place.

"Life is not like that, I'm afraid. It's not so simple."

"The autumn is coming," he said a little sadly. "Piotr said it is on the way."

"It's going to be a hard winter, they say." Zaroushka looked out over the soft green earth and the trees still decked with shivering leaves. Soon it would be all gone, the earth dead.

"The birds will fly away because it is getting cold," Sasha said, then looked at her for a moment, his face dimpling. "Race you to the statue," he called, and was away like the wind.

In retrospect the conversation surprised her for Sasha did not usually like to be serious. He avoided the unpleasant and rarely spoke of personal feelings.

But he was correct, Zaroushka thought. It probably was all her fault. She was unsociable. She was difficult to get along with and sadly lacking in charm. She wished she could change her nature but feared it was too late.

Autumn was well advanced. The foliage had changed colour. Shimmering copper-coloured leaves hung trembling on the massed trees in the palace park, shuddered then slowly fell and were blown into drifts on the gravelled walks, to be raked up by an army of gardeners.

When the first snows came she went back to the house on the Neva. Her father came to the Alexander Palace to fetch her. He was in a towering rage.

"You are not fit to be her mother," Zaroushka heard him tell Anya angrily. "Mademoiselle says she knows nothing. You never speak to her. You ignore her presence. Remember, Anya, she is my daughter."

"But not mine," her step-mother replied. "She hates me, that child. I sometimes think she is in league with the devil. She fixes those great eyes on me and ..."

"Don't talk nonsense! Mademoiselle says she has a good mind. It's just that she knows nothing."

"Is that such a bad thing, Alexei? Do women need education when men keep them firmly in their power? Of what use is knowledge when all we can use it for is dreaming dreams?" Zaroushka heard the familiar sound of Anya's ice-tinkle laugh. "As I say, I am not her mother and you cannot fault me on my son's upbringing. Sasha is very clever. He absorbs knowledge. He speaks English, French and German with a good accent, and the Grand Duchesses adore him. He is their little pet."

"I wish you could find it in your heart to lavish such time and attention on Zaroushka."

"Oh, my dear, you know by now that I am quite heartless. Except with Sasha I have found love to be a thankless and risky emotion. It opens you up to such pain. I am not grown-up enough to endure it."

"Will you never forgive me for being the wrong man? Why do you take it out on me when I had nothing to do with the affair of Boris Brunewski? All that happened before we met. Your parents separated you, deprived you of him, not me. His suicide was none of my doing. Yet you have never ceased to be angry with me."

"I was honest with you, Alexei. I told you I could satisfy your lust, nothing more. You took me on those terms. It is too late now to complain."

Zaroushka made of this conversation what she could. It was very confusing. She had begun to realise that her step-mother's ill-temper and wanton ways had something to do with a broken love-affair before she married the prince. This Boris that she had heard her mention before obviously had something to do with her dissatisfaction with life.

Zaroushka did not feel in the least bit sorry for Anya. She believed there were other ways of getting over broken romances. She had no pity in her heart for the woman who had deprived her of the love and warmth all children are entitled to. But it made Anya more understandable to her step-daughter. She ceased to be a witch and became a human being. Thoughtless, selfish, but a human being nevertheless.

"Well, I have come to take her away. She will be better off in St Petersburg."

Her father collected her. Zaroushka left without saying goodbye to the princess Anya. But leaving Sasha was hard. She loved his company so and his companionship had saved her throughout the summer. She hugged him, tears in her eyes.

"I love you, Sasha."

"Me too, Zaroushka."

"I'll try to get Father to bring you to St Petersburg too."

He pulled away from her slightly. "But I don't want to go. I like it here."

She kissed his cheeks and mouth, and after one last hug climbed into the coach.

Maminka as usual travelled with them. Piotr hauled the basket of clothes on top of the equipage. Zaroushka wore her fur hat low on her forehead. Maminka pushed it up.

"You'll get a headache with it like that," she said. Then clamped her teeth together, hoping the Prince would notice and give her an opportunity to tell him about her pain and perhaps arrange a visit to the dentist.

On their way back they saw a company of Cossacks charging across the horizon. The sight of them standing on each other's shoulders as they rode full gallop, shrieking their halloos to the bright morning, their tall black hats remaining perfectly secure a-top their heads, thrilled Zaroushka.

"Are they our friends?" she asked her father.

He nodded. "For the moment, *golubchick*. For the moment. But we do not know what will happen eventually. These are the Tsar's men. The soldiers at the front are deserting now. Everything is very unsettled. Time will tell."

Zaroushka shivered. Quite suddenly she remembered the dark corridor and the saturnine face of the Baron, the stale smell of wine and tobacco on his breath. 'If anything happens, remember I am your friend. I will help."

Zaroushka resumed a life without the companionship of young people her own age. She did not go out much in St

Petersburg. When she did she could not help but notice the poverty and despair of the people and the angry protesting crowds. A terrible winter marked her seventeenth year and it seemed to Zaroushka that all these people were waiting for just one signal before their anger erupted and violence broke out like a volcano. We have a responsibility to them, she thought. Our world is opulent and they live in squalor. Surely it is not right.

Sometimes she caught the gaze of someone in the crowd as she rode by on horseback or in the carriage or motor car, and there was resentment as well as dull despair in their eyes. The face of poverty was ugly. There was something about these people that made her feel uncomfortable.

Once when they were driving down the Embankment of Vasilyevsky Island a crowd closed in upon them. They came quite unexpectedly from a side street that led to the University on the nearby University Embankment. They were a motley assembly of poor and desitute, sprinkled liberally with rabble-rousing students. They jostled the carriage and someone shouted through the window: "Down with Tsar Hunger. Down with war."

Maminka was choked to the core. She pushed up the window with a snap.

"How dare they?" she cried. "They should know how to speak to their betters, or else not speak at all."

Maminka always identified herself with her employer the Prince.

Then Zaroushka was told she should not go out any more. "There has been fighting in the streets," Maminka said. "Piotr knocked two Bolsheviks' heads together and left them both senseless. They are stupid people."

The footman Ilya said it was the fault of the Bolsheviks. "Kerensky is all right," he said. "The Soviet Party would change Russia, bring her into the twentieth century. The workers would get a decent wage and there would be bread again. But the Bolsheviks! They are too radical."

Ilya was well informed about politics. He chatted to them when he brought their polished boots in the morning. He told them that Lenin, the leader, was in hiding in Rapino. Or Razlov. But her father said he was in exile in Switzerland. No one knew for sure. Rumours abounded and in the house no one knew exactly what was happening.

A new governess came and went. She could not stand the angry crowds nor could she stomach being unable to venture into the streets. She fled back to Paris from 'the land of barbarians', to use her words.

They were told that St Petersburg was now Petrograd but Zaroushka did not know why. Her father seemed elated and his excitement communicated itself to his daughter.

"Great days are coming, my dear. Great days."

"But, Father, you said that our soldiers are freezing in the trenches and the people in St Pet ... sorry, in Petrograd, are short of bread. How can you say that great days are coming?"

"You'll see, my darling, you'll see."

That was the trouble with her father; he never explained.

Ilya, a positive mine of information, said that the streets were full of people demonstrating and that the workers had all gone on strike. They were disillusioned with their 'Little Father' for the Tsar's government had done nothing to ensure supplies for the homeland and they were running out of what little they had.

'It's the Tsar's war,' they cried. 'End it.' They wanted nothing to do with it.

But all this happened outside in the streets. Zaroushka heard it all second hand. Nothing interrupted her day-to-day routine. She found it hard to credit some of Ilya's tales even though Maminka swore he was an honest boy and never lied. There was a war raging in Europe. Thousands of Russians fighting and being killed every day and thousands more deserting and sneaking home. The people of her country were crying: 'Enough is enough'. They were angry and starving. Out there in the streets outside her lovely home there were riots and demands for justice. Blood was being spilt. Russian was killing Russian. And as usual, she thought, she was isolated. Out of life. Protected in her glass shell.

Chapter Four

One morning Anya amazed Zaroushka by bursting into her bedroom, white-lipped with fear. Her hair was an amber banner, flowing behind her unbound; her sables were wrapped tightly around her shivering body.

"Where is Prince Alexei?" she demanded. "I have looked for your father everywhere and I cannot find him. Yet here you are abed so late. Disgraceful!"

"What has happened?" Zaroushka asked, sitting up in her nightdress and rubbing her eyes. "What is the matter?"

"The Tsar has abdicated, God help us. We must go. There is such trouble. It is terrible. Oh, where is your father, Zaroushka? Why is he not here when we need him?"

Maminka awoke and rose from her pallet at the foot of Zaroushka's bed, yawning and scratching herself. There was a joyful scream from behind Anya and Sasha erupted into the room, throwing himself on to his half-sister.

"Oh, how lovely!" Zaroushka cried. "To waken and find you here, Sasha. How are you, my sweet, sweet boy?"

"Oh, Zaroushka, it's been so exciting! Running away in the dark. We've had such adventures." His eyes were round and shining. "It's been such a time. The Tsar has abdicated. Mama is in a state."

"The Little Father gone?" Maminka screamed, the truth dawning on her. She blessed herself and fell to her knees, setting up a moaning. "Ach, God help us all, we are doomed. It is the hour of the Beast. The demons will rule.

87

Satan is in command."

Sasha was still bouncing up and down on Zaroushka's bed. "It's all very exciting, Zaroushka, isn't it?" he cried. "On our way here the streets were crowded and everywhere they were taking down the double-headed eagle."

"Oh, Sasha, be quiet, do. I came here to find your father and find him I will."

Anya's determination was quickly met. They were finishing breakfast an hour later when the Prince arrived home. He looked tired but there was a tremor of excitement beneath his obvious exhaustion.

He greeted them all, clearly happy to see Sasha again, though a frown creased his brow when he saw his wife.

"What brings you here?"

"The Tsar has abdicated," she said dramatically.

"He has been prevailed upon to go, my dear," the Prince said calmly. "I have been in the Winter Palace all night. There is movement for reform throughout Russia. Perhaps now we can hope for a more democratic regime. Ah, bread and butter and caviar. A perfect breakfast!"

Anya looked at him impatiently. Zaroushka was watching them both while Sasha munched the food, oblivious of anything else.

"But what should I do, Alexei? You must tell me. Is there danger?"

He looked at her wearily and with some pity. "There is no danger, Anya. The Cossack rifles did not fire on their brothers. Their drawn sabres were waved in comradeship with the crowd. The Tsar has, as you say, abdicated. All is peace. You've had a wasted journey, my dear. If I were you I would return to your friends. They'll need you now. You cannot desert them. It would be dishonourable."

Anya took her husband's advice. She went back to the Alexander Palace. She took Sasha with her and Zaroushka found herself once again alone in the house in Petrograd.

A provisional government had been set up in the Winter

Palace and the Prince spent a lot of time there. However, they were together much more than they had ever been before. It gave Zaroushka great joy to know that her father would be home most evenings and that he would sup with her alone, just the two of them in the big dining room. Each evening she dressed carefully, wearing the gown that her Aunt had bought for her in Moscow and that a maid Valenka had altered for her, adding bands of Swiss lace here and there to accommodate Zaroushka's changed shape.

To her dismay she had a very boyish figure but she had grown upwards and so was taller. She loved to stand by her father and note that she had reached his shoulder and could kiss his cheek by standing on tip-toe.

She loved those tête-à-tête dinners. The Prince gradually unbent to his daughter and often discussed with her the state of things in Russia. He seemed to enjoy her company, her quiet attentiveness, her ability to listen and absorb what he said. He was surprised too by her knowledge gleaned from servants' gossip and conversations overheard.

"You have a good mind, no matter what Mam'selle says," he told her.

"She's not here any more, Papa," Zaroushka reminded him, and he nodded, his mind obviously elsewhere.

"I was never more surprised in my life than to see those Cossacks join the strikers," he continued as if there had been no interruption in his flow of thought.

"Tell me about it, Papa."

"Well, a crowd of demonstrators came into Pushkin Square, led by students and shouting for bread. A young dark-haired man was leader overall. He had a red rag on a stick which he waved high in the air, his head thrown back. The Cossacks came. They were grouped together in tight formation and I thought: Oh God, they'll shoot him. Oh, please God, don't let them shoot him.

"There is nothing worse, Zaroushka, than a man, a soldier, it does not matter, firing on his fellow countrymen.

89

So I prayed but I had little hope. The stage was set for bloodshed. The Cossacks, the tattered crowd, the student with his red rag. I thought: Oh God, he is so young. In ten years' time he'd have forgotten his anger and his compassion and concern. He'd have a plump belly and a plump wife and his biggest problem would be to make enough kopecks to feed the five or six children they'd have."

"Is it not better to die young for your ideals, Father, than to live on and become disenchanted? A cynic?" She hesitated, then shrugged: "A fat *bourgeois*?"

The Prince threw back his head and laughed.

"Ah, Zaroushka, how romantic! But you know a death like that is such a waste."

"I know, Father. I'm sorry to interrupt." She thought better about arguing. She wanted to hear what happened to the student with his head thrown back, the red rag on a stick in his hand.

"What happened to your young student?"

"Well, my romantic young student stood there, waving his ridiculous red rag on his equally ridiculous stick, a thousand hungry despairing faces behind him. They faced the Cossacks and for a long moment, there in Pushkin Square outside the University, there was silence. The snow fell. There was no sound and only one splash of colour. Then with a cry the officer leading the soldiers pulled out his bayonet. His men followed his example. My heart stood still, Zaroushka."

"Oh, Papa, please go on," she cried eyes wide with excitement. She had heard the story a dozen times by now, but it still had the power to keep her spellbound.

He gave her a special smile that told her she was loved.

"Well, after they had all unsheathed their bayonets the officer, instead of giving the order to attack as we all expected, suddenly whipped a piece of scarlet material out of his pocket, impaled it on his bayonet and held it aloft." The Prince shrugged. "Why he did so I'll never know. Had he intended it or was it an impromptu action? Where did the piece of scarlet material come from? Who knows? All I do know, Zaroushka, is, I saw it."

"But what did everyone do?"

'They cheered. There was a spontaneous burst of comradeship, the soldiers saluting the workers and vice versa. It was strangely beautiful."

One evening he mentioned a man called Kerensky who had taken over the leadership. Zaroushka remembered Ilya saying the same name.

"He is a man of words rather than deeds," her father told her. 'He moves everyone with his eloquence. They are carried away by his rhetoric. Heartened by his words, seduced by his enthusiasm, no one asks how the job is to be done, how Russia can be governed and become economically viable.

"Oh, Zaroushka," he said, leaning back in his chair, his face tired, "I wish he could succeed. I will him to succeed. All that worries me is the growing power of the Bolsheviks. The Mensheviks and the Soviet Democrats, all the rest, are moderate. But Lenin, Trotsky, those two – they know exactly how they want the job done. They present no idle threat. We all hoped a new era would dawn." He smiled mirthlessly. "But if the Bolsheviks sieze power then we, the class that still has so much to offer Russia, are doomed. It will be over for us."

"You and me, Father?"

He nodded sadly. "You and me, *golubchick*. And life as we have known it." He glanced at her and added, "But then, the life you have known has not been so wonderfully sweet, has it?"

She shook her head. "It was not your fault that Mama died."

"Dearest Olga," he sighed. "You are very philosophical, Zaroushka."

"Please, Papa, call me Zara now. I'm quite grown up and Zaroushka is my nursery name. I would like to be Zara."

"Very well, Zara Arkadova Vashinskova, Princess. You will be called what you will."

They got to know each other better during that lull in the storm. She plucked up courage and asked him about the Baron.

"He is a very brilliant man, Zaroushka. An Austrian who has always been sure that the Germans will lose this war. He saw it coming and he sees the end. He is of the opinion that Germany is about to enter a terrible period of economic and social decline, but he sees it triumphing in the end if it takes twenty years. Germans are constituted to work for and achieve success, he says." The Prince pressed his lips together a moment. "He is not a popular man but that does not worry him. He is indifferent to public opinion." He glanced at her sharply. "Why do you ask?"

"I have met him once or twice and each time he has made me feel ..." she sought for the right word, "... uncomfortable."

The Prince nodded. "Yes, Klaus is like that. He cuts straight to the heart of things. He is, I think, rather a cruel man. But he is also extremely intelligent and a very good friend."

Soldiers, deserters from the front, began to filter back into the city and there was growing unrest.

"It could go either way, Zara,' the Prince said one night as he poured himself some brandy. "It is chaos now, but something will develop and emerge from this. Let us pray it is the right thing for Russia."

"Maminka says the German Army is approaching Petrograd," Zaroushka told him. "Perhaps after all the Baron was wrong?"

"I have never known him to be," the Prince pronounced firmly, then added, "I want you to go to Pesochny."

He saw her face crumble into piteous protest, "Don't look like that, Zara. I thought you loved Danya Bolovna?"

"Don't send me away, Father, please. I couldn't bear it!"

92

The Prince looked away from her into some far-off place where she could not follow him. "I must, sweet girl, I must."

"You always say that but it isn't true. You could keep me here with you if you really wanted to, you know you could." Her eyes were full of tears.

"I am afraid to, my darling. The Baron may be right after all, and the Germans may lose this war, but if they succeed in coming here it would be terrible for you. Also, there is a lot of unrest at the moment and I would feel happier if you were at Pesochny." His voice was firm and she knew that once his mind was made up it was useless to argue with him. But she tried once more.

"Father, please let me stay with you. I am not afraid. I am so happy with you now. I don't want to leave you."

He looked into her big dark eyes, wet with tears like flowers in the rain, and sighed,

"I know, and I have been so happy here with you. I do not want you to leave either. But I am responsible for your safety and if you remained here your presence might hamper me. Don't you see? You would be my main preoccupation while it is Russia which must be paramount in my mind now."

After that she ceased to argue. Maminka prepared for their departure. She still had not found an opportunity to ask the Prince about her teeth and was crochety with pain.

They left Petrograd the next week, Zara's heart brimming with a melancholy sadness that would not allow her the luxury of tears. As she grew older she found the sudden outbursts of childhood were a relief denied to her now. A dull hopelessness overwhelmed her spirits and she accepted her dismissal with bowed head. Her father hugged her and kissed her forehead.

Everything, everyone that gives me love and makes me content is taken from me, she thought. I am unlucky. I am not meant to be happy.

"I do not ask for very much, Maminka," she said aloud.

"Only to be with kind people like the Rostovs, or to be with my father. It is little enough. Why will God not listen?"

"I do not ask for very much either," Maminka replied tartly. "only some relief from the pain in my teeth." She patted Zaroushka's hands and added, "The Lord's ways are not our ways. They are mysterious ways and we must not question His wisdom." She smiled and nodded sagely.

Zara did not feel that she had been any help at all.

Life at Danya Bolovna, the hunting lodge near Pesochny, was dull and uneventful. There were no visitors and the seventeen-year-old Zaroushka had no companionship at all. Her only pleasure was playing the piano. She practised morning, noon and night. There was nothing else to do.

She daydreamed about her father and the Rostovs and in those lonely months, cut off from everyone, she fell in love with the memory of her cousin Dmitri. She had a photograph of him with Nina and their parents and she lay for hours on her stomach, gazing at the sepia reproduction of the Rostov family. She touched the handsome face with her fingers and yearned for him, remembering every conversation they ever had and whispering to him in day-dreams, mooning over the photograph as she lay on her bed. She felt full of longings she did not understand and emotions she had little control over.

Maminka was worried that the girl seemed to burst into tears for no good reasons that she could see and as quickly recover. She lost her temper too and was petulant for the first time in her life. She had depressions and periods of unexplained elation.

"I've never seen you like this before. Cross as two cats. What is the matter, Zaroushka?" the old nurse asked, shaking her head.

"Oh, leave me, Maminka! Just leave me be." And she would go back to her bedroom and lie there, dreaming of life, adventure, love and Dmitri and fretting against her solitude.

This state of affairs, mercifully, did not last too long. The

Princess Vashinskova arrived with Sasha, announcing that they intended to stay for a while. Zara was enchanted to see her brother but did not look forward to the Princess Anya's living with them in so confined a space. Danya Bolovna was by far and away the smallest of their homes.

However her step-mother was curiously subdued. She was a-twitch with nerves and restless as a caged leopard, spending a lot of time in her room and having her meals sent up to her. Everyone was aware of her presence even though they did not see much of her.

"There's disaster in the air," Maminka said with a fatalistic air of enjoyment. "Mark my words."

Zaroushka did not care what disaster struck. She had company again. She forgot Dmitri in the joy of having her beloved brother to talk to.

"We came here because they have taken the Tsar and Tsarina and the family to the Urals, no one knows where. I think they are prisoners, Zaroushka," Sasha told her. "The poor Tsarevitch is always sick. They think Rasputin is dead. Murdered."

He sat with his sister in front of the big roaring fire in the living room where once the gypsies had feasted with the Prince and Zara. 'Mother is very upset. She is devoted to the Empress no matter what impression she gives. She likes to pretend that she cares for no one but it's not true." He shook his blond head vehemently.

"She does not care for me, Sasha," Zara said quietly.

He put his arm around her shoulders. "I know, dearest. I don't know why. I've heard her say that Father has always loved your mother more than her. 'He lusts after me,' she says, 'but he loved her.' She told me once that if your mother, Zaroushka, looked anything like you, that would be enough to keep a man enthralled."

Zara looked at him, surprised. "Why, what a compliment!"

"Yes. I told you she's not all bad. She cannot help herself,

95

I think. But do not let us talk any more about mother. How are you, Zaroushka? What have you been doing?"

She rolled her eyes heavenwards.

"Nothing. Absolutely nothing. Oh it's so good to see you, Sasha. So good."

She hugged him to her fiercely. "If only we knew where Father was."

"Oh, in Petrograd or Moscow, trying to solve the problems of the world."

"The problems of Russia, you mean," Zara said, and sighed. "I wish he'd come. I feel anxious about him and I don't normally."

"Well, it's an anxious time."

How precocious he was, Zara thought. Poor boy, his upbringing had been nearly as odd as her own. He had lived a cossetted life, surrounded by adoring females. The Tsarina adored him, the Grand Duchesses petted him, his mother doted on him. He must have been aware, too, of Anya's bizarre sexual habits, yet he forgave her and loved her and had an almost protective attitude towards her. He was, Zara thought, a very sophisticated young man. Had he, like herself, lost his childhood somewhere in the palaces, lost forever the chance to be careless and innocent, joyous and irresponsible? It was no use asking such questions. The answers would change nothing.

"Have you been in the forest?" Sasha asked. Zara shook her head. "Maminka would not let me out. She said Father would kill her if anything happened to me, and if I went into the forest I would be tempting providence."

Sasha and she loved to penetrate a short way into the green-gloom of the forest, terrifying themselves as shadows leaped from the dense undergrowth and twigs crackled underfoot. They never dared go far. It was uncharted territory and the wild animals who inhabited the depths were an ever present danger. They carried guns when they went. Their father insisted on it. He had showed them how to fire the weapons though he had made them promise never to use them unless there was no alternative.

But they loved to go a little way until the path petered out. The roots of trees, fallen branches, logs left by the woodcutter, moss and a thick carpet of decaying leaves soon took over. Even in winter, when it lay under snow, the forest was a magical place. There was no indication of direction in the ever-shifting olive depths, daylight eclipsed by the thick tangle of branches overhead. They felt enchanted then. Magic children. They made up fantasies, enacting them in the hushed and muted stillness.

"We'll go this week, Zaroushka, on an expedition without telling Maminka? Are you game?" Sasha whispered.

She nodded. "Oh, yes. Sasha, it's so lovely to have you here."

The next day the Prince arrived. It was totally unexpected and his arrival sent Zara into transports of joy. But the wonderful unity of those weeks in Petrograd seemed broken, fragmented. The Prince kissed her absentmindedly. He seemed even more preoccupied and worried than usual.

"I'm hungry, Maminka," he said. "I have been travelling day and night."

Dinner was about to be served and the Prince joined them but did not speak to anyone. He seemed not to hear Sasha's merry chatter or his daughter's gentle questions. He wolfed down his meal then rose and summoned his wife.

"Perhaps when you are finished, my dear, I could have a word with you in your room?" and without waiting for a reply he left the room.

Anya followed soon after and when she had gone Zara hurried to her room and unashamedly put her ear to the wall. Something was very wrong, she could tell. If only her father would stop treating her like a child. She could hear the Prince's voice clearly.

"It is bad, Anya. The situation is becoming worse for us every day."

"How, Alexei? What has happened?" The Princess sounded subdued. The autocratic tone she usually used to her husband had gone and in its place was a fearful note.

"In one word: Lenin. The Bolsheviks are in control, Anya. We must leave Russia."

Zara's heart began to thump uncomfortably.

"You are mad, Alexei, quite mad! Leave Russia? Have you lost your reason?"

Even as she heard her step-mother's incredulous question Zara realised that the Princess was the most Russian person she knew. It was inconceivable to picture her outside the country she loved.

Sasha came into the bedroom and Zara motioned him to be silent. "We have to leave Russia," she whispered to him almost inaudibly.

"Listen."

"I will *not* leave Russia." It was the Princess's voice, raised in anger.

"We have no choice." The Prince's tone was cold and firm. "I have no desire to go either. How do you think I feel about this? Or don't you care? A life's work in ruins. Listen, Anya, try to understand. The Bolsheviks have introduced new laws, effective as from now. All our land and possessions are confiscated. All our property is gone. It reverts to government. It does not belong to us any more. That means we have nothing. Nothing, do you hear? It is over for us. We must bow gracefully to the inevitable and go."

"I will not." Her voice was stubborn.

"Then you will find yourself homeless, penniless and very unpopular. They are not killing us – yet. But they may get to it quite soon. Klaus says they have probably done away with the Imperial family."

"Oh, no. No! They cannot. They would not do that," she moaned.

"My dear, it seems they can and they have. We must be practical. We have to think of the future."

"We should have gone with the Rostovs. We should have left then."

"Well, we did not. We could not."

"Because *you* wanted to stay. Now see what it has brought us! Skulking out of our country by the back door. It is monstrous. And the Tsarina … Ah God, that dear lady, the children. I cannot bear to think of it."

"Listen, we cannot delay. They will start on the city properties first but soon they will remember Danya Bolovna. We must fly."

"But if they have taken our money and possessions, how are we to manage?"

"I have been transferring money to Switzerland. Tomorrow morning we will leave here. There will be a boat waiting for us in the Gulf of Finland. We will cross the channel then try to reach Zurich. Quietly, without pomp and ceremony. No fuss, dear Anya. You must leave your more flamboyant clothes here. Take only your simplest things."

"Oh, my God, the world has come to an end," she sobbed. "What about the children?"

"They, of course, come too. But I don't want them frightened or upset. We will tell them all about it tomorrow.' He paused then said, "The Baron is coming with us."

"Klaus? Why?"

"It is he who has arranged our escape. He has the contacts. Let the children have a peaceful unworried night's sleep. Zara broods so. She becomes anxious and I don't want to upset her unnecessarily."

Zara and Sasha looked at one another guiltily.

"You always think of your daughter first," the Princess said. "What about Sasha?"

"He is a happy carefree boy." Sasha pulled a face at his sister. "I have no fears for him. He is a credit to you, my dear."

There was an ironic note in his voice. They heard him leave, then the click of the door as he closed it behind him.

Sasha, who had been rolling his eyes about comically since hearing his name mentioned, collapsed on Zara's bed in silent mirth. "Happy," he chortled, "carefree. Oh heavens!"

"Hush, Sasha. Your mother might hear us."

She still had her ear pressed to the wall. She could hear Anya crying aloud: "Damn! Damn! Damn!"

Sasha had quietened down. After a pause he asked Zara what she thought of the news.

"Oh, I don't know. I won't like leaving Russia too much, but I expect it will be exciting. Switzerland ... I wonder what it is like?"

"Mountains and chalets and it's pretty, I think. Oh, and snow."

"Not snow again," Zara groaned. "How I long for the sun. Warmth. Still, maybe I'll be happier there."

The next morning everyone was up early. The Prince came into Zara's room and told her they were leaving.

"I know, Father. Sasha and I heard you last night."

He gave a little snort. "What a naughty boy he is. He never said a thing to me when I spoke to him just now." The Prince shook his head and looked into her wide guileless eyes. "But you would never dissimulate, would you? Ah, you are very special, my darling. I love you very much, do you know that?"

She nodded, her heart full.

"You are so like your mother. You have Olga's smile."

Perhaps in Switzerland they would be close all the time, as they had been in Petrograd.

"I love you too, Papa."

"Now get up. Don't bring anything with you that is not entirely necessary."

"But I have nothing to bring, Father." She looked at him, proud and happy to be so helpful and accommodating. "I have the dress Aunt Sonya gave me, and the earrings. That's all, really."

100

He looked at her and an expression of great sadness crossed his face.

"Nothing else?" he asked.

"No Father," she said proudly. "Nothing at all."

"Well, when you are ready go down to Maminka and have a good breakfast – it will be quite a journey. Then I'm going to send you and Sasha into the forest a pace and you will wait for us there."

"Why, Father?"

"In case anyone is watching. We have to be careful. We don't want to be seen all leaving at the same time. Anya and I will take the carriage. The motor car would be too conspicuous. We'll drive past that pathway there. Come and see."

He crossed the room and Zara padded to the window behind him. "Look," he pointed, "where the tall oak rises above the others. Wait for us there."

"But no one is watching, Papa dearest. I don't understand."

"Look, Zara, just do as I say. The Baron has suggested that we do things this way. He has been so good, making all the arrangements, and I trust him. This is a dangerous time. We must do as we are advised.'

The Princess was cross and out of sorts with everyone at breakfast. "Zaroushka, your manners are abominable. Stop rubbing your mouth with your napkin. Sasha, you are stuffing yourself again! Do you want to get fat? Alexei, can't you stop tapping your spoon like that? I have the most appalling headache this morning."

"I am sorry, Anya," the Prince said.

"Will we never see the Tsarevitch again? Will we never live in the Palace?" Sasha asked.

Anya pressed her handkerchief to her lips and gave a little moan.

"Now, now, Sasha," said the Prince. "We do not know what will happen. But you will be with Zara. You must do as she says. You will take care of him, won't you?"

She nodded her head fiercely. "Yes, Papa. Of course."

Maminka bundled Sasha and Zara up in their fur-lined coats and hoods and gave them woollen shawls for their legs in the coach in case they got cold. Zara felt waves of excitement grip her stomach. She thought of the journey ahead of her with fearful but eager anticipation. Perhaps at last they would be all together, a warm cosy family in a small house in Switzerland. She would even forgive Anya if she could always have Sasha and Papa near.

She and Sasha went out into the icy bright morning hand in hand. The world was silent and silver-white beneath their feet. The snow sparkled and their breath came in bleached clouds of vapour.

Obediently they did as they were told and walked towards the forest. Zara glanced back at Danya Bolovna. It rested in the snow, quiet and peaceful, a wisp of smoke trailing from the chimney. If anyone was watching they would see nothing out of the ordinary.

"It's all right," she said to Sasha. Her lips were stiff with cold and she could feel the sharp air in her nostrils.

"I can't feel you," patting her with his mittened hand, he said, "Here, put your arm in mine. We're like the Babes in the Wood."

"Oh no! Don't say that," she cried, and suddenly felt a shiver of apprehension course over her skin and down her back.

When they got into the forest thick silence enveloped them like a cloak.

"We haven't got our guns with us," Sasha whispered.

"I know. I wish we had."

The trees were white-laden except where the snow could not reach the pines and evergreens. There was no birdsong here and Sasha and Zara tiptoed in, skidding a little on the leaves and moss underfoot. Sasha stopped.

"Let's watch and see the carriage brought around," he said. "Then we'll cross to the oak."

She nodded and they turned. The house looked small and like a painting from where they stood. They were hidden by the trees and Sasha pulled down a branch which obstructed his view. A flurry of snow fell off on to Zara's face. She was busy wiping it off with the back of her gloved hand when he gripped her arm.

"What is it?" she asked.

"Look there. There," he whispered. She followed his gaze and at first could not understand the alarm in his voice. The carriage had come round to the front of the lodge and she could see the Prince and Princess standing near the old brougham with the stout figure of Maminka and the small Valenka behind them. Piotr sat in the coachman's seat up top. But what Sasha had remarked was a company of about ten soldiers galloping towards them from behind the lodge. The little family group in front of Danya Bolovna were obviously completely unaware of the newcomers riding on to the scene.

For a moment Zara stood silent and perplexed, not really comprehending what was happening.

"They're drunk," Sasha cried. "Oh God, they're drunk!"

They had heard tales of drunken deserters, marauders roaming the countryside causing havoc wherever they went. Zara looked at the band of men. They swayed on their horses and most of them were holding bottles which they raised to their lips every now and then. They were shouting and laughing and the brother and sister could hear their voices carried on the wind: raucous, menacing.

The soldiers spotted the carriage. What happened next was so swift, so sudden, that Zara and Sasha were never sure afterwards exactly what precipitated it. They stood frozen to the spot, unable to believe their eyes.

The men rounded the house and for a second the group of people, black against the snow, stood frozen in tableau. The leader of the ragged band said something. They saw the Prince gesture. The soldier replied, seemed to be arguing, when another soldier still on horseback drew his gun. They saw a sudden flash, a puff of explosives, and the huge figure of Piotr slumped over in the driving seat of the coach.

The leader too had a pistol in his hand. It popped with a flare of red, and yellow smoke. Like broken dolls, the figures of the Prince and Princess fell into the snow.

Flashing in front of her eyes Zara saw the wolves again. Blood in the snow. Oh God, the snow splashed scarlet with blood. The blood, oh dear God, not the blood of her darling Papa. Oh no, sweet Jesus, not that. She opened her mouth to scream and a hand was instantly clamped over it. She tried to bite, heard a muffled curse. She was held in a vice-like grip as she watched, helpless. Two more blasts of gunfire and then the plump figure of Maminka and the childish one of Valenka crumpled pathetically where they had stood.

Zara could not scream as she would assuredly have done if the strange hand had not held her fiercely an unrelentingly. By now she did not care what happened. She was perfectly sure that she was in the hands of more soldiers and that she was lost. It did not matter. Nothing mattered now.

She sucked in her breath and bit down as hard as she could. She took another breath preparatory to screaming loudly. Sasha was somewhere near. She would struggle and fight for his life even if her own meant little to her now. But as she was about to yell out she felt herself hit hard on the chin and lost consciousness.

When she came to she was in a carriage jogging along at a leisurely pace. She had thought she would be bound and gagged as she regained consciousness. Memory came flooding back quickly – too quickly. To her surprise her arms were free and there was no restraint on her at all. Next to her she saw Sasha, sitting up, looking out of the window at the snowy landscape. His shoulders were shaking and she knew he was crying. She had never seen him weep before and did not know what to do. She waited. When his sobbing had diminished she leaned across and put her hand gently on his arm.

He turned at once to her, brushing his eyes which were swollen and red.

"Oh, Zaroushka, Mother and Father are dead. What will become of us? We are all alone now."

She drew a deep breath. She would not think of her father yet. It was not the time. She might die of grief if she thought of that. Not yet. Not now.

"Where are we going?" she asked her brother.

"To the boat. As Father intended."

"But how?"

"The Baron was in the woods. Father had told him to be. He was going with us. He had made all the arrangements and we were going to stay with him until we could get to Zurich. Father had told him to save us if anything went wrong. The Baron said Father was sure something would go wrong. He had an instinct. At any rate he was afraid you would scream and the soldiers would come and get us. They would kill us too for we had seen what they had done. He had to knock you out. Oh, Zaroushka."

He drew a jagged breath and she squeezed his arm. For the first time she became aware of the ache in her jaw. For some reason she was glad it hurt. It focussed her attention on a pain other than the one of loss.

"Yes, I would have screamed," she said, "I thought it was the soldiers."

Her brother nodded. "We waited a long time in the woods, the Baron and I. You were out cold. The soldiers ransacked the lodge. They took everything they could carry then set fire to the house. It's funny how quickly it burned. Yes, we waited a long time."

Burned. All those memories. Memories of her father. All gone in smoke as if they had never been.

"When the soldiers went away," Sasha continued, "the

105

Baron carried you to the coach. We left you there with the coachman and the Baron said he was going back to see Mother and Father. He wanted to make sure that they were …" He gave an involuntary sob. I said I wanted to go with him. He understood."

His voice became very shakey again and Zara put her arm around him. She was numb with pain, feeling that somehow this was all a dream and that she would soon wake up and call Maminka.

"When we came to the lodge we saw them there, lying in the snow. Even Piotr had fallen off the coach. Maminka was holding Valenka's hand, their fingers were intertwined. Stiff. Very stiff. They all lay there, broken, quite dead. It was as if they had gone somewhere else and left only a shell behind them. It was awfully lonely, Zaroushka. I wonder where they went."

Sobs overtook him again and he turned in her arms and buried his face in her shoulder. She held him to her fiercely. I will not cry, she told herself, I will not. Sasha needs me now. Besides, if I start I will never stop. There are not enough tears in the world to rid me of my grief.

After a while he raised his head. "We couldn't *do* anything about them. We just had to leave them there, in the snow," he said. "The house was burning. We could have taken them and put them in, hoping the fire would consume them, but there was no time. The Baron said every moment was precious."

"Where is he now?" she asked. It was getting dark. She felt dull and dry-eyed and her head and chin throbbed unmercifully.

"He's sitting up in front with the coachman," her brother answered sleepily. His tears had exhausted him and his eyelids were heavy. "He thought we might like to be alone for a while," he added.

"That was thoughtful of him," she said. He had not seemed to her a particularly considerate man, but perhaps she had been wrong.

Her jaw began to ache badly. She stared out of the window of the carriage. The clouds were black and angry, racing across the face of the moon. She had wanted to begin again, but not this way. Her hopes for the future had been so high.

"Where are we going?" she asked.

He shrugged and pulled the rug closer over his knees and up around his waist.

"I don't know eventually, but for now I think we're going to Narva. There is a boat there for us." He yawned. "I'm so tired, Zaroushka. So very tired."

"It's all right. You can sleep now," she soothed him, and his head sank on to her shoulder.

The journey over the trackless landscapes, white under the moon, seemed endless. When at last they came to a halt, Zaroushka put her head out of the window to see where they were.

Under the stars a small village slept. The houses were blanketed with snow and she could see an onion-domed church at the far end of the main street. It looked like a picture postcard but the cold nearly froze her face rigid and she pulled her fur hood closer around her cheeks, covering her nose with one velvet-lined side.

The door of the coach was opened and she saw the Baron in a heavy caped overcoat, his fur hat firmly on his head. It made him look taller than he really was. He motioned her to descend. She shook Sasha awake and he turned his sleep-flushed face to her. "Come on. We're here." She helped him out of the coach.

The snow crunched beneath their boots and their knees felt weak after the long drive. The Baron guided them into an inn.

A sleepy host who had obviously been in bed before being rudely awakened sat them down before a dying fire which he proceeded to build up. He was a plump many-stomached man, stubble-faced and red-eyed. He bent to stoke the fire with heavy arms as if he were still asleep. As he worked to coax the blaze into full brilliance his wife came bustling down the old wooden stairs. She was full of concern and motherly cluckings, and although she was almost as fat as her husband, with hanging jowls and a pendulous bosom, she was of quite a different character. She had a jolly and consoling manner and hurried about cutting great swatches of pink ham and cured meats, hacked them thick slices of black bread and poured them wine both red and white.

It was difficult to understand the dialect she spoke but they managed somehow to communicate and she fussed and cooed over them.

The Baron seemed to have disappeared. Zara and Sasha sat silently eating and drinking, allowing themselves to be mothered by the stout landlady.

There was a big clock on the wall over the mantelpiece. Its ticking was the loudest sound in the room. Zara watched the pendulum swing and the minute hand click around until her eyes watered. The room had a deserted look. It smelled of stale alcohol and the smoke of pipes and cigarettes.

Zara shivered. She wished she could feel something, anything, but there was nothing inside her now except numbness. She wondered briefly where the Baron was but somehow couldn't be bothered to concern herself too much over his whereabouts, even though their fate depended on him.

She found it difficult to swallow and so drank deeply of the wine, partly because she was very thirsty and partly to help the bread and meat down her dry throat.

Sasha was half-dead with fatigue, the aftermath of grief and shock. His chin kept drooping down upon his chest, his head hung heavy. They were just about to go to bed, the landlady having said their rooms were ready, when the door opened and the Baron came in stamping his boots and shaking the snow from his long overcoat. Zara felt too tired to ask where he had been and simply stared at him without interest.

"Have you been well fed?" he asked. She nodded.

"Sasha is very tired. He is exhausted," she said.

"Well, I want to speak with you a moment, Zara. Alone. Will you take him up?" He looked at the innkeeper's wife who nodded.

The Baron gestured to Zara to reseat herself opposite him in front of the fire. His face was severe and remote. She sat gazing at him, feeling stupid and a little woozy from the wine. He took her limp hand between his.

"Zara, we have a problem."

She did not care. She could not seem to rouse any emotion at all. Surely she should be worried? But she sat there and stared at him unblinking. Eventually he let her hand drop. Her gaze seemed to disconcert him. He glanced away. The fire by now was blazing and leaping, red-centred with golden tongues licking and consuming the logs. Poor logs, she thought, remembering what Maminka had said about them being in pain. But Maminka had gone. Gone. There was no more Maminka.

"Zara, did you hear? I said we have a problem." There was anxiety in his voice. "Here, have some more wine. You look like a ghost." He poured her a glass full and when he pushed it towards her he spilled some ruby drops on the white tablecloth. Blood on the snow, she thought.

"I expect you'll take care of any problem, Baron von Eldrich."

He stared at her a moment. "It's about you, Zara. You have no papers. Sasha has his from the time he was in Europe with his mother, but you have none. Well, you have never been out of Russia. You cannot go anywhere without papers."

"Well then, what shall I do?" She sounded completely indifferent.

"It means we would have to leave you here. We could not take you with us." He was watching her intently. As if he is a cat and I a little mouse, she thought. And shrugged.

109

"Perhaps the landlord and his wife would let me work here." She nodded to herself. She thought it a good idea. How nice it would be to live in this cosy little inn, be mothered by the fat landlady and not have to think any more.

He stared at her, nonplussed. "Zara, have you forgotten who you are? Your Father was Prince Alexei Alexandrovich Vashinskov. You cannot possibly work."

"Then what can I do?" She did not sound very interested.

He took a deep breath. "You can marry me."

She looked at him, at last a little startled. "Marry you? What on earth do you mean? I do not wish to be married. Are you mad?"

"It is the one way we can get you to Helsinki, to Finland. As my wife you can travel anywhere and there will be no problem. It would, of course, be in name only."

She shrugged again. "All right," she said indifferently. Her voice was dull and listless and she lifted the wineglass to her lips and drained it. "You were my father's friend. Whatever you decide will be all right."

He seemed disconcerted by her sudden capitulation but recovered quickly.

"I have visited the church," he said. So that was where he had been. "I told the priest and he agreed to perform the ceremony early tomorrow morning. He said it was all very irregular and was most reluctant. But I told him we had been affianced for some time."

"Did money change hands?"

He glanced at her, startled. "What? Well ... yes. I gave him a contribution."

"Why did you tell him we were engaged? It was a lie." He was startled to hear contempt in the voice of the young girl he had thought deep in shock.

"It was the only way to get him to agree. Listen, Zara, I don't think you realise how serious our situation is, or rather yours. We *have* to get out of here, out of Russia. It is the only way."

"I don't care much what happens to me."

"You will, Zara. You will. At all events, think of your brother. He needs you. If I have to leave you behind, he'll never forgive you or me."

"I said all right."

"Then I'll get the inn-keepers to call you at five o'clock in the morning. I'm sorry it's so early but if we are to make a start it is necessary."

"I quite understand. I'll be ready."

He looked at her curiously. Her face was pale and turned away from him, yet he could have sworn the expression on it was contemptuous.

"God, Zaroushka, you're a cold fish! You have not shed a tear over your father's shooting. And you agree to this without argument."

"Never call me Zaroushka," she said, her voice was as sharp as a steel blade.

"Whatever you wish," he said as coolly.

She sat motionless, hands clasped loosely in her lap.

"You should get some rest," he said finally.

She nodded obediently and went upstairs.

Chapter Five

The next morning the landlord knocked at her door as the first crowing of the cock shattered the silence of the dawn. The Baron, in overcoat and boots, stood behind him. The landlord carried a tray on which were fresh baked *blinis*, some caviare and a large cup of steaming coffee.

They were both surprised to hear a gentle 'Come in', and entered to find Zara standing in the middle of the room. She was all in white. She wore the lace dress that her Aunt Sonya had bought her in Moscow and the pendant pearl earrings. The Baron stared at her, a perplexed frown creasing his forehead. She did not move but stood like a virgin martyr awaiting execution.

"I thought I should dress like a bride," she said, and he saw her lips tremble. "It's all I've got."

"Come along now. Where's your coat?" he asked gruffly. He strode over to the wardrobe and took out the fur-lined garment. "Come along," he said again.

She followed him meekly out of the room and down the stairs and only once spoke before they reached the church, to ask if Sasha would be coming.

"No, I thought it better not," the Baron said. "He's still asleep."

"Oh. Did you tell him?" she asked.

"No." He shook his head.

No more was said. He took her elbow and they stepped out into the street and began to walk down to the onion-domed church that lay directly ahead of them. Yellow light fell across the pristine covering of snow from the bright little windows of the houses humped in their protective mantle. The moon was still visible, pale in a calm cloudless sky. The Baron's giant silhouette was thrown before them as they walked. The landlord and his wife walked behind but Zara was not aware of them. She felt outside all experience, impervious to what was going on. It was a play, a painting, a man and a girl walking down the long snow-covered street at dawn to the church at the end.

The door was open, the priest there to meet them. They walked out of the cold silver shimmering into the warm light of icons and candles and cloth-of-gold. Yellow beams glittered on luminous walls; incense burned over a crimson flame. It was nevertheless colder inside the church than out.

The main protagonists – Zara, the Baron and the priest, bearded and grand in his glittering vestments – spoke as if hypnotised. The ceremony was short. There was no music, no ceremonial, no pomp, nothing except the bare essentials. The priest seemed reluctant, almost boorish, and his hands shook.

The landlord and his wife acted as witnesses. They were obviously troubled by the strangeness and coldness of the performance. In a very short space of time all the correct words were said, all the pledges were exchanged and it was over. No kiss was given, no tender gesture went from one to the other, no glance of mutual understanding showed that the pair were agreeing to love, honour and obey, that they were intending to spend the rest of their lives together. The landlady felt profoundly shocked without understanding why.

The icons glowed under the candlelight and the smell of the incense made Zara feel faint.

The papers were signed and the landlord and his wife made their mark. The Baron led the little party from the ante-room where the paperwork was completed back into the church. At the altar-rail he took Zara's elbow. They paused for him to pick up her coat. When he turned back to drape it over her shoulders, she had slumped to the floor. She lay on the cold mosaic, still and pale, in a crumpled heap of white lace.

She did not remember much about the journey. They had been at sea, she knew. It was stormy with huge slate-grey waves. Thunderous black clouds filled the charcoal sky.

The boat was a dirty tub, rusty and smelling of tar. It was cold and damp, a piercing cold that sliced into the body and a damp that made her bones ache. She had always hated the cold but had never known such a death-like chill.

Life held no reality for her. She felt as if she were watching herself from the outside, looking at herself from a distance with little interest and less concern. She felt totally indifferent. She did not notice what was happening around her and Sasha said he was fed up. Talking to her was like talking to a lamp-post.

He spent his time feeling sea-sick. He was uncomfortable and miserable and not afraid to complain. He had been used to servants hurrying to supply his every need. He was used to cossetting and petting. So he demanded this and that, clean napkins, hot-water bottles, drinks of water, all of which he got, and for the sea to calm down, which he did not.

He spent a lot of time weeping for his dead parents, shaken by anger because they were dead. But his sorrow alternated with moments of excited anticipation. He drove the Baron to distraction with questions about their destination.

He, however, would not commit himself and Sasha had to be content with the certain knowledge that they had left Russia and were on their way to a remote property of the Baron's somewhere in Northern Europe.

"Why won't you tell me where?" Sasha insisted. "Why?"

But the Baron remained silent and did not even reply.

"He is a strange man, Zaroushka," Sasha said to his sister.

115

"Why do you say that?"

"I don't know. He is devious, I think. I believe also that often he does not tell the truth."

Zara nodded. "I think so, too, Sasha, but what can we do? We have no family, no friends other than him, no money, nothing. We don't even know where we are. He is all we have and I suppose we must make the best of it."

Sasha nodded in reply. He noticed the ring on her finger and in time asked about it.

"I married him," she said tonelessly.

Her brother was incredulous. "Married the Baron? Why? He's old enough to be your father."

She knew this was not precisely true; knew also what he meant.

"I had no papers. You had. There was no other way to get me out of Russia, he said. I had to do it."

Sasha was still shaking his head. "But when? Where?"

She told him all about it and still he stood shaking his head, his hands clenching and unclenching.

When she had finished he said softly, "There is something strange here."

The journey seemed interminable. They hardly saw the Baron. The sea heaved and threw them about and they clung together in their fear and loneliness.

They were in a mountain range and it snowed all the time. They had been travelling for days and nights. Zara had lost count of time. They had jogged along in the coach, their bones rattling, then taken a train, then crossed another sea. They had been met by a motor car, driven through a city and changed again to a train and then a carriage. They had slept on the way and twice in a hotel and on the boat. They had eaten in the same haphazard way, on the trot as it were, travelling, travelling, until they were bone weary of the road and the sea and the droning of the engine and the endless rocking and jolting.

And now they had arrived. Another palace, Zara thought. It looked like a schloss, a turreted fairy-tale German castle from the outside. Inside it could have been Petrograd or Tsarskoye Selo; high ceilings, gloomy portraits, bad plumbing, cold, damp, inadequate lighting.

On their arrival they were greeted by the Baron's aunt, a plump lady in her fifties who seemed delighted to see them.

"So this is your bride, Klaus?" she twittered, standing on tiny feet as if poised for flight.

Zara was still stunned after the long journey, but that did not matter. She was infuriated at the remark and took an instant dislike to Aunt Gertrude. The woman had an ingratiating manner and was clearly nervous of her nephew. Her black eyes darted to and from the Baron while she kept up her unceasing and pointless chatter, interspersed with flattery and little pleas for attention directed towards the Baron and totally ignored by him.

"Oh, it is so nice to have you here, my dear, but not as wonderful as having Klaus home again," she said to Zara. "And you, my young Prince, how handsome you are! Nearly as handsome as Klaus when he was your age."

"Is everything prepared as I instructed?" the Baron interrupted. His tone was brisk and cold.

When had he let her know the arrangements? Zara wondered. But she gave up the thought. She was too tired and bone-weary from her travels, and too worn from emotional shock and the uncertainties that faced her.

"You need not change for dinner tonight," the Baron said casually to Sasha and Zara as they stood, forlorn and exhausted, in the great echoing hall. The floor beneath their feet was of black and white marble, chequered like a chessboard, and the chandeliers that sparkled above their heads were enormous. The size of it and the giant squares dwarfed them and Zara felt she was a child again, without resources or rights. They had arrived at their destination and she knew things had to be faced. But now she dimly felt that what was being asked of her was obedience.

"Where is that stupid girl?" the Baron asked impatiently. "Katya!"

A small square-faced girl appeared through a door presumably leading to the servants' quarters. She had a closed peasant face and wore a maid's cap and apron. She curtseyed to the Baron, her head lowered.

"What took you so long?" he asked in a sibilant whisper, "Why were you not here, as you should have been, waiting for me?" He lifted her chin between his fingers and jerked it sideways, letting it go in what Zara thought a vicious little jerk that must have been painful.

"Get Bonner to bring the large trunk up, Katya, and you take my wife's basket and her brother's ... if you can manage it," he added sarcastically.

Zara looked at him in surprise and as much anger as she could muster in her exhausted state. There was that word again: 'wife'. What did he mean by using it? Their marriage had been undertaken as a mere formality. What was happening? All the Baron's previous urbanity seemed to have disappeared inside this house. He stood tall and dominating in the chequered hall and she felt suddenly afraid.

He turned away abruptly. Aunt Gertrude twittered again, something about Zara herself as his wife and bride.

"We will have a light repast in the dining room and then it will be time for bed. I'll see you both in there in ten minutes," he said to Sasha and Zara, pointing towards a room on the right of the chequered hall. Then he entered it, leaving them with Katya in the hall.

He had spoken in German and Sasha tried to engage the little maid in conversation in that language. She looked at him with hostility and behaved thereafter as if she were deaf and dumb.

It did not strike Zara on that first night in the snowbound castle that it was odd that her bedroom was so far away from

118

her brother's. Achingly tired, she splashed her face with cold water from the ewer, noted that the room was large and comfortable, put a clean collar on her dress and went down to the dining room. She met Sasha on the way.

"Where is your room?" she whispered.

"Up there." He pointed to the floor above hers. "Right at the end of the corridor. I wish we were nearer each other."

They dined in silence. The Baron sat at the head of the table. The dining room was huge and the table long. He put Zara opposite him at the bottom and Sasha and Aunt Gertrude on his right and left side respectively. No one spoke. The silence was broken only by the clink of cutlery and glass, and the greedy slurping and chewing of Aunt Gertrude whose eating habits revealed an obscene greed. She attacked her food with table manners that drew glances of contempt from her nephew.

Zara never remembered what they ate that night. At last when the meal was over the Baron nodded.

"You may go to your rooms now."

It's just as if Sasha and I were the same age, Zara thought.

"I'll see them up." Aunt Gertrude drew her gaze from the last almond tuille, half-rising from her chair.

"No need to deny yourself the last biscuit, Aunt," the Baron said in a cutting voice. "Zara and Sasha are quite capable of finding their own way to bed, *hein*?"

"Yes, sir," Sasha agreed briskly. Zara could tell he was trying to keep his voice manly and free from the tears she felt sure he wanted to shed. He's only eleven, she thought. He's been through a lot.

At the top of the first flight of stairs she kissed him and held his hands. They looked at each other wordlessly.

"We'll be all right, won't we, Zara?" he asked in a quavering voice.

She nodded. "He was a friend of Papa's," she said firmly, and kissed him again.

"Then it must be all right,' he said, a doubtful expression

on his face. "I just wish I could like him better. Goodnight, Zara."

"Goodnight, dearest," she answered and went into her room.

She took off her clothes, missing Maminka. The old woman would have clucked and fussed over her and helped her with buttons and over-the-head. She would have picked her things up off the floor where Zara now discarded them. She pulled on her flower-printed flanelette nightgown and fell into bed, sinking almost immediately into that semi-consciousness she had become used to. In that condition there was no pleasure and no pain for her, no sadness and no happiness. It was more terrible than anything she had ever experienced before. It was a state of non-being.

The door opened. There was no knock. She sat up, startled, and saw the Baron at her bedside.

"What is it?"

She could not think what he was doing there. He stood looking at her coldly. He was wearing a long wine-coloured brocade dressing-gown.

"What do you want?" she asked through stiff lips.

He laughed. "My conjugal rights, my dear."

At first she did not understand what he meant. Realization came when he slipped open the sash of his dressing-gown and let it fall to the floor.

He was quite naked underneath and she gasped in horror for she had never before seen a full-grown man without his clothes. She remembered briefly the cries of the men as they leaped into the waters of the Neva. Her Uncle Vassily, the Kutuzov brothers, Dmitri, those nice men. They had been hidden behind the leaves and branches that grew on the promontory but there had been nothing alarming in their nakedness, she was sure.

This was different. Her soul shrivelled from the sight so brutally thrust upon her, her mind rejecting the implication of his words.

"Oh no," she moaned softly.

"Oh yes," he replied. "I saved your life. There is always a price to pay."

"That is not what Father taught me," she cried through trembling lips. She drew the bedclothes tighter under her chin.

"Your father — ach! He was a foolish idealist. And because of that he is dead and I am alive."

With one swift move he pulled the sheets and blankets away from her. She sat shivering with fear and outrage. Another quick movement and she felt his strong fingers catch the neck of her nightgown. With a vicious jerk he tore it from her body. She screamed, one short sharp scream, and as she did realised that no one could hear her. Was that why Sasha was so far away?

"Oh, please don't! Pity, please," she cried, trying to appeal to his better nature. "Don't do that to me."

For some reason this seemed to excite him and his breathing grew heavy and audible.

Hardly realizing what she was doing, Zara leaped away from him and jumped out of the other side of the big four-poster bed. She ran to the door, naked and trembling. He caught her, and jerking her round hit her with the back of his hand across her face. She remembered her step-mother's blows but they were mild compared to this one. She could taste the blood in her mouth and for a moment everything was concealed in a haze of indigo pinpricked by darting specks of light. He caught her wrists together in one hand and dragged her across the room to the bed.

He picked her up and threw her on to the sheets. She tried to dart away again but he pinned her arms cruciform, leaning on her, smiling to himself. There was no sound in the room but their heavy breathing interrupted by her piteous cries.

He did not treat her as herself, Zara Vashenskova, but as

an object that he hated and was manipulating for his own satisfaction.

She screamed as he entered her, assaulting her brutally, taking her unaware and unprepared. He cried out his satisfaction at his thrusting and her wincing agony. It was loathsome, what was happening to her; her whole being revolted against this terrible violation. She struggled, pain overwhelming her, but it only seemed to stimulate him and he took her at his leisure while she wept for the first time since her father died. Her lips mumbled a prayer for her ordeal to be over or for God to let her die. Every so often, panting, he would stop, then with a grunt resume the dreadful penetration of her body with renewed vigour and animal cries that disgusted her. Pain pierced the centre of her being. She wanted to die.

At last with a cry he collapsed on top of her, inert and heavy. She stared at him with revulsion. Almost at once he rose. Without looking at her he picked up his dressing-gown from the floor where he had dropped it, donned it and left without a word.

She was covered in blood. So were the sheets, her nightdress and the bedclothes. The pain was intolerable. She moved herself to the edge of the bed, each movement an agonizing effort, and swung herself off. She tried to stand but her legs buckled beneath her and she collapsed on the floor.

The carpet smelled of dust. It assaulted her nostrils and she sneezed violently. The spasm shook her body and activated sharp tremors of acute pain that shot through her and made her lose consciousness momentarily. When she opened her eyes she knew only one thing: she must wash.

The ewer of cold water and a basin stood on the washstand across the room. It took her a long time to cross to it. She had to lie on the floor for about ten minutes before she mustered enough strength to crawl across. She managed to pull herself up the wooden legs of the stand, inch by painful inch. Finally perpendicular, she held on to it as waves of nausea and cold chills, stabbing pains and throbbing bruises, overwhelmed her.

When at last she could control the trembling and the pain had lost its piercing sharpness and become general again, when at last she could bear to move, she splashed her face with the ice cold water and dried it with the towel, then set out slowly to sponge herself down. She had to take a break every five minutes or so and when she had finished her body was raw and red from her scrubbing and in the basin the water turned from pink to crimson with her blood.

Moving slowly as if she were a broken doll she searched the drawer until she found her other nightdress which she pulled over her head. She went back to bed, and slowly, agonizingly, but with a determination worthy of her father, dismantled the bed, piling the bloodied linen into a mound in the corner. Taking the eiderdown which had been thrown back she wrapped it around herself and lay on the mattress. Cocooned in the cover, she closed her eyes against the horror of the last hours and slid into unconsciousness.

Chapter Six

"Will you go to his bed tonight?" Sasha asked, looking at her curiously. She shook her head. "No. But he will come to mine." She stared at the ceiling, her voice expressionless.

They had been in the fairy-tale palace for months now. Her life was a nightmare that had become routine. Zara did not know how much her brother knew. Or guessed.

The terrible ordeal was almost a nightly occurrence. She struggled and screamed. She had bitten him, scratched him, to no avail. She had wept and begged but it was no use. He was impervious to abuse, pleas, violence on her part – which did him no real harm in any event. She was petite and fragile, his strength like iron.

He often beat her. He liked to hurt her. She remembered her father saying he was a cruel man. The memory of Papa was what she found unbearable. She did not want to think of the Prince. It was too distressing. She felt ashamed before his memory, guilty and besmirched. All she could do was try to suspend all feeling except her hate.

She fed on it. It sustained her. She knew that without it she would perish. It was a red-hot palpable growth within her, a pulsing energy-giving power. One day she would destroy this man. There was no doubt about it in her mind. She knew she would annihilate him and the thought kept her alive.

Where they were they still did not know. It was not Germany, Austria or Switzerland. Sasha said they had not

125

travelled long enough to have got very far south in Europe, and the climate was wrong. He thought they were in Norway or Sweden. Zara did not care where they actually were. It was not very different from Russia. The same snow. The same large imposing rooms. The same absence of comradeship. The same loneliness. But here she was virtually a prisoner. Here she was a victim, tortured and persecuted. Oh, their movements were not curtailed in any way, but they were high in the snowbound mountains and there was nowhere to go if you left the castle. They were trapped as surely as if they had been bound and gagged. At least in Russia she had been free. She might have been lonely, unhappy, but she had been free. Sasha had led a social life at home and now he missed it acutely.

The staff did not speak French or Italian and of course they had no Russian. Zara and Sasha's schoolroom German was not fluent enough to help understand the maid's and Katya refused to communicate with them. They could not comprehend the other servants gabbled dialect. That it was Swedish or Norwegian, Sasha was fairly sure.

"The Swedish Ambassador was a friend of the Tsarina, and he had just such a lilt in his voice," he told Zara, who shrugged.

Sasha read. He at least had that compensation. The Baron had a large library. But books for Zara were a chore and so her only recreation was the piano. Even playing that ceased to be the delightful and satisfying pastime it had once been for the Baron often came to listen.

He would glide in to the music room and sit quite still, a frown of concentration on his face, that dark cold face she had come to loathe. She would become aware of his presence and her fingers would grow stiff, the music cease to flow. He terrified her. He was implacable, incomprehensible, a grotesque demon who towered over her with his obscene manhood that tore her body apart, crushed her spirit and filled her soul with hatred. He defiled and

126

humiliated her to the depths of her being.

Nowadays there was always a knot of fear in her stomach. It never unwound and grew like a tape-worm in her belly. All day her apprehension increased like a cancer spreading within her until bedtime came, bringing with it the horror of her nightly ordeal. Her days were spent husbanding her strength for the inevitable gross assault, the unforgivable insult to her maidenhood.

There was no hope of escape but still she fought and each night lost the battle. She was left bruised and beaten, mentally and physically.

One night, to her horror, after she had been pinioned to the bed during the Baron's onslaught, her body, seemingly of its own volition began a strange response to his. With disgust she fought the involuntary reflex movements and her terror increased. It gave rise to a latent dread she had lived with since this sexual subjugation began; namely, that she was like her step-mother, that she had been somehow contaminated by the things she had seen as a child. That something in her manner or bearing had invited the Baron to treat her thus. It was a vile and harrowing thought and she was tormented by it.

She did not think beyond each day. Sasha plotted escape but she was too tired, too bruised, too defeated to join him in this fantasy.

Not beaten though. She still fought her persecutor, each night, still mustered enough energy to try to fend off the violation. The staff and the Baron's aunt all treated her as a blushing bride. It caused her grave emotional pain that there was this total misunderstanding of her situation. To them, she was the Baron's young bride. They believed she was entitled to a period of adjustment but when, after a time, she showed open ingratitude, they were intolerant of her. They thought her lucky. She had a wonderful husband, a handsome man who had rescued her and brought her out of Russia. Saved her life and that of her brother, as well as

127

marrying her. He had brought her to this beautiful castle. She should be grateful.

Sasha, after a few months, was able to understand some of what the servants said to each other. And of course he and Zara could talk to Aunt Gertrude who spoke French tolerably well. They came gradually to understand her place in the house. She was obviously a poor relation, and as such dependent on the Baron for everything, a roof over her head, food in her belly. It was impossible to speak freely to her. She adored the Baron, or pretended to, but was obviously terrified of him and equally frightened of upsetting him. She never inquired about Zara's bruises and injuries. When she tried to speak of them Aunt Gertrude firmly closed her mouth and shook her head.

"Don't you dare to involve me in husband and wifely disputes," she said firmly. "It is none of my business. Klaus is an angel to me. I will not listen to a word against him. Whatever he did to you, Baroness, you deserved."

As she spoke the woman's eyes darted around in alarm as if there were spies behind every door.

"Is it possible to go shopping here?" Zara asked her one day after tea.

Aunt Gertrude looked surprised, "Why should you want to go shopping?"

What a stupid woman she is, Zara thought. She had watched her gorging herself on cream cakes when lunch had been at one and dinner would be at eight. It was now four o'clock.

"I would like to go out and do some shopping," Zara reiterated.

"Well, you'll have to ask Klaus," Aunt Gertrude said. "But I don't think he'll be pleased. He likes to have everyone here." Again her eyes darted about. "Under his control."

It was a strange thing to say and she immediately became contrite and tried to rectify the slip of the tongue. "I mean, he likes to know exactly where we all are."

128

Zara did not want to ask the Baron's permission to go out. She guessed he would say no and it would be one more humiliation for her, one more manifestation of his power.

She did not know when Sasha had cottoned on to what was happening to her, they never spoke of it.

One day her brother had said something to the effect that he hoped the Baron was not too tough with her. She had glanced at him, startled and embarrassed. He blushed and looked away. His face was immensely sad. There was no doubt about what he meant. A long silence fell between them. At last she had said, "No, Sasha, it's all right. Don't fret for me."

And in a very small way the nightmare had lessened. The Baron stopped coming to her bed nightly. Now he came about three times a week. He would arrive within half an hour of dinner ending, or else not at all.

Zara waited breathlessly each night. If his footsteps sounded outside her door her heart-beat skidded to a halt, then renewed itself with a vigour that shook her thin chest and threatened to tear it apart. During the ordeal that followed no words were spoken. She often cried or screamed, moaned or cursed him, but he never engaged her in conversation, never talked to her except to tell her to be quiet.

On the other nights she would wait, breath held, every muscle tense. "Oh please God, please," she would pray watching the minutes tick by on the ormolu clock on the mantelpiece. She would lie still as a corpse beneath the bedclothes which, if he came into the room, would be torn from her frantically gripping hands. As the minute hand approached ten-thirty she became more and more tightly strung, her body rigid as if awaiting execution. If the hand passed the six and he had not arrived, bit by bit she would relax, her body unclenching, and her heartbeats steadying.

She usually cried a little then, softly, in relief. In reprieve her tense body stretched itself in the vast bed, luxuriating in its release.

129

With the realization that tonight she would not have to endure the agony and humiliation came self-pity. She dreaded the arrival of these waves of weakness. She knew that sobbing, 'Why? Why?' did not achieve anything. She fought the feeling of reproach she felt towards her papa at those times. Why had he not warned her about the Baron? Reason told her that perhaps he had not known. But he had said that the Baron was cruel. Why then did he leave his son and daughter to this man's protection? It was pointless telling herself he could not have known what would happen. He was not a stupid man. He should have considered all contingencies. He was after all, their father, their guardian.

Her total confidence in her father was shaken, her complete faith disturbed. And he was not there to answer her accusations.

Most nights she eventually succeeded in shaking off the black cloud of doubt and then, for a glorious while, peace would descend. She could drowse, and send up a prayer in thanksgiving for these precious moments of peace.

The days passed uneventfully. Zara and her brother walked in the castle grounds. Behind and before them rose mountains, snow-capped vistas claustrophobic and impenetrable. There seemed to be no roads and even when the snow melted all they could discern were little trails and paths that petered out and led nowhere.

The terrain was very like that a couple of miles from Danya Bolovna. Zara sometimes wondered if they had travelled in a circle and were really in Russia all the time. Perhaps Papa was still alive, wondering where they were ... But when she confided this to Sasha he shook his head.

"I wish it were so, Zaroushka, but I saw him. He was dead. I told you, there was no mistaking. We are in northern Sweden or Finland. Somewhere like that."

Aunt Gertrude was with them a lot. Zara was sure she was watching them at the Baron's order. Her incessant chatter drove them mad. She talked of nothing, rabbited on and on, and stuffed herself with nervous greed at every opportunity as if she expected a famine. She hid her dislike of them under a joviality that rang as false as her pretended concern for them. Her whole life was a performance, Zara thought, even her protestations of devotion to the Baron were insincere.

She was never still for a moment, creating an air of unease. She addressed Zara as 'Baroness' despite the girl's insistence that she was not. Aunt Gertrude merely smiled at her denial of the title.

"I know it's a great honour," she would twitter, flashing raisin-like eyes to right and left and up to the ceiling. "I know you feel unworthy, dear, but I have seen the certificate and indeed you are the Baroness Hoffen von Eldrich. It's all there in black and white." And with a satisfied smile she would bob her head vigorously.

Zara knew that the woman hated them both and wished they would go away. She gathered that before she and Sasha had arrived at the castle the Baron had been away a lot and his aunt had had the place to herself to do as she pleased. She was resentful of the intrusion. She had to keep up appearances and she found it a strain.

"Before you came here ..." She often began, "before you came here my nephew was away a lot. Most of the time, in fact. Paris. London. Moscow. Of course, there was no war then. He would bring me bon-bons from Paris, Bath Olivers from Fortnum & Mason in London, caviare from Russia. My days were peaceful then." She sighed, glancing slantwise at them, her meaning clear.

"Is the war still on in Europe?" Sasha asked. Or "Where are we Aunt Gertrude?" or "Where is this place?" She never gave a reply. She would parry the questions or change the subject, saying: "Ah, well, I can't sit here gossiping all day" or "I wonder if it is nearly time for tea". The questions remained unanswered.

They spent long aimless days; Sasha reading, Zara playing

131

the piano. Sometimes the Baron spent a few days away. Zara would sit in the window and stare over the wastes of snow. In the spring she watched them melt and the green emerge – so many shades, olive, emerald and apple – as life came to the countryside.

From its fixation with her father and his real or imagined inadequacies, her mind had turned to thoughts of escape. Flight seemed, on the surface, to be impossible but it became her obsession. She spent hours discarding plans, exploring possibilities. All her ideas so far had to be cast away as unworkable but she persisted. There seemed no way out but still she searched for a solution.

She told Sasha. He had changed, she noticed. She supposed it was inevitable that he should. It was not a healthy way for a boy of his age to grow. There was about him – a cowed, trapped look. His shoulders slumped, his eyes slid from hers as guiltily as Aunt Gertrude's and he had lost that sunny candid frankness that had been so charming. He had become thin and it did not suit him. He needed flesh on his face. He was pale where he should have been rosy. His body, once lithe and limber, had lost its energy and drooped, overwhelmed by a lassitude he seemed incapable of shaking off. His brightness and quickness had dimmed and slowed and there was a bleakness about him that worried her.

"We'll have to escape from here or we'll both go mad," she said.

He did not seem optimistic. "We wouldn't get very far," he said, "it's all open country. Then the mountains. There's nowhere to hide. We have no money. Where could we go?"

"Anywhere is better than this," she said fiercely.

He took her small hand between his and pressed it. "I know it's hard for you, Zaroushka. Very hard."

He always called her Zaroushka when they were alone. If he forgot and used the long soft-syllabled name with the others present the Baron reprimanded him severely and Aunt Gertrude corrected him as if he were retarded.

132

Zara snorted at his remark. "You don't know what it's like or you wouldn't call it 'hard'. 'Hell' would be better!"

"I'm sorry, dearest sister. Nothing I say will help, I know that." There was a sob in his voice. Instantly she was apologetic, regretting her brusqueness. She put her arm around his thin shoulders.

"Dear little Sasha, I'm sorry. It's not your fault." She looked at him earnestly but his big eyes dropped under her gaze.

"We must try to escape. Don't you see? If I don't try to plan it, I'll go stark staring mad. You do understand?"

He nodded tiredly. "Of course, and I want to escape as much as you do. But how? It's hopeless. There's no way."

"Well, I've been thinking. There must be cottages. Everywhere in the world there are cottages. Some of the servants leave at night. Some go away for a few days. Couldn't you try to learn their language? Make a friend?"

He shook his head. "I tried that," he said wearily. "There is a footman, he is a valet to the Baron. He seemed a friendly sort of fellow. I used to talk to him in German. I asked him about ways out of here, where we were and so forth. But he told the Baron." Sasha paused and stared out of the window. She could see he was near to tears.

"He was very angry with me," he whispered.

Zara felt a surge of blinding rage overwhelm her. The thought that the Baron might hurt her little brother filled her with a new and terrible fury. She tried to keep her voice calm.

"You never told me this. How dare he! What did he do to you?"

Sasha's face was a mask. There was no expression in it.

"Nothing. He said terrible things. He will kill us if we try to get out of here, I'm sure of that." He looked at her hopelessly. "And who would care if he did? We are quite alone, Zaroushka. No one gives a damn what happens to us."

133

"We do!" she said emphatically. "We do, Sasha. I care. I care about me and I care about you. You care about yourself and me, otherwise you would not be so unhappy." She screwed her face up in pain. "And I want to get away. Across those mountains. To freedom."

They both looked out over the new snows and the wall of mountains that circled them. Her heart filled with a burning ache to escape and be free, to fly away from her purgatory and like an eagle soar her way to the sun.

"I've thought and thought, Sasha, and there is only one way. We must wait until spring again, or better 'til summer when the land is green and kinder than it is just now. Remember last year? It looked so pretty out there and there were berries and green things growing and there must be streams. We must wait 'til then. When we think the time is right we will go."

He lifted his hands, palms upward. It was a gesture reminiscent of Anya and Zara looked again at his sad face. He had loved his mother and must miss her. She felt full of sympathy for the boy whose bright and cherished life had changed so dramatically.

"If we walk from here to there, Zara," he said irritably, pointing to a tree not a hundred yards from the window at which they sat, "someone would see us and there would be a hue and cry."

"Not if we leave before first light. In the night even. If he ... when he ..." She hesitated, seeking her words carefully and trying to control the tremor in her voice when she spoke of that man. She continued in a rush, "When he comes to my room, he usually stays about an hour. That would make it eleven-thirty. Say he takes another hour before going back to his room, settling to rest. Allow another hour for him to sink deeply into sleep – making it one-thirty. We could leave then. By the back door. We could walk as far and as fast as we could. We could try to find a cottage, or perhaps a carriage would pass."

"I'm going to try anyhow. I've got to. It's all that keeps me from despair. If you don't want to come with me, you don't have to."

"Of course I will, Zaroushka, you know that. It's just that I'm not the bravest person in the world. I'm afraid of his punishing me, you see. I'm afraid of what he might do."

"Yes, but we must not think of that now. If we do, we'll never succeed. Father used to say that you should always believe that you will succeed. He said that it was half the battle. So, little brother, we must be confident that we can do it, and if we are we'll win. You'll see, we'll win."

The snows melted. They had passed their second winter under the hostile roof. The Baron went away and Zara made a few sorties out and about but realised quite soon that they were watched much more closely than they had ever dreamed.

Once when she had wandered some way across the snow she had suddenly found her arms being gripped and, turning, found a burly kitchen maid pinioning her in an iron grip. She had seen the servant around the castle but had paid scant attention to her. Now she was hustled on to a sledge driven by the German-speaking footman. She looked as innocent and outraged as she could while trying to explain to them that she had merely gone for a walk. She met only stony implacable faces. They did not listen to her and when the Baron returned and they were having dinner that night he stared at her with a cold amused expression in his eyes.

"You must not walk too far from your home, Zara. It is dangerous. There are wolves in this vicinity."

She looked at him, raising her eyebrows, but said nothing.

"In any event I do not like it," he continued.

"A good wife is obedient to her husband," Aunt Gertrude said smugly. "You are a well brought up young lady. You should know that."

She glanced at her nephew for confirmation, her head

bobbing, but he was staring at Zara, his thin dark face full of mockery.

He loves this power over me, she thought. He loves to prove that he is the master. But she said nothing. To make any comment would be a sign of weakness. So she simply lowered her head and remained silent.

He came to her that night. She lay paralysed with fear, listening to his footsteps approaching her door.

The dreaded ritual commenced. But tonight, for the first time, she did not struggle. He pulled the bedclothes down with his usual abrupt movement and she let him, lying there without protest. She felt too tired, too depressed, to fight him. He told her to take off her nightdress and she obeyed him. She felt indifferent. He pushed her back and she lay inert, like a dead thing, waiting.

He seemed curiously disconcerted. "Fight, you little bitch. Fight me!" he cried through his teeth.

She made no movement.

"What's the matter with you?" he hissed, shaking her. She flopped like a rag-doll in his grip. "Got to like it like your step-mother? Underneath you are all the same."

She said nothing. It was the first time he had spoken to her like this. He tried to anger her, insulting her, saying things he knew would hurt her. To no avail. She had learned something. She had a weapon against him. He had enjoyed her resistance, been stimulated by the fierce fight she had put up during the eighteen months they had been here. Tonight, for some reason, she had been too indifferent to fight and had closed her eyes the better to shut him out. It had worked in her favour. She had thought he wanted a passive acquiescent wife. She had been wrong. That night his conquest of her was quick and obviously unexciting for him. Inwardly she rejoiced.

One of the things that had most distressed her was how accustomed her body grew to the battering it received. She resented the fact that physically she had become inured to his

136

rape. Her soul still suffered.

She watched him go, her body bruised but not as battle-torn as usual, her feelings somewhat less outraged.

He came to her for the next two nights. Experimenting she became putty in his hands, like a doll or a puppet. She emptied her mind and read pages of music in her head, lying stone-still as he laboured above her.

He hit her but it had no effect. He screamed obscenities at her but she did not respond and behaved as if she were deaf.

It worked. He spent himself but there was no vicious erotic triumph.

She bided her time. On the following night she waited for him but he did not come to her.

She could not sleep. She was full of her little victory. It was tiny, a minute triumph. She realised she was still his plaything, a human being he treated as an object and subjected to foul misuse. Nevertheless she was elated. She felt that hitherto he had taken everything he wanted from her. He had achieved sexual relief in her body without her consent and she had thought that there was nothing she could do about it except fight him. That fact diminished and humiliated her nearly as much as his sexual abuse of her. Now she found that she could, in some small measure, spoil it for him and the fact filled her with unholy glee.

She decided she would tell Sasha. If he could be beaten like that then perhaps he could be tricked in other ways. He was not, after all, all-powerful.

It was summer. They could plan their escape. It might work. She would wait until next week. The next time the Baron came to her she would fight him again. Exhaust him. Let him have his last victory. When he had left her he would be bound to sleep deeply. They could go then. They could creep away out into the night. Away to freedom. Her heart beat faster and for the first time she felt a surge of hope and a real belief that she and Sasha might make it.

She got out of bed. She had never left this room at night.

She was in no condition to if the Baron had been with her, and if he had not, she had been worried in case she should draw his attention. Tonight she decided she did not care if he heard her. He could rape her again but she had made up her mind that she would not be here much longer, that she was prepared to die rather than remain.

She put on her dressing-gown and went to the door, opening it inch by inch.

There was complete silence. Not the breathless silence of a waiting house but the calm silence of a sleeping one. Her door creaked a little and she paused, trembling.

Nothing. She moved again. Slipping out into the passageway she closed her door carefully behind her. She remembered Russia and the palaces, the long corridors flanked with mirrors. There were no mirrors here. She remembered the sights she had seen and shivered. She hurried up the stairs to her brother's room.

She was inside before she realized he was not alone.

The scene that greeted her was worthy of the Princess Anya. Zara froze, unable to absorb what was happening before her eyes.

The Baron was naked. So was Sasha. Her brother's small face was piteously creased and his naked body, joined to the Baron's in an obscene embrace, looked white and frail. The large black-haired familiar frame of the Baron cleaved to the fragile milk-white boy in a sacriligious dance. The man held Sasha around the waist, grunting, moaning, quivering. Zara knew from bitter experience that he was nearly finished. Sasha's eyes met hers in a wild and agonized glance, but one that was glazed too and out of focus.

Stunned, she grabbed the handle of the door and tried to turn it. It slipped in her trembling fingers, so she used both hands. The sounds behind her mounted, profaning her ears. She left the room as fast as she could, closing the door behind her.

Her knees buckled under her. She sank to the floor and

vomited. Her stomach heaved and she could not get her breath. When the spasm was over she got up, intent on reaching her room. The door opened behind her. Whimpering, her body shaking, she turned to run but the Baron's hand descended on her shoulder and he spun her around. He hit her then and she sprang at him, trying to tear his face with her nails, choked by dry tearing sobs. He laughed at her hysteria and caught her wrists in fingers of steel.

"Your brother is just as much a whore as you are. Didn't you know? Didn't he tell you? I thought you might have compared notes."

She wrenched her hands free of his grip, clawing at him, trying to damage him. There was a mist before her eyes and her shock, horror and disgust had turned to blinding rage. He laughed again.

"I like it when you're like this. A tiger cub. But you will learn who is master here."

He dragged her kicking and screaming down the corridor. Sasha had come to his door and when he saw what was happening, ran after them.

"No, no! Zaroushka, don't. It's what he wants. Don't! Please leave her alone. Oh, leave her alone."

Zara had gained control of herself. The sound of her brother's voice calmed her. She became quieter.

The Baron dragged her down the corridor, opened a door and shoved her inside. Then he pushed Sasha in after her. She stood, trembling but calm, as he came in after them.

"You have been let off lightly up to now,' he said. "You have been fed, housed, given every comfort. Isn't that true?"

He stood leaning against the closed door, staring at them. The room was a study of sorts. The walls were dark and pannelled and there was an Indian carpet on the floor. A large mahogany desk with writing materials stood in the centre with a large leather chair behind it. It was obviously well used and had an air of comfort.

"Is that not true?" the Baron repeated. He took a whip

from a stand beside the desk. It held walking-sticks, other whips, shooting-sticks and similar paraphernalia. Sasha and Zara shrank behind the desk as he flexed the whip then cracked it through the air. It made a singing sound, like the wind in the turrets.

She could see he was enjoying himself. He was master here. She shivered, desperately afraid. She had angered him, disturbed the routine and thus given him licence to behave as he pleased. He would feel entitled to do as he wished and punish them both for her resistance. Sasha would suffer too. Poor little brother. No wonder he had changed.

The whip sang through the air again.

"Answer me," he commanded.

"Yes. Yes, you have," she replied dutifully. Resistance now must be wrong.

He advanced a step towards them and she gripped the edge of the desk. It helped her to stand for her knees were weak.

"No one could complain of my behaviour," he said. "You, you feeble creature, are my wife. It is your duty to please me. But you don't seem to understand that."

He stared at them both, his black eyes snapping. For some reason she did not understand, he was angrier than usual. She lowered her eyes to the desk.

"I saved your lives," he continued. "If not for me, you would be lying there in the snow with your father and Anya."

She saw it then and could not believe the evidence of her eyes. A gun. There, on top of the desk, half-covered in papers. A surge of excitement coursed through her. Terrified lest her face reveal anything she kept her eyes lowered, her hands on the edge of the desk.

"They're dead now. You are alive, and you are my creatures. You belong to me."

For a moment she wondered if he were mad. Then she concentrated on the gun.

She moved her hands a little way forward on the desk. The Baron continued his tirade. He was carried away on a stream of self-justification, not really looking at them.

Suddenly she realized, more by instinct than anything, that Sasha knew what she was about. For one horrible moment she thought he was going to give the game away.

"We didn't mean any harm," he said, moving forward and a little to his right thereby concealing her hand and drawing the Baron's attention to himself. The strategy worked. The Baron took a step forward.

"Shut up, you little bastard!" he cried. Then his voice dropped and he said softly, "Come here, little man. It's time you were taught a lesson."

He took another step towards Sasha, a gloating expression on his face. As he did so Zara grabbed the pistol, praying it was loaded. She fumbled with the safety catch as her father had shown her, aimed the gun as steadily as she could, and fired. She had only used a gun a few times in her life but she had never forgotten the lessons. Anger and pure hatred drove her on. She did not even flinch from the recoil. The gun was loaded.

The Baron had not understood. He had not seen her actions. He took another step as a bright red stain appeared on the white vee of his chest visible beneath his dressing-gown.

His eyes bulged. His face changed colour. He stared at her in amazement and put his hand to his shoulder, making hoarse little grunts low in his throat. She saw he was trying to breathe. There was silence in the room except for the sounds the Baron was making. Sweat trickled down Zara's body as she pulled the trigger again. And again. She went on until the gun clicked emptily, then she dropped it. She stood panting a moment then turned to her brother.

He stood staring at the Baron who now lay motionless on the floor. A pool of blood, dark, almost black, was spreading from his body.

Zara shook her brother. "Come on, Sasha. We must go. Come on!"

She pulled him away towards the door. His eyes were glazed again and he was sobbing.

"Sasha, it's all right now. We're free. Free."

She stood, her breath coming jaggedly, her whole body trembling, over the body of the man she had hated, repeating over and over again: "Free, free, free!"

Chapter Seven

About to leave the room, Zara wondered if anyone had overheard them. She hesitated. Logic told her that the servants and Aunt Gertrude had been told to ignore alarming night noises or else had been located where they could not hear. The latter seemed more likely.

Zara struggled to control her shaking body. When she had regained a modicum of calm she looked around the study. She opened all the desk drawers. Eventually she found some gold coins. She put them in her dressing-gown pocket. She found some more in a silver box on the mantelpiece and took those too. Then she cried, "Our papers," and frantically ransacked the desk until she found what she was looking for.

Sasha was still transfixed, staring at the Baron on the floor. "He stirred," he said suddenly in horror. "He moved."

"Nonsense!" she said briskly, and bent to feel his pulse. She was filled with loathing at the feel of his skin under her fingers, but there was nothing, no quickening of life. "It was a trick of your eyes," she said. "Come along, Sasha. We'd better hurry. There's no knowing who we have wakened or who might come around snooping or checking. Go back to your room and pick up just the bare minimum."

"What?" He looked at her stupidly.

"Just your coat and a jersey and warm socks and a hat. Oh, think, Sasha, think!" She shook him gently.

"Please, help me. We cannot stay here now. I've committed murder, don't you see? We must go. We've got to escape."

He nodded. "Yes," he said. "Of course." But still he did not move.

"Go on then." Her voice was frantic. "Please."

Galvanised suddenly he left the room. They crept down the corridor together. The castle was silent. Now and then a window rattled in the wind, no one stirred.

Zara pushed her brother into his room. "Five minutes," she mouthed. "Meet me in the hall." Then, as he hesitated, "Hurry!"

When she left him she tiptoed down the stairs. A step creaked under her foot. She stopped, hardly daring to breathe. The sound seemed like thunder in the silence of the night. She continued cautiously until, with a sigh of relief, she reached her room.

For a moment she stood with her back to the door, as the Baron had stood in the study above, memories chasing and jostling each other across her mind. The wolves howling in the night, their blood dappling the snow. The bodies of her stepmother and her father, Maminka and Valenka, lying on the red blanket of their own blood. Then it was the Baron lying face downwards on the study floor, staining the carpet crimson, dark, dark crimson that turned to rust as his life's blood flowed away. And she had murdered him. She looked at her shaking hands. Was her life always to be punctuated by acts of violence? But she would not worry about that now. She would achieve nothing if she dwelt on those horrors.

Zara glanced around the room that held the secrets of her humiliation and defilement and drew a long, shuddering breath, closing her eyes for a moment to dispel the images. Then she smiled. She realized she was glad. She did not regret what she had done.

In a second she was cool, calm and purposeful. She

144

dressed hurriedly. She put on warm clothes, reasoning that she could discard more easily than acquire. The money she had taken from the study would help but there was not much of it and she did not know its value. She had never handled money in her life. She hoped it would buy food and pay for lodging. She wrapped herself in her fur-lined coat and put the coins carefully in her pocket. She would have liked to pay a visit to the kitchen to take some provisions but did not dare in case she disturbed anyone.

She had nothing to take with her. She remembered the sadness on her father's face when she told him that at Pesochny. It seemed a lifetime away. Well, she still had nothing to take with her, not even the precious lace dress this time. It reminded her of her wedding morning and the terrible times since, so she left it. But she did take the earrings. She slipped them into her pocket with the money, then left the room in which she had lost her innocence and her childhood and hurried down the main staircase to the hall.

Sasha was there before her. He looked pale and frightened. "Where will we go?" he whispered fearfully. She looked at him, exasperated. Then the sight of his wan shocked face brought home to her the strain he was under. He had suffered so much. He was not like her, used from babyhood to alarms and frights, loneliness and sudden changes.

Until they had come here he had been protected and cherished, petted and pampered. The change must have been bewildering for him, and the shock of his father's and mother's death was something he had never really had time to get over. In front of the Baron there had been no opportunity for him to grieve.

She gave him a quick hug. "Away from here, my dearest," she said calmly. "Far away."

She had not the least idea of where they were going or how they would get there but she did not want him to know that.

She could not open the front door. To her horror it was locked and bolted. She was terrified lest she disturb the servants now so looked around the great chequered hall for another means of escape. Sasha pointed to the window near the cloakroom. It was old and the catch was weak. Zara let out a long breath of relief when it gave beneath her grasp and opened quite smoothly.

She motioned Sasha to go first. It was a small window and she was grateful that they were both so thin. She pushed him through then followed, jumping on to the gravel. Their feet made sharp, crunching noises that sounded like thunder as they began to run down the drive.

Zara glanced back. A light had come on in the servants' quarters in the right wing.

"Oh God! Oh God, Sasha,' she cried, panicking. "They'll find us. We can't escape."

She stopped and looked around the flat green landscape that surrounded them. It was bathed in moonlight that looked blue and there was nowhere at all to hide.

Sasha clung to her making little whimpering noises. For a moment they stood still as badgers dazzled by a brilliant light. Then Zara had an idea.

'Come on," she cried with renewed energy. She took Sasha's hand and ran with him as fast as she could back to the house. She circled around it and pulled her brother after her to the stable wing at the left of the castle. She drew him into the yard just as they heard the front door open and voices call out and the crunching of gravel beneath hurrying feet.

She could smell familiar stable scents and glimpsed a wild-eyed stallion in its stall. She pushed Sasha into the huge pile of straw that was kept at the back of the yard and began heaping handfuls on top of him. She lay beside him and covered herself in the same way. The straw was prickly and uncomfortable, but at least they were concealed.

"They'll never think to look here," she murmured in his ear, holding his body close to hers. "They'll think we have run away. No one would imagine that we would stay so near.

146

Only the Baron might guess that and he is dead." She felt a tremor pass over Sasha's body and smoothed him gently.

It was not long before someone came into the yard, calling out loudly. They heard a horse being saddled and the sound of someone galloping away. The minutes ticked by. Zara was afraid to move. Her arm felt quite dead where Sasha lay on it. It had gone to sleep and was beginning to ache but she dared not take it from beneath him. The straw might be disturbed and she could not be sure that no one was watching.

She realised that Sasha was asleep. She shifted, one tiny movement at a time, and when her arm was free tenderly cleared a space so that he could breathe more easily. As time passed she realized they were in a worse predicament than ever. After murdering the Baron they were trapped here in the confines of the castle and the flat basin of sward it was situated in, a hopeless position.

She fell into the sleep of despair until Sasha stirred then tried to turn in his sleep, and finding it impossible woke them both up with a start.

"Hush," she said, and saw comprehension dawning on his white strained face.

Zara came to a swift decision. They would go now. It was nearly morning and they had no option but to take their chances. They would most probably be caught but they would have a try.

She stood up, gently helping Sasha to his feet. She shook the straw from her coat and they walked out into the yard.

"Mein Gott!"

Zara stood still in horror. It was Katya, the square-faced housemaid. She stood stockstill, her hand to her mouth, staring at the brother and sister who had risen from the straw. She said something in her own language then turned as if to go. Fearful that she would raise the alarm, Zara moved to her side quickly and whispered in German, "Please don't give us away."

It was a slim chance, Zara knew, but she was desperate. She watched the girl's face working, hardly daring to breathe. Katya shook her head, suddenly smiled, put her finger to her lips and motioned them to the door.

"They have come for the Baron and everyone is at the front of the house. There is a commotion. The woman Gertrude found him." She spoke to them in moderate German, her eyes glittering. She nodded her head once. "I hated him too. The Baron," she said and looked meaningfully at Zara who blushed. There was no doubting what the girl meant.

Katya pointed through the heavy barn doors. They were open a crack, just wide enough to have allowed her entry. A shaft of sunlight poured through.

"Sven," she whispered. "My friend."

They did not know what she was talking about but she gestured them closer and they peered through the door.

The milk-cart was outside. A wooden cart, bare save for some monolithic pewter churns in the back, ladles clattering against the side. it was drawn by an ancient nag who moved with rheumatic slowness. It had already commenced its departure.

"We could not hide on that," Sasha said.

"No, listen. Quick, take these." Katya picked up some sacks and shoved them at Sasha and Zara. "He'll not notice. He's a bit thick. Watch me and use your wits." She ran out of the stable and across the cobbles. Her boots clattered like castinets on the stones. The boy held the nag's reins loosely between his fingers. When he heard footsteps behind him he slowed the horse and looked over his shoulder. Katya waved and the cart drew to a halt.

She ran around until she stood in front of it and placed her hands on her hips in a provocative manner. She said something to the boy who jumped down from the cart. She said something else and he laughed and drew her into his arms. She held him, his back to them, and looking over his shoulder waved them on while kissing him thoroughly.

Zara beckoned Sasha and they both ran as fast as they could, bodies bent, until they reached the cart. Scrambling on they concealed themselves in the sacks, putting one over their heads and another up to their waists. They lay still, trying to be inconspicuous on the floor of the cart. There was nothing remarkable about a pile of sacks. They would draw nobody's attention. The only fear would be if Sven noticed them near his milk churns and to do that he would have to come around to the back of the cart.

However, Katya had taken care of that. She suddenly pointed to the castle, broke away from him and began hurrying him up, urging him to go. He climbed up on his driver's seat, a little dazed, clicked his teeth and coaxed the old horse forward, Katya still shouting at him to hurry.

Zara could see through the wide mesh of the sack. She edged herself over to the side of the cart, and tried to peer through the slats. She could not see much but thought she would know when they arrived at a village.

She heard Sasha whisper but could not hear what he said. She thought that her best course was to stay alert, and when the chance came, take it.

They bumped along for what seemed hours. There were no stops along the way. Either Sven had finished his round or the castle had been his only delivery. Zara felt bruised, but for the first time there was a glimmer of hope in her heart. They went jogging along, their bodies bouncing on the bare planks, the harsh sackcloth irritating their faces.

At last they heard Sven calling to the nag and the cart began to slow down. Zara swiftly pulled the sack from over her head and shook Sasha who followed her example. They wiggled out of the lower sacks and dropped over the back of the cart, rolling into a ditch at the side of the road. They were scratched and stung by the bushes and brambles and nettles, but they were free.

It was about mid-day, Zara guessed. The sun was directly overhead and it was quite hot. It was suffocating in her fur-lined coat but she kept it on. She knew the night would be harsh and she might have great need of it. Brambles had torn her cheek and the scratches stung. There seemed to be no one about.

The ditch was beside a lane. A small track off it led to a cottage. She saw the cart stop there and Sven dismount. A woman came out of the cottage and they greeted each other, then went inside. Zara reasoned that it would be unwise to go there and ask for help, even if they could make themselves understood. If Sven were to be trusted, Katya would have told him about his passengers. The fact that she had not done so meant that she was not at all sure of him and they could not risk it.

Sasha was pulling on her sleeve. She turned and saw he was pointing. She shaded her eyes with her hand. On the other side of the ditch the land dropped and there, at the bottom of a green and verdant slope, she saw what Sasha indicated. A stream, silver in the sun, was bubbling its way across the land, cutting through the fields, gurgling over stones.

She nodded to a hedge that divided one field from the next, and they crept along keeping their heads down until they got to the side furthest from the cottage. Thus concealed, they slid down to the water.

They were desperately thirsty. The water was fresh, cold and clear.

"I'm so hungry, Zara," Sasha said wearily when he had drunk enough.

"Well, we'll just have to put all that out of our minds," she replied briskly, hoping she would have enough will power to conceal from him just how ravenous she herself felt.

She had never fended for herself, never studied the countryside, and had no idea where to find food. There were berries on a bush nearby but she did not know whether they were poisonous or safe.

She took off her coat and bade Sasha do the same. At

least she had a quick and logical mind and could work out certain obvious things for herself.

"We will have to travel by night," she said. "The police or the Baron's men will not look for us then. They are bound to search by day. So if we conceal ourselves and sleep during the daylight hours we will be safe."

He nodded. "There's a thicket over there," he said. "We can lie down on our coats and rest."

Across the stream there was a stand of trees and bushes. They crept beneath the hedge and tucked their coats under their heads. The earth was alive with myriad movings and rustlings, creakings and shiftings. A vast imperceptible activity of plant and insect life breathed around them.

Sasha could not sleep, he was too hungry. Zara promised that as soon as it was dark they would cross the fields and try to steal something from the cottage.

She slept fitfully. She would doze off then jerk out of her descent into unconsciousness and look with wide brown eyes at her brother. She drew him into her arms and cradled him there. She heard him sucking his thumb, making little smacking noises with his lips, and held him closer until finally the smacking stopped and his head became heavy in the crook of her arm. Sasha slept.

The sun slanted in through the curtain of leaves and she wondered what would happen to them. She looked at her brother's defenceless face and was filled with a quiet determination that somehow they would escape and find a way to live a happier life.

Somehow they would survive.

She let the sunshine play on her face and emptied her mind of doubt.

"I will succeed," she promised. "Somehow I will succeed, and you and I, little brother, will be happy and at peace together."

It was the sound of birds that awakened her. They had set up a

151

cacophony of chirping and calling to each other at the end of day. A chill wind had blown up and it sang in the tops of the trees. Zara was stiff and cramped but full of energy and determination.

She shook Sasha awake. He murmured and protested in his sleep and seemed reluctant to leave it. Zara helped him on with his coat. Together they went to the stream and drank again.

They were desperately hungry by now. Zara wanted to leave Sasha there in the copse and go and forage for food, but he would not be parted from her. He clung to her limpet-like, terrified that if she went she might never come back.

They crept up by the side of the hedge. Darkness had fallen with its thousand creeping shadows. They started at strange noises. An owl hooted and there were rustlings in the under-growth. Unused to the countryside, Zara and Sasha were frightened by the nocturnal activity. They did not understand it. A badger scuttled through a gap in the trees and Zara nearly screamed. They reached the little garden patch beside the cottage. There was a chicken run and a vegetable garden.

They crept nearer. Then something moved on the other side of the plot of land and Sasha gripped Zara's arm, his eyes wide with fear. The rustling continued.

"There's something there," he whispered. She nodded.

They nearly jumped out of their skins when a sudden wild outburst tore the silence of the night. The chickens squawked and screamed, there was a banging and clattering, and a plump old peasant woman came out of the cottage brandishing a broom.

The light from the doorway revealed the cause of the commotion. A fox was revealed, caught in the middle of its attack, the bloody carcass of a chicken clamped firmly between his teeth. It took off while the woman waved the broom and yelled in a language they did not understand, stamping her feet and shaking her fist.

At last the rumpus died down. The woman went back

inside the cottage. They saw the light go out downstairs, and a moment later come on in the room above. Then it went out and all was quiet again.

The moon hung in the sky, remote and mysterious, veiled occasionally by dark purple clouds that drifted across its face, cloaking the world in darkness.

Zara waited about half an hour. Then she tiptoed up the garden path followed by Sasha. She planned to creep into the kitchen and steal some bread and cheese but halfway up the path a dog suddenly set up a shrill barking, a loud alarming outburst that sent them scuttling away. The light came on again in the tiny upstairs window.

Thoroughly alarmed and nearly in tears the two ran as fast as they could until they reached the edge of the wood. They fell down on their empty stomachs, panting for breath. They were too afraid to venture further under cover.

"The Babes in the Wood," Zara murmured sarcastically to herself, but there was a catch in her voice.

Frustrated and starving, they looked at each other in mute despair. They moved together, twining their arms around each other in mutual consolation. Whether it was lack of food or their habit of trusting one another, when they lay down they fell quite unexpectedly asleep.

Someone was prodding them. An old woman was poking them with a stick. It was dawn. A cock crew raucously. The first faint pink light tinged the sky.

Zara was too confused and hungry to think of running away. She simply sat up and stared at the apparition before her. Sasha moved, rubbing his eyes and yawning, until he too focussed on the old tramp. Or so she appeared. Her skirts, layered and multitudinous, were brown and green and a mouldy olive. She had many shawls over a torn black blouse and her head was encased in what looked like brown woollen stockings wound round and round and tucked in under her chin. She wore enormous black boots caked in mud, the tongues hanging out, the laces, or what remained of them, untied. Over the stockings that framed her face a squashed hunting hat perched precariously. On her hands she wore mittens, torn and unravelling, revealing fingers gnarled as the limb of a tree, with nails which were broken and blackened. Her face was leathery and brown. In the middle of this two milk-blue eyes twinkled with slightly crazy glee. When she saw the two were awake she sat down beside them and inspected them.

She stared for a long time, saying nothing.

Zara and Sasha did not speak either. There was no point. They did not know the language, and were too tired and hungry to care what happened to them any longer. They were trapped. Suddenly the woman gave a satisfied nod. She smiled at them and they saw that one large ivory-coloured tooth graced her otherwise bare gums.

She was carrying a knapsack which she proceeded to unpack. She took out some rolls of black bread, a hunk of cheese and a bottle, re-corked, half-full of wine.

Sasha put out his hand towards the bread and she smacked it sharply. They waited while she carefully divided bread and cheese into three equal portions. She then handed them their scrupulously even allowances and nodded again. Sasha fell on his but Zara told him to eat slowly. The old woman then passed the wine bottle around, having taken a first deep gulp herself. Zara felt a thrill of reluctance about putting her mouth to the neck of the bottle directly after the old woman, but, fearful of offending and desperately grateful for the food, she closed her eyes and went ahead. The wine warmed and calmed her.

They ate until all the food was gone. The cheese and bread seemed the tastiest meal they had ever consumed. Then the old woman rummaged in her bag again. She gave a triumphant smile, revealing her one tooth dyed red with wine, and produced two apples, giving one to each of them. She pointed to the tooth and shook her head and Zara realised that she was not capable of eating the firm fruit. Their benefactress smiled again and watched while brother and sister munched the sweet fruit.

When they had finished and taken their last swig of wine the woman stood and shook her skirts. She took some crusts of bread and cheese rind that Zara was planning to pocket against future need and scattered them, making a funny crowing sound in her throat. The air was suddenly full of birds. They fell on the remains and fought and squabbled over each crumb while the woman laughed and called to them. She looked like an old scarecrow, the air around her full of birds.

She turned to the children then and winked broadly, beckoning them. A little apprehensive, they followed. She led them through the wood, over fallen logs and thick layers of pine needles, through interlacing branches that snapped in their faces and dense foliage. They were not afraid of her. She was surefooted and confident in the green gloom and knew the little paths.

When they reached the other side she stopped and pointed. Zara and Sasha could not see at first what she was indicating. But suddenly their hearts leapt. It was a railway track with a small station in the distance. Why or how she showed them the station they puzzled about later but never came to a satisfactory conclusion. She must have guessed that they were runaways and having opted out herself was automatically on their side. In any event she pointed the way to escape. "*Danke. Danke*," they cried, and followed the direction she had indicated.

Zara had a brief struggle with herself. The woman was obviously poor, but so were they. Finally she dug deep in her pocket and took out one precious golden coin.

The old crone looked at it, smiled her crazy smile and shook her head. She closed Zara's fist over the coin and turned and left.

"*Danke. Danke*," Zara cried after her. She wondered

whether she had done the right thing or not. Perhaps the woman was insulted? But she turned and waved, showing her large single tooth in a friendly grin, then continued on her way.

They followed the track until they neared the station. There they concealed themselves in an outhouse a short remove from the platform. The station was decorated with floral borders and hanging baskets and as the hut they were in was full of gardening tools, Zara decided that whoever took care of the gardening was probably the station-master. The train would slow down as it approached the station, she reasoned, and hoped they could jump on the back without actually having to enter the station. There could be a picture of them in circulation or a description might have been issued.

The first train seemed very full of passengers and did not stop. Zara was getting worried. Reason told her that two young people in the mess they were in, scratched by brambles, their clothes stained with earth, would not pass unnoticed.

Their luck held, however. The next arrival was a goods train which slowed as it entered the station.

Zara seized her opportunity. Pulling her brother by the hand she left the hut at a run, bent double in case anyone was looking. They were able to clamber into an empty freight car. The train gathered speed and rumbled along, clickety-clack. Zara looked at Sasha in amazement.

"We got away," she whispered, unable to believe their luck, "We got away!"

She stared at the countryside racing past them. Her heart raced joyously in time.

"I wonder where we are going," Sasha said, not expecting a reply.

"I don't know, dearest, but we have escaped, and the further we go the safer we are." She grinned at him. "Don't look so worried. If we can escape the Baron we can survive. The worst is over, you'll see."

They were in luck. They were on a goods train which stopped at a dockside to be unloaded. When Zara and Sasha jumped off their nostrils were assailed by the sharp iodine and salt smell of the sea. They could see across the cobbled quay the tall masts and funnels of ships against the slate-grey sky.

All was hurry and scurry. Nets were strewn everywhere. Stone bollards had ropes thick as a man's arm wound around them. There were wooden crates and iron-hooped barrels, burlap bales and canvas-covered rolls. There were sailors everywhere. They wore jerseys, boots and oilskins, most of them smoking evil-smelling pipes. There were women in shawls with creels of fish carried on their heads or under their arm, resting on a hip. At one end of the dock stood a table, unbleached wood on thick legs, where women gutted and cleaned fish, throwing them into huge baskets on the ground beside them.

No one paid any attention to Zara and her brother. She found the smell of fish overwhelming but in the grey and misty day was aware that she was very hungry again. Sharp pains gnawed her belly and she had a stabbing headache.

Sasha held her hand. He looked around, taking everything in. "What'll we do?" he asked her, not understanding their good fortune in ending up here.

"We stow away," she said, her voice filled with excitement.

"But if we're caught?"

"Well, we'll be somewhere else by then, won't we? We'll be accused of stowing away not murder. No one will know us. Oh, Sasha, our luck is holding. But first we must get something to eat."

She saw a street trader selling hot sausages cooked over an iron brazier. Digging into her pocket she took out a golden coin. She held it out to the trader and the sausage seller took it eagerly, tested it with his teeth and smiled happily. Zara thought then that the coin was probably quite valuable; at least that it would buy more than a few sausages. Still, food was what they needed most right now and she caught on enough to demand a second and a third helping. The trader seemed pleased enough to give them all they asked for, but no change. He even gave them a swallow or two from his tankard of beer, laughing jovially all the time, a big redfaced fellow whose bulbous nose was studded with warts and whose level of intelligence was obviously low and did not lead him to question the young pair. The acquisition of the gold coin had clearly brightened his day so he felt warmly towards the brother and sister.

They did not, however, understand a word he said. Zara was still worried about being seen and recognised. There were newspapers about and she remembered her father once pointing to a smudged indistinct face on a front page, saying, 'That is someone wanted by the police.' She felt that they were still too close to the Baron's home. He was dead and his murderer would be hunted down, she felt sure of that, but she did not think that they would look for her in another country.

She wondered briefly if the war was over, then thought that it did not really matter to them whether it was or not. They ate heartily, the jovial fellow pressing more food on them, until finally they were full.

Zara looked around. She knew little about ships but reasoned that it would be a good idea to find one that was carrying a soft cargo so that they could conceal themselves without too much discomfort. Secondly she wanted one that was going as far away as possible. She saw signs everywhere saying 'Goteborg'; over a warehouse, on an inn, and realised that they were probably in Gothenburg, Sweden. She saw cargo boats too. She walked along the wharf, reading the names: *Isle de France, The Queen Bess, Circe, Madonna Rosa, Chicago Clipper*, and finally one loading bales of wool and sheepskins, *Der Wilhelmina*. 'Hook of Holland' was inscribed on the cargo's burlap wrappings.

Zara made up her mind. They would take their chances with that one. She racked her brains for ways of sneaking aboard. In the event it was easy.

They hung about the quays all day. No one paid any attention to a scruffy girl and her young brother. Gulls screamed overhead, fighting over the fish-heads thrown to them by the women. People called to each other, but no one bothered them. They went back to the sausage-man. He had disappeared for a while and when they found him again was drunk, his bulbous nose bright red in the cold. He greeted them like long-lost friends, and was only too happy to supply them with more sausages. Zara forced herself to eat them although by now she never wanted to see another sausage again.

When twilight came and the women had gone home and most of the men had disappeared into the tavern, Zara took Sasha's hand and bravely crept up the gangplank of the ship. They did not need to conceal their actions. The deck was deserted except for one young sailor who was either drunk or fast asleep. They could hear raucous singing from the tavern and a beam of golden light streamed through its windows. Otherwise it was dark, and growing darker by the minute. They crept like shadows into the hold where they concealed themselves, comfortably cocooned among the bales of wool.

"We're getting better at this," she whispered to Sasha as she arranged the rolls around them so that they would be cushioned and covered them with a couple of loose sheepskins.

"But will it ever stop?" he queried.

"Once away from here we can stop running."

"How will we live?"

"We have the gold coins. They will last a while. Then I'll get a job," she said doubtfully.

"But you've never worked. You wouldn't know how."

"Well, I'll learn," she said, tired of his objections. "We'll manage, Sasha. And then everything will be all right."

She held him loosely in the crook of her arm and yawned. It was not long before they both began to doze. It had been a long day. They had been there about an hour when they were jerked from their light sleep into wakefulness. The boat had suddenly throbbed into life. An engine roared and pulsated, voices shouted, ropes could be heard slapping the deck.

They smiled at one another and drew in a deep breath. They were on their way.

PART II
Holland

Chapter Eight

They did not escape undetected aboard *Der Wilhelmina*, but after Zara had parted with a couple of the gold coins the captain treated them fairly, allowing them to use a small locker room as a makeshift cabin, and feeding them the same pickled herring and stale ship's biscuit as his crew.

In Amsterdam the gold coins did not last very long. Zara knew that she was mismanaging them. She could not haggle or bargain or even ask for change. Though she held out her hand after she had passed a coin, the expectant palm was usually ignored. People seemed to know she was not capable of demanding her rights. They knew they could take advantage.

The problem once more was that they did not speak the language.

Amsterdam enchanted them. It was autumn by now, and bronze and amber, gold and scarlet leaves flurried on to the streets and covered the parkland or floated down the canals like bright confetti. The houses, Zara thought, were like doll's houses, just the sort she had always wanted to live in, as unlike palaces and castles as you could get.

They spent a week in an hotel but found it too expensive. They went to a cheaper one and that, full of unsavoury characters, frightened them, so they started to look for lodgings. Zara set about finding a well-maintained house with a kind landlady.

They found an apartment in Prinsengracht. Frau Kettner had a notice in the window of her pristine little house. The German woman herself was friendly and seemed honest.

Zara had tried to look as grown-up as she could when they knocked on the door and pointed to the sign. The fact that it was in German, which they could both speak after a fashion, had a lot to do with their choice. When they addressed Frau Kettner in that language she was so delighted she invited them in at once and made a big fuss of them.

She had, she said, one room left for rent. It was an attic, under the eves, a small room with a sloping roof. It was simply furnished but pretty. Frilled curtains at the window patterned with yellow sunflowers. A bedspread to match, bright and cheerful. Woven rugs covered the floors and there was a big wardrobe at one side and a table and chair near the window.

Frau Kettner apologised because it was so small but Zara clapped her hands and told the woman that it was exactly what she wanted. The landlady was a sandy-coloured person with salt-and-pepper hair and eyebrows, a thin face with a double chin that wobbled, faded lashes and worried blue eyes.

"If you could put another bed under the window for my brother, Frau Kettner, I would be very pleased," Zarah told her.

The girl's tone was unconsciously imperious and the German woman guessed that they had been used to a grander way of life and had obviously suffered a loss of fortune.

Ah, well, she sighed to herself, the war has left some sad flotsam and jetsam floating about.

She nodded her head and went to get the spare fold-up bed she kept for just such a contingency.

They put it by the window, under the sloping roof, and Zara thought it perfect. Through it you could see the stars at night and a shimmering piece of sky. The floors and walls

164

were wood, old beams weathered and polished, and there was a blue and white stove in the corner that Frau Kettner said was from Delft but reminded Zara of those in the Russian palaces. Of course it was much smaller but then everything here was and Zara liked it that way.

When she said as much to Sasha he looked sharply away from her and she remembered guiltily his childhood love for the Alexander Palace and the courtly lifestyle there. There was no denying this new life was different but Zara believed that, given time, Sasha would gain as much comfort and satisfaction from it as she did.

Frau Kettner moved the table, put it near the stove and added another chair. She put the bed where the table had been and covered them both with multi-coloured patchwork covers. There was a toilet and bath at the bottom of the passageway that led to their room, five flights up. They shared these with a student at the University who lodged below them.

Dirk Van Holstein was a friendly chap from the Hague. He had a mop of brown curls, round brown eyes and a good-natured face. He always wore large tortoiseshell-framed glasses and was, they discovered, serious and kind, intelligent and a little shy.

They explored the city, more confident now that they had lodgings. They marvelled at the quaintness of the town, wandering up cobblestoned streets and strolling up and down beside the canals, kicking up the leaves in golden and russet flurries. They stared at the Royal Palace.

"It's very small," Sasha said disdainfully, but seemed interested for some reason in the Post Office nearby. They explored Kalverstraat, wandered about the Beguinage, sitting on the low wall that surrounded the patch of green grass and the statue of Jesus in the middle. They went inside the Oude Kerk and the Westerkerk and found them austere and very far removed from the golden, onion-domed, gloriously icon-filled churches at home. Sasha said it was a mortal sin even to go inside a Dutch church and they would be punished.

They strolled through the Vondelpark and watched the ducks on the lakes and the scattered leaves, dampening and drowning.

"Tsar Peter the Great lived here once. In Amsterdam," Sasha said. He knew things Zara did not and sometimes she was jealous. She would have liked to be able to read so easily.

Then they would return to the house in Prinsengracht. It had little steps up to the door and an oak tree grew before it. The green waters of the canal meandered past but Zara and Sasha were too high up to see it from their room.

They crossed the bridges and drank coffee in a cafe and had hot chestnuts from the street vendors, rode the trolley tram and peered in the shops on the Rokin. They bought some warm clothes; jerseys and scarves, new trousers for Sasha and a plain dress for Zara and although they bought quite a lot in the shop this time they got change.

At first they were suspicious of everyone, Dirk Van Holstein included. But Frau Kettner, who had shown them much kindness, thought the world of him. "He is so bright. Clever." She shook her head admiringly. "And so helpful. Ach, he is a nice boy. He will be your friend."

They liked the landlady for her soft freckled face and sandy hair and the sheer plainness of her. She was like a woman in a painting by Pieter de Hooch. Her calm acceptance of them, and most of all her good humour, endeared her to them and they felt that if she liked Dirk Van Holstein they should too.

They smiled at him when they met him on the stairs and said '*Guten haben*' in pleasant voices. He bowed and beamed at them under his thick spectacles.

The whole house was narrow so they had literally to squeeze past each other when they met. Dirk had a habit of thrusting his head forward. It always seemed to be slightly

166

ahead of the rest of him, and twisted and turned to each of them as they spoke.

The autumn died and winter came. The wind was bitter and the gold coins were disappearing fast. They were sitting on their beds one night, wondering how to go about finding a job, when there was a knock on the door.

Zara leaped up to answer it. She felt it must be Frau Kettner but any unexpected visit still had the power to startle and frighten her. She was always afraid it might be the police.

She wanted to see Frau Kettner and give her three-quarters of what was left for she was afraid the money would dribble away and then what would they do? Frau Kettner was kind to them but Zara did not think she would be so kind if they could not pay their rent. The thought of being homeless terrified her. Her experiences en route to Amsterdam had convinced her that she was not born to be a travelling woman like the old crone they had met. She wanted a roof over her head, food in her belly, and above all warmth.

When she opened the door it was to find Dirk. He stood there bashfully, holding a bottle of wine at arm's length. He thrust it into her hands.

"I thought we could drink together," he said in a rush. "But perhaps your brother is too young?"

Sasha laughed and Zara said, "No, it's all right. He is quite used to wine." Then, "Please come in."

He entered and Zara closed the door. They stood looking at each other, speechless with embarrassment for a moment. Then Zara remembered her manners, "Please sit down," she said, sounding unconsciously very polite and formal. Then looked at him, suddenly radiant. "It is the first time in my life I've ever had a visitor. Oh, welcome!" The ice was broken and everyone laughed.

Sasha elected to sit on his bed since they had only two chairs and Zara took out some glasses and filled them with wine. They toasted each other and soon were chatting amiably.

"Let's ask Frau Kettner up and make it a real party," Dirk said. Zara was delighted at the idea and Sasha ran down to fetch her. She was only too willing to leave the front parlour where she sat watching the world go by through her window. She followed him up to the attic where they settled her in one of the chairs while Sasha and Zara sat on their beds. She sipped her wine, smacked her lips and said, "Ah, this is good."

Dirk encouraged the brother and sister to talk. "We know all about each other, Frau Kettner and I. You must tell us about yourselves."

For a moment Zara was overwhelmed with fear. Suppose the police had been trying to find them and asked the landlady and Dirk to try to trap them? But looking into the kindly eyes of the landlady and the friendly ones of the student she pushed her fears aside. If she could not trust these people then life was not worth living anyway.

They talked of their past, leaving out the worst of it. They confided how they had seen their father and Anya shot in the snow in Pesochny, and how they had escaped with the Baron. They were a bit vague about the next part of their story but Dirk and Frau Kettner were tactful and did not press them for more detail.

Zara could see that the good Frau was moved to tears at their story, and Dirk shook his head and sighed.

They said that they left the Baron in Sweden, and had journeyed to Gothenburg where they stowed away and come by boat to Amsterdam.

Reliving their travels made Zara emotional. With a sob in her voice she said, "The money we had is almost gone."

She went to the drawer in the table where Dirk and the landlady sat. She sorted the coins out, kept one and pushed the rest towards Frau Kettner.

"It's all we've got left. Please take it, Frau Kettner. I'm so afraid of being without a home."

The landlady wiped the tears from her eyes. "I'll never put you out, *leiblings*. Would I do that?" She shook her head. "Would I, Herr Professor?" She always called the student that.

Dirk shook his head. "No, you would never do such a thing. But," he looked at Zara and Sasha solemnly, "you would be unhappy to live off the dear Frau's charity. What you need is a job."

Zara nodded. "Yes, exactly. But how do we go about it? I have no idea. I'm not trained for anything. Sasha isn't either." She looked at her brother who shuddered delicately. "I can hardly read and write. I'm a little slow. So what use am I to anyone?"

Dirk smiled at her. "Not much, I'm afraid," he said cheerfully, "But I have an idea. One of my friends at the University has a brother who works in the Mander Hotel. They are always looking for bell-boys. Sometimes my friend has to work there in the vacations. He has very little money. You could do that, Sasha."

Sasha's expression was blank and uncomprehending. Work was something that peasants were born to. True, his sister had said she was willing to try but he had never believed it would be necessary in his case.

Unconcerned Dirk turned to Zara. "They always need chambermaids as well. The thing is, could you do it? It would be very hard work but you would certainly get the jobs. No one will even ask you for papers."

"Papers? But I have them," she cried triumphantly. "Why did you think we would not want to show them?"

Dirk shrugged his shoulders. He had been aware of the telling gap in her story – why they had decided to leave the man who had saved them in Russia. "I think you don't want anyone to trace you. I don't know why and I'm not asking. But, put it this way, if you do not wish to be located, it is an ideal job for you."

Zara nodded. "Yes, I see." She looked at him with wide worried eyes. "But our papers? If anyone did ask ..."

"Listen, don't worry. Let us take one thing at a time. First, do you want me to try to get you a job?"

"Oh please, yes," she cried. The gratitude in her huge black eyes was overwhelming.

"We'll see you through," he said, "don't worry." He felt he could not bear it if the brave Russian girl had to suffer further distress and made up his mind to smoothe her way for her.

The party went on until late. Frau Kettner told them about her husband Gustav who had left Germany in 1900 to come to Amsterdam and start a bakery; how he had caught a chill and ignored it; how she had remonstrated with him. "I told him and told him to take care." She sniffed, and dabbed her eyes with her handkerchief. " 'The winds here in Amsterdam are bitter,' I said, but he would not listen. He was stubborn that man! We had this nice shop. He went every day. When he got ill he still insisted on going, and the wind was like knives; as cold as it is now. 'Listen,' I said, 'miss one or two days, what will it matter?' We had bought this house. We were doing fine. There was no need, going every day like that. But he insisted. He loved his work. 'They depend on me. Best bread in the whole of Amsterdam,' he said. You know what men are," she told Zara, who didn't. "Paid no attention to me. So, the chill developed. He got pneumonia. In three days he was dead." She clicked her fingers. "Three days. He was gone."

There were no tears in her eyes by now. It was an old story that she had told many times.

Dirk told them he was studying physics at the University. He described some of the experiments he was conducting and they did not understand but listened anyway, feeling only affection because they liked him.

They all felt closer when the little party broke up and in the next weeks and months took to popping in and out of each other's rooms whenever they passed by. Dirk's room was spare, containing only a white-covered narrow bed, a desk and a chair, but it was full of books. On the shelves, on the floor, on the desk, on the bed – books, books everywhere. Frau Kettner received them in her parlour which had a *chaise-longue* and innumerable knick-knacks, silver-framed photographs of her dead husband and of a pretty fair-haired girl whom they took to be her in earlier days.

Dirk spoke to his friend. Within a week they had interviews and both of them got jobs. They were given uniforms and told briskly to start the next day. The work was hard as Dirk had promised. Sasha spent his days carrying the guests' cases up and down to their rooms. He wore a grey uniform and a peaked cap edged in gold braid.

Zara's days were spent tidying the rooms, making the beds, changing linen. It was back-breaking work. The maids were on their feet and active all the time. It was a long hard day.

Since leaving the Baron Zara had been plagued by phantasms of blood on the snow, amber figures dancing obscenely in a golden glow, sheets stained crimson. Images of horror paralysed her with fear every night. There was no escape in sleep. She was at the mercy of her dreams. Worst of all were her nightmares about the Baron: on top of her, his face turned away, the pain of his assault piercing her loins; or joined to Sasha, violating her loved one, despoiling the innocent. Last of all deathly still on the floor, his head twisted grotesquely, a pool of his own blood spreading and staining the carpet. So much blood.

She had grown accustomed to being awoken from her nightmares by Sasha's voice calling to her, asking her what was wrong. But soon after they started working the nightmares stopped. Whether it was her exhaustion at the end of a gruelling day, whatever the reason, they ceased. The brother and sister sank into unconsciousness each night as soon as their heads hit their pillows.

They worked six days a week and had Tuesday off. Mevrou

Kloof the housekeeper had wanted Zara to take Wednesday as her day off but she explained that the new bell-boy was her brother and as his day off was Tuesday it was the only time they had to spend together, she would be much obliged if she could have the same day. The housekeeper who was a fussy woman and a strict disciplinarian was nevertheless kind and gave in. She liked Zara who was never lazy, who cleaned the rooms thoroughly, who never complained but strove to please. Also she was a quiet girl, not the saucy, boy-chasing type that the maids so often turned out to be. They were the bane of the good woman's life, a lazy, shiftless lot whose only ambition was to catch a fellow, anyone whom they fondly imagined would take them out of the hotel and install them in a life of comfort.

Zara worked with another girl. Her name was Hannetjie and she was stupid but well-meaning, a great lump of a girl who wore her straw-coloured hair in braids around her head and had a placid and docile temperament. She was good to work with because she was strong and could turn the mattress with a flourish and shift piles of linen while Zara tucked and turned, counted and oversaw.

Each morning, led by Zara, they tackled the rooms, made the beds, dusted, put fresh towels in the bathrooms and paper in the toilets. They swept and polished and cleaned. They sorted the linen and towels for the laundry and checked the supply that came back. They sorted it, sent worn stock to the seamstress and made sure there was enough left in the cupboards in case of emergency.

They hardly ever had time to rest for the hotel was large and the guests needed all manner of services: fetching and carrying, washing and ironing. And if all that had been satisfactorily done there were plants with hard green leaves down the corridors that had to be kept free of dust, and endless vistas of pearl grey carpet to be attended to. Everything must be perfect.

Sometimes the gentlemen guests made overtures to Zara

but her frantic reaction was enough to put them off. Besides she was skinny and had a strange imperious manner that was off-putting in a chambermaid. They thought twice before they touched her and any that did instantly regretted it. She almost jibbered in her panic and was obviously prepared to scream, and that was not what the gentlemen had in mind!

Hannetjie was not skinny, and far from nervous. One day, Zarah saw her friend leave one of the guest's rooms, smoothe down her skirt and slip something into her bodice. When she spied Zara she smiled at her and winked.

"It pays," she said laconically, showing Zara the note she had tucked between full breasts that threatened to burst from the black uniform.

"It's easy," she said later during their short break. "I just lie back and open my legs. Takes five minutes. But first I open my bodice. They just love my boobies. It makes them hot. Then it's zip-zap and over, and this.' She waved the note under Zara's nose. "Is a lot for a little, no?"

Zara shuddered. She did not think so. But she kept her thoughts to herself. Also, she thought, Hannetjie had not been forced. She willingly offered herself. Perhaps that made a difference. Zara did not know and did not want to find out.

They had one break in the middle of the day, provided there was no rush on. They were given a plate of food to eat in a little pantry next to the kitchens. The food was good, leftovers from the restaurant.

Sometimes she saw Sasha. Her heart swelled with love mixed with a twinge of pity as she caught sight of him, spruce in his smart uniform, marching down a corridor, suitcases in both hands and sometimes under his arms, or pushing a huge pile on a trolly. His delicately boned face was thin now, all plumpness gone. His blond hair in the neat cut the hotel had made him get, his large eyes earnest and intent, made her feel obscurely guilty that he had to do so menial a job. But his looks and good manners made him a lot in tips.

173

Christmas was coming. Dirk suggested they should all spend it together. He was studying for exams and did not want to waste a minute by going home where, he told them, he would be fussed over and pampered and effectively prevented from studying.

Frau Kettner said she would buy the food and do the cooking. A goose, she suggested, and cabbage and potatoes.

Zara and Sasha who had saved quite a lot from Sasha's tips, their wages being just enough to exist on, said they would buy bon-bons and fruit, nuts and candy, biscuits and any other goodies they could find in the Rokin. Dirk said he would bring the wine and the beer.

The week before Christmas a lot of the male guests in the hotel drank a little more than was good for them. They were sales gentlemen and predictably some of them became amorous. It so happened that Mevrou Kloof was a witness to Zara's terror. One evening in a corridor on her way to fetch some linen the housekeeper rounded a corner to see a gentleman, slightly the worse for wear, lunge at Zara. She watched as the girl froze in terror against the wall while the man, a goodhumoured fool, tried to cajole her into kissing him. The girl's reaction was quite out of proportion to the man's fairly harmless overture. She seemed transfixed, unable to move, her eyes wide in horror, making little mewling gasps of anguish. At that moment Hannetjie came hurrying down the corridor from the other end and with a few tart words prized the man away from Zara. Taking his key from his slack hands she opened his door and pushed him into his room, shutting the door firmly behind him.

Mevrou Kloof shook her head. That girl had had some bad experience with a man, she thought. Some bastard had frightened her out of her wits.

Mevrou Kloof did not like men. She had worked in the hotel business to support herself and her ageing mother all her life. She had started just like Zara as a chambermaid and worked herself up the responsible position she now held. All her life she had received a salary smaller than her male counterparts. Her father had been a sailor, away most of the time, drunk when he was at home. He gave her mother nothing, or a pittance, depending on his moods, and it had fallen to her to provide for her parent in her old age.

She never complained. She accepted her situation as her duty. But she had no time for men, the brutes. When a trembling Zara asked her later in the day if she could have Christmas off, Mevrou Kloof readily agreed. Normally she would not have countenanced such a concession, only people with great pull got off on Christmas day. But she felt so sorry for the girl that she gave her permission. As Zara got to the door she called her back.

"I'm not prying, don't think that, but you are Russian, yes?"

Zara nodded timidly.

"Well then, why don't you get in touch with other Russian *emigrés*? Make you feel at home. There is a café, the Café Russe." She frowned and tapped her forehead with her pencil. "Now where is it? Ach yes, around the corner from the Leidseplein, opposite the American Hotel, down a side street by the Opera House. You go there. You might see a friend." Then, embarrassed, for it was not politic for the housekeeper to be on friendly terms with the chambermaids, she said: "Now get back to your work, girl, and think yourself lucky."

Sasha had the day off too. The bell-boys were not busy that day. People arrived before or after Christmas, seldom on the day itself. The other boys had a poker game going and Sasha did not play cards. He was an earnest timid fellow who worked hard. The others thought he might be shocked by their gambling so when Meneer Van Daniken asked who would be let off they volunteered that he should be the one. Sasha was surprised at their gesture. They were not given to generous impulses. They fought him for every customer, but he had become adept at outwitting them, which they did not like. He got tips twice as large as theirs which they did not like either. He kept his distance which irritated them. But all in all he did not suffer too much at their hands. There simply was not enough free time. He did not question their generosity, neither did either Zara or Sasha tell the staff or their friends at the lodging house that in Russia they celebrated Christmas a week later than in Holland. It did not seem relevant and their manners were too good.

Christmas was a great success. Zara and Sasha went to buy presents for Frau Kettner and Dirk. Darkness fell early in the city and the shops were Aladdin's caves, decorated with holly and ivy, festive bells and silver tinsel. There were Christmas trees in every window. They wandered wide-eyed through the fairyland city, shivering despite their fur-lined coats for the wind was sharp as a knife. Deep down they were thrilled to be buying presents. It was something neither of them had ever done before. They wanted to give pleasure and were quite anxious over their choices. For Frau Kettner they bought a pair of fur-lined gloves. She had only an old pair of mittens and often complained of the rheumatism in her fingers. For Dirk they got a Norwegian sweater.

"It came on a boat like ours," Zara said to Sasha and suddenly, overwhelmed by emotion, she gave him a bear-hug and kissed his cheek.

Afterwards Christmas seemed the happiest time she could remember, excluding the period spent with the Rostovs. The day was a glowing little oasis in the middle of their drudgery.

They spent it in Frau Kettner's parlour and dining room. There were candles on the table which was adorned with pretty plates of dates and candied fruit, wine in decanters and silver tinsel around the candlesticks. The goose was fat and crispy, the stuffing succulent, the potatoes browned to a turn.

Everyone laughed all the time, Zara never remembered about what. Only Sasha seemed a little sad, but that was often his way nowadays. But even he laughed and kissed her after they had sampled the wine Dirk had bought. His round face never ceased to be split by a grin and Frau Kettner, flushed from cooking, became a tiny bit tiddly and then weepy as they toasted her dead husband.

Sitting around the table in the crowded little room, the glow of candlelight bathing their faces, Zara felt tranquil for the first time. It seemed you could feel safe if you were surrounded by friends. She decided that she too would get a little tiddly and with tears of happiness in her eyes raised her glass again and said, "To us all here. May we be as happy as we are this day for a long time to come. Dear friends, thank you."

Chapter Nine

It was on January the fourth that Sasha disappeared. It was snowing, making Zara think of Russia, but here the snow was quite different. It melted on the ground under the wheels of cars and horses' hooves and turned to slush before it could settle. The street vendors blew on their fingers, their noses red. Breath came in little puffs and everyone hurried about their business in a serious abstracted way.

Mevrou Kloof came to Zara when she and Hannetjie were changing the linen on the beds of guests who had checked out.

"Do you know where your brother is?" she asked, poking her head around the door.

Zara looked startled. "Yes," she said, "he's here. He came with me this morning."

'Well, he never reported to Meneer Van Daniken. No one has seen him. Do you suppose he might be sick?"

"It's not like him to be," Zara replied. She was worried. Usually she knew Sasha's whereabouts. Cold crept into her heart. Everything had been going too well. She thought of his face on Christmas Day, shadowed despite the candleglow, and shivered.

He was still missing at the end of the day which was one of Zara's late ones. By now she had made up her mind that he had been taken ill. But why had he not left a message for her? She would have left a message for him if she had been sick.

Then she realized that she really did not know what her brother would do. She had grown so used to thinking of him as somehow indivisible from her that she had rarely considered how he might act autonomously.

But she was sure he had played truant. That must be it. He had decided to have a day off. But why? He would not do a thing like that unless he was very unhappy. He was not the sort of boy who naturally got up to mischief. He had stared at Dirk in disbelief when the student told them stories of his escapades as a youth. Sasha wouldn't think of something like playing hookey.

He would be at home in bed when she returned, she was sure of it. When they had parted in front of the hotel that morning he must have felt ill and gone home. She would scold him for being so thoughtless. Then she would hug him and hold him close and ask him to tell her what he was feeling.

But he was not at home. She raced up the five flights of stairs, opened the door and found the room empty. She felt a lurch of panic, of acute apprehension then thought: Perhaps Frau Kettner has him downstairs. Or Dirk. Perhaps they are looking after him. Yes, of course, that's it.

But Dirk was out and Frau Kettner astonished.

'No, I have not seen him, *leibling*. Now, do not get yourself into a state. There is a reasonable explanation, I am sure. Here, have a cup of chocolate and we will wait together." She thought a moment and then said, "Perhaps he played truant?" But she shook her head at once without waiting for a reply from Zara. "No, no. He is not like that. Not Sasha. Ah, but there will be a good reason, you'll see."

Zara drank the hot chocolate but did not even realize she was doing so. She felt numb with fear, the old apprehension returning. Waiting was a nightmare, each minute agony.

Dirk returned from the University. Sasha was not with him as they had foolishly hoped. Nor had he seen him. He was just as shocked as they by the disappearance.

Zara jumped up, trembling now. "Where is he then?" she asked. "Has he been murdered too? Has he been killed? Oh, I will lose my mind, I will lose my mind if I don't find him!"

Dirk laid a timid arm around her shoulders. "You must not panic, Zara. You cannot help Sasha if you do. You must remain calm."

She turned to him, her eyes wild. "How can I be calm when my brother has been kidnapped? *They* have come. The Baron's men have come. The police will be here next, you'll see. Oh, it will all start again."

Dirk shook her gently and she burst into tears.

"I'm sorry," he said, "I did not mean to hurt you. But you must calm down."

He held her arms above the elbow to steady her and fend off her blind panic.

"Now listen," he said, his head thrust forward, "before you jump to wild conclusions, have you checked his cupboards?"

Zara was outraged. "What are you suggesting? Are you saying he *left*? He just left? Without letting us know? Are you mad?"

Dirk shook his head. "What I thought," he said calmly, "is that if we go to the police the first thing they will ask us is did we check his wardrobe? The police, the hotel, anyone would ask that. We must be able to answer." Zara glared at him, then in angry silence led the way upstairs.

She flung open the wardrobe door indignantly, without bothering to look at its contents. She saw the expression on their faces …

Sasha's side of the wardrobe was empty. She went to the drawers and pulled out the one he used to store his underwear. Empty. She looked on the bureau and saw that the little icon Dirk had given him a week ago was missing.

She sat down abruptly on the chair beside her. She looked at Frau Kettner and Dirk, saw the sympathetic understanding in their eyes, and a moan escaped her lips,

"Ah no," she cried. "Ah no. Dear God, no."

She and Dirk talked endlessly. It took Zara a long time to accept the fact that Sasha had obviously left of his own volition.

For a long time she was convinced it was a plot. He would not do that to them, she tried to convince Dirk. Never, never would he leave without letting them know. He must have been seized, by force. Dirk said that there had been no signs of struggle in the room. Even the rug which moved if you sneezed was in perfect place. Zara's hairpins were undisturbed on the bureau beside the icon. It was just not possible.

She hated Dirk for not pretending to consider abduction but he would give her no easy options. He knew she would suffer more later if she did not face up to the facts now.

But she could not understand it. Why had Sasha gone without a word? He must have known how heartbroken she would be, how worried and despairing. Yet knowing she would feel all these things he had still gone. With whom? He knew no one. And where?

Dirk suggested back to Russia, but she told him to read the papers and see if it was likely that Sasha would go back to that torn country. Not in a million years. Besides there was no one there that he knew any longer.

Zara could not understand it. Dirk let her go over and over events, speculating and pondering, arguing with herself. The only thing he would not let her do was fudge the facts. She confided in him a great deal. Everything she left out of her story previously, she revealed to him in the weeks and months after Sasha's disappearance.

She told him the details of her childhood, showed him the colour and fabric of her life, the shadows that haunted her, the violence that had followed her at every turn. Dirk, who had never known such horrors in his life, listened, shook his head and said nothing.

Then she told him of the murder and that she felt no remorse, that she had never regretted what she had done.

"I am a monster, Dirk. I lost no sleep over his death. Why do you bother with a terrible person like me?"

He shook his head, eyes troubled. He longed to comfort her, to say the right words, to soothe and make her feel better. But no words came. He just listened without realising that it was the very best thing he could have done.

They walked beside the canals holding hands, Dirk's head bent forward earnestly the better to hear her words. They sat opposite each other in cafés on the Kalverstraat or the Café American on the Leidseplein, and in the attic room in the little house at Prinsengracht.

In winter the main canal, the Singel, was frozen over. The boats were icebound, going nowhere. Then spring came and the ice dissolved. Little shoots of grass pierced the snow and the trees began to bud. With the thaw, Zara's proud reserve melted. It was the sight of the spring flowers that made her cry for the first time since her brother disappeared.

Dirk found her one day, kneeling on the canal bank over a group of violet and white buds around the base of the oak tree. The first crocuses. Zara's shoulders shook. He realized that the final guard had come down and knelt beside her, holding her in his arms as all the tension left her body and she wept hopelessly.

He knew then that what he wanted to do more than anything in the world was to kiss her. To hold her in his arms and make love to her. And he knew it was the one thing he must not do. Dirk realised as the weeks went by that he was taking the place of her brother. She needed him to be her friend, her family. He knew that that was all she wanted of him. He had taken the place of her lost father, brother, nanny. But he had fallen hopelessly in love with her.

He dared not tell her. She would take fright and run. She was too vulnerable, too raw. She was, for the moment, incapable of forming a romantic attachment. She needed all her energy to recover from the brutality she had endured at the Baron's hands. Sadly he realized she was not now and perhaps never would be capable of a natural response to romantic love. The Baron had spoiled that for her forever.

Dirk was Zara's devoted friend, her confidante, her constant companion. No more, no less.

He supported her too, helped her fight her fear of arrest. The murder of such an important person as the Baron could not go unpunished, she knew that. Society would demand retribution. Also Maminka's God, the Church she had been brought up in, would exact punishment no matter what he had done to her. However cruel he might have been, she should not have murdered him. Would the Dutch police have been told? Dirk doubted it. Would they suddenly one day come for her? He said it was a thousand to one chance.

Zara would shiver in fear and pray that God would not condemn her. She lived in constant fear, jumping when someone knocked at the door or accidentally touched her. Mevrou Kloof saw the girl's raw nerves and came to a decision.

"You are a good girl," she told Zara, "not flighty and scatterbrained like most of the others. That Hannetjie for one. Such as her are only here *en route*. Where they think they are going I don't know, but it's certain they won't get there. They dream of some rich handsome man falling in love with them and taking them away from all this. Ach, what fools they are! They end up walking the streets.

"There is no short cut to affluence, Zara, remember that. You are different from those foolish girls. It is sad about your brother, though. He had his eye on other things." She looked at Zara shrewdly. "He was not like you. He felt we were not good enough for him here."

Zara wanted to scream 'No, no, you are wrong', but she did not know any longer what her brother had been. So she kept silent.

"I have noticed you since he disappeared. You have been jumpy and nervous. I am anxious about you." Mevrou Kloof's plain spinster's face was filled with concern.

Zara protested, fearful that she would lose her job. "No, Mevrou Kloof. I'm all right. Really I am. I'll be better, you'll see."

The housekeeper shook her head again. "I have spoken to Meneer Van Daniken and we both think you might be better off and of more use to us in the dining room. At least we can be sure you will not flirt with the male customers there and upset their wives. We've had to sack Beatrix Vingboons for doing that just once too often. And you'll not be bothered by unwanted attention there as much as in the corridors and rooms up here. God, men are beasts!" She drew her lips together in a straight line, relaxed and then smiled. "You'll get better wages and better tips."

Zara was grateful for the promotion. She preferred the work in the restaurant. The room was wood-panelled with long gilt-framed mirrors. The napery was damask, the lighting discreet. Tables were set within semi-circular banquettes. The low murmur of the diners' voices blended with the gentle clink of cutlery and glass, and mellow tones of the head waiter as he spoke to the guests. Zara found the work more congenial after the rush and fuss, the haste and dash, of a chambermaid's life.

They ate together, Dirk, Frau Kettner and Zara, every night when she returned from the hotel. Often she brought home little luxuries saved from the kitchen. The Chef liked to clear away food that would spoil and was quite happy for the staff to take what they wanted of the perishable foods, but woe betide anyone who took so much as a biscuit without permission. They would be dismissed on the spot without a reference.

Zara thought this quite fair. She liked exact rules and regulations. That way she knew where she stood. Everything in black and white and no uncertainties.

And they were kind to her. Her past, the fact that she had never experienced the hurly-burly of average family life, made her unsure of herself, and vulnerable, but the staff at the hotel taught her all about comradeship and their friendliness touched her.

They were so sympathetic when Sasha disappeared. They did not say anything much but Mevrou Kloof and Meneer Van Daniken and the others pressed little treats on her: a bon-bon; a handkerchief; a posy of flowers. They gave her a friendly pat on the arm or a smile of encouragement. They lent a hand when she seemed in distress and she noticed each little kindness and appreciated it, more than any of them realized.

Their support and Frau Kettner's and Dirk's constant sympathy kept her from losing her mind. The work exhausted her which was a good thing. By the time she got home and had eaten with Frau Kettner and Dirk, she usually collapsed into a deep sleep.

Dirk met her each night at the back entrance of the restaurant. If the weather was fine he walked her home and if it was bad they caught the tram. Often they did not exchange a word. Sometimes Zara would sigh, remembering something, and Dirk would touch her arm just under the elbow and give it a gentle squeeze. Zara would smile at him, that enchanting smile that lit up her small face. But it made him feel she was as remote from him as the moon.

Dirk's happiness became dependent on her. He knew how stupid he was being. To let her see, even by the flicker of an eyelid, that he desired her would, he realized, throw her into terrible confusion. So he remained, very carefully, her friend.

He often watched her across the table, her eyes weary as she picked daintily at the kitchen leftovers that constituted their supper. He ached to lighten her expression, bring that wonderful smile to her face, but rarely succeeded. Her loss had left her mistrustful and depressed and there seemed no way to get her out of it.

Then Dirk had an idea. He remembered Zara telling him about Mevrou Kloof's suggestion. She had told him in a hopeless defeated tone of voice one day when they were having coffee in the Café American how kind the manageress could be.

"She's really nice to me, Dirk," she said, stirring her coffee. Then leaning across the table she pressed his hand. "As you are. So kind. I'll never really be able to thank you. And it's not as if I'm good company. That is why I won't try to find the Russians. Mevrou Kloof told me they meet in a café." She looked out of the rain-splashed window. Across the street the lights of the Opera House shone palely in the puddles and people hurried into taxis.

"Down there." She nodded and pointed across the street.

"Oh, it would be nice to hear the sound of the language again. So good." She sighed and rubbed a drop of coffee on the marble-topped table 'til her finger had absorbed it.

"Then we must go. We must try to find it."

She shook her head. "Oh no, Dirk. I'm such a failure, a nobody. Once I was the Princess Vashinskova. Now I'm a waitress." She seemed to shrink into her black coat, her small face half-concealed by the collar.

"So are they, Zara. Most Russian exiles are working as waiters and waitresses, cooks, chauffeurs ... anything at all, I've heard, in order to live."

"Where have you heard?" she asked curiously.

"At the University," he said. "From the French. Most of the Russians go there ... to Paris. And apparently most of them get jobs as waiters. Oh, other things as well. The lucky ones are art dealers or journalists, a lot *are* waiters. I'm not making it up, Zara. As for the women, Professor de Rochas said that there were a lot of dancers in the South of France. Perhaps ..."

But she was shaking her head vehemently. "No lady would ever have been allowed in the ballet. It was not possible. The ballet dancers, even the stars, were emphatically not of the nobility. It would have been impossible for me although I would have loved to dance.

187

Well, never mind. I think my fellow-countrymen are better off without me."

She stood up and they left, emerging into the rain and running to catch a tram.

But Dirk was not at all sure she was right. He thought that contact with her fellow-countrymen might cheer her up, improve her spirits. He decided to find out where this café was and it did not take him long. A lecturer at the University told him it was just around the corner from the Leidseplein. He looked it over to make sure it was the kind of place he could take Zara to, then seizing his opportunity one evening when they had been walking along the banks of the Amstel and it had suddenly begun to rain, put her on a tram and took her there.

It was not a success. The café was filled with old bearded men who played chess. As they opened the door a bell tinkled and a cacophany of Russian assaulted their ears. Zara flinched and shrank back as if she had been struck. Dirk did not know whether the tears in her eyes came from the sound of her mother-tongue or the smoke.

She looked at him, her expression fearful, and he said, "It's just a café, Zara. We can have a coffee and go."

The room was small. Each table was occupied. A large man in a velour coat with an astrakhan collar made room for them, nodding and smiling. He had large bushy eyebrows and a broken front tooth.

"Borscht!" Zara cried looking into the bowl from which he was eating. The way she said it made them all laugh. Dirk asked her if she would like some.

"No," she said. "No. Just coffee, please."

The windows of the café were steamed up and there was a strong smell of damp clothing drying out.

The waitress was a large-bosomed woman in a shiny black satin dress. She bustled about serving people and exchanging pleasantries with them. She addressed Dirk in Russian. Zara quickly replied for him.

"I have asked her for two coffees. Is that all right?"

Dirk nodded. He did not know what to say or do. He wondered what he had hoped to accomplish by bringing her here. What had he hoped would happen? Eureka, and Zara's sadness would have vanished? He shook his head and felt her hand cover his.

"Oh, my dear, don't look so disappointed. I know you meant well. I know why you brought me here and I do appreciate it. You are so good to me and I am so undeserving."

She smiled at him and he thought, At least I have won that from her. He felt foolish to be grateful for so little.

The man in the astrakhan-collared coat leant over. "Are you Russian?" he asked in German, the language in which Dirk and Zara had been speaking.

"No," replied Dirk.

"But you are, little one?" he asked Zara.

She nodded, looking at the man curiously.

"It's good to hear the mother-tongue, no?"

She nodded again.

"But painful?"

"Yes."

"I know," the man said sadly. To Dirk's alarm he looked as if he might cry. "We come here for a little comfort and it only makes us lonelier than ever. Why do Russians find exile such agony? I tell you, I don't know the answer." He shrugged his shoulders and spread his hands, looking at them with large mournful eyes, then returned to his borscht with a resigned sigh.

They drank their coffee quickly. Zara looked about her all the time, swift little bird-like glances as if she were under threat.

They left, walking through the grey sheets of rain in silence.

It rained for a week. Zara began to fear she was being followed. A slight inconsequential man in a raincoat seemed

189

to be everywhere she went. She could not even describe him; he was too innocuous-looking, too average, too inconspicuous. He just seemed to be around. When she had looked through the window of the Café Russe, he had been standing under a lamp post in the rain outside. When they jumped on a tram, they left him standing in the rain on the pavement, yet when she arrived for work the next morning she saw him leaning on a low wall some distance away. In the evening she thought she could see him further up the street; and once he stood motionless against the oaktree outside the house on Prinsengracht.

She thought perhaps she was imagining things. Dirk said she was sometimes paranoid. She did not know exactly what that was but understood the context in which he used the term and so did not tell him of her shadow. Then, suddenly, the little man ceased appearing. Zara decided his appearances must have been coincidental and put them from her mind.

Some time later Mevrou Kloof came upon Dirk as he sheltered from the drenching downpour under the awning at the side of the hotel. He always collected Zara and this evening he was shaking his umbrella and stomping his feet when Mevrou Kloof emerged through the kitchen exit.

"Meneer Van Holstein," she acknowledged him, and started to walk away. In the act of putting up her umbrella she stopped, changed her mind and came back to him.

"Could I speak with you for a moment?" She had galoshes on her feet and her raincoat was buttoned to the top so that it pressed her double chin out in an exaggerated fashion, making her look a little like a turkey. Her wobbling cheeks and the red cloche hat she wore increased the resemblance, but her eyes were kindly.

"Come to my office, please," she said, turning back into the building. "Zara will not be finished for another half hour."

He followed her through the kitchen. No one looked up.

People in white jackets and hats ran about, dishes clashed and utensils clanged. Waiters and waitresses came through the swing doors with trays piled high with dirty dishes and left with bread in baskets, chicken and lamb under silver covers, vegetables in warm dishes, desserts in cut-glass bowls.

Dirk did not see Zara. He obediently followed Mevrou Kloof down a corridor, stepping over cardboard boxes, an empty ice-cream churn, and stacks of empty wine and brandy bottles. She led him into another corridor and, eventually, a small office. She sat, pulling off her gloves, and indicated a chair in front of her.

'Please sit down. You must forgive me for approaching you like this. We do not really know each other.'' So far they had only exchanged greetings when Zara's exit coincided with her boss's. Mevrou Kloof got straight to the point. "I'm worried about Zara," she said abruptly, looking at him with anxious eyes.

"I am too," said Dirk, "but I don't know what to do."

He was glad to have the opportunity to discuss it with this sensible woman. Not that Frau Kettner was not sensible; far from it. But she was old and sentimental and nurtured a negative way of thinking. Her method with Zara was to sympathise and assure her she had every reason to be sad and depressed, which got them nowhere.

"Who wouldn't?" she was fond of saying. "Your parents shot before your eyes, your home taken away, your brother leaving you in the lurch like that ... oh, it would take a stronger woman not to sink."

"I don't know what to do either," the housekeeper said now, "but we must do something. That girl is wasting away. Oh, she's an excellent worker. Too good. Sometimes I would like her to rebel a little, it would do her good. But no, she's as biddable as a sheep, and as docile, and anyone can see her heart is breaking." She compressed her lips and frowned. "There now, I've upset you," she said contritely.

191

Dirk's eyes pricked with tears. He blinked and bent his head. "It's all right. You are quite correct. Ever since her brother ran away she has been in a deep depression. But what can I do? Tell me that."

"Has she tried the Café Russe?" Mevrou Kloof asked.

"Yes, it did no good at all. She was uncomfortable there. It was painful to see."

The woman clicked her tongue against her teeth. "Too bad. But I'm afraid it's your only chance." She drew a deep breath. "Look," she said earnestly, "she's Russian. Of the nobility, yes?" Dirk nodded. "Well then," she continued, "someone, sometime, will go into that place who knew her, her family or their friends. Someone will eventually come who will know someone else who knows her. They will help. Do you not see?"

"Yes, I do. But what can I ...?"

"Go yourself if you cannot get her to. Make friends with those people."

"I don't speak Russian."

She looked at him impatiently. "Then speak Dutch or German or French. They will speak another language. I'd do it myself but," she gave him a chilly smile, "I do not have as much time as you. In fact, I am here morning, noon and night." She narrowed her eyes. "Now listen, life does not owe us anything. We have to manage as best we can, get on with it. But don't you see, Zara is different? She has a soul that is sick. She may die of all this."

He looked startled. "Die? That's taking it a bit far, don't you think?"

"No, I don't. I believe that the life-force, the will to live, is the greatest power on earth. Without it people simply succumb. They are carried off, no fight in them. I've seen it scores of times," she continued sadly, "the ones who don't survive. They come here looking for work. They are usually quite good at it for a time, and then they begin to despair. They seem to lose colour, become lack-lustre. Drab. Dull.

192

Then they fade away. Sometimes it's the canals. Sometimes pneumonia or a fever. Something quite simple. The will to live is gone, you see."

She stood up and Dirk knew the interview was at an end. "We don't want that to happen to Zara now, do we?" she asked and without waiting for a reply added: "Goodbye, Meneer Van Holstein. Thank you for your time. I think we understand each other."

She held out her hand and he gave her his. She gave it a hearty shake.

"I really must go," she said, "I have a sick mother at home who will be waiting anxiously for me."

The touching scene this conjured up reminded him of how alone Zara was. Mevrou Kloof obviously found her sick mother both a heavy responsibility and an irksome tie, but caring for her was her *raison d'être*.

The conversation had shocked and frightened him. It was unbelievable to think that Zara could die, just like that. Yet he knew the housekeeper was right. He felt it in his bones. Daily Zara seemed to be less and less vital. Her eyes, dominating her small white face, were empty of expression. Sometimes she did not hear what he said. She did everything mechanically, showing little interest in the world around her. She neither laughed nor cried. Not since the day he found her weeping over the crocuses had he seen her express any emotion at all.

So Dirk took Mevrou Kloof's advice. He went each evening for a coffee to the little Café Russe and talked to anyone and everyone who would have a conversation with him. He became well known there, an *habitué*. He chatted with the fat waitress, the owner's pretty daughter and Astrakhan Collar who came in every other evening. He spoke to princes and men who merely claimed to be titled, women old and young. Winter melted into spring. Zara lost weight and was so thin her light skirt fell to the floor over her hips after she had fastened it up. Dirk was becoming desperate.

Then one evening when the leaves were beginning to dress the trees in tender green and the breeze from the Amstel had a satiny feel, a most unlikely fellow – obviously a working man, probably a servant – said to him: "Vashinskov? Vashinskova? Yes, I remember. They came to stay with us in Moscow, the Prince and his daughter. With my family, the people I worked for – Rostov. Cousins they were, I think. Princess Rostova was Prince Vashinskov's sister."

He smacked his lips and Dirk hurriedly ordered another beer for him. The genial follow was only too pleased to talk. "Yes, I have a very good memory. Many peoples say so. They live in France now. The South of France. Nice, I think. I was with them there then I left. I am a good mechanic, sir. I was the chauffeur then. I drove the little Princess Vashinskova from the station to her aunt's. I remember it as if it was only yesterday. But, you see, I can get more money as a mechanic. Everyone has cars now. Everyone. So I left them. Went to Germany then here. I married a Dutch girl."

A broad beaming smile crossed his face and he took another swig of the beer. "I am very happy here, sir. It is more like Russia. I was not happy in France. Not at all. It was too hot. I am uncomfortable in the heat.

"No, I do not have the exact address, but let me see ..." He searched the ceiling with his bulbous eyes, then scratched his head under the cap he wore without taking it off. "The house was behind the town. Something about roses ... Villa de la Rose, I think. Villa de la Rose, Nice, France. That would get them, I think. Yes, Rostov, Villa de la Rose."

Dirk kept the news of the Rostov's wherabouts to himself for about a week. He knew he had to tell Zara and was happy that he had found for her the part of her family that she truly loved. He had heard her speak of the Rostovs. Her stay there was, she had told him, the one time in her life she had been supremely happy.

He loved Zara and wanted more than anything else to

make her happy again; if not as completely happy as she had been with the Rostovs then at least as content as she had been before Sasha had run away. Yet he knew he was about to lose her. He knew that in all probability she would leave Amsterdam and go to Nice, out of his life. He agonised over his secret, hugging the news to himself for days, reluctant to tell her yet knowing he must.

She was standing in her little attic room when he broke the news. She was holding a cup and saucer in her hands and let them fall. They shattered on the wooden floor, white ceramic pieces bouncing everywhere. Zara did not notice. Her hands flew to her face and she whispered, "Rostov, Rostov," as if she were unable to believe her ears.

"Who told you? Where is he? Oh, I must find out where they are." She stared at Dirk, then ran to him and hugged and kissed him. "Thank you, dear, dear Dirk! Oh, how can I thank you? It never even occurred to me to try to find them. I thought it would be impossible. I didn't imagine it could happen. Oh, let me find them!"

It was not difficult. Professor de Rochas made a phone call to his friends in Paris and they were able to trace the family. They contacted the Russian Church in Paris who contacted the Russian Church in Nice. They verified that, yes, indeed there were Rostovs living there. They gave the address as the Villa de la Rose, Nice.

Zara wrote. While waiting for a reply, her mood swung from ecstatic excitement to despair and back again.

"Oh, it's all a dream. A dream. It could never happen. Never. How could it? I am building up my hopes and I will find that it is all a mistake. If it's a mistake, Dirk, I'll die. I'll just die."

This changed the next day to, "They're there, I know it! My beloved Rostovs. I'll see them soon, Dirk. Imagine! Oh, you cannot comprehend how I love them all. Dmitri and Nina. Dearest Aunt Sonya and Uncle Vassily. Oh, Dirk, come with me to meet them. Do, Dirk, do. You would love them and they you. Oh, come with me, please. I don't want to lose you." And she would gaze at him with wide pleading eyes.

His heart nearly broke. He wanted to go with her, stay by her side, never let her out of his sight. But he knew he would not. He could not leave his studies. He could not leave the University. His mother and father were making great sacrifices to send him there and support him while he was studying. He could not leave at such an important moment in his life, just before his finals.

"I cannot, Zara. You'll have to go alone."

He saw she hardly listened but accepted his decision lightly. He felt bruised and hurt. She did not mean to be cruel to him, he knew, but she was. He knew she had never been in love with him the way he was with her and it was not her fault, yet it wounded him when she took the thought of their parting so casually. His hopes would rise when she clung to him suddenly, begging him to stay with her. Unconsciously then he hoped she would not go, that she would change her mind and tell him that it was enough for her that they could be together. But her dependency upon him only lasted a moment and then she would weep with excitement over the prospect of seeing her beloved Rostovs and Dirk would feel abandoned and lost. He began to hate the very name Rostovs.

Eventually Zara received a reply. The letter was addressed to Princess Vashinskova. Dirk brought it to her in her little room. Seeing the title on the envelope made him feel inferior. She never used her title here in Amsterdam and he knew he was being unreasonable but he felt that in that moment he had truly lost her. Receiving the envelope addressed 'Princess', she was suddenly outside his orbit.

She held the letter in trembling hands. When she opened it two bank-notes fell out. Dirk picked them up and handed them to her. She took them absently, intent on reading the letter that accompanied them. It was from her Aunt Sonya.

You must come to us at once, *chérie*. Bring your Dutch friend with you if it is possible. We would love to meet him. Anyone who has been so kind to you is held warmly in our hearts.

Go to Paris and take the Blue Train for the South. I enclose money to cover expenses. Please hurry to us! Send a telegram with arrival time. All of us are enchanted to hear from you and await your arrival eagerly.

Dmitri and Nina send love and Vassily and I also, and our deep desire is to see you soon.

Your loving aunt, Sonya

When Zara had scanned the letter she read it aloud to Dirk, then flung her arms around him, hugging him and kissing his cheeks. He had never seen her like this before – her eyes alive and sparkling, cheeks flushed. She had changed completely and he realized for the first time how beautiful she was.

For Zara the days passed in a whirl. She felt as if she was flying. All encumbrances fell away from her. The chains of despair, hopelessness, and earth-bound pessimism disappeared. She felt euphoric and full of breathless excitement.

Amsterdam had never looked so pretty. The sky was a pale madonna blue and the chestnut trees were in bloom. The breeze from the Amstel was warm and a primrose sun picked out the water in the canals in pinpoints of light, little golden shafts, dancing and twinkling in perpetual motion.

She made her preparations in a heady mood, like a drinker with his second cocktail; the first had been drunk fast, this one was to savour.

Dirk made all the travel arrangements for her. It was his last opportunity to be of service. He wished he could go on making the arrangements forever, refusing to think of her actual departure. He could not believe it would really come, and what he would do when she left he could not imagine. She had taken up so much of his life.

Zara told Mevrou Kloof and Meneer Van Daniken her news with barely concealed emotion, quite sure that they would be pleased for her. She was not mistaken. Her vulnerability had touched and disarmed them and they felt protective of her. They were not used to feeling like that about other employees, and were surprised at their own emotion.

They both embraced her and Mevrou Kloof had tears in her eyes as she said: "I'm so glad for you. So very glad. And, remember, if it does not work out for you, let us know, eh?"

Meneer Van Daniken ducked his head and could not look at her. His voice was husky.

"You will come back here? Remember, you will always have friends in Amsterdam, and a place if need be. You have been a very good girl."

Frau Kettner held her in her arms and wept copiously over her. She too assured Zara of her friendship and a place always in the little house in Prinsengracht.

"I'll remember. I'll never forget you, dearest Frau Kettner." Zara cried, kissing the landlady's soft wrinkled cheek.

On the day she left, Dirk took her to the station.

"I love you, Zara. You know that," he said, his face screwed up in anguish.

She nodded. "Yes." She felt awkward suddenly, realising he wanted so much more from her than she could ever give him. She wished she could love him passionately, it would make things so easy, but she could not.

"I'll write." She said the trite words sadly and added, "I wish you could come too. They did ask you."

He shook his head. "No, I would be out of place there. They are your family. I would be an outsider."

She knew he was speaking the truth, that when she saw them she would have no time for him. Her throat tightened at the thought of how much she cared for him and would miss him, and how impossible it all was. She clung to him, afraid suddenly to part.

He pushed her on to the train. "Is there anything you need?" he asked briskly.

As much as he had wished that the departure date would never come, now that they were in the station he longed for her to go, for this agony to be over.

Zara shook her head and he heard the train doors slamming and the piercing shriek of the whistle. She leaned forward and kissed him, putting her hands on either side of his face. He felt the touch of her lips on his, sweet like the taste of an apple. She smiled into his eyes.

"Write," she said. At that moment he would have died for her. All he said was, "I will. Let me know how it goes."

Still she held his hands in hers.

Everyone was ready. The last door had been slammed and the train shuddered into motion. Dirk stared into her white face, leaning out of the window towards him. The train began to move. Their hands were dragged apart. Zara raised her arm in salute as it steamed out of the station and waved as they gathered speed.

"Goodbye," he called after her though it was too late for her to hear him.

PART III
France

Chapter Ten

Zara felt no pangs of separation as the train chugged out of Holland. The flat countryside sped past her bright gaze; a windmill standing alone, awkward and cumbersome on the horizon. She admired its sheer power but there was no sweet regret at leaving this land only exultation as she travelled south.

At the Gâre du Nord she left the train, easily able to carry her little case. She never remembered what she did in Paris that day. It was mild there but she still huddled in her warm fur-lined coat. She knew she did not venture far. Her mind was centred on thoughts of the Rostovs. She wandered about looking at the shops which were not very exciting in that quarter. She was hardly aware of where she was going or what she was doing. She ate a *brioche* and drank coffee though she could have afforded a four course meal in the best hotel. But frugal habits die hard, and anyway she had no interest in food. She could only think of reaching her destination.

In an expectant haze she boarded the Blue Train for Nice. She had dinner but did not know what she was eating. She slept, a deep dreamless sleep, and awoke to the sound of the porter crying: "*Attention! Attention! Arrive à Nice. Ici Nice.*"

She stepped off the train into glorious sunlight. She turned up her face and bathed in its welcoming warmth. She had never been in a place like this before. The air was warm, the very earth warm, the sun a benediction. She felt she had come home.

A chauffeur in white drill trousers, white jacket and peaked cap met her at the exit. He was carrying a large piece of cardboard with her name printed on it: VASHINSKOVA. He took her battered little case and brought her outside to the long, gleaming Dusenberg.

Nothing had prepared Zara for the South of France, but she knew as soon as she set foot outside the train that it was the place she had been aching for all her life. She had so hated the cold and now she had arrived in this place of colour and sunshine.

The shimmering light was molten gold on the sea, the dancing waves a deep almost navy blue crested with silver foam. Swaying palm trees lined the Promenade des Anglais with its pink buildings decorated with wrought-iron balconies and white shutters. They drove past the Negresco. Zara sat luxuriating in the cream-coloured seats as the Dusenberg turned by the hotel and left the Promenade and the glittering dancing water, driving past splashes of pink and white oleander. The sighing sound of the sea followed them as they climbed into the hills behind Nice.

The smell of the trees perfumed the breeze and assaulted Zara's senses. Nowhere she had ever been before had smelled so sweet. She leaned out of the window of the elegant car, sniffing the aromatic air, filling her lungs with the scent of herbs and lemons and flowers. Her eyes feasted on the colours, the brightness, the sheer sparkle of the place. She felt so full of joy she thought she might burst. Warmth flowed around her, embracing her through the open window of the car so that at last she had to remove her coat. It was like balm to her, the warmth of the air, and she felt wrapped in well-being just being here. And always, shining upon her, this new and brilliant sun.

They did not have far to go. The Villa de la Rose was perched on the side of the hill surrounded by trees; olives, bent and grey-green, scented eucalyptus, summer magnolia, umbrella pines, mimosa, bay and cypress. It was a square building painted pink with a terracotta-tiled roof, green shutters and a pillared terrace surrounding it.

As the car drew up Zara's composure shattered. They all stood there waiting for her; Dmitri, Nina, Vassily and Sonya, surrounded by servants in uniform. She thought her heart would burst. It seemed to swell within her at the sight.

They moved towards her, a group of slim fashionable people dressed in white, looking cool in the sun. She flung herself towards them, opening the door before the car came to a halt, a black-clad whirlwind of excitement as she hugged them and kissed them, tears streaming down her face. She had to touch every member of the family before she would believe they were real.

Aunt Sonya's greeting began in a dignified manner but her eyes filled with tears at her niece's waif-like appearance, her trembling need, and she swept Zara into her arms. Her transparent white organza hat tipped sideways as she murmured endearments in Russian. The traces of Prince Alexei in his sister's face brought tears of sadness as well as joy to Zara.

Uncle Vassily frankly and unashamedly blubbed. He mopped his eyes with a large white handkerchief, took off his panama hat and buried his face in Zara's neck while she patted his fringe of grey hair, saying "There, there, Uncle", over and over again.

Dmitri was handsome as ever in his cream linen suit. He kissed her cheeks and called her "Dearest little cousin". And then there was Nina, slimmer, lovelier, blonder, smiling at her through tears.

"I'm so glad to see you here, dearest Zaroushka. So very glad."

"Is this all you have?" Sonya pointed to the battered little case.

Zara nodded.

"Goodness gracious! Then I see that our priority must be a shopping spree. And here are Drushenska and Maya, Mikhail and Boris – they remember Princess Vashinskova. Zaroushka, you know them, of course. But no, how could you remember?"

"Oh, but I do. I do," Zara cried, overwhelmed. She shook the servants' hands and kissed Drushenska. "Oh, Aunt, you don't know … you cannot imagine …"

She found she could not continue. "I'm so happy to see you," she cried feebly as she tried to control her laughter and her tears.

It was Vassily who recovered first. "Come along. Come along," he said, blowing hugely into his handkerchief, making a trumpeting blast that startled everyone and changed Zara's sobs to a giggle. "There," he cried, "that's better. Laughter. We have some wine. We speak Russian. What could be better?"

"A rest and a meal," said his wife tartly. "She is skin and bone."

"The most fashionable way to look, darling," said Nina, sighing.

"Now be quiet, Nina. Don't go filling Zara's head with nonsense. She needs a few square meals. She's not healthy-looking."

"It's not done to look healthy," Nina insisted.

"That's enough. I'll not have you talk like that. She'll eat or I'll know why." She looked into Zara's small pale face. "You must tell us all that happened to you for we know nothing." Then, seeing her niece's expression, she added hastily, "But not yet. Not until tomorrow when you are rested."

Nina put her arm around her cousin's waist, "I'll show you your room," she said.

Zara was enchanted by this new unimaginably exotic world. The villa's rooms opened on to each other. From the cool paved hall where they were standing she could see through to a lounge that gave directly on to a patio where the family obviously ate. There was a marble table there, set squarely in the middle with chairs arranged neatly round it. On it stood a huge flower arrangement, freesias, carnations, lilies and laurel, scrupulously mixed to give a delightfully careless effect. Zara could see that from the table the view was of the mountains, the sea, Nice and the bay. Immediately beyond the patio she made out a fountain playing, bright red geraniums in terracotta urns and a magical garden full of colour and scent.

"We have prepared the most adorable bedroom for you, dearest Zaroushka," Nina said, squeezing her hand. But Zara stood and gazed, disoriented and as if in a dream. It was such a different world. The cramped little attic room, the cold grandeur of the palaces and castle she had lived in, the bleak Northern skies, the long grey days she had endured threw this brilliant place into stunning relief.

Her room was cool, with cream-coloured walls and a marble floor. There were bright blue curtains before the shuttered windows and sprays of wine-coloured Sweet William in Mediterranean blue vases on a little desk and dressing-table. There was a blue-tiled bathroom off the bedroom with fluffy white towels hanging beside the bath, washbasin and bidet. The taps were gold and shaped like swans. Water gushed from their open beaks. Chinese vases made into lampstands stood each side of the bed, topped with cream shades. The bedspread was silk damask, a brilliant blue to match the curtains.

There was a white dress laid out for her.

"It's a sort of fit anyone dress," Nina said, "but Drushenka will put in tucks for you. We never thought you would be so thin, though we thought you might not have a dress ..." She shrugged in embarrassment and Zara gave her a brief hug.

"Thank you, it's lovely." She looked around the room, lost for words to express how moved she was, how welcome they had made her feel. As if divining her thoughts, Nina held her cousin's hands,

"Oh, Zaroushka, has it been awful for you?"

Zara bit her lip.

"Well, don't think about it yet. Have a rest, a bath. I'll send up something to drink then you can change for lunch. I'll leave you now."

When she had gone Zara undressed and bathed. A maid brought in a silver samovar on a silver tray and Zara poured herself tea and sipped it, feeling cosseted and loved as she had not since last she saw the Rostovs. But she had never before known such luxury and beauty, manmade and Godmade to excellent perfection. She could smell the scent of the bath soap on her body, feel the softness of the robe she had found hanging on the back of the bathroom door. She stared at the shaft of sunlight piercing the open window where the breeze caught and played with diaphanous white curtains. Her body was aching but it felt light and she was full to the brim with happiness.

They would take care of her. Her Aunt Sonya and Uncle Vassily would take the responsibility from her shoulders. She would tell them everything. They would protect and look after her. It was a lovely thing to know. Zara fell into an exhausted, dreamless sleep.

She did not hear Nina come into the room. She did not hear her leave and return with her mother. She did not hear them draw the curtains nor feel them cover her lightly. She slept dreamlessly, released from the burdens that oppressed her.

She did not awaken until the day was almost over. She stirred and felt the familiar fear jerk in her stomach, but when she opened her eyes in the cool blue light and saw her cousin watching over her, relief flooded in.

"Mother says it is good you slept. We did not disturb you. It's nearly dinner. Would you like to eat with us? But only if you are up to it."

Zara stretched and smiled. She realised she was ravenously

hungry. "Yes," she said. "Oh yes, please!"

They ate under the stars which scattered a blue-black velvet sky. A new moon hung silver-gold above them.

Zara never forgot that first meal. Forever afterwards she could close her eyes and visualise the long marble table and deep blue plates scattered with breadcrumbs. There was silver on the table, candlabra with flickering white candles. There were blue napkins and Venetian glass, fine as tissue, on the white tablecloth.

They ate calamari with salad, then quail and wild rice, French cheeses of all kinds, followed by an apricot compôte and ice cream. They drank champagne and red wine from the province and finally thick Turkish coffee. All the time the conversation flowed, desultory, unstructured, casual.

Below them Nice sparkled, a string of lights like a glittering necklace hanging over the sea. The mountains were etched against the dark sky, mysterious and remote. Cannes, Cap Ferrat, St Tropez, Villefranche, Monte Carlo ... they were all there, showing themselves off under the stars, some with their feet in the sea, some hidden behind the headland, some peeping from a glittering distance.

"You remember the night of the ball?" Dmitri asked her. He was the first to broach the past. The conversation up to then had been about the local social events, the beauty of the view, and comments on the excellence of the chef.

"I remember," said Zara softly. "I have never forgotten a moment of it. You brought me champagne. I danced with Papa."

The butler was refilling their coffee cups and Dmitri gestured to him.

"This is Feydor who pulled you away from the window, remember?"

Zara looked into the smiling face of the servant. "Oh, yes, I remember you."

"It is good to see you here, Princess. We are all happy you

escaped."

There was silence after he left the terrace. Zara cleared her throat.

"I would like to tell you here and now what happened to me."

"Only if you feel like it," Nina cried.

Zara waved her hand, "We cannot be at ease with each other until I have told you everything. You are all so afraid of hurting me, and you don't know which particular things will cause me pain. Before I do, I want you to know that for the first time in years I feel safe, here with you."

Vassily leaped to his feet. "We feel privileged to have you. So glad. So happy."

"Sit down, Vassily, and allow her to continue," Sonya said sharply.

"Of course, my love. Sorry."

Zara gathered her thoughts and began. At times she faltered; at times paused to drink some champagne or coffee. The others sat quite still, transported by her words.

She told them of her father's death, which Sonya had guessed; she said she had known almost to the moment when his heart had stopped beating. She told them how Anya and Maminka, Piotr and Valenka, had died with him.

Vassily pressed his handkerchief against his eyes and murmured, "Ay, ay," in a gentle moan. Sonya shook her head, her fine eyebrows drawn together in a frown. Nina covered Zara's hand with hers, then took it away when her cousin did not react to her show of sympathy.

But Zara did not even feel the clasp. She continued, telling them of the terrible journey culminating in her wedding to the Baron Klaus Hoffen von Eldrich.

Vassily sucked in his breath. "But this is monstrous!" he said.

"Was it true? Was it the only way?"

"Be quiet. Let her finish before we ask questions," Sonya chided.

Zara was glad it was night and the last candle guttering. Their faces were all in shadow. She could not see them and that helped her recount the rest of what had happened to her. She carried on, told them of the further journey, their destination and what followed. She left out nothing but the most lurid details, and she did not cry.

She told them about Sasha, and about the murder. She could hear them draw in their collective breath after she had described the scene in the library. Her Uncle Vassily sobbed and Aunt Sonya cried: "But ... but ..." Zara hurried on over her aunt's protests.

"We escaped to Amsterdam," she said. "That is the worst part over now. I'm very tired. I'll tell you about Amsterdam tomorrow. There's nothing much. Just that we got jobs and lived quietly, avoiding the police, and then ... Sasha disappeared." Her throat had tightened again and she took a deep breath. "Then I found out about you. Or Dirk did.

"But you may not want me here now that you know. I am, after all, a murderess."

Uncle Vassily patted her hand. "You poor, poor child," he sobbed. "That beast! That monster!"

"Hush, Vassily dear," his wife said soothingly.

"But, Mother, didn't you say ...?" Dmitri sounded puzzled.

"Dearest, you are not a murderess," said Nina triumphantly.

"And even if you did kill someone who treated you like that, do you really think we would blame you?" said her aunt grandly.

Zara was perplexed. "What do you mean?"

"You didn't kill him," said Dmitri.

"Of course I did! I stood there, shooting bullet after bullet into him. There was blood on the floor. The carpet was stained. His body jerked and was still."

Dmitri stood, came around the table and knelt beside her chair. "He is alive, Zaroushka. Mother saw him."

211

Zara looked at her aunt. She felt confused and wondered if perhaps she was dreaming.

Sonya nodded. "Yes, I spoke to him. It was in Baden-Baden. Vassily and I were there for the waters.

"The Baron Hoffen von Eldrich was in a hotel there, the Grand or the Palace, I can't quite remember. I saw him in the dining room having breakfast but he avoided me. The hotel said he had booked in for a week but had just told them he had been suddenly called away. Now I understand why. He had seen me and wanted to avoid me at all costs.

"At the time I thought him very ill-mannered. He had visited us in Moscow, yet when he spotted me in the dining room in Baden-Baden he almost ran out. I wanted to ask him about your stepmother, Zara. If she had escaped, where she was now, if you were with her? I knew they were friends.

"The porter said he was just leaving and I caught up with him as he was getting into his car. I thought his manner exceedingly strange, abrupt, almost rude."

She gave a little snort. "Now I know why! He could not have known then that I had not seen you. He probably thought you had told me the whole story. In any event, his attitude changed when I asked him for news. I told him I knew that Alexei was dead, but asked about Anya and you and Sasha. He said that Anya was dead, and that you and Sasha had probably not survived. We were shattered, all of us. I'll never forgive him for that. Never!"

"Thoroughly rotten vile creature!" Vassily said heatedly.

"We had never ceased to look for you," Sonya continued, "but he seemed so certain that you had not survived that we accepted what he said. At the time there seemed no reason for him to lie. Imagine our surprise and delight when we got your letter!"

"Oh, we were so pleased. So pleased," Nina said. She had come to her cousin's other side and put her arms around her. Dmitri stood and clasped both girls in a brief embrace.

"Come along. Bed time," Sonya said briskly. "Zaroushka

must be tired. In fact, we are all worn out." She patted her niece's head. "You can rest tonight, secure in the knowledge that the police are not looking for you and you have not committed a murder."

Zara felt a wave of happiness wash over her. There had been such relief in the telling of what had happened. She was amazed that she had not succeeded in killing the Baron. The revelation relieved her anxiety but deep down there was a shadow of regret that she had not killed the man who had used her so badly, that he inhabited the world she lived in, that he was still free and alive.

Chapter Eleven

The full story of Zara's years in Amsterdam emerged over the following weeks. She talked of Dirk and how he had helped her, and of Frau Kettner's kindness. Sonya wrote them letters of thanks and encouraged Zara to write at once to them both, inviting them to the South of France whenever they wanted to come.

They replied by return, each turning down the invitation but for different reasons. Frau Kettner wanted to go to Berlin and would not leave her little house in Prinsengracht for any other destination, Dirk said he must study and that he would spend the summer in the mountains with his parents. Perhaps, he said, he would take them up on their invitation at a later date.

They wrote to the hotel and thanked Mevrou Kloof and Meneer Van Daniken. They said that anything they could do in the future, the housekeeper and manager need only ask.

Princess Sonya sent Zara's measurements to Coco Chanel and a few weeks later took her niece to Paris for fittings. They stayed in the Ritz and Zara could not believe the change in her fortunes. It was so strange to be treated as the spoiled darling of a rich and powerful household after her recent years as virtually a slave, and after that little better than a skivvy.

She was enchanted by her new clothes. The Princess had all Zara's thick dark hair chopped off and she found the new light bob made her feel free. In Paris they went shopping every day.

"Are you sure?" Zara would ask. "I may have all this? Isn't it too much? It must be so expensive."

"Nonsense! It's the very least I can do. There is nothing too good for Alexei's child."

The Princess was pleased with herself, and delighted with the change in Zara. She looked so beautiful, so exactly right for the fashionable clothes.

Nina, her Nina, had always been lovely: blonde and curved, pink and white, like a gorgeous doll. Sonya was delighted with her. Every eligible young man on the Riviera was mad about her and her mother had no fears of finding a match for her.

Zara's appearance had appalled her at first. She had looked like a starving gutter-snipe when she arrived but after she had confided in them she seemed to regain some of her bloom . She stood taller. Her movements lost their servility and became untramelled and graceful. And now, dressed in couture clothes with her hair bobbed, her aunt saw that Zara possessed a rare and exciting beauty.

The girl gradually learned to relax, and that helped too. She lost the terrible anxiety and fear that had changed the lines of her face, becoming more outgoing. The sun brought out her latent gaiety. The dazzling flowers, the colours of the sea and trees, the golden light suffusing everything, brought her vividly to life as she had never been before. Her huge eyes sparkled with animation, and if sadness lurked in their depths also, she did not speak of it.

She was a perfect shape for the times. Nina was a little too feminine and curved to be entirely at home in the straight little slips of dresses that were fashionable. Zara had the figure of a boy. Slim as a sapling, bony, long-legged, with her large dark eyes and cap of shining hair, she epitomised the modern flapper on the Cote d'Azur.

She began to enjoy herself and the lifestyle that riches brought. The Princess entertained lavishly; the Prince was

216

gregarious and had an exuberant child-like love of people. He liked nothing better than to fill his beautiful villa with the rich, fashionable and artistic people who lived or holidayed along the coast and up in Provence. The Rostovs could afford to live well. They had transferred their money and possessions out of Russia in plenty of time.

"We saw it coming, Zara," Sonya said. "We begged your father to leave, but he was an idealist. He really believed in reform, in a Russia run by the people for the people. He thought the aristocrats who knew a little about it would be kept on to help and advise. They were, in the Kerensky government. Alexei would gladly have given his services. Russia lost a great man in him. But in a way it is better he did not live to become an exile. He would have died away from Russia." She added after a pause, "So would she."

"Do you hate her, Aunt Sonya?" Zara asked.

The Princess shook her head. "No, I don't hate her. She could not help herself. The one man she loved, Boris Brunevshi, was taken from her. She did not want to marry Alexei. He persuaded her, much against her will. He offered her position, a dazzling name, wealth ... It would have taken a far wiser woman than Anya to refuse what he offered.

"In the event, she made up her mind her life was ruined. She had decided it and she hung on to her grief. She would not let go of the tragedy. Boris had committed suicide because he could not have her, so she was never going to be happy again. Poor Alexei could not satisfy her. Sex used as a drug is as addictive as morphine or opium. Once you acquire the habit ... Well, it destroys. Ah, child, she was a sad woman. You cannot hate such a person. You can only pity her."

Zara had never been conscious of money until Amsterdam. In Russia she had accepted the material grandeur together with the isolation in which she lived. It was all she knew. She had never handled money in Russia. In Amsterdam she had become aware of the value of money and the privation brought about by the lack of it. Here money was not even spoken of, was never mentioned. Yet the signs of it were everywhere. It brought comfort and luxury, it bought time and freedom. It bought leisure, good food and wine, it brought with it friends and fashionable company, entertainment, music and laughter. It bought everything except happiness and release from the past.

She woke up each morning to the excited chatter of the birds. Throwing her shutters open she looked at the gardens below her ablaze with misty blue plumbago mingling with purple bourgainvillia, massed white and pink oleander and crimson and yellow hibiscus. Palms with huge white cones of blossom fringed the gardens and below them were borders of scarlet geraniums and pink, blue and cerise petunias; jacaranda and night-scented jasmine splashed the green of the lawns with colour.

Jean-Pierre, the brown and gnarled old gardener worked, back bent, in dark blue shorts and a white shirt, a battered panama on his head. The fountain splashed serenely in the sun, already up, and far in the distance the sea twinkled and danced.

Her cousin Dmitri taught her to play tennis. The others laughed a lot at her ineptitude. Zara did not mind for their mirth was loving amusement at a cherished one's mistakes. She remembered how she had fancied herself in love with her handsome cousin and thought now that all she felt for him was a deep family affection. He was the only young man she allowed to hug her. She shied away from casual embraces.

It was instinctive, this shrinking from anything more than mere friendliness. Zara was inwardly terrified of any suggestion of a sexual overture. The young men about the Riviera misunderstood. They called her a beautiful, heartless witch, toasted her and vied with each other for her elusive favours.

218

Nina fell in love. According to Princess Sonya it was a regular occurrence with her. This time it was the young Henri, Comte de Montaigne. He was handsome, effete, and intent on being the 'blonde goddess's' slave. He sent her roomfuls of red roses, wrote her poems and mooned about driving Nina wild, for in the middle of the most exciting game of tennis he would fall into a trance of speechless adoration and became totally unable to return a ball.

"He is pathetic!" Dmitri said to Nina. "Just when Zara is becoming a terrific player and we *could* have beaten Maxwell Clover, who's brilliant, he goes all moony and makes a hash of a really exciting game."

"Ha! You're just jealous," Nina laughed, delighted at the situation.

"Jealous? Of gormless Henri slobbering all over you. Ugh!"

Vassily laughed. "Now, now, Dmitri. Leave your sister be. She can have whoever she likes in love with her. It's a wonderful time for her. She is young and beautiful and she can have any young man in Nice …"

"Exactly," Dmitri said triumphantly. "She could have *any* young man in Nice. Instead she has hopeless Henri, so wet he's soggy. Anyone, *anyone*, would be an improvement."

"If you think I'm going to choose a boyfriend just to suit you and your precious tennis game, *mon frère*, then you are wildly mistaken. Maxwell Clover is a know-all who hates to lose. Henri is sweet and gentle. He worships the ground I walk on."

"I'd rather you preferred Chuck Kenelly. He's a good tennis player and he also 'worships the ground' you walk on."

"Chuck Kenelly is an American," Nina said with finality.

He was, indeed, American. Tall, muscular, goodlooking in an almost chocolate-box way, he resembled a hair tonic advertisement. He was gentle and courteous, and a week later Nina was to be seen hanging on his arm in public, gazing at him with adoring eyes. Poor Henri was relegated to the crowd of also-ran contenders for her hand.

Half of the smart set were in love with Nina and the other half with Zara. She was considered the 'in' person. Because of her mysterious past, her elegance and style, she was adopted as the leader of fashion, the arbiter of good taste.

Zara had not sought her position, and did nothing to encourage it. She felt the fashionable crowd's restlessness. They were constantly partying, intent on their own amusement, yet became quickly tired and easily bored. She was reminded of Russia. She remembered her father saying that the rich there frittered their money and time away on useless pleasures and trivialities. It seemed to Zara that they were doing exactly the same thing here.

These people spent money prodigally. They bought newer and newer clothes, had their homes redecorated at a whim or fancy, entertained lavishly, outdid each other in grandiosity and expense. Each party was a competition with newer, more outrageous themes. Negro bands were imported from New Orleans. Fancy dress parties were held in surroundings designed by Picasso or Cocteau.

Evening dresses designed by Schapiarelli and Chanel, Molyneux and Vionnet, were worn for one evening and ended up on the scrap-heap. Food was often quite unnecessarily imported, exotic and out of season. Even for the Rostovs, who were far more conventional than the majority, wastefulness was a way of life. The quantity of things thrown away was appalling: pears with one bruise; a napkin with a wine stain; a dress that had been dirtied or torn.

It was not only things that were short-lived. Songs, in one day, were out the next. Fashions in couture and home design were hurried along by the rapid increase in demand. There was a high frantic note to everything. Music and conversation became loud, echoing the voracious greed of the society that produced it. People drank too much, experimented with drugs and sex. Zara thought of the Princess Anya and knew she would have fitted in here.

She herself took life more quietly. She stayed close to Dmitri, veering away from emotional entanglements. She was grateful to spend time with the older, more leisurely generation, particularly her uncle and aunt. Zara stayed on the periphery of the social engagements that ate up the days and nights, allowing people to seek her out rather than seeking their attention.

The Rostovs were inundated with invitations. They gave parties. They went to the ballet. They saw "L'Aprés Midi d'un Faun" with Nijinski, were properly scandalised, gave a party for the Ballet Russe de Monte Carlo, chatted wth Diagilev, Nijinski and Nijinksa, and were horrified when he had his breakdown. Horrified and excited. They drank champagne, danced the charleston, the tango and the fox-trot. They smoked cigarettes through long holders and drove fast cars, and who cared if their laughter was a little hollow.

The inevitable happened. Dmitri, dazzled by his radiant cousin's remote and untouchable beauty, flattered by her exclusive choice of him as partner, driven by the fire in his loins and the urgency of youth, fell seriously in love with Zara.

It was the usual type of party. The Marquis d'Arrent had a villa on Cap Ferrat, a lovely pink hacienda-style building surrounded by pine trees, more typical of Spain than France. It had arched ceilings supported by clematis-entwined pillars and courtyards in which fountains splashed. The white-crested sea below was of a blue so deep as to be almost purple.

They had piled into cars, the Rostovs and Zara in Henri de Montaigne's Bugatti. He had by now recovered from his infatuation with Nina and was madly in love with Solange d'Arrent. Nina fancied herself enamoured of Nickey

Orandreou. Solange's father the Marquis was a gambler and played most nights either at home or in the Casino. He kept open house and was always pleased when his children, Pierre and Solange, brought their friends home. Pierre was often heard to remark that the longest running party on the Riviera was at their home.

This evening they had dined at the Rostovs' and were on their way to Cap Ferrat. Dmitri had had quite a few glasses of champagne. It was not his usual style but Zara had been driving him mad and though he was not drunk he was not entirely sober either.

The perfume of the girls' warm bodies combined with the wine to make him light-headed. For so long he had held himself in check, for so long he had treated Zara like a sister, for so long he had restrained himself when she kissed his cheek or pressed his hand.

Now he stared at the flesh above the sheen of her stockings. She sat half on top of him, with Nina beside her on Nickey's knee. Dmitri felt a huge knot of desire overwhelm him. He caught her face in his hands and clumsily tried to kiss her open lips.

Instantly she seized up, rigid as a catatonic, turned to stone by the demand of his lips on hers. To his horror, she started to shake. She shook from head to toe as if she had palsy. Her teeth chattered. Her breath came in short harsh gasps.

He did not know what to do. No one else noticed. Nina and Mickey were indulging in some heavy petting beside him. The car sped on its dizzy way along the coast road from Nice to Cap Ferrat. Lights shimmered and a comet streaked the sky.

They were singing in the front, Solange and Henri, 'Poor Butterfly', and their singing was punctuated by shrieks of laughter and excitement as they rounded bends too fast.

And still Zara shook. Dmitri tried to get someone's attention but they were all too high to hear him. He tried to soothe her but she simply went on trembling, teeth clicking like castanets.

At last they wound down the drive to the villa. Everyone but Dmitri and Zara tumbled out of the car as the tyres screeched to a halt.

The noise from the house was deafening. Saxophones wailed, drums pounded, cymbals crashed. A Negro voice sawed the air. From open windows came the parrot chatter of people competing to be heard against a band and the sound of popping corks. The other passengers in the car hurried to join them.

Dmitri and Zara still sat in the car. He was appalled now by what he had done. She had trusted him and he had betrayed her. He understood, belatedly, that her past experience with the Baron was to blame for her reaction and tried to get the girl out of the car. But when he touched her, she shrank from him. She did not seem to recognise him.

"Can I help?"

The man peering into the car looked adult and capable. In a panic, Dmitri was only too glad of someone's help.

"Thank you. She's in shock, I think." He blushed and stammered as he spoke. "But there's a very good explanation."

"Never mind that now. Let's get her out and take her somewhere quiet."

Dmitri knew he was English by his clipped accent. He had a neat little English moustache and his teeth gleamed very white in his tanned face. He looked rather rakish and Dmitri felt a moment's doubt. Then he decided he had little choice in the matter; he needed help too badly.

The newcomer helped Dmitri to get Zara out of the car. He lifted the girl gently in his arms and carried her around the house to a deserted terrace. There was a cool fountain playing at its centre. The noise of the party was cut off here, the only other sound the whisper of the waves. A stone bench ran the length of the terrace facing out to sea. There were occasional cushions scattered here and there. The tall stranger laid Zara down on the stone and put one behind her head.

"Get some water, and a blanket or rug," the man said. "Don't draw any attention to yourself if you can help it. The last thing we want is that mob hurtling out here agog with curiosity."

Dmitri blushed again. He wanted to explain away the question in the man's clear blue gaze.

"Well, hurry up, my boy. Make up your mind to trust me," the man said impatiently, then added, "Look, if it will make it easier for you, I know your father well: Prince Vassily Rostov. I've forgotten your name. We met briefly at a ball at Lady Forbisher's. The name's Tom Armitidge. Now go. She's safe here, but she's cold. Hurry!"

Feeling a fool, Dmitri hot-footed it up the curved staircase. From there he could hear the driving music and the party sounds on the other side of the house. He took the stairs two at a time and hurried down a corridor until he reached a bedroom. He grabbed the coverlet off the bed and took a carafe of water covered by an inverted glass.

When he came down the stairs again a couple was sitting on the bottom step. They were kissing, the boy's hand halfway up the girl's skirt. She had her arms around his neck, a burning cigarette between the fingers of one hand and a glass full of champagne in the other. She was laughing excitedly through the kiss. They did not seem to notice him, or if they did they did not care.

He hurried back to the terrace. The man called Armitidge had taken off his dinner jacket and covered Zara with it. He was holding her firmly in his arms, cradling her as if she were a child who had been hurt and whom, by the sheer force of his clasp, he could make forget her pain. He was rocking her gently to and fro, murmuring something Dmitri could not hear. He felt a stab of jealousy, fierce and agonizing, shoot through him, then Tom Armitidge saw him.

"Oh, good man," he said, "give me that. She was freezing."

He wrapped Zara around with the coverlet then tilted a glass of water to her lips. She seemed to come a little more to life, taking a sip.

"Good girl," he said softly. "Now you'll feel better." He laid her gently back on the seat. When he stood, he towered over Dmitri.

"Will you tell me what this is all about?" His voice was hardly above a whisper. Dmitri looked into his blue eyes and decided to trust what he saw there.

"She had a terrible experience," he whispered. "She was er ... molested violently." He faltered to a stop.

"When?"

"Some years ago. She's been afraid of men ever since."

"And tonight?" Tom Armitage looked at him kindly. Dmitri felt that he already knew and simply wanted confirmation.

"I ... I kissed her. That's all! Others were at it in the car and ..."

"Good heavens, Dmitri, no one can blame you for that."

"But she trusted me, sir, and I betrayed her."

Tom Armitidge shook his head. "No. She'll recover. She has to live in the real world. You may have done her a favour. Forced her to face up to the past. Who is she?"

"My cousin, Princess Zara Vashinskova."

"Ah, well. We'll drive her home, eh?"

Dmitri looked embarrassed. "What shall we say when we get there? I mean, what reason shall we give for coming home so early?"

"The truth, my boy. Vassily will understand. Your mother ..." He shrugged. "She'll not mind too much. Don't worry, you have not harmed Zara. Someone else did that, poor child."

Dmitri thought how childish he felt beside Tom Armitidge who could not have been much older than him. Some men were born adult, he thought, no one ever called them boys.

Armitidge leaned over Zara. She was quiet now. The trembling had stopped. She remembered the panic that had overcome her when she had felt Dmitri's inexperienced mouth over hers. The more she had fought the terrible trembling, the worse it became. There was a ringing in her ears and her teeth were chattering. She was afraid again. The Baron was alive in the world. He might find her and persecute her. She remembered those nights of pain and humiliation, the agony both mental and physical she had suffered at his hands, and the shaking got worse.

Then the man had lifted her out of the car and carried her to this hard bench. She could smell the sweet breeze and he took off his coat and wrapped her in it and held her so strongly, so firmly, that she felt suddenly safer than she could remember since her father died. He smelled the same as her father, too. Cigars, hair oil, an indefinably masculine smell. She trusted him and the trembling went.

He carried her now to a car, a big car she had not seen before. He put her in the front seat, tucking her in carefully. Her face was pale under the moonlight and the huge eyes had difficulty focusing.

"Dmitri?" she asked.

"I'm sorry, Zara," he said. "So sorry." He was in the back of the car. He put his hands on her shoulders then pulled them quickly away.

"No, no," she protested. "Give me your hand. *I'm* sorry. *I'm* the one who should be sorry. Oh poor, poor Dmitri. What a fool you must think me."

She held his hand as if he were the one who should be comforted. Tom Armitidge put the car in gear and rove off.

They took the coast road, lights glittering, sea and sky sheets of dark velvet, scattered with stars and touched with milky wave-crests.

"What about this?" Zara asked, fingering the coverlet. "It's theirs, isn't it?"

"We stole it," Armitidge said coolly. Dmitri giggled. Zara still held her cousin's hand, idly playing with the gold signet ring on his finger. "You'll take it back though, Dmitri, won't you?"

"Do I have to, sir?" Dmitri was not at all keen on the idea. "How can I explain?"

"Stop calling me 'sir', for God's sake! Tom's my name. Plain simple Tom. All right?"

"All right, si ... Tom."

"And you can explain your possession of it any way you please. Say it was a bet, a rag, a wheeze, I don't know! Heavens, man, that lot won't think twice about it. I'm confident you'll come up with something."

There was no one at home in the Villa de la Rose except the servants. Dmitri need not have worried. The Prince and Princess were in Monte Carlo and Drushenka took Zara to her room. Dmitri told the servant that Zara had become ill at the Marquis's and that she needed a hot bath and rest.

"Thank you for your help," Dmitri said to Tom when they were alone. "I don't know how I'd have managed without you."

"Well, you didn't have to." He walked to the door then turned.

"I'll let you off the hook for once," he said, smiling. "*I'll* take back the coverlet. How's that for service?"

"You don't have to do that." But Dmitri could not keep the relief out of his voice.

"Well, I'm going back to the villa in any case. Truth is, I left on a winning streak and I'm keen to return to it. So, you're in luck."

"I am, sir. Goodnight."

"Tom. Goodnight."

"And thank you," Dmitri cried after him, but Tom Armitidge had gone.

227

Chapter Twelve

Zara opted out of the fast and furious social life led by Nina, the d'Arrents and their friends. Dmitri and she became inseparable. It was as if they shared something intimate and binding. The incident in the car had brought them together instead of driving them apart. The Prince and Princess were pleased. Nothing would have gladdened them more than a marriage between the cousins.

The pair spent long hours sitting in the shade in white rattan chairs, breathing in the scent of flowers. They went for walks, arms loosely entwined, or drove the car along the coast road, wind blowing through their hair. They went to parties and drank champagne but remained aloof, on the periphery.

People watched them, aped them, exclaimed over their beauty and similarity to each other. Their appearance was totally in tune with the times. They were both the same medium height, both slender. Zara wore her hair in a short thick bob while Dmitri's was long for a man. In their stylish white clothes they made a remarkable couple, always together, the family resemblance strong.

They talked little, companionably silent. They held hands and were tranquil together. Zara was content with Dmitri, sure of him now, aware that he knew his place in her waking life.

In her dreams at night, or swinging gently in the hammock, dozing under the shade of the white canvas umbrella, she dreamed of Tom Armitidge.

Dmitri never tried again to kiss her. He knew it was forbidden. Sometimes she would turn to him, her huge dark eyes full of sweetness. His heart would miss a beat, startled by the power she wielded over him. He was in love with her but dared not overstep the invisible line between the affection she craved and the sexual attention which terrified her.

And then there was Sasha. Zara missed him every day. Her hurt at his defection had not healed, her maternal love for him never diminished. She chided herself that she had not paid enough attention to him when they had been in Amsterdam. Yet she knew there had been no more time available to devote to him. They had been working too hard in order to survive. She asked herself whether, if she had asked him this or that question, if she had not said or done this or that, he might still be with her. She could not know and it was a useless waste of time, yet she could not stop herself wondering.

Prince Vassily and Princess Sonya told her that they had hired people to look for him. No expense was being spared. It appeared, to date, a lost cause. No one in Amsterdam seemed to have seen Sasha. Railway porters, tram conductors, hotel staff, servants, train guards … no one had any recollection of the boy. Dirk and Frau Kettner said in their letters to Zara that people had been to question them about the young Prince, but they had nothing new to say. It was as if the canal had opened and swallowed him up.

Zara loved to hear from the inhabitants of the Prinsengracht house. Mevrou Kloof too sent the odd card with 'Greetings' or 'Best wishes' on it, and always added that Meneer Van Daniken sent regards from Holland. Zara propped the cards up on her mantle. They brought back a time that seemed strange and remote but also curiously happy. She could not understand it. Here she was, surrounded by luxury, looking back on her hard life in

Amsterdam with nostalgia. Perhaps, she thought, it was because Sasha had been there.

The summer passed. The Rostovs often swam, shrieking and leaping in the water. Afterwards they would sit beneath the umbrella Drushenka had erected for them on the beach. She had to do it slowly for her back was very bad these days. Enjoying the easy pace of her life, Zara realized she had almost forgotten the Baron. His ghost had been laid, temporarily at least.

Nina often came to her cousin's room at night. Tired after some late and hectic party, she would remove her earrings, necklace and bracelets while she lounged on Zara's bed and chatted. She would talk about her boyfriends and who she was currently in love with, and Zara wished she could join in such careless happy activities, but knew she would never have such an untroubled attitude. She lay back on her pillows and listened, feeling curiously adult. Her own experiences had set her apart from the jazz-minded, joyously unconcerned young party-girl that Nina had become. The truth of the matter was that Zara had grown up and Nina had not.

However, they loved each other and Zara always thought of her cousin as a younger sister whom she needed to protect and guard.

"Do you like sex, Zara?" Nina asked her one night. She wore Zara's dressing-gown and her hair was wet. Georgio Lampelli had pushed her into the fountain at the d'Arrents' villa and Zara was towelling it dry for her.

At the question, she pulled her hands away. "No." The answer was involuntary. "No, I …"

"Oh, I'm sorry," Nina said softly, "I forgot. How on earth could you? But, Zara, you can't let what happened put you off for life, can you?"

"I don't know. I simply don't know." Zara shook her head as if to rid herself of unwelcome thoughts. "But you, with your boyfriends? Aren't you afraid?"

Nina laughed. "Oh, I don't go the whole hog. No, that would be too dangerous." She blushed a little and hung her head. "I just fool about. My knees go all weak, little electric shocks go all through me and I feel faint. It's all done … outside. The boys are careful." She looked at Zara's expression. "Are you shocked?"

Zara shook her head. She was not. How innocent it all sounded. Without violence. And Nina obviously loved whatever it was. It made her feel excited and good.

Zara was a little jealous of her cousin. She longed to be able to 'fool around', experiment, explore, and wished that the inevitable backlash of disgust would not overwhelm her if she even thought about it. It must be nice to enjoy preliminary petting, to be able to wriggle about in the back of cars with boys who were careful. If they were careful it meant they put your feelings high on the list of priorities. Yes, that must be nice.

"You'd better go to bed, Nina," she said.

"Oh, I *have* shocked you. Or upset you." Nina was instantly contrite. That was the trouble with Zara. You could never have uncomplicated chats with her. You always had to worry whether what you said would upset her.

"If you must know, I was wishing I could be like you."

Nina shrugged. Sometimes she could not understand her cousin at all. She kissed Zara lightly on the forehead and went to her own room, dragging the ruined dress behind her.

Zara brooded over her cousin's words. She made up her mind she would have to change. Her hatred of the Baron could not be allowed to deprive her of a pleasure others took for granted. But what must she do? She decided to ask Dmitri's help.

He joined her in the garden one day. She was lying under the trees on a rug, reading 'Pride and Prejudice'. She did not notice him until he flopped down beside her and picked up the book. He looked at the title and grimaced.

232

"Read it in school," he remarked. "Like it?" He knew she had difficulty in reading.

Dmitri's white shirt was open at the neck and his cream-coloured linen trousers were crumpled and had a grass stain at the knee. His vivid young face was beaded with sweat and he fanned himself with the brim of his straw hat while he lay beside her, resting his weight on one elbow. They were shielded from the house by a row of lime trees.

"It's a bit difficult," she said. She could smell a faint sharp trace of his perspiration. She shivered, not knowing how she felt, and leaned closer to him. "Dmitri?"

"Yes?" He opened his eyes and was startled by the closeness of her face. He looked into those dark eyes, drowning in them.

"Dmitri, I wanted to ask you …"

"What?" He had not intended to sound so harsh.

"It's just … Oh, hell!" She pressed her face into his shoulder and felt him flinch. 'It's about … that," she said. "Could you … touch me?"

Merely getting the words out had taken some of the fear away. They stimulated her in some strange way that she did not understand. She had had sexual intercourse many times yet still did not know the first thing about it.

Dmitri seemed uncertain.

"Please," she said. "Help me."

He touched her lips with his. The kiss was featherlight, his uncertainty communicating itself through the gentle meeting of mouth upon mouth. She could feel his nervousness and it encouraged her. He put his hand over her breast. It was small. Hardly there at all, Nina had once remarked enviously.

His fingers moved over the small mound, back and forth over the silk of her blouse. She could feel the friction through the soft material. It was a nice feeling. Little throbs descended from that private place, down to her knees. She half lifted herself towards him in response. She felt his teeth

233

against hers and tasted the wetness of his tongue. Her back arched.

Then he put his hand on her knee and suddenly she felt her body tense. He misunderstood, taking the movement for a shiver of passion. He slid his hand up her smooth bare flanks and she felt the probing fingers reach upward and inward ... She pulled away.

"For Christ's sake, Zara!"

"I'm sorry, Dmitri. I want to so much, I really do. I'm trying hard. It's just that ..."

"It's tough on a chap," he sighed. "And you did tell me to."

"I know. I was trying to be normal, like everyone else. Then ... I couldn't."

Tears slid from the outer corners of her eyes into her hair.

"At least you're improving," he said softly. "You didn't go into shock this time."

Overcome with tenderness at his forbearance, she turned to him and kissed the side of his mouth. "Oh, Dmitri, you're so good to me. So understanding and patient. You always were."

He smiled ruefully. He did not want to be understanding and patient. He wanted to possess her and achieve release from this terrible tension whenever he was near her. He wanted to hold her close, so close, hearing her cry out in passion.

But he knew it was useless. She had been deeply damaged.

His body throbbed. He concealed his irritation and patted her head. He knew what he would do to relieve his pulsing loins and it filled him with sadness. She must feel unfulfilled too but there was nothing they could do about it. He left her there. Alone.

Autumn came. Every so often the winds blew and strained the shutters, slamming the doors and whistling through the chimneys and shutters. But the *mistral* lasted only twenty-four hours and the mild clement weather returned and the

English came to Nice for the winter. Parties were given by the English colony and the season picked up. Sonya took the girls to *soirées* and balls in Cannes and Monte Carlo, and the young set endlessly racketed around the dances and parties.

Zara often cried off these affairs, and when she went was inevitably accompanied by Dmitri. Though still admired the couple were given a wider berth for Nina, unable to hold her tongue, had blabbed about Zara's rape. Not in detail or in so many words but she had mistakenly confided in a friend. It had sufficed to make Zara, once a creature of mystery, a trifle too exotic and untouchable. There was something not quite the thing about a girl who had been raped. Inexperienced young men felt that if she had been a real lady it somehow couldn't have happened. Her experience alarmed them so they kept their distance and she was left with her cousin.

Winter melted into spring. The English returned to London for the season there: Henley, Wimbledon, Glyndebourne and, of course, Ascot. But the parties on the Cote d'Azur survived without them. The French arrived, and the Germans. To Zara, pleasure-seeking became routine. 'Ice Princess' she was nicknamed. Many of their set were engaged now, or had married. There were new arrivals on the scene: younger sisters and brothers launched and ready to take their elders' places.

Princess Sonya began to complain. She disliked how open Riviera society had become. Used to the rigidly controlled Russian society where no stranger, however moneyed, was permitted to enter, she found the nabobs and *nouveau riche* who infiltrated the South of France distinctly disagreeable.

"One never knows where they've come from," she said, her forehead creased in a frown, "or even *who* they are. It makes one very uncomfortable."

She pulled her gloves up over her elbows, pressing between her fingers and smoothing the fine kid over her arms. Zara sat on a little Louis Quinze vanity stool and watched her aunt. She began to clasp diamond and emerald bracelets over the cream-coloured gloves. Nina, not allowed to sit on her mother's bed, was sprawled on a *chaise-longue* picking at the jet beads on her black chiffon gown. She liked the young, fast set. Unlike Zara, who enjoyed evenings in the sedate company of the Prince and Princess's contemporaries.

"I wish you'd listen and learn, Nina," Princess Sonya said. "You are far too free."

She sighed and shook her golden head. "Oh, Mother!" She was going steady with Chuck Kenelly now. Nobody knew who his antecedents were. Nina didn't care a fig. He was beautiful. That was all she cared about.

The Princess took some cigarettes from a rosewood and silver box and put them carefully, one by one, into her small silver cigarette case. It had the Rostov crest engraved on one side and her initials on the other. She put it and a slim silver and platinum lighter into her beaded bag as she spoke.

"You know what I mean, Zara. In Monte Carlo they'll be out in full force. 'Breaking into society.' Ha! As if one could. They are the type who never really *see* you, only what you are, what you represent. They collect titles, don't understand about breeding. That is why I would be so happy if you and Dmitri ... Ah, but I don't want to push you together."

"*Push* them," shrieked Nina. "They're stuck together like glue. Never out of each other's pockets."

"Hush, Nina. Please control yourself." The Princess took a handkerchief out of a drawer and put it into her bag. "Come along. Let us face the savages!"

The party that night was in the Hôtel de Paris in Monte Carlo. Lady Abercrombie was giving a ball for her daughter Lucinda's twenty-first birthday. Sonya liked Amanda Abercrombie and was fond of Lucinda. The English lady had no money at all and Sonya had decided that Lucinda, pretty and bidable with impeccable breeding, would make a very suitable match for Dmitri if things did not work out between her son and Zara.

The Rostovs had no need of an alliance with money for they had more than enough of their own. Vassily's financial advisors in Switzerland had been instrumental in doubling his fortune since he left Russia. So what Sonya wanted in a daughter-in-law was a girl she liked and felt she could mould. Someone, too, who would fit into their social circle. Lucinda was such a girl.

"It's such an odd thing, holding a party in an hotel."

"I think it's swell," Nina cried.

"Oh Nina, please! Don't use those awful Americanisms you learn from Chuck Kenelly. Although I must say he is a very personable young man and has the most delightful manners but he speaks in an idiom I can scarcely understand." She fixed her daughter with a meaningful look. "It's about time you made up your mind which of your admirers you prefer. It's time you were settled down and having a family."

In the sand-coloured marble entrance to the Hôtel de Paris with its smoked mirrors and peacock glass dome the Rostovs stood a moment, preparatory to being announced.

Amanda Abercrombie was a plump Englishwoman with amazingly soft skin and an optimistic disposition. Her heart's desire was for her beloved Lucinda to marry wealth and position. These attributes were abundant in the person of Prince Dmitri Rostov who also possessed more than his fair share of good looks so she had fixed her hopes and ambitions on the young Russian. Now she came hurrying eagerly across the hall. The party was well in progress and she was filled with relief. She had thought for a very tense hour and a half that the Rostovs were not going to show.

"There you are, Princess Sonya, I have been awaiting your arrival anxiously." She had not the guile to conceal her hopes from them. When she realized that Dmitri was not with their party her expression was so comical in its dismay

237

that Nina stifled a giggle. Princess Sonya hastened to reassure their hostess.

"Vassily and my son are in the Casino. They said they would join us here at ten o'clock."

Lady Abercrombie looked relieved. She glanced at her wristwatch.

"Oh, good. It's nearly that now."

To the Princess's amusement the Englishwoman made as if to go towards the entrance of the hotel from which she would be able to see the Casino.

"Don't you think it would be wise to await the men here?" asked Sonya mildly.

Lady Abercrombie's plump cheeks quivered with embarrassment. She was far too good-natured to mind the implied criticism. It was, Sonya thought with amusement, impossible not to like her.

"You're right, Sonya. Yes, of course," she said. Nevertheless she kept craning forward, casting anxious eyes at the entrance.

Princess Sonya took her arm firmly. "Come along, Amanda. Your other guests will be waiting."

"Oh, they won't notice whether I'm there or not," she said absently. "Tom is with them. He said he'd help out for a while. You have no idea how difficult it is for a poor widow alone."

"Tom?" Sonya raised an eyebrow.

Lady Abercrombie's lineage might be impeccable but she was so gregarious that, like a puppy-dog, she made friends very easily and sometimes indiscriminately. Sonya had had to rescue her more than once from an unsuitable attachment.

As if she guessed the Princess's thoughts Amanda Abercrombie looked away from the entrance and gave her friend a hard stare. "Tom Armitidge. Lord Lionel's youngest. He's a charmer, if a bit of a gambler."

Zara, standing behind Sonya, pricked up her ears at the familiar name. She glanced at the ballroom and, as if on cue,

238

Tom Armitidge strode out and over to their group, a wide smile on his face.

"What a handsome man he is," whispered Princess Sonya.

Amanda Abercrombie giggled a little. "Oh, yes, isn't he?" She introduced them. "Princess Rostova, Tom Armitidge.

He bowed over Sonya's hand.

"Tom, dear boy, this is Princess Rostova's daughter, Nina, and her cousin, the Princess Zara Vashinskova." Amanda gave a breathy laugh, pleased to introduce people she liked to each other, pleased to have acquitted herself well in the pronunciation of the difficult Russian names.

Princess Sonya decided she liked this man but knew she shouldn't. He had an abundance of charm and good looks but there was, too, an irresponsible air about him. She sensed he was a flirt. It was obvious he adored women. Not just some but women in general.

She had no time to speculate further for at that moment she heard her husband's voice and the patter of his pumps as he crossed the foyer. To Lady Abercrombie he said,

"Ah, there you are, my dear. Sorry if we're late. Dmitri was winning."

"Dear, *dear* Prince Vassily, no, you are not late. I have just been telling your wife how she should cosset you." Sonya's eyes widened at her temerity but Lady Abercrombie hurried on, "Ah, Dmitri. How lovely to see you. Lucinda is so looking forward ..." She caught Sonya's glance of warning. "Not that ... she has been dancing continuously. So many admirers," she finished lamely.

Vassily and Tom Armitidge greeted each other as old friends. Dmitri coloured and stammered, seeing their handshake. His mother was very surprised that her sophisticated son should suddenly prove so gauche but Lady Abercrombie was already shepherding them into the ballroom. Dancers whirled around the floor. Against the clink of glasses, the buzz of conversation and the orchestra, Zara heard a voice say: "How lovely to see you again."

She looked into the blue eyes of the man beside her. Her heart was beating at the memory of their first meeting, and she blushed.

"Don't be embarrassed," he said. "I would not dream of …"

"I never thought you would," she told him candidly.

They stared at each other, and Dmitri, watching, felt a chill steal over his heart. This man, he felt suddenly, might be able to unlock Zara's reserve. He shook the thought away angrily.

"Dance with me?" he asked. He knew she usually liked to. Tonight she was not looking at him at all but focussing all her attention on the man beside her. Her dress caught the light from the branches of tiered candles, sequins and crystals shimmering. The beaded juliet cap on her head was glittering too, surrounding her head with tiny pinpoints of light. The big, dark eyes holding Tom Armitidge's gaze were unfathomable. Dmitri felt a wave of despair. There was besides a tiny flicker of relief. He had loved her for so long, so very long. He had held himself in check. He had been bruised and hurt and he was a little tired of it all. Zara was a heavy load to carry.

He turned to Lucinda. Her candid and eager little face under its mop of red curls was pretty and uncomplicated. Her light green eyes told him she admired him above all men.

"Will you dance with me?" he asked.

She dimpled and nodded.

"I *love* the tango," she said breathlessly. "Don't you?"

"Come and talk to me," Tom Armitidge said to Zara. Watching her cousin sweep Lucinda away, she sensed his relief and suddenly felt a dreadful sense of loss. It was as if she had said goodbye to her protector and stood, vulnerable and uncertain, facing the challenge of this tall stranger.

Tom was authoritative. "I loathe dancing. No good at it. Never was. The English aren't in general. So come and talk to me."

She let herself be led from the ballroom back into the lobby. He sat her in an alcove of ornate design. "Now don't move a muscle," he commanded.

She was happy to obey him and sat very still, waiting for him to return. The amber lights were low and diffused, the glow from them blending with the tinted mirrors. She was reminded of Anya, of Russia, of the corridors she had hurried down, fleeing from seeing her step-mother by firelight, naked in passion. She shivered and looked up to see Tom, two champagne glasses caught between the fingers of one hand and a frothing bottle of champagne in the other.

"What is it?" he asked softly, instantly divining her distress.

She shook her head. "Nothing. The past." She smiled, but there was a plea beneath the surface. "I'm plagued by ghosts."

"Well, we shall have to do something about that, shan't we?"

He seated himself, put a glass before her and the other in front of himself. He poured a little champagne, seeming intent on his job, but somehow she knew she was the focus of his eyes. He waited for the foam to disappear then added more champagne and put the bottle on the table.

"Cheers," he said, raising his glass.

"That's not very romantic." The words were out before she could stop herself.

His eyes widened in amusement. "Ah," he said. "Romance."

She was appalled. "I didn't mean … I wasn't suggesting … it's just a figure of speech."

"I know you didn't," he said solemnly. "Now stop being silly and drink your champagne."

She suddenly felt very at home with this man, as if she had known him a long time.

"You are very beautiful, Princess," he said.

"Zara."

"Zara." He rolled the name around. "Zara. Lovely sound. Don't you like sounds? You speak English well."

"I picked it up. In Russia I was, well, sort of taught French and German. But I never learned to write them. I was hopeless." She shrugged, that sad expression he had seen before shadowing her eyes. "I started to understand languages when I was very young. When I left Russia I had a smattering, I suppose. In Amsterdam, when it became necessary, I found they all came back to me."

"We have so much in our heads, we know so much more than we realise we know." They both laughed at his portentousness.

"Are all the things they say about you correct?" he asked after a pause. She looked up, startled by the directness of his question.

"What do they say?"

"They say you saw your mother and father shot in Russia, that you were rescued from the Cossacks and raped by a wicked Baron."

He was watching her intently, his blue eyes narrowed. "They also say it affected you so badly that you cannot bear anyone except your cousin to touch you."

"So that is what they say," she said softly. He waited silently, giving her time.

"It's true, some of it," she said at last after a sip of champagne. Surprisingly, she did not feel embarrassed or uncomfortable.

"I saw my father shot. I loved him very much. But it was my step-mother who was shot with him, not my mother. She died when I was very small. I hated my step-mother. She was *une diable*, and a nymphomaniac."

He burst out laughing. "Where did you hear that word?"

"I don't know … Chuck Kenelly, the American. But it's true. She could not leave men alone. Her whole life was a series of *liaisons*."

"Poor little girl," he said. "Another reason to …"

"I am not a little girl," she said defiantly.

"I'm sorry. Please go on."

242

"It was drunken soldiers who killed them. Deserters from the front. It was in the snow and the Baron would not let me go to them ..." she faltered.

"Quite right. If there were drunken soldiers, how could he?"

"He raped me though. Again and again." She looked at Tom whose eyes had widened.

"That I did not know. Poor little girl." This time she did not correct him.

"He married me first, you see. I suppose it does not count as rape when you are married?" She looked at him, wide-eyed and questioning.

"Good God, of course it does!" He could see this point had troubled her and now she was relieved. "It's an appalling thing to do, whatever the circumstances. A husband has no right to behave like that."

"When he raped my brother, I shot him."

She looked up in surprise as he cried, "Good for you. Well done!"

She felt suddenly more cheerful. "I *thought* I had killed him, but it appears he is alive. I thought I had murdered him so we ran away, Sasha and I. We ended up in Amsterdam. We were poor and had to work very hard to survive. Then my brother disappeared. I don't know why. He just took all his things and left."

A sob caught in her throat but she resolutely swallowed it down and looked at him, her eyes shining with unshed tears. "I just went on, from day to day, until I discovered my aunt and uncle were here in the South of France. But the last bit ... you asked ... I don't like men. I don't like sex. I wish I did. You saw me ... that night. That is all."

"That is all, you say. Oh, my dear. My sweet girl."

He looked at her across the table. She avoided his gaze but he took her chin and drew her to him.

"Listen to me. You have been through enough to fell an ox. Poor brave little girl, I know precisely what you need."

He looked down into the childlike eager face. "But you must trust me. From the first moment I saw you I was attracted to you. You were to me, too, I know. You can't be wrong about a thing like that. Let me love you – no, don't be alarmed. I won't lay a finger on you, yet. Never, if you don't want me to. Until you want me, I'll not touch you. When and if you do, I'll teach you so gently, so slowly. I'll introduce you to love. But not yet. Will you trust me, Zara?"

Tentatively she put out her hand and slipped it into his.

"I'll trust you," she said.

Chapter Thirteen

Tom came into her life and took over. So, she remembered, had the Baron. In bed that night after they had returned from Monte Carlo the thought made her shudder. Could she never act of her own volition? Was she always to be led? But she put such ideas from her and gave him a chance to succeed for more than anything else she wanted to be able to think and feel like a normal woman.

The next morning she was awakened by a shuffling noise, crackles and swishes and scratching sounds as if the room had been invaded by an army of mice. She opened sleepy eyes to see that it was full of roses. They were everywhere, longstemmed, red. Baskets and vases of crimson blooms, a sea of red velvet petals, their perfume drenching the air.

Drushenka and Maya were grumbling and giggling respectively as they arranged them.

"Nowhere left to put them ... thinks we still live in a palace ... falling over them ... all up the stairs. The man must be mad," Drushenka muttered under her breath.

Zara knew at once who they were from. Tom! She felt a surge of delight. She jumped out of bed and circled around the flowers, smelling and touching them.

The card said 'A new beginning' and was signed 'Doctor Tom', which made her laugh. She was elated as she bathed and dressed. Nina came in. "There are roses all down the stairs and in the hall. I thought you'd died."

"They're from Tom Armitidge," Zara said noncommitally.

"I know," Nina said lightly, tapping the card. "A bit excessive. Oh, don't mind me. I'm jealous, that's all. Wish Chuck would do something so extravagant. What does 'Doctor Tom' mean?"

But Zara merely said, "Aha", and put her finger to her lips.

Dmitri said nothing at breakfast and she felt guilty at the sight of his closed face. She knew he was trying very hard to conceal his feelings. She wanted so much to make everyone else as happy as she was, to share her excitement, but that was not possible, especially with him.

"Did you have a nice time with Lucinda?" she asked, watching him crumble a croissant between his finger. As soon as she had said it she realised how crass it sounded.

"Yes," he replied, giving her a brief smile.

Nina was too excited about the flowers to worry about her brother's feelings.

"Did you see the roses?" she cried.

"One could hardly fail to."

After breakfast Sonya asked Zara to come to her room. Zara sat on the *chaise-longue* where Nina had sat the previous evening. She watched as Drushenka removed the peach satin *peignoir* Sonya had worn at breakfast. Her aunt sat in her camiknickers of cream *crêpe-de-chine* edged with Brussels lace. She brushed a little powder across her pale skin, then coloured her lips carefully. Drushenka held out a cross-over taupe crêpe dress ready for her mistress. Sonya stood, then slipped the dress on and waited patiently as Drushenka fastened it and fixed a huge artificial pink cabbage-rose at her hip.

There was silence in the room. Zara watched her aunt's graceful movements intently. She loved moments like this: the shared intimacy; the silence. This must be what it was like to have a mother. Sitting watching her dress, no need for words, comfortable in each other's presence.

246

Sonya picked up a crystal perfume spray. It had a tassle on the little round ball at the end. Sonya sprayed some perfume behind her ears and into the vee of her neckline.

"You may go, Drushenka."

The maid put down the taupe suede pumps she was holding beside her mistress's feet. She bobbed and left the room.

"She still holds on to the old ways," Sonya remarked with a smile as the door closed behind the servant. "I've told her not to do all that bobbing and bowing but she disregards my wishes." She slipped her feet into the shoes, then picked up some bracelets from the dressing table and slid them over her hands.

"Zara," she began, then hesitated.

"Yes, Aunt?" She had an idea that her aunt wanted to speak to her about Tom Armitidge. She waited patiently while Sonya put a pair of diamond earrings in her ears and clipped a Cartier broach to the right of the draped vee.

"This is difficult. I care very much for you, my dear, and you must forgive me if I am blunt. You see, I look on you as a sacred charge. My brother adored you. He would never have forgiven me if I allowed harm to befall you."

"Dearest Aunt, you have been so kind, but after all I am not a child. I am twenty-six years old and well able to take care of myself."

"Zara, I don't think so. I always think of you as younger for you are such a waif. So tiny. You are *not* competent to take care of yourself. You have been through experiences which have given you – well, a warped view of life."

"Oh, Aunt, am I never to be allowed to forget? I want nothing more than to leave my past behind."

"That is what we want for you, too. But there are the boys of our own set to help you."

"No, Aunt, they have not helped – the boys of 'our set', as you call them, have never let me forget for a moment what happened to me. If I flirted with them, there would always have been a third person present."

247

"Zara," her aunt admonished, "I really cannot have you speaking like that. Now sit down a moment. Listen to me."

She waited until Zara resumed her position on the *chaise-longue*. "My dear," she began, "Tom Armitidge is one of the most attractive men on the Riviera, or anywhere for that matter, and it is obvious he has taken a fancy to you. His attention is very flattering, I'm sure, and all those roses ... quite a gesture. But, my dear, you must know his reputation."

"No, I don't, and I don't think I want to."

"Now that is silly." Zara had realised it was foolish the moment the words were out. Sonya continued, "You should be forewarned. What kind of a guardian would I be if I did not inform you? You must know what kind of a man that charmer is, although there has never been any scandal attached to his name. Once I have enlightened you, then you may do as you please; I will not stop you. You are, as you point out, old enough and I have never believed in separating people. It rarely works and sometimes causes tragedy." She spread her hands and opened her eyes wide. "Look at Romeo and Juliet," she said, then added, "although you are hardly that. Tom Armitidge is much too ... experienced for you, though of course you know that already. He is also a gambler, a professional one. He is a younger son and, as if all that were not enough, he is a womaniser. He has had affairs with half the women on the Côte d'Azur. And London. And New York. And Paris."

It hurt to hear that. Even though she knew it was silly and all this had happened before she had met him, it nevertheless hurt. But she said nothing, waiting for her aunt to finish.

"He has no money. Heaven knows how he survives. He has a small allowance from his older brother and something from his father and he gambles it all away." She shrugged. "Sometimes, of course, he wins. Then it's roses, roses all the way." She waved her hand towards the hall, "But there's no stability there. No security."

"Oh, Aunt, when did I ever have stability or security?"

Sonya looked at her in surprise. "Heavens, child, you have it now. And you have money behind you. It was always there though you never seemed to have a stitch to your back or anything of your own. I well remember when you arrived in Moscow with that pathetic little basket ... I blame Alexei for that. My brother was a dreamer, he lived in his head. The practicalities of life passed him by."

Zara could see a new thought had struck her. Sonya frowned. She seemed to be working something out in her head. Then she said. "What did Alexei do with all his money? Do you know?"

Zara shook her head. "That morning, you know, when we were to leave Danya Bolovna, he said something about having lost everything. About the new law being something about forfeiting our money and our lands and possessions."

"But you were leaving Russia. He must have arranged funds for that."

"Yes. He said something about Zurich, I think."

"If he was getting you out of the country then he had money somewhere and Zurich is most likely. I wonder which bank?"

"You mean, there is money somewhere that is mine?"

Sonya crossed the room and kissed Zara's forehead.

"I will get Vassily on to it. We must find out. Don't get your hopes up, Zara. I'm sure you care as little as we do whether you have money or not."

She left the room and Zara could hear her going down the landing, calling to her husband, her heels clicking on the marble floors.

To Sonya, Tom Armitidge had ceased to be of paramount importance.

He telephoned midmorning. The Prince and Princess were closeted together, presumably getting in touch with their bankers. There was a basket of red roses at the side of every step of stairs and a giant one on the telephone table in the hall.

"You got them?" he asked. She smiled into the phone without answering. His voice was so attractive, so familiar to her already.

"One thousand. Did you count them? There are one thousand red roses there for you,"

"Really?"

"Ah, there you are. I thought I was talking to air. No, I tell a lie. I could hear you smiling."

"Oh, Tom!"

"Am I right? Were you?"

She nodded. "Yes."

"And now you are nodding."

"How do you know?"

"Because I know you, my darling?"

"Tom ..."

"Stop saying my name like that, else I'll ravish you, and you know I promised I wouldn't."

She found herself laughing.

"That's what I like to hear," he said, "a good belly-laugh. Now don't say 'Oh, Tom' again."

"No, but this isn't all a game to you, is it?"

"Will you lunch with me? Of course you will! I'll pick you up at eleven-thirty and I'll take you to the Colombe d'Or in Saint-Paul de Vence. It is a delightful restaurant and we can sit overlooking the mountains. You'll love it. Lots of kisses. That's allowed, isn't it, over the telephone? See you eleven-thirty. 'bye."

And she was left sitting in the hall, surrounded by roses, cradling the receiver in her hands, her question unanswered.

They lunched in the Colombe d'Or, high up on the terrace, gazing out over a patchwork of greens – the pale grey-green of the olive trees, the dark green of the cypress and the emerald of the plane. All around them flowers bloomed. Bright blue scilla vied with the luscious, laden branches of wisteria, drooping heavily in a sea of misty mauve. They ate langoustines and salad and finished with fruit.

On their first outing they discovered little details about each other, likes and dislikes. All that week they lunched out in the hills and in the small villages around the coast: in the little fortress hamlet of Haut Cagnes; in the old town of Frejus; in a little café on the waterfront at St Raphael; and in the grandeur of the Hotel du Cap in Antibes.

They walked arm in arm up cobbled streets and strolled through seaport markets where they bought cheap souvenirs.

On every occasion he delivered her safely back to the Villa de la Rose for tea or at siesta time. He did not ask her out at night.

"I'm being careful of your aunt. She can't complain about lunch. Lunch is innocent," he said.

Sonya, however, tartly remarked that Mr Armitidge had better things to do with his evenings.

"He gambles, *chérie*, that is the truth of it. However, you seem to enjoy your little lunches and you are certainly exploring the south of France."

Tom was amazed at her ignorance of the countryside. She had lived in it without really seeing it.

"What an ignoramus you are," he chided her. "I don't know how you managed to see so little. It's quite an accomplishment. This is some of the most beautiful country anywhere in the world. The trouble is, my darling, you take yourself too seriously. You are so immersed in your own problems that you do not appreciate the world around you."

He glanced at her quizzically, his strong hands on the wheel of the car. The tyres screeched as they rounded hairpin bends climbing up into the mountains, the turquoise sea below. They had the hood back. The wind whipped their hair around their faces.

"You're probably right. But I'm making up for lost time," she said, smiling at him.

"What did you *do* before I came along? Where did you go?"

"To friends' houses. Their villas. Hotels for the big affairs. And the *thé dansant*. And home, of course. That's all." Impulsively, she laid a hand on his arm. "Thank you for these weeks. You've shown me so much. It's been beautiful."

He grinned at her. "You talk as if it was over." But he knew what she meant even if, as he suspected, she herself did not realise what she was saying.

He had seen her desire for him grow. He had deliberately planted the seed then left it. He had allowed it to increase, nurtured by his lack of response. He knew it was the best way to feed her appetite for him. The night of the ball he had planted the idea firmly in her mind that he desired her and that he was aware she was attracted to him. She could not, therefore, look on their relationship as merely platonic.

"I don't make passes at women unless they encourage me," he said on their first outing. "I don't need to. So stop worrying."

She had relaxed after that and a short while later began to make little impulsive touches on his arm or shoulder, forgetting her reticence in her excitement at the beauty around them; on other occasions lulled by wine, she would lean over and lay a hand on his bare arm or hold his hand and let his fingers lace hers. He noticed each little relaxation, how the gestures became premeditated and how she began to want to touch him more and more. And he ignored it. He pointed out the magic of a cathedral arch or an old fountain in a courtyard or the loveliness of aged and polished stones, as if he took for granted her little affectionate gestures.

Her eyes then took to journeying over his face, lingering on his mouth. He would say, "Look," and draw her attention to a giant evergreen fig tree with a twisted green trunk and branches sinuous and strong, or to ivy-covered stones on a ruined castle wall. Now all her gestures showed she was ready. One day he turned the car off the main road, past Saint-Paul de Vence. It bumped over a dirt track to a little villa with a pink-tiled roof. The place was tiny, no more than one large room. In the surrounding pines birds squawked loudly and cicadas hummed.

"Whose is this?" she asked.

"It's mine," he said with a smile. "I need to get away sometimes and this is tiny and private and no one knows about it. Except you."

His smile was warm but no more than that. Zara faltered a little, confused. She had thought, This is it, but saw no hint of intimacy in his eyes. She took his hand and they walked over a thick layer of pine needles to the verandah.

"It's very peaceful here," he said. "The old biddy who sold it to me said she was off to the desert. She was a tough old party who thought the south of France was becoming too crowded."

They went inside. The single room which ran the whole length of the house was covered in brightly coloured Greek mats. There was a bed under a sloping roof, a white cotton spread draped over it. There was a range at the other end, tucked into an alcove, and a huge sofa with brilliant shawls on it before a fireplace full of pine cones. On the wall were two pictures whose colours were as bright and sunny as the place and seemed to belong there.

"They're beautiful, aren't they?" he said. "Gauguin and Derain."

"They are! But you leave the door open?" she asked, astonished. He burst out laughing. "No thief worth his salt would break in here. With the Cote d'Azur awash with millionaires this place is unlikely to be given a second glance. The paintings would only be recognized by a connoisseur. No, I think they are safe here.

"Sit down, I'll get you a drink. There are a few more paintings I bought in Paris over there. Face to the wall, I'm afraid. I haven't had time to hang them and they simply would not fit in with the decor in my apartment in Jermyn Street. It was my great uncle's before me and his father's before that. Very dark and heavy."

He chuckled and went on pouring the drinks. She had gone over to the wall where the canvases were stacked. She turned them to face her one by one.

"What do you think?"

"I don't know," she said doubtfully. "I'm used to more ... I love the Gauguin and the Derain."

Tom let her study the paintings undisturbed. He gave her a drink and sat on the sofa, looking at her as she examined them.

"I think these are wonderful, but I don't know why," she said.

"The Matisse and the Miró? It's the colour, I expect. They are so full of life."

"These I'm not sure I understand."

"Ah, the Picasso and the Braque. But do you *feel* them?"

Zara nodded. "Yes, I do. Can you tell me about them? What the painters are trying to do?"

He did not touch her. They talked and sipped their drinks, side by side on the sofa. She ached to lean forward and run her finger over his lips or cover his hand with hers. But he kept his distance and continued the conversation about art. He was erudite and interesting and held her attention when it threatened to wander. At last he looked at his watch.

"Your aunt will be anxious," he said. "Come on, it's time to go. Where are you dining tonight?"

"With the Marquis in Cap Ferrat," she said, sighing, wishing she did not have to go, aching to stay in this room with him, longing to have him hold her in his arms.

For the next four days it was the same. After lunch among the olive groves of Contes or in the mediaeval town of Roquebrune-Cap, they would go to his villa. They travelled miles in his fast little car and sometimes when they got to the

254

villa in the hills it was quite late and they spent only ten minutes or a quarter of an hour there. Zara wondered what he was doing but did not ask.

She had come to the conclusion that he did not want her when, about a week later, they lunched early in Mougins. Full of lobster and strawberries and a superb Pouilly Fuissé, they paid the bill and drove fast to the villa.

When they arrived Tom lifted her up in his arms and carried her into the house, dropping her gently on to the bed. He sat beside her, looking into her large startled eyes. Zara reached out to touch his face. He caught her hand and kissed the fingers one by one, then ran his tongue over her palm. Relaxed by the sun and the wine, the familiarity of the room and the confidence she had in him, she allowed the desire she had felt for him and that he had gently nurtured to sweep over her. When he leaned towards her and took her face between his hands, she wanted him as she had never wanted a man in her life. He kissed her lightly. He unbuttoned her blouse and for a moment she wanted to hide the tiny breasts from him but he bent to them and she felt the wetness of his mouth on her body. She drew in her breath sharply. Darts of pleasure pierced her body. Still he took his time. He fonded and caressed her, seeking areas of new pleasure and arousing her until, more than ready, she was aching, trembling for him.

"Oh, please, please, now," she whispered and he entered her, holding the curve of her behind in his hands and sliding into her with no effort at all. It was like nothing she had ever known before. The Baron's tearing into her dry body was an experience so remote from this as to be another act altogether.

Tom's body inside hers, arousing her with its tempo, searching for pinpoints of pleasure, bore no relation to the obscenity of the Baron's forced entry, his indifference to her pain or pleasure and his cruel domination of her defencelessness.

Now she was part of another, of Tom, of the man she loved, the man whose every feature she knew, whose smell was familiar, whom she wanted to devour. Now they were riding together on the crest of a huge tide of arousal, of passion. And he was careful not to leave her. With every nerve in his body, with fingers and lips and words, he urged her on, drew her with him, until, unable to hold back, reaching a mighty crescendo they both called out in the quiet room, and shouted again, and panted to a shuddering halt.

They did not speak for a long time. Drenched in sweat she was overwhelmed by what she had just experienced. That so frail a container as her body could be capable of such tremendous upheaval astonished and delighted her. She felt fear and tension leave her. It simply vanished. Suddenly she was strong and brave and confident. Ready to fight giants. She also wanted to laugh for joy. The fun of it. The glory!

He lit her a cigarette and they lay, side by side, smoking. Wave after wave of tenderness for him swept through her. He had liberated her. She was a part of him and totally herself for the first time. She had no doubts about herself now. She knew he had shared her tremendous experience. She only had to look into his eyes to see the tenderness there.

Zara giggled. Tom raised himself on his elbow and looked at her, smiling.

"Better now?" he asked, and she burst out laughing with him.

"Yes. Oh, yes," she said.

She was late back to the Villa de la Rose that evening.

"You'll have to hurry," Nina said. "We're due at the Marquis's at nine-thirty."

She looked at Zara who stood in her slip before the long mirror scrutinising herself, now this way, now that. Nina was already dressed.

"Oh, Zara, you're so lucky you're thin," said her cousin.

Zara breathed "Oh, yes," and wondered when she'd said that in those tones before, then remembered and giggled to herself. But Nina did not notice.

"I have such a battle," she continued. "It's so difficult. I don't suit the dresses. You need to be straight up and down like you. I'm all curves."

Full of goodwill to everyone, Zara kissed her cousin.

"You are lovely," she said, "and I haven't heard any of the boys complaining. They like you just as you are."

Nina brightened. "That's true," she said. "Now hurry, Zara. Mama will be ready in an instant so get a move on."

Zara laughed. "Oh, Nina, you and your American expressions," she cried.

"Well, it's all the rage."

All through the boring dinner at the Princess's, while she made small talk to her right and her left, Zara's head was full of the memory of love. Once or twice she forgot her manner enough to allow her mind to wander and said 'What?' abruptly to her table companion when she lost the thread of the conversation.

She collapsed in a fit of giggles when Andrew Fyfe-Warrington on her right told her she had the reputation of being a 'cold fish', as he put it. This was because she stood on his foot when he put his hand on her knee. Her laughter disconcerted him as nothing else could and he withdrew his attention and turned to Nina who was seated next to him on the other side. The two swiftly engaged in a robust and flirtatious exchange much more suited to Andrew's rather school-boy tastes.

The next day, consumed with excitement, Zara waited for Tom. He came at the usual time, mid-morning, tooting on his car horn in front of the villa. She ran to greet him.

"Let's go to your little home right away," she said as she jumped into his car. He burst out laughing.

"But we must eat."

"Not today."

"Tell you what we'll do," he amended, "we'll buy some cheese and wine and fresh french bread, and eat there. How's that?"

"Perfect," she sighed, content.

It was a blue day. The sun shone, the sea glittered, the air around the little villa smelt of pines as she lay on the bed, waiting for him.

"Good heavens, Zara, I'm not a machine. You have to learn to enjoy yourself," he told her, looking at her expectant face.

"I enjoyed myself yesterday," she smiled back at him.

"Of course you did," he said, "it was a wonderful new experience. It was a release. Now you must learn to arouse me. We must complement one other. You must learn to experiment, not just lie back and wait for me to do it to you."

She looked at him, frowning. "I didn't do something for you yesterday?" she asked doubtfully. He lay beside her, naked and warm to her touch.

"There was nothing wrong with yesterday and you know it," he said, "But that was yesterday. Today I don't intend to do all the work." He lay back on the bed, stretching his arms behind his head.

She looked at him uncertainly. "What will I do?"

"Look at me," he replied. "Think of something. What do you *want* to do? Touch? Explore?"

"That, and that, and that," she cried.

She was happier than she had ever been before. Her eyes were the eyes of a woman in love. Her Aunt Sonya shook her head, uncertain how to proceed. It never occurred to her that this was anything more than an innocent falling in love. That Tom and Zara might be lovers was unthinkable. With Nina she worried that her boyfriends might 'go too far', but with Zara's background it never dawned on Sonya that she had anything to worry about.

"At least he is not as dowdy as the rest of the English

aristocracy," she was heard to remark, "but I am a bit surprised by the frequency of these romantic lunches."

Then she received news from Zurich which filled her with dismay. She bearded Vassily in his small study one afternoon at siesta time. As usual Zara was not at home at this hour. Vassily was dozing in a deep armchair near the open French window. A cool breeze blew from the sea and the room was shaded by a fat palm tree. It was called Vassily's study because he was usually to be found there. He went there to sleep. Everyone knew that and they knocked before they entered. He liked to doze in the comparative quiet over a vodka in the afternoon. He also used the room as a retreat from problems and his wife, yet here she was, breaking all the rules, entering without knocking and wanting to talk to him in the very middle of his siesta.

He knew precisely what she wanted to talk about and he had hoped to avoid the discussion until a more civilized time, or even better to have no discussion at all. He had often remarked that things had a habit of sorting themselves out, if you left them alone.

Sonya had spent a fortune trying to locate Zara and Sasha but nothing had come of her search. Vassily had told her it wouldn't. Zara had written, out of the blue, just as things should happen, he thought.

His wife settled herself firmly in the chair on the other side of the window and stared at him in exasperation. He lay sprawled in his chair, his linen suit crumpled, his good-natured face full of sleep, eyes hazy.

"Really, Vassily!" she said.

"What, my love?" He blinked at her.

"Look at you."

"I say! That's a bit difficult."

"Don't be facetious, dear. It doesn't suit you. You are a mess. Your suit is like a dish cloth."

"Well, I'll be bathing and changing for dinner presently," he said equably.

"It's only four o'clock."

He decided it was useless to argue. She was not angry with him, he knew that. She found him lazy, it was true, but she was agitated about something else and was taking it out on him.

Vassily took refuge in silence while Sonya sat examining her fingernails for several minutes. He was just nodding off again when her firm voice drew him back from the blissful slide into unconsciousness.

"Should we tell Zara about the money?"

"Of course, my love. It's hers."

"I don't mean tell her there *is* money," she sounded exasperated, "of course we'll tell her that now that we've traced the bank. What do you take me for? No, I meant, shall we tell her the whole truth?"

"You mean about the withdrawals? Well, my love, I don't know. What do you think?"

Sometimes this worked, getting her to figure out her own solution.

"The thing is, I don't understand it myself. Over the years … half the yearly allowance. It's amazing! It can only be Sasha. The letter says the withdrawals of half the interest on the capital were 'correct', which means there was no hanky-panky. Perhaps Alexei left the money to someone else?" Sonya paused and frowned. "But who? He didn't have a mistress, did he? He might have told you. Not wanting to shock me or some such thing."

"Oh no, my dear. I don't think so." Vassily pursed his lips and blushed as he remembered his own philandering. "We'd have known. They hated him so at the end. The gossips were dying to discredit him. They did everything to dig up some dirt on him, but they could not. No, I doubt it. And he knew you loved him and would have been delighted for him if he had someone who loved him, or at least made him happy." He cleared his throat loudly then added gallantly, "'sides, you're not shockable. Not at all, my love."

"Quite right, dear. Well, if there wasn't a mistress, who

else except Sasha could have legal right to half the income? And if he is withdrawing the money, it uncovers a veritable hornet's nest. How does he know about the account? Who told him? Why doesn't he contact Zara? And if we tell her, what will happen then? Will she feel she must go tearing after him and perhaps be badly hurt again? Oh, Vassily, I don't want that to happen. Indeed, I don't. She's so happy these days. All that gloom has lifted. Poor child, she's never had the chance of happiness until now.

"Her Father … oh, you know how I adored Alexei, but he was not, even I have to admit, the ideal family man. Then there was the dreadful Anya! I know you did not think so, Vassily, and there is no need to look so uncomfortable. It's all in the past."

He wished it were so. But every time his sister-in-law's name came up, his wife could not resist having a dig. "Then the murder and that terrible Baron and all he did to her. And Sasha going off and leaving her like that … well, she has had more than her fair share of tragedy. Now I do not approve of Tom Armitidge, as you know."

Vassily nodded dutifully. He thought Tom Armitidge a capital fellow, always cheerful, always paid his gambling debts, never let a chap down. But he prudently kept his opinion of the Englishman to himself.

"He's a gambler and a womanizer," his wife continued, "but he is charming. And honourable. He would never shirk his duty."

Vassily permitted himself a dry chuckle but Sonya, in full flow, did not notice.

"Tom Armitidge has succeeded where everyone else has failed. I don't mind telling you that I have despaired at times. My heart has bled for the girl and the burden she carries. But I have also lost patience with her. Dmitri is, after all, my son. God forgive me, I have felt sometimes that I could shake her. And now the miracle has been worked. Tom Armitidge has made Zara's melancholy disappear.

Thanks to him, she shines."

Sonya smoothed her skirt and patted her hair and drew a deep breath. "Well, Vassily," she said, "I think you are right."

He looked at her, mildly surprised. He did not think that he had said anything.

"I think we'll tell her about her money but say nothing of half of it being 'correctly' withdrawn. At least not yet. Let us leave it for a while. There now! I feel much better. It always helps to talk things over. A trouble shared ... I know you hate to be disturbed but you have been invaluable to me. Thank you, dear."

She rose and left the room, pausing only to plant a kiss on his forehead. Vassily sighed and with a gulp emptied his glass of vodka. He started to drift, drift, drift into blissful nothingness.

Chapter Fourteen

Zara was delighted about the money. It gave her a certain independence although Vassily and Sonya adamantly refused to accept any of it from her.

"Under no circumstances. It's yours, absolutely yours."

"But you've been so good to me."

"Well, and do you think we expect to be paid for that?"

"But my clothes alone ..."

"You may buy yourself luxuries, extra clothes, if you wish," Sonya said. To Zara's surprise, tears came into her aunt's eyes. "I look upon you as a daughter. You are part of the family. I expect no repayment." The tears threatened to fall.

Zara put out her arms. "I'm sorry, Aunt. How crass of me. Of course I think of you as my family too. You are the mother I never knew. I didn't mean to hurt you."

"It's just that money is so ... I'd rather not ..."

"Let's not talk about it any more," Zara said, "I won't have you upset at any price."

She patted her aunt's back a little clumsily, realizing that she had begun to take this dear family for granted. So no more was said on the subject of the money except that it was on deposit, and that Zara had a large sum in interest accruing to her available to spend.

Life with Tom got better and better. For a time all was well. She was content, fulfilled. But as the months passed, spending a few hours at lunch time, eating their picnic feast and making love afterwards, was not enough for her. She wanted more of him, much more.

Her father had once told her that human beings are constituted to aim at something they want and having achieved it quickly take it for granted, adjust and aim for an even higher goal. She found out how correct he had been. She had ached to be able to love, fully, like other women. Having achieved that, now she wanted to become a permanent part of Tom's life. To her consternation she found that this was not going to be as easy as she had assumed.

He was a fascinating man, an interesting talker, amusing and entertaining. He was the perfect host. But that was all he was, a host. There seemed no deeper commitment on his part.

"Why can't we spend the evenings together?" she asked.

The room was dark, the shutters drawn. The scent of the pinewoods mingled with that of their bodies. The remains of a baguette and some half eaten fruit and cheese lay in disarray on the table with an opened bottle of wine.

"Why?" she pressed.

"Because, my darling, I am a gambler," he replied lightly. "I make what little money I have that way, and gambling is an evening occupation. Would you rather I was a stuffy banker or a postman?"

"Yes, if it meant I could see more of you."

"He looked at her seriously. "I cannot change myself, Zara. You know that."

She supposed he was right. Then she forgot about the odd pattern of their liaison and for days was content to meet him like that and make love in the small villa in the hills. But the path had been taken, the seed of discontent, though tiny, had nevertheless been sown. A small voice within her refused to be silent.

"Your skin is like milk, my darling," Tom said, kissing her. "No, not like milk, like cream, and I will drink you all up."

She ran her hands over his chest. "Golden hairs ... who

could imagine anything more beautiful? Every muscle, every bone of you, I love. Look at you!" she laughed. "You're beautiful. Once Nina said that men were beautiful. I didn't know then what she meant. Now I do."

She had lost all her shyness.

"You're brazen," he told her, teasing, "a brazen lass. My shy, frightened fawn has become a predetory lioness."

She nudged him with her head.

"We must get back, Zara," he said suddenly, looking at his watch.

"Oh, why?" she moaned. "Why can't I live with you all the time?"

"Because you cannot," he replied.

"But I don't understand. I want to live with you. Why won't you live with me?"

He wasn't angry. She had thought he might be now that she had made her feelings clear.

"And what would your aunt say to that?" he said patiently. "What would Princess d'Artelli say? What would Lady Frobisher and Amanda Abercrombie say?" With the mention of each name he tickled her, and in five minutes had her laughing so much that it hurt.

They ended in each other's arms, laughing, kissing, twining themselves about each other until the sounds of mirth changed to moans of passion and Zara was late for dinner.

After a few more days of lovemaking and peace, of long drives and animated discussions about all the fundamental things, she took the irrevocable step.

"I want to marry you, Tom. I love you."

There was silence in the little room that had become so familiar to her, so dear. They sat across the table from each other. The silence lengthened. She could hear her heart thump against her ribs.

"Well, say something. Please." She was afraid now. If she lost him she would die.

He sighed. He looked across the table at her, seeming older suddenly.

"I'm not the marrying kind," he said. "You move in more elevated circles. Oh, I don't mean that I'm not as well-bred, but you and the Rostovs are used to money. You are cossetted by it. It is part of your life. I have none. Truth to tell, I don't really want to be filthy rich. I'd only gamble it away. I could give you so little."

"All I want is this." She spread her hands and looked about the room." I am more alive here than anywhere. I have been happier here than I ever thought possible."

But he shook his head. "No, my love. You would not be for long. Don't you see that?"

She felt anger and tears rise up within her, panic and fear. This was all she wanted, all she would ever desire.

"It's because of the Baron," she said. She knew this was not true but said it anyway, hoping to make him feel bad, perhaps instil in him a sense of obligation.

He came around the table to her, squatted beside her chair and wiped away her tears with his handkerchief.

"No, how could it be?" he said, soothing her.

"Don't treat me like a child," she said, pushing him away. She was behaving petulantly, she knew, but could not stop herself. "I'm not a baby to be shushed. I'm a grown-up person and I'm angry."

"Because you are not satisfied with what I give you now. Don't you see, it will always be like that? It's human nature. We want a bicycle. We dream of it. We feel we'll never be unhappy again if we get our bicycle. Then we receive it. Within a week we want a car."

She remembered her father saying much the same thing, and pushed the thought away.

"No. I *know* I would be happy if I was married to you and we lived here simply. I would wait for you to come home. I would learn to cook beautifully. And I would do everything to please you."

266

"What about yourself?"

She looked startled.

"You say 'to please you.' It's all to please me," he said. "What a responsibility! Surely you've learned with me that doing something, living in a certain way, to please someone must also please you. Otherwise it's a disaster. Resentment creeps in." He went to the french window. "Oh, Zara, when I met you first all you wanted was to be released. To feel like other women. Not to be afraid. Well, all that's been accomplished. Why can't that be enough?"

He stood with his back to her, looking out over the pine trees.

"Oh, darling, it would be if only you married me," she said.

"That's what you say now. Soon you'd want a better villa, more money. For me to be more like other men. Then what would I do? Oh, never mind. I don't blame you. It's human nature. It separates us from the animals."

She ran to him and pressed her cheek to his shoulder.

'Oh I'm sorry. Forgive me. I'm stupid and selfish. Please forgive me."

He sighed. "You're so extravagant in all your emotions, Zara. There's nothing to forgive. It's natural to want a husband and children. It's natural that you look to me to provide for you. But, you see, I'm not that type of man. I'm sure your aunt told you."

He loosened her grip and turned and walked to the sofa, leaving her feeling deserted. He looked at her wryly. She felt awkward under his gaze. So far away. So separate. "I'm a bad catch, Zara. I live a rackety life. I gamble. I have affairs with women." He saw her flinch. He could not bear to see the hurt in her face. "Never one like this though," he said to console her, and found to his surprise that he meant it.

A radiant smile broke over her face and she said, "There, you see," and sat on his knee and kissed him, biting his bottom lip and rubbing herself against him. She knew how to

267

arouse him. Soon she had him gasping in excitement and pleasure. Their bodies took over and arguments were forgotten. But afterwards she felt bad for some reason. As if she had played a trick, done something less than honourable.

She did not return to the subject for a long time. She had been frightened. She felt he might leave her, quite suddenly. He spoke sometimes as if she were an incident in his life while she knew quite definitely that he was the only man she would ever love. Her talk of a permanent relationship alienated him, yet that was what she wanted more than anything in the world. At last it was too much for her to bear in silence.

Aunt Sonya had begun to grumble. "You cannot go on forever eating lunch with that man."

Nina asked, "Are you going to marry him?"

Zara said to him in the car one day, when all her instincts screamed at her to keep silent, "I have money."

He knew at once what she meant. He understood the thought processes which had brought her to that remark. The car screeched to a halt.

"If you think you can buy me, get out now," he said coldly. It was the first time she had seen him angry. He glared at her and his eyes were cold as ice. As if they were strangers. Terrified, she leaned towards him.

"Tom, I didn't mean it. Tom, please!"

"Zara, we have been all through this. I am not the marrying sort, will you understand that? I have nothing to offer you. Let me be frank with you."

She was already sobbing. She did not want him to be frank with her yet ached to hear what he had to say. It was always like that, as if she was pushing further and further towards her own destruction. He must, she thought, be getting fed up explaining to her over and over again that he would not marry her and why. One day she would push him too far and he would leave her forever, yet still she insisted on pressing him. She looked at him now with solemn eyes.

"You're married," she said.

He burst out laughing, all anger gone.

"Oh, Zara, ever the female logician. I won't marry *you*, ergo I'm already married. For heaven's sake, no! Don't you ever listen to me? Do I have to repeat myself over and over again? Can't you get it into your head that marriage is out for me? That we would be at each other's throats in no time at all? Imagine it. First it would be a larger house, nearer town. nearer your aunt."

She knew a little thrill of fear for she had thought of that already. She had thought now nice it would be if he bought, with her help, a little house, nothing grand, just perhaps a little larger than his place in the hills. And it would be behind Nice, near Aunt Sonya and the Rostovs. It would save them time. She could prepare the food and they could have a maid for the heavy work. Sometimes his little villa was messy. She didn't like the remains of yesterday's food to be there when they arrived. It would be like that today. The cleaning woman only came in twice a week and neither yesterday nor today were her days. So there would be a mess. If they had a house nearer she could buy flowers ... new linen ... She glanced at him to see if he read her thoughts but he was gazing over the bay at the sparkling sea and the soft curve of the Cap.

"Then it would be children," he continued, "a nanny, other things you were entitled to. Oh God, Zara, when I started this thing with you it was to set you free, not bind you to me!"

She suddenly felt sick.

"What do you mean – started this thing?"

"I mean there was a moment – there always is, no matter what the romantics think – when you can draw back. What I thought then was that I could teach you not to be afraid of sex. I could unlock you. And then, when we tired of each other, you would find someone else – a charming boy, your cousin perhaps. He loves you so much, and he is a much more suitable match. I thought you would marry him and have your secure monied life together. No ripples."

She felt shocked and numb. He sounded so casual. He was talking about choices when for her there was only one course possible. He was talking calmly of her marrying someone else. What kind of a love was that? What did he feel when he told her he loved her? He obviously did not feel as she did. He could not. The mere thought of him being with another woman made her feel physically ill, yet he seemed to feel unattached.

"You don't love me at all," she said. "You don't care about me. You never saw us as a pair. As a couple. Only singly."

She got out of the car on trembling legs, slamming the door, and started to walk back the way they had come. She knew he watched her in disbelief. He did not understand the extravagant gestures she made. He thought she was 'over the top', as he called it. She wondered if perhaps he was not capable of feelings as deep as hers. She wondered if perhaps he was shallow.

"What the devil!" he drove in reverse until he reached her. "Don't be so bloody silly," he shouted. "Get in and let's talk about it at least."

But she was too hurt, too angry, and paid no attention to him, knowing she was being stupid, yet unable to stop herself. She went on walking, ignoring him.

"Oh, bloody hell! I'm not going to play your silly little game." And he drove off and left her walking in the sun.

It was hot though it was autumn. Soon the English would be back, she thought, his buddies. Her feet in her chubby-heeled pale apricot shoes and silk stockings were soon swollen and hot. There was a tight feeling in her chest and a panicky flutter in her stomach. Terrified by her own actions she wanted nothing more than to rush to him, apologise, take it all back. She had no pride in regard to him. She wanted a piece of him and the smallest piece was better than nothing at all. She wished ruefully she could undo the whole conversation, but realised conversely that it

270

was impossible and undesirable. She had meant what she said. She felt she had been justified so why should she recant? Was there no hope for her then? Were they forever to be driven apart by their individual wishes so that no peace was possible between them? They could not spend the rest of their lives meeting for lunch in his little villa in the mountains. Time stands still for no one. A relationship has to develop, but what could she do if he refused to see that? She was not at all sure that he loved her enough to give in to an ultimatum. She certainly did not have enough courage to issue one in case it did not work. She could not face the consequences if he said that in that case he would not see her any more. If that happened, she would die inside, she knew it. The pain in her heart thinking of life without him, an empty world, was so fierce that she gasped.

She stopped walking. There was no one in sight. A deserted landscape spread before her, a vista of indigo sea and verdant mountains swam through a golden haze. She could see tiny boats on the water, still, as in a painting. The smell of flowers was overwhelming, the light in her eyes blinding.

Why hadn't she got pregnant? She had hoped against hope that she would. Aunt Sonya said Tom was an 'honourable man'. Then he would *have* to marry her. But there was no sign of that. Once or twice she had hoped, there had been a false alarm and her excitement ran high, but the hopes proved groundless. Why were all the people she loved taken away from her? Her Father, Sasha, and now Tom.

But he had not been taken. She had sent him. The sweat trickled down her neck and slid from under her arms and she began to sob. She had never felt so helpless in her entire life and it was all her own fault. She began to walk towards Nice, the sun in her eyes, and soon the walk turned to a limp.

Five minutes later she heard a car draw up and brushing her eyes with the back of her hand she turned.

It was him. Her breath caught and her heart leaped and such relief flooded her body that she thought that she would fall. She would take him on any terms.

"Oh, get in, you silly girl," he said softly. "Get in."

She climbed into the car and threw herself into his arms. He kissed her temples then put the car in gear and drove with her arms about his body, clinging to him like a limpet to a rock.

In the car outside his villa she began to open his shirt. She could not wait. Her fingers were everywhere; her lips searching, passionately demanding. They hurried to the bed, panting for each other, hot with their mutual desire.

It was a fierce short mating, a wild crescendo, soon over.

"What a sexy little lady you are," Tom said, and smiled at her. He seemed cooler with her, a little distant and less tender.

"Should I not make love to you like that?" she asked.

He sighed. "It was good, my darling, but oh so possessive. Do you really want to gobble me up?"

She felt again the lurch of fear. It was exactly what she had felt. She had not imagined he could divine such desires.

"Yes, I do," she said, but she kept her tone light. She saw the trap. She knew that, whatever else, she could not bear to give him up. She would put up with anything rather than be without him. So she smiled lightly and said, "And then you can gobble *me* up. Remember our second time? You informed me that you were not going to do all the work."

He was diverted. "Did I really say that? God, what a bastard I am."

She was going to say, 'Oh, no. It wasn't like that. It was so tender, so helpful to me. Don't you remember?' But she stopped herself in time, holding the words in check. It was sad, this deception. Was life to be like this now if she meant to keep him? Lies and dissimulation? At the beginning it had been so spontaneous, she could say anything she liked. Now she had to censor her words.

272

She needed to be in control when she had none. She needed to be detached when she was passionately involved. She was not sophisticated enough for the game she was trying to play. It exhausted her.

"Do you see women in the Casino?"

No, no, no! Shut up. Don't ask. Don't even think.

But it was said. Lying across him, tracing his eyebrow and the lovely curve of his mouth with her fingertip.

"Why do you ask?" he said, not replying directly – (he would if he were innocent, she thought) – a tiny edge to his voice.

"Oh, no reason. I wondered. Does my aunt go there sometimes?"

Better. She had got out of it. She could feel his body relax.

"Yes, I see her sometimes with Vassily. I'm very fond of your uncle."

"So am I."

"But your aunt can never resist a little dig about us."

"You can hardly blame her." Oh no!

"What on earth do you mean?"

"Well, she wants to see me in a conventional arrangement. She wants me to be married."

Oh God, no. Why am I doing this?

"Well, Zara, you have the answer to that. I told you you should marry your cousin or someone like him. I agree with her."

His voice was cold. Why was it like this? Dear God, why?

It was so complicated now, not being able to say what she thought or felt. Yet each time she saw him was exciting, and she saw him every day except Sunday when the family went to the Russian Orthodox Church in Nice. The sharpness of her delight, the sudden overwhelming feeling that now he was with her all was well, never faltered. It was worth everything to keep those strong arms about her, feel his heartbeat under her ear, feel his possession of her so deep that he was part of her.

Her aunt finally asked Zara what Tom's intentions were.

"You'll have to sort it out, my dear. You are the talk of the Riviera. It's not right, you know, even in this permissive age, to go racketing around the countryside with a man whose reputation leaves so much to be desired. I've been glad to see you happy, so I haven't said anything. But, my dear, for the last month you have appeared a little drained. Is anything the matter?"

Sonya was worried about her niece. The pale face was paler and the skin almost transparent. She was like a piece of delicate Dresden china, as fragile and as breakable.

"No, Aunt, no. I'm fine. I don't want to talk about Tom, that's all."

"Well, you can't refuse to discuss it forever. It's got to be faced soon, my dear. You never go out with anyone else. You are long past the marriageable age. You will be left on the shelf. Not that we mind, my dear, indeed we do not. But for your own sake. You are becoming *persona non grata* on the marriage market for no one else will marry a girl who has been on the arm of the same man for over a year now with no results. You forfeit a home and family of your own. Don't you think you are being a little short-sighted?"

Zara did not reply and went her own way.

He was with her daily, so she argued he must be content with her. But she did not want him to be merely content. It was not enough. She wanted him to be madly, passionately in love with her, unable to live without her, desperate to marry her, be with her forever and have children by her. And she knew he did not feel that.

"I saw you smiling at Solange d'Arrent at the ball last night."

"Did you?"

"Yes. You did not know that I was there. We were in the blue room."

"Yes, I went to gamble. I only left the card room once. That was when I saw Solange."

"But you were laughing."

"Why on earth not?"

"I never laugh when you are not with me."

"How sad for you."

"What were you whispering?"

"To Solange? That, if I may say, is none of your business."

"Were you flirting with her?"

"Zara, stop this now. If you don't trust me there is nothing more to be said."

"Oh, I do, I do. But you were laughing so much and I knew I couldn't be so happy …"

"Zara, I don't think we should pursue this any further."

"Oh, darling, darling, don't be so cold. I'd die without you. Let's forget I said it."

She wished she could confide in her aunt. Sonya was worldly wise and would know what to do, but Zara had not the courage to unburden herself. Nina was no help either.

"Do you, you know, fool around with Tom?" she asked her cousin. "Chuck and I do a lot of snogging. It's bliss."

Zara looked at her. The girl was light-years away from her in experience, yet, Zara reasoned, when she felt contemptuous of her cousin, Nina's experience was more in keeping with her age and breeding. 'Snogging' was such an awful word to use in the context of passion that Zara felt disgusted, yet Nina's pretty face shone and she gave a sexy little wiggle that spoke volumes. Perhaps what they did, Chuck and herself, in the back of the car was as precious to Nina as what Zara and Tom did in the bed in the villa. Even Nina was considered a trifle fast by some of the mamas in polite society along the Riviera. But it was fashionable to be fast and shocking so Nina did not worry.

Nina pestered her with questions about Tom. Some of them she could truthfully answer. No, he had not asked her to marry him.

"All my boy friends pester me – to get married, I mean. I wish they wouldn't. Tom is so mature."

Yes, she was in love with him.

"Gosh, you're lucky you're so sure. I can never make up my mind. I'm almost certain, then I get doubts. So many of the boys are gorgeous."

No, there was no suggestion that she meet his family.

"Mama says he doesn't get on with them. He's more or less penniless. I think it's wonderful that you have some money so you won't have to worry about that."

No, she did not know if his intentions were honourable.

"You mean you don't know what he wants eventually? Well, ask him, Zara."

After one interrogation which had been especially gruelling, and during which Zara had found it increasingly difficult to hold her temper in check, Nina remarked, "You're very testy these days, I must say." She was swinging gently in the hammock, her face speckled with green and gold light. Is it something in particular I said?"

Zara shook her head. "No, Nina. I just don't like being questioned, that's all."

"But we're family. Naturally I want to know all about it. I thought at first love suited you but now I'm not so sure. If he doesn't ask you to marry him soon, I'd chuck him if I were you." She rolled down her gossamer fine stocking and peeled it off, wiggling her freed foot. Zara, echoing her aunt, said, "Nina, where do you pick up such expressions?"

"Oh, you! You're far too old for your age." Then, instantly repentant, she blew a kiss to her cousin. "I'm sorry," she said, "it's just I'm having a difficult time making up my mind whether to marry Chuck Kennelly or not."

Zara was instantly agog. A wedding in the family was just what she needed. She would get Aunt Sonya to ask Tom and when he was there, actually at the wedding, he would want to get married himself. Weddings were so romantic. She would be a beautiful bridesmaid. Oh, dear. Here she was, just as Tom had accused her, writing the story in advance instead of waiting for what happened and accepting it. But how could anyone in love do that?

"Oh, Nina, how wonderful! Oh, how lovely for you. Do you love him?"

"Well," Nina swung in the hammock squinting at the sun's shifting rays between the branches of the trees, "yes and no."

"You can't love someone 'yes and no'. Either you do or you don't.

Nine was giggling. "No, listen to me, Zara. See, it's like this. First, I'm getting old. I can't go playing the field much longer, Mama says, and I'm sure she's right."

"I'm sure she didn't phrase it like that."

"Well, anyway, I made a list and Chuck Kennelly came out ahead of all the others. Then I made another list … no, Zara, don't laugh. I'm being practical. I made a list of the reasons for and against marrying Chuck. And guess what? I had loads of reasons *in* favour and only two against. I think that means I love him."

"What are the reasons?"

"For or against?" Nina asked, then without waiting for a reply she continued, "I'll tell you anyway. One, he's gorgeous. I just love the way he looks. I could live with that forever. Two, he's fun, fun, fun! We spend a whole lot of time laughing. Three, he's nice. He's a nice human being, kind and considerate. Four, he's rich. Oh, I don't love him for his money and I have my own, but it helps. He's got lots so I'll always be comfortable and never have to worry. Five, he's a divine dancer. He dances beautifully *and* he knows all the latest steps."

Zara burst out laughing. "And what are the two reasons against?"

"Well, both the same really. America and America."

"But you're sure to love America. It's where all the new music comes from, and movies. You're mad about all that, and if he's rich then …"

"Oh, it's not that, Zara," Nina said impatiently, "I'm sure

I'll love America. It's the journey I dread. I hate travelling, I hate the sea as you know. Even a little river quite unnerves me, and the thought of that vast ocean … brrr! But that's reason number two. Number one is …"

"What?"

"Can't you guess? Gosh, Zara! It's leaving all of you, of course. Being so far away from Mother and Father and dearest Dmitri. And you. I love France and the Villa. All of it. It's so pleasant, so protected, so safe. I'll *hate* leaving."

Zara had not thought of that because it would not have mattered to her. If Tom Armitidge crooked her little finger she would follow him to the ends of the earth with scarcely a backward glance. She felt ashamed as she acknowledged this to herself.

"Oh, Nina, I'm so awful!" she cried suddenly and caught her cousin's hand, nearly yanking her off the hammock.

"What a silly thing to say," Nina chortled when she had righted herself. "Goodness, you are the most serious creature. Still, I understand. I don't know how I'd have been if … ah, well. Stop accusing yourself and feeling guilty. You can't live life as if it was a three act drama, for heaven's sake."

Tom had said a similar thing to her. He had told her not to take everything so desperately seriously. He had also accused her, albeit lightly, of being possessive. When Sonya told her one evening that Dmitri was going to marry Lucinda Abercrombie she knew he was right. She was overcome with a wave of emotion so intense that she thought she was going to be sick.

But he's mine, she thought, even though she had hardly been aware of his existence in the past year. "Mine," she whispered, and knew he was not.

"No one belongs to anyone," Tom had said when she had told him she belonged to him. "No one belongs to another human being. It's not healthy. If you want to possess the ones you love, you only lose people. Hold on tight and you kill. Let people be free and they'll come back."

She had been hurt when he had said it but she knew he had been right. She was terrified of losing the ones she loved. It was fear that made her possessive. Perhaps that was why Sasha had run away. She did not want to be like that. She wanted to be pleased for Dmitri and Lucinda, but deep within herself she hated the fact that he loved another, even though she did not want him for herself. Oh, it was all so complicated!

Her time with Tom was now laced with a desperate passion, Zara's tension communicating itself in an intensity of emotion that shook them both and also aroused them. She wondered what would happen to them eventually. We can't go on like this forever, she thought, no matter what Tom thinks. It's just not possible. Then, frightened to dwell on the consequences, she would shiver. Let it be a good ending for us, she prayed, but deep in her heart she did not have much hope.

Chapter Fifteen

It took Zara a long time to realise that nearly half the money was withdrawn from her account regularly. At first she never looked at the bank statement. She opened the envelope, glanced at the balance and threw it away. As she received the statement quarterly, she was not often concerned by it. Her mind was preoccupied with her own emotions and with Tom. Sonya, who was anxious to protect Zara from the knowledge and the perhaps painful implications of the regular withdrawals, told her that the bank were extremely careful and she need not worry that they would make a mistake.

But as time passed Zara noticed that an amount equivalent to half the sum credited was regularly withdrawn. The amount credited was, as her aunt explained, the interest from the capital her father had left her. She saw the amounts for the cheques that she had written. They were uneven, arbitrary sums of money. And there were bank charges, her aunt had explained that. But slowly she became aware that the gross amount was halved on a monthly basis. Surely this could not be right? She asked Sonya about it. To her surprise, her aunt was evasive.

So she asked Tom. She often asked him about the most simple things. He never laughed at her ignorance, seeming to accept it. When she broached the subject to him, he wanted to know if she minded him seeing the statement.

They had made love and were smoking a cigarette. She

looked at him fondly. His eyes were closed and his lashes rested against his cheeks. He looked defenceless, she thought, and very vulnerable, but she knew that he wasn't. If he didn't want to do a thing he would easily avoid it. She walked, naked, to her envelope-bag to remove a stiff piece of paper from it.

"Here. Look."

He looked at it a moment. "Wow. You're rich," he said, grinning at her.

"Oh, pooey!"

Then he whistled. "Odd," he muttered. "Very odd."

"I thought they were bank charges. Or, really, I didn't think about it at all. I sort of left it to the bank. But when I began to notice, I mean really notice, it seemed a bit expensive," she said.

"No. These are not bank charges. What does your aunt say?"

"She was rather evasive."

"Would she take some of your money ... you know ... for expenses?"

"Oh no," Zara was emphatic. "No indeed. I offered her some and she was horrified. She was hurt. No, I'm sure it's not that."

"Well, I can tell you for certain that these are not bank charges." He looked at her. "And the bank is not going to allow any unauthorised person to remove sums of money from an account. There is no doubt about that.

"Zara, is there anyone, was there in your father's life, anyone with as much a claim to his money as you? Why, darling, what is it?"

But he knew. As he said it, he knew. He saw her face pale and she began to tremble. He held her to him, trying to still the shaking.

"Sasha," she breathed. "Oh, Tom, it's my darling Sasha!"

"Hush, dearest. We don't know that."

"*I* know," she said, suddenly firm. "I know. I've got to find him. From this. How can I?"

Tom looked at her. "Listen, if this is Sasha then I don't think he wants to see you. No, don't be hurt. Face facts. Oh, Zara, will you stop living in your dream world? In life things don't turn out the way we want them to. Look, if Sasha is making these withdrawals then he knows about you, he probably knows where you are. And still he does not get in touch with you. It must be because he doesn't want to."

She pulled away from him. "Oh, you! Always telling me what other people want. Why should *I* care what *they* want? It's what *I* want now. You expect me not to try to find my brother?"

"I'm only thinking of you. I don't want you to be hurt."

"How could he hurt me?"

"He might reject you."

"Why? We loved each other."

"I don't know why, Zara. I only wonder why he has not contacted you. He must have known that he could find out where you are, and he didn't. Why? As I said, I don't want you to be hurt."

"You're always saying that, but you hurt me all the time and you know it."

There was silence. He did not reply. When, after a pause, he looked at her, her dark eyes were sparkling and she seemed to have forgotten her grudge against him.

"Of course! He was like me. He didn't look. He thought they were bank charges too. Sasha was even worse than me. Much worse. He couldn't tie his own shoe laces. He had no conception of things like bank charges and withdrawals. If it took me all this time to find out, it would take him even longer. Don't you see?

"Anyhow, Tom, sometimes we have to be hurt. Life is not all meant to be easy and untroubled. You accuse me of hoping it will be. Well, you try to arrange yours to suit you exactly, you can't deny that." She smiled at him. "I can find my brother and ask him. I can do that surely? That way at least I'll know."

"Have you the strength, Zara? Will you be able to cope if ..."

She looked at him calmly. "I haven't done too badly up to now, have I? I want to find Sasha no matter how hurt I get."

"Then let me come with you."

For a moment she doubted she had heard him correctly.

"What?"

"Let me come with you to find him. The bank will tell you where the withdrawals go. You have a right to know."

She must have misheard him. It had been a misunderstanding. Tom Armitidge leave his beloved South of France? Tom Armitidge give up his routine for anyone? Tom Armitidge stop gambling to devote himself to helping someone? Nonsense!

But he said it again. "I insist I come with you. I cannot allow you to go off to meet your brother alone. It will be a highly emotional encounter to say the least. Even if everything goes well, it will be difficult for you. You are easily overwhelmed, Zara, and I want to be with you. All right?"

She nodded, her face illuminated. Such a little thing, she thought, and she was transported to another sphere, another realm. The pain inherent in the fact that Sasha, her beloved brother, had chosen to run away from her, and now, probably, did not want to see her, vanished. Now all she could think of was that Tom, her darling Tom, was going to accompany her, support her through the ordeal. An enormous flood of gratitude swept through her. She wanted to throw her arms around him ecstatically but she had learned to think before she acted. He might think it was a trap. He might change his mind.

"That would be very good of you, Tom," she said in a small voice.

He took over the detective work. It was not long before he could report success. The young Prince Vashinskov, was, indeed, making the withdrawals. He lived in Berlin. He had contacted the bank a long time before his sister.

Prince Alexei Vashinskov had been very specific about his money. Everyone was to be treated equally: Anya, Zara and Sasha. The bank's instructions were that the money would stay lodged in securities and investments, and that the interest would go into an account. Each of the benefactors could withdraw one-third of the interest on the capital monthly, or cash cheques up to the total of one-third. In the case of decease of one or two of the beneficiaries, then the interest would be adjusted. On Anya's death the sum would be split in half. If Sasha or Zara then died, the whole would go to the surviving member of the family. If they all died the whole would revert to the Rostovs. The capital could only be touched by agreement between surviving parties.

Yes, the bank did have the prince's address and would be only too pleased to let the Princess have it. The bank only gave Tom the information on instructions from the Princess. And yes, Prince Sasha Vashinskov had his sister's address in France. He received an exact copy of the statement the Princess received quarterly and he had inquired after her when withdrawals had begun to appear on them. He had asked her whereabouts and the bank had furnished him with the information. They trusted that they had done the right thing? They felt the letter of their instructions could only be carried out if all parties were cognisant of their partners' whereabouts. But the Prince had asked them not to reveal his whereabouts to the Princess. They had said that that was impossible. What they could do, however, was keep silent about it unless directly asked. Which is that they had done. They had been informed by the Prince that the Princess Anya Karenska Vashinskova was now deceased and therefore the only two parties relevant were the Prince and Princess.

It was a lot to take in. It showed, unequivocally, that Sasha had known where she was and had chosen not to contact her. Zara fell silent a long time when she had realised the stark truth, time spent waiting for the pain to stop. She thought of his face, his golden hair, his blue eyes, his sweetness, and there was a tight band around her heart.

"I'd better write to him, I suppose," she whispered, "ask his permission."

I took care of you, she thought, like a mother. I loved you. What did I do wrong? I'm your only living relative and you don't want to see me. Oh, God, what did I do?

Tom frowned and looked at her.

"No," he said. "I don't think so. If he's avoiding you perhaps it would be better not." Then added when he saw her desolate expression. "He may have a very good reason we don't know about. Don't jump to conclusions. But let's say, just for argument's sake, that he has been hurt and does not want your pity. Or he is ashamed – something like that. Then a letter would only alarm him. Make him refuse to see you. I think it's better to take him by surprise. Then, whatever his reasons, he cannot avoid you. You will know the truth. I only hope, Zara, you are up to it."

The Rostovs were giving an engagement party for Dmitri. Lady Abercrombie was ecstatic. The villa was not large enough to accommodate the crowds and Princess Sonya decided to have the party in the Negresco.

The hotel had decorated the ballroom with roses, lilies and carnations, and Sonya remarked that it was more like a funeral than an engagement party. However, the pair were on clouds of happiness. Lucinda looked beautiful in a pale leaf-green dress by Patou, and now Zara wished her joy. She really meant it. Since Tom had asked to accompany her on her journey to Berlin she had been in a state of euphoria. They were away together. Morning, noon and night she would be with him. It was all she wanted, all she cared about.

She set him free. She no longer, even subconsciously, made demands upon him. In a wonderful burst of trust and love she found she had complete confidence in him and all her restraint and awkwardness fled. She became as she had been in their first days, joyous and carefree. She did not project, she lived and loved within the day.

They laughed a lot. They made love with joyous abandon. They were happy. The dark atmosphere vanished, the emotional tension fled.

Sonya insisted that they wait until after Dmitri's engagement party.

"I think you should stay for it, Zara, otherwise people might think it was sour grapes."

She laughed. "I don't think so, Aunt. I think most people have guessed I'm not romantically interested in Dmitri. If not they are blind."

"How can you laugh about it, Zara?" her aunt asked. "You gallivant around, not caring what people think of you. I don't know what your poor father would think of me if he were alive today."

"Well, he's not. And he might have surprised you, Aunt Sonya. Papa was always a modern man. Anyway, I had intended staying for the party. I love Dmitri and I hope he will be very happy with Lucinda. I want to be there to celebrate with them."

"Heaven knows what people will think of me when word leaks out that you are going to Berlin with Tom Armitidge," Sonya mused.

"Don't worry, dearest, they'll know you disapprove. I'm a woman after all and they know you cannot stop me. If you like I'll say you tried."

"Oh, Zara, you'll be the death of me," Sonya smiled. "You have an answer for everything."

"No, seriously, Aunt, I'm desperately sorry if I am causing you pain. It's the last thing I want to do. But, you see, I love him."

"No, my dear, you are not causing me pain. Oh, I grumble, it's true, but if I'm honest about it I love seeing you

287

and Tom together. You make such an attractive couple, and you are so good for him. Not that he realises that. I think in the end, you'll tame him and get your heart's desire."

She smiled at her niece and pressed her hand. Zara was surprised at how correctly Sonya had read the situation and thought she had probably underestimated her aunt's intuition.

"Besides, the gossips must be tired of Tom and me after all this time."

"I doubt it." Sonya shrugged. " 'The Princess and the Gambler' they call you. But it's true they have far more scandalous material to speculate about these days. The sixty-year-old Marquesa d'Aurto Mendoza has taken her butler to bed. What's more she is flaunting him, not being in the least discreet about it. She's driving society wild for they have to greet him, receive him. He's a Cockney, I think they call them, from London, and he seems very pleased with himself *and* her, which they cannot bear."

Zara laughed and her aunt continued, "Still, she's taking attention away from you, so good luck to her I say. She's a doughty old thing – wonderfully amusing. I hope he makes her happy." She sighed, "stranger things have happened."

Dmitri's party was a great success. Everyone was there including the Marquesa, Zara saw, with her handsome butler, who had not a clue how to behave and who flirted outrageously with his mistress to the righteous consternation of the guests.

"It is quite remarkable," Sonya said. "In the South of France a party is not complete without the Marquesa and she will not come without her butler. How extraordinary life has become."

It was the first time that Tom had accompanied Zara to a party; she was happy to stay quietly beside him, but she danced with Dmitri. They danced superbly together and people stared.

"I hope you'll be so very happy, Dmitri," she said,

meaning it. He nodded. "Lucinda is wonderful. She's gentle as a lamb," he said. "She's right for me, Zara." She nodded and he continued, "I was in love with you for so long. I thought I'd never love anyone else, ever."

"Never is a long time," she said.

"But it would not have been right. I could never have coped with you, Zara. You needed someone more mature, wiser."

She nodded again. "Yes, you're right. Tom is wonderful for me."

"I hope so." Dmitri sounded doubtful.

Lucinda was watching them. Every time Zara glanced in her direction she was watching Dmitri. She was trying to pretend that she wasn't but Zara could see her covert glances. Tom, however, was oblivious of Dmitri and herself in the centre of the floor. He had his head thrown back, laughing at something Vassily was saying, or he was bending down solicitously to listen to Sonya. Or, silent, he was looking at the orchestra. Whenever Zara glanced at him, his attention was elsewhere.

When the dance was over she accompanied Dmitri back to the family group. Lucinda was chatting to her mother and Sonya. Zara kissed the girl impulsively.

"I hope you two will be very happy," she said, and saw an expression of relief cross the little redhead's face.

She's as in awe of him as I am of Tom, she thought, amazed. She gave Lucinda a hug before she went to find her uncle and Tom.

"She's a sweet gel, your niece," said Lady Abercrombie, who had missed nothing.

"She is," Sonya said, glad as always to smoothe and reassure. She was grateful for Zara's impulsive little gesture towards Dmitri's fiancée. "Tom Armitidge is a very lucky man."

Oh dear, she thought, now everyone on the Riviera will say I have sanctioned this unholy alliance between my niece and Tom. Still, all in a good cause. Poor little Lucinda Abercrombie is pea green with envy and she'll never find happiness with my son until she ceases to think of Zara as a threat.

The Abercrombies, mother and daughter, heaved sighs of relief. As Lady Abercrombie said to Lucinda later as she pressed her marcelled waves and secured them firmly for the night with long hairgrips. "It's good to know that that unhealthy relationship is quite cold. Never did approve of in-breeding, m'self. Well, it looks as though we're home and dry."

Lucinda cast a despairing glance at the ceiling.

"Oh, Mother, don't talk as if you were at the horse show! I love him. I love him with all my heart." Her little face was flushed and earnest.

She doted on Dmitri and wished her mother would be more romantic about her engagement, but all she could say was, "Poppy-cock! As if that were important." Lady Abercrombie kissed her daughter. "You'll get over that soon enough," she said briskly, "Breeding is what counts. Money and breeding, m'dear. Don't you forget it."

Chapter Sixteen

They were together all the time. Tom's face was there beside her when she awakened. Zara saw him shave for the first time, slicing the razor up and down the strap, scraping his jaw with the newly sharp blade, and could not look in case he hurt himself. They walked the streets together, hand-in-hand. They looked in shop windows, admired what they saw or grimaced and shook their heads. They ate breakfast and lunch and dined together. They went to bed at night together and she had never in all her life known such happiness could exist. She was part of his life, he was all of her.

Zara struggled with the guilt she felt as she realized more and more that she did not want to reach Berlin and Sasha yet. It might be the end of this peaceful time with Tom, and she did not want that.

She could not think what would happen after meeting Sasha. Would Tom return to the South of France and the old routine? It would not be enough for her any more, she knew that. And when she actually saw her brother what would happen? The closer it came, the more she dreaded it.

But in the meantime she had everything she wanted. Tom even accepted money from her.

"It's for our expenses," she explained, as firmly and authoritatively as she could. "You must accept this draft. I could not be comfortable else. This is *my* problem and I will not have you out of pocket on my account."

"But it is far too much," he said dryly, one eyebrow raised.

"I'm used to the best. Don't quibble. I hate vulgar arguments about money."

They stayed in Paris two weeks.

"You're not in a hurry, Zara, are you?" Tom looked at her anxiously. "I have some people to see. Nothing important. It can be put off if you …"

"Oh, no," she cried, enchanted to stay here with him, meeting his friends and sitting at sidewalk cafés to drink coffee as the fashionable crowds passed by. Tom loved to show her off. She could see he was proud of her and the fact gave her pleasure. He had a run of luck at the casino so he bought her a diamond broach from Cartier.

They stayed at the Ritz and she bought clothes in the Rue Faubourg St Honoré at Molyneux and Patou, and gloves in the Rue de la Paix. "We'll pick them up on the way back," he said.

The way back. She did not want to think of it. She wanted time to stand still, wanted to hold on to these shining moments forever.

She had become used to the little bed in the villa in Saint-Paul de Vence. It was dark there, the villa shaded as it was by the pines. Now she found the brightness of the hotel room, the sun shining through the tall windows, the crispness of the sheets, a delightful incentive to lovemaking. Always passionate, their lovemaking took on a new ardour.

Tom enjoyed revealing Paris to her. She told him about her first and only visit there.

"I've changed so much," she mused, amazed as she thought back to what she had been then. "Scrawny … I was like a scarecrow! My clothes were cheap and too long and my hair was the same, very unfashionable. I was a frump." And, as Tom gave a little disbelieving laugh, she added, "No, really, I was. You cannot imagine. I had no money for luxuries. Oh, Aunt Sonya had sent some but it held no reality for me. I am a different person now. You, the Rostovs and the South of France have changed me out of all recognition. It's terrible, you know, Tom. I got used to it all, the life of comfort and luxury, as if it was all I'd ever known."

He nodded. "We change very quickly. I told you that."

"Yes, well, I did. Now I take it all for granted." She smiled ruefully. "But remembering how I was before ..." She shuddered. "Oh, Tom, you cannot imagine."

They sat at a table outside the Deux Magots. The afternoon was cool. An autumnal chill in the air made Zara draw her coat closer around her. Tom looked at her speculatively.

"You must have been thrilled to find them," he said. She knew he meant the Rostovs.

"Yes. It was such an accident. I didn't want to go to the café. If it hadn't been for Dirk ..." She looked at him, suddenly struck by an idea. "Darling, could we ... it would only take a few days ...?"

"Go to Amsterdam?" he asked non-committally. "Um. Don't see why not. *Garçon, l'addition s'il vous plaît.*"

Again she was amazed. Tom had divined her wishes and agreed, he who was normally indifferent to her wants. She said nothing and lowered her gaze to conceal her excitement. But he sensed her triumph. He lifted her chin and his eyes were impersonal as they sought and found her guilty gaze.

"Don't read anything significant into this," he said. "I just feel that as we are here, so near, it would be nice to stay a weekend at the American and see your friends." He let go of her chin. "Please don't play those games with me again, Zara."

"Of course not," she said, slewing her eyes away from his knowing look. She knew she had not deceived him; nevertheless she felt optimistic and exultant. He would be hers eventually. He would! He would get used to having her

293

around. He would see how well she fitted into his life, how limited her demands were.

During their stay in Paris she urged him to go gambling if he wished. She wanted to let him see how magnanimous she was. "I know you are trying to show me how accommodating you are," he said with a grin, and she blushed.

They took a train to Amsterdam. Zara felt her heart thud uncomfortably against her chest as they drove through the familiar streets.

"Autumn," she said, "I can smell it. Autumn in Amsterdam. Oh God, it brings back memories! Such pain, yet there was happiness too. Sasha was here."

He took her hand between his, holding and patting it as he would a distressed child's. The sky was heavy with grey clouds and against its low mass the leaves shook themselves free. There was an atmosphere as sad as Zara's face, Tom thought, and made an effort to shrug off his mood of ennui.

In the hotel, lights blazed and music came from the lounge. "Do you want to freshen up?" he asked.

She had shrunk into herself, her chin disappearing into the soft fur of the lynx collar on her smart coat. She looked all of a sudden as if she did not belong in it, like a maid in her mistress's finery. The emerald on her finger, a present from the Rostovs on her last birthday, looked like an imitation and her make-up stood out on her face as if she were a painted doll.

"Are you all right?" he asked her, a little shocked at the transformation. She just stared at him, her enormous eyes dark with memories.

"Oh, my dear, come along. This will never do. Let's have a cocktail."

He put his hand under her elbow and asked the way to the cocktail lounge. The music was coming from there and the sound of it was cheering. Tom settled Zara in an alcove seat at a table obviously designed for discreet flirtation.

When he returned with the drinks she had regained some of her natural warmth and colour. Though pale at the best of times, at least now her skin had lost its greenish tinge.

"Drink that. It's champagne and brandy. Do you good." He looked at her anxiously. "Are you all right?"

She sipped the drink, then smiled at him, a little tremulously. "Yes, I'm all right."

"What was wrong? I would never have brought you here if I'd thought …"

She put her hand lightly on his arm. "No, don't say that. I just faced some ghosts, that's all. I never realized how affected I could be. Coming back here, all the fear, all the horror, returned. I had forgotten the depth of my pain. Oh, Tom." She turned to him, her eyes naked in their expression of love and gratitude, and there was no way he could resent the look she gave him, or its implications. She was too guileless, too honest. "If you never do another thing for me in the whole of your life, know this – I suffered most brutally, I had forgotten how much. I was damaged, broken, as if someone had smashed me. And you mended me. You healed me. Thank you."

"Steady on." He was embarrassed before the intense straightforward gratitude. She laid a finger on his lips.

"No, don't. I know I embarrass you. The thing you did for me was very important, you see. It was a very big thing, and I sometimes forget that. If you try to minimize it, you minimize my pain. Do you see?"

"Yes. Yes I do. But remember …"

"Hush," she said, "I don't want to talk about it any more. I want to have a bath. Do you realize I never had a proper bath in Amsterdam? Do we have the bath-salts we bought in Paris? Well, I want to use handfuls. Extravagantly. I shall smell like a tart, so there! Then I'll wear my new Chanel. Then, my darling, I want you to buy me the most divine dinner. I want to pamper myself and feel like a princess. I want to exorcise the little waitress."

The next day she went to Prinsengracht. She had written to Frau Kettner to say she was coming to see her. She did not say exactly when as she did not know herself, but just to expect her. However, Frau Kettner was waiting for her, sitting in her front room window.

Zara had gone alone. Tom wanted to accompany her but she did not want him there. It would, perhaps, embarrass the good woman, make her self-conscious, Zara explained to him, and he stayed behind.

Nothing had changed. When Frau Kettner saw her through the window she hurried to the front door, beaming a welcome. She wrenched open the front door and wrapped the girl in her arms, hugging and kissing her and weeping copiously all the time.

"*Leibling, leibling, leibling*, let me look at you. Dirk, Dirk, she's come."

"Is Dirk still here?" Zara's voice was rough with emotion. "Oh, I did not think I should be so lucky ..."

"She is here," Frau Kettner shouted. "Dirk, she is here! But come inside. Come inside." She closed the door, drawing Zara into the well remembered parlour.

"He stayed in. Three days now he waits, afraid to miss you. He goes nowhere." She raised her voice again, calling, "Dirk! Dirk!"

Zara looked around. Everything was exactly as it had been when she left: polished surfaces; velvet hangings; the beaded lampshades; the pot plants; the ornaments and silver-framed pictures. There was the thunder of boots down the stairs and Dirk burst into the room. She was swung aloft and around and around, eliciting cries of, "Careful, Professor. Careful," from Frau Kettner.

It seemed as though Dirk or Zara must knock something over in their wild embrace.

"Hey!" When her feet touched the ground she held his face between her hands. "What's this I hear? Professor?"

He blushed and nodded, peering at her through his

296

spectacles. "Yes, I'm a teacher. Don't you remember? I wrote."

She remembered instantly and was ashamed. It had seemed unimportant in the context of her new life. Amsterdam, Dirk, Frau Kettner had seemed so far away. They became unreal and insubstantial against the fashionable glitter of Nice, and she had been so overwhelmed by doubts and uncertainties about Tom that she had barely registered Dirk's graduation. Now she was contrite but Dirk and Frau Kettner were so patently glad to see her that she could not feel guilty for long.

"When you live far away the achievements and tragedies and dramas of old friends are distant," Dirk said. "It is natural." He was saying it to make her feel better. She knew it was not true but the kindness in his eyes told her he forgave her all and only wanted her to be comfortable.

He continued. "Do not worry, Zara! Yes, now I teach at the University. I have a seat." He grinned widely. He was much plumper, she saw, his mop of soft brown curls as unruly as ever but slightly peppered with grey.

"We are very proud of him," Frau Kettner said.

"But you," he cried, holding her at arm's length and looking at her, "you look wonderful. No need to ask how you are. So elegant. A great lady. Isn't she, Frau Kettner?"

Frau Kettner smiled happily. "*Ja*. Beautiful. A real princess."

Zara stretched out her hands to both of them and they held each other, palm to palm.

"You never accepted my invitations," she said.

"Can you blame us?" Dirk asked. He was not apologizing or on the defensive; he was just stating the obvious. "We would be out of place. Uncomfortable with your grand friends. And you who are so kind would be uncomfortable for us. No, no, it is not our world. But it is good of you to come and see us."

"But I'd love to have you," Zara protested feebly.

297

"No. We go to Germany in a year or two. We plan a trip. A long one."

"Really? I'm going there now," Zara said.

Frau Kettner went to the door. "Let me get tea." She bustled out then poked her head back in. "Don't say anything interesting while I'm making the tea," she begged. "I don't want to miss anything."

"We won't, Frau Kettner," Dirk assured her. "And even if we do I'll tell you every word afterwards." He looked at Zara as Frau Kettner disappeared. "We talk about you often, dear Zara. You and Sasha."

There was a pause then she confided in him: "It's because of Sasha that I am going to Germany."

He frowned. "We heard nothing new. You obviously did."

She nodded and told him about the account and the withdrawals.

"You mean you need never have been poor?" He shook his head. "Fate is peculiar. But be careful or you might be badly hurt."

"How?" Zara asked though she knew the answer.

"He has rejected you for some reason known only to himself. He hurt you once. I saw, remember? I'd hate to see that again."

"Anything is better than not knowing," she said. "I want to hear his reasons. I deserve that at least."

Dirk shrugged. "Then I'll not try to stop you. But, remember, curiosity has destroyed many, from Pandora to the proverbial cat."

"Curiosity? Curiosity?" Frau Kettner came back into the room carrying a heavy tray laden with teapot and cups, sliced cake and *gebäck*. "And you talk of Sasha? What news?"

"We have heard that he is living in Berlin," Zara said.

"Ah, Berlin! How I miss it. But, does he wish to see you?"

"I don't really think so, Frau. I don't know. But I must see him."

"Leave well alone, I'd say. But if you must, you must. Here's your tea, Zara."

"Tom said that I must be prepared to be disappointed. You both tell me that and I understand. But, don't you see, it's a mystery that I want to solve?"

"Who is this Tom?" Frau Kettner's eyes twinkled shrewdly as she passed round a plate of cakes.

"He's a dear friend," Zara said, blushing, then amended. "No, that's not fair to you. He's the man I love."

She saw the flicker in Dirk's eyes. Regret? Loss? Then he beamed. "Congratulations! That's very good. There is someone you love."

Frau Kettner kissed the top of Zara's head. "Oh, it's good, good!" she cried. "Just what you needed."

They wanted to know more about him and her answers to their innocent questions were not reassuring.

"When will you marry?"

"Well, I'm not … he's not … you see …"

"Don't tell me he is married already?"

"No, of course not. Though he might as well be …"

Bit by bit the story of her relationship with Tom emerged. She realized how unsatisfactory it sounded to Dirk and Frau Kettner. She could see the realisation of the true situation dawn in their eyes and how they perceived Tom's character from her replies to their questions. They saw him as an irresponsible gambler who did not want to marry her. She tried to correct their impression but it was no use; perhaps, she thought, because it was the correct one. It irritated her and spoiled the happiness of the reunion.

They were too polite to criticise. They let the questions drop, unwilling to embarrass her further. The atmosphere was awkward when tea finished.

"Well, that's enough about me," Zara laughed a little nervously.

She did not like the picture of Tom that had emerged any more than they did. She wished with all her heart that she could have told her friends that she was engaged to be married. She even thought of lying, but a glance at their loving faces and trusting eyes made her ashamed of her desire to deceive.

"What about you?" she asked.

Frau Kettner talked of arthritic joints, her longed for trip to Berlin and the fact that the young people today had no manners.

"And you?" Zara asked Dirk. "Have you anyone yet?"

To her surprise he blushed and nodded. She felt that sinking feeling again, similar to the way she had felt when Dmitri got engaged. What did she expect the men who loved her to do when she refused them? Become monks? She thought she probably did.

Oh dear, what kind of woman am I? she asked herself, trying to smile and be happy for Dirk.

"Gerda Hauptmann. She is a lecturer in the University. Modern Languages." He beamed at Zara, his good-humoured moon face full of tenderness. "Ah, she is lovely! She comes from Bavaria, in the mountains near Innsbruck. She is kind and beautiful." His eyes grew misty. "She is so good to me. We plan to marry in the spring." He looked at Zara and she put her arms around him and embraced him.

"I'm so glad for you, Dirk. So glad. We'll always be friends though, won't we?"

He smiled at her. "Of course, *leibling*. Of course."

"And if ever you need me, you've got my address, you know where I am?"

He nodded and assured her that if ever he was in the South of France he would contact her, but she knew that they would seldom see each other, their lives were too far apart. This girl he loved, this Gerda, he would cherish. He would make her a cosy home and she would fill it with children. They would be mentally compatible, she thought, as well as physically, and they would laugh a lot. She did not know how she knew all this but she was sure that that was the kind of girl Dirk would pick for a wife. Frau Kettner said as much.

"She is perfect for him, Zara, a good girl, a bright girl, and she loves him very much. I will miss them when they marry."

Dirk looked at her fondly. "We will have to live here for a while, until I can afford something of our own. After that we will visit every week." And Zara knew he would keep his promise. He turned to her. "If ever you need us, Zara, we'll be here," he said. "Don't hesitate to call."

She knew he would keep that promise too. There seemed no more to be said so she left shortly afterwards.

She walked along the canal taking the old familiar route to the hotel. She stared at the turgid water and the sad drowning leaves that were being borne along willy-nilly. Like us, she thought. Like us. Did anybody have any real control over their lives? Even people like Dirk who seemed to choose more wisely than she did.

The hotel looked seedy to her now. She had thought it quite grand but compared to the Negresco and the Hotel du Cap it was a dump. She stared at its façade and sighed. Time had changed her.

Mevrou Kloof welcomed her with open arms.

"My dear Zara, it is good to see you again. Sit down and have a sherry."

She poured a glass of sweet sherry for Zara and sat back expectantly but there was little to say. She eyed Zara's clothes but did not ask her about them. Conversation proved difficult. Zara realised that they had little in common except a shared past. They talked of incidents that had happened when Zara was there. Meneer Van Daniken had been offered a better job in a bigger hotel and had accepted.

"I put in for his post," the housekeeper said. "I could easily have done it. I know how to run this hotel backwards.

301

I often stood in for the Meneer when he was ill or on holidays. But they couldn't see their way to letting me have the job."

"Why not?" Zara asked. Mevrou Kloof gave her a withering glance. "Why do you think? I am a woman, that's why. God, it makes me angry!" She gave Zara a shrewd glance. "But you wouldn't know anything about that," she said. "Lucky girl ... tell me what you are doing."

There was a deep bond between the two women, but the social gulf yawned. Zara's conversation was stilted because she was afraid of saying something that sounded like boasting, and Mevrou Kloof could not help but be envious of the beautifully dressed woman Zara had become.

She stayed only a short time, then left the hotel where she had worked so hard for so long. She walked away from it without a backward glance.

Chapter Seventeen

They left Amsterdam the next day. Her encounters with Dirk and Frau Kettner and particularly Mevrou Kloof had left Zara feeling an outsider. The conversation about Tom had opened her eyes and forced her to see him, however unwillingly, much more objectively than she cared to do. She had to face two facts: the first, that she was helplessly, hopelessly, passionately in love with him; the second, that he was far from being a good choice. In fact he was selfish and thought only of his own desires.

The thought gave her a headache. The happy, carefree mood that had blessed them in Paris and touched everything they had done with magic, was gone. They were silent and separate from each other. From the moment she had stood in the hotel in Amsterdam and felt the cold hand of the past clutch her heart she had harboured a premonition of disaster.

Tom seemed curiously nervous of her, as if she was a stranger he did not know how to handle. She supposed he had never seen her alone like this, without the powerful protection of the Rostovs. She must appear vulnerable and defenceless.

Berlin seemed to Zara a dark, depressing city and she did not like it.

"I die out of the sun," she said. They stayed in the Adlon, a hotel on the Unter den Linden. It was full of military. Tom said that you would think there was a war on. At dinner that night she said to him, "When I went to Nice for the first time, Tom, my heart lifted. I saw all that light, that sun, that clarity. I was warmed into life." She glanced at him to see if he was laughing at her but he looked at her seriously, his blue eyes steady.

"I felt the same. I was sick to death of the rain and the foggy gloom of England, especially in winter. When I came to the South of France I thought 'home' and I've stayed there ever since. I do know what you mean." He was emphatic. He glanced around the dining room. Under an enormous chandelier the mirrored room was full of light and the reflections of the guests in evening dress. It was an opulent scene. The women were jewel-laden and many of the men sported medals. The uniforms were seductive, Zara was thinking, when Tom said,

"They are imposing uniforms. They take themselves very seriously, don't they?" He sighed. "I'll be glad when our business is over. I'm uneasy here."

"I'm sorry," Zara found herself whispering, "I've dragged you into this."

"No, don't always take the blame. I offered. I wanted to come with you and I'm glad I did. I would not want you alone here, and the damndest thing is I don't know why."

She sipped her wine and said, "I'm sorry I've been so down. I don't know why either."

"I do." He smiled at her reassuringly. "You are going into your past. It's a frightening past, not a joyful one. Obviously you are apprehensive and scared. It's natural that you should be."

"But I shouldn't take it out on you."

"Dearest girl, I'm a big boy now. Don't worry about me. Just get what you have to do done, and return to the sun. It's your element. You are happy in the sun."

And then what? she thought. Back to making love at lunchtime. It would never be enough again. Not after these weeks of living with him. Not after Paris. She glanced up and saw him watching her. She wondered if he knew what she was thinking. So often he guessed her innermost thoughts.

"Let's have dessert," she said, smiling at him.

That night he came to her as usual but they did not speak. Zara tried to be gay but the laughter rang false. He was very gentle with her as they made love. She had to curb a desire to hurt him, scratch him, bite him, cause him pain. She had never wanted to do that before. She shuddered and thought of Anya, then of the Baron. Afterwards she clung to him.

"I'm frightened, Tom," she said.

"So am I a bit. These Nazis are a formidable bunch. We'll see Sasha tomorrow and then you will have your answers and we can go home."

Despite her lack of sleep Zara dressed carefully the next morning. Sasha would find her very changed. Would he recognise the smart fashionable woman she had become? Her hair was now in the thirties fashion, rolled up at the temples with soft curls in a cloud to her shoulders. He would remember her with all that heavy hair pinned up under a waitress's cap.

The address the bank had given her was in a very elegant district. They got a taxi from the hotel. Tom took her hand and held it in silence as they cruised through the streets. There seemed to be flags everywhere, huge swastikas on a red and black background, fluttering in the cold wind. She snuggled into her coat, hugging the fur around her ears.

"Oh, can't he hurry?" she cried.

"He's driving as fast as he can," Tom replied. "Calm down, Zara."

She was pulling at the fingers of her gloves and he covered her hands with his, steadying them.

The house was set behind high iron gates. The façade was of grey stone with pillared balconies, long windows, and a gravel arc before twin flights of steps leading to a heavy studded front door. They paid off their taxi, pushed the gates open and went up the short drive. The gravel crunched beneath their feet.

Zara went up one of the flight of stone steps to the huge double doors and rang the bell. She could hear no sound. Tom had sprinted up the steps opposite and now stood beside her. He was about to ring the bell again when the door opened.

The butler did not glance at Zara once. He looked only at Tom. She felt her stomach clench and her heart beat in sudden panic. She took Tom's hand furtively, trying to hide her gesture from the servant, feeling like a terrified juvenile.

The butler asked whom they wished to see. She told him in a quavering voice but the butler ignored her and still looked at Tom for an answer.

"Prince Sasha Vashenskov, please," he said.

"Prince Vashenskov. Yes, sir. Who shall I say wants him, sir?"

"Mr Tom Armitidge."

"This way, sir."

He led them across a vast marble hall. There were russet-coloured marble pillars and alcoves with exquisite marble statuary. He showed them into a panelled drawing room, curtained and carpeted in rich crimson. The furniture was of gilded walnut. There was a tapestry on the wall after a design by Boucher, a Savonnerie carpet, and a terra-cotta statue of Cerberus on a marble pedestal between the floor-length windows.

The butler picked up a crystal decanter.

"Sherry, sir?"

"Yes, thank you."

Tom nodded, met Zara's questioning eyes and shrugged.

She could not understand the magnificence of the place. She had envisioned Sasha in surroundings quite different from these. The grandeur was quite overwhelming, even to one used to luxurious houses. The butler presented their small crystal sherry glasses on a silver tray. He bowed to them and left the room, his movements slow and unhurried.

306

There was silence except for the ticking of an elegant French clock on the russet marble mantelpiece.

"Why didn't you give my name?" Zara asked in a whisper.

"So that he would not refuse to see you," Tom answered in his normal voice, looking at her with curiosity. She knew he thought her behaviour strange. She thought so herself and did not know why she was acting like this. She felt afraid and the house disturbed her. She looked at him in panic.

"What have I done?" she whispered. "I must be mad."

He shrugged and gave her a sympathetic smile.

"Have to go through it now," he said. "Matter of principle. Can't chicken out. Never forgive yourself if you did."

Neither of them heard his arrival. Zara simply turned and he was there. And she saw Anya.

Sasha was perhaps more beautiful than ever. The blond curls hugged his head, making him resemble a sculpture of Apollo. His blue eyes were startling, the colour of a midnight sky, but they were veiled, no welcoming smile in their depths. The cupid's bow curve of his mouth seemed petulant though the precisely angled bones of his face were exquisite.

He was beautifully clothed; his suit grey flannel pin-stripe, his shirt white silk, his tie the same blue as his eyes. He wore hand-made shoes shined to a brilliant polish and on one finger a gold signet ring. Tom in his tweed jacket and cavalry twill trousers looked almost shabby beside him, but he made the boy look a little flashy, a tiny bit outré, a little too perfect. Sasha lacked the casual nonchalance of the English gentleman. Zara decided that it was Anya's blood in him.

Then all the old affection overwhelmed her and she flung her arms around him, holding him tightly to her.

"Sasha, Sasha, Sasha," she cried, tears spilling down her face. She kissed his cheeks and touched his hair until she suddenly realised his lack of response. She held him at arm's length. "Sasha, what is it? Aren't you glad to see me?"

His face held the same withdrawn look.

"Zaroushka, why did you come here?"

"Oh, Sasha! Sasha darling, I'm your sister. I love you. Why wouldn't I come?"

The closed pale face was half turned away, presenting a perfect profile. "I made it plain ..." a slight hesitation " ... I thought you'd understand. I don't *want* to see you." The voice was cool as a mountain stream and it withheld something.

"Do you have a drink?" he resumed, his voice light and conversational, as if they were little-known guests who had called at an inconvenient time. Which they were in a way. He's holding something back, something he doesn't want his sister to find out, Tom thought. He speculated on what it might be and tried to catch Zara's eye. He knew what she must be suffering. He realised the devastating blow her brother's cold reception must be. She surprised him by challenging Sasha.

"Look at me."

He sighed. Long lashes fluttered over the blue eyes. "I'm sorry, Zara. I don't want to. All that is past."

"I'm your sister, for God's sake. That's not the past!" She sounded almost hysterical and Tom crossed the room to her.

"My half-sister," a calm voice replied.

"Come," Tom interrupted, "let us sit down and talk about it calmly." But Zara pushed him away.

"Let me alone. How could you, Sasha? How could you run away and leave me alone? Not knowing where you were." The anguish of that anxious time overwhelmed her again and filled her voice with pain. The young man blushed.

"I'm ... er ... sorry about that, Zaroushka. Very sorry. But you would have followed me, brought me back. I wanted to stop you." He looked up at her directly for the first time. "You always tried to control me. Keep me so close. I was stifled by your love."

He could not have said anything more devastating to her. He could not have chosen more cruel words. The cry that escaped her was agonised.

I do destroy those I love, she thought, the knife in her heart twisting. She felt old and very, very tired.

"I'm sorry, Zara. There, you see, I'm apologising all the time to you. You always made me feel guilty. I had no freedom. It was always what *you* wanted for us, your plans, your dreams, as if they were automatically the same as mine. And your plans were always the *right* ones."

The eyes flickered again. Tom thought of snows and glaciers and frozen wastes.

"There is another reason. I don't want you meddling ..."

Zara sat down abruptly.

"I don't want you to take all the blame on your own shoulders, Zara. You always do that, you know."

She flinched, the nerves in her face quivering. Tom had watched while expressions of naked fear and grief, rejection and pain, had crossed her face. Anyone else would have stopped, seeing her like this, but her brother continued.

"So you must hear the rest. You must hear it all so you will see it was not your fault. It was no one's fault." Sasha, unlike his sister, was cool and unruffled. Tom went to her side and put his hand on her shoulder. She did not look at him, however, concentrating on her half-brother, trying to understand what he was saying to her. He lit a cigarette, then looked at her through the smoke. The blue eyes glittered.

"I had to get away, and not just because you were smothering me with maternal love." Tom felt Zara flinch. The fragile bones of her body drew themselves inwards as if she had been hit.

"Don't you think enough's been said?" Tom asked, tightening his grip on the girl's shoulder. But she shook her head and seemed to straighten.

"No," she said, "I want to know everything."

This seemed to amuse the young man. He gave an incredulous little snort.

"I doubt it," he said, then his eyes met Tom's and he

shrugged. "All right," he said, "I am a homosexual. So! You see."

Zara shook her head back and forth, back and forth. Then, with a puzzled expression on her face, she said, "So?"

"Don't you understand?" Sasha showed emotion for the first time. "I am a homosexual."

"Why on earth should that matter?"

"Well," he shrugged again, "you've certainly changed. I thought you'd have a fit."

"Who cares what you do in your private life." Zara seemed puzzled, "We have friends like that in France. We also have promiscuous ones. What difference does it make?"

Sasha looked confused. She's thrown him, Tom thought. He's spent years underestimating her understanding and compassion and now he does not know what to do. And yet there was something else, a final veil of secrecy behind those pale expressionless eyes.

Zara seized Sasha's hand and pressed it. "Oh God, is that all that's kept us apart? You're not harming anyone. I don't expect you corrupt the young? Unless you do, I don't see that it is anyone's business except yours. I certainly can't get worked up about it. That is unless ..." she bit her lip "... there is unkindness or cruelty."

Sasha looked uncertainly at his sister. Tom thought there was little resemblance between them. The blond boy with his ice blue eyes and his curly golden hair, his choir boy looks, was totally dissimilar to the thin dark-haired Zara whose black velvet eyes dominated her elfin face. As if to confirm what Tom was thinking Sasha said, "I'm afraid I'm very like my mother, Zara. There was something else too." For some reason he looked at Tom. "Money," he said.

"Money?" Again she was puzzled.

"Yes, sister, money. I had to have it, you see. I was incapable of struggling and pennypinching like you, Zara. I did not have your courage, your independence, call it what you will. How I loathed slaving in that seedy hotel." His face was animated now, full of a petulant fury. "I used to listen to you in disbelief when you walked home with me or when you talked in our bedroom. I hated sharing it with you. I wanted to be alone. On and on and on you went! You never stopped. Talking *at* me." He was pacing the room, up and down, in quick, jerky movements. Now Tom could see Zara in him.

"You never told me," she said, looking at him in horror. "You could have said."

"You never listened! I tried once. You told me not to be silly. That we had no alternative. I knew we had. But you never asked for my opinion. You always said, 'When we'. You took it for granted that I thought the same as you, wanted the same things as you, had the same goals. But, you see, I didn't. I didn't *want* to struggle on in squalor. 'We'll get there some day, Sasha, on our own merits,' you'd say. Well, I didn't want to get anywhere on my own merits. 'We'll find the Rostovs, Sasha,' you would say. I didn't want to find them. I didn't *know* them. You forgot I'd never met them. Just because you loved them did not mean I had to."

"My mother used to laugh at Vassily Rostov. She called him the 'dithering man'. I knew that Aunt Sonya might not be too keen on me. But you never thought of that. And that gruesome hotel." He gave a shrill laugh. "You were *proud* to work in that foul place with the smell of vegetables, of stale perspiration, of a hundred bodies sweating in the night."

Her face was pale and cold and her lips felt stiff. She had never felt so shocked. Not even when her father had been shot. She knew it was because she recognised that what he said about her was true. She had never asked him what he wanted. She had talked at him, taking it for granted that he wanted what she wanted. A chill slid over her body, making her skin prickle. Wrong, wrong, wrong again. How could she have been so obtuse, so crassly unaware of another's needs?

He stood before her now, accusing her, and she saw for the first time little things about him she had not noticed before.

The almost girlish beauty of his face. The feminine cast of his features. The cool, selfish, beautiful eyes; no compassion in their ice-blue depths, no laughter, only mockery. The small inward-slanting teeth and petulant mouth. The soft, smooth hands with their manicured nails. She remembered now always being vaguely aware that he took meticulous care of his hands. She remembered too how he had hated working. But she had always brushed aside his complaints. She took a deep shuddering breath and proudly tilted back her head. Tom's heart went out to her.

"Well then," she said, after a pause, glancing up at him, surprised by the look in his eyes, "I'm sorry, Sasha. I suppose there's nothing more to be said. We will go and leave you in peace."

He had gone to stare out of the window, his back to them. Tom realised that Zara's body was shaking though she was trying her hardest to control it. He took her arm.

"Can't we be friends?" she asked, her voice steady.

"Oh, yes. I think fondly of you," he said.

How cold it sounded. How bleak.

It had begun to rain. It pattered sharply on the window-panes, a hard tattoo.

"Can't we meet sometimes?" She knew she shouldn't ask, that she was only going to be hurt. Sasha had made his position crystal clear. She could feel Tom's hand signalling restraint but she could not help herself.

Sasha turned and faced them. "No, I don't think so. That would not be a good idea. While you idle your time away in the South of France, great things are happening here."

She heard Tom's disbelieving exclamation of "Good, God!" and looked at Sasha as if he were a stranger.

She knew now she would have to let him go forever. He was no longer the little brother she had adored. Had he ever been who she thought he had been? She did not know. She felt only the sorrow of a great loss. She was parting forever with her little love, the boy who had shared the hardest part of her life with. She stared at him, seeing a stranger. He seemed uncomfortable under her gaze. "I think you'd better go now."

She rose. Tom's hand fell from her shoulder.

"Yes, I suppose we had better," she said sadly. Then, tentatively, "But you haven't told me where you went … you had no money."

"Does it matter?" he asked. "Now?"

She supposed it did not yet she would have liked to know. Sasha looked at his watch. He seemed uncomfortable, Tom thought. The icy façade was cracking slightly. He glanced down into the street.

"Go now, please," he said, his voice urgent.

At that moment there was the sound of the front door slamming to, then the murmur of voices and firm footsteps in the marble hall.

Zara said, "Goodbye, Sasha. I hope you'll be happy. I'm sorry I did not listen. Things might have been different if I had not been so selfish."

Sasha looked very pale now. Perhaps after all he did care, Tom thought.

"It's useless to speculate on that now," said Sasha, glancing nervously at the door.

It opened. Tom looked at the man framed there, his sentence of greeting dying on his lips.

Zara cried out, whimpered an agonised animal-like sound, and Tom knew at once who this was. He felt a surge of rage overwhelm him, an immediate desire to kill, to wound. He felt Zara's body sag against his and said fiercely, "Don't faint. Stand up." She obeyed him automatically, and he saw the man in the doorway assimilate the little scene before him and smile.

"Well, well, well," he said smoothly. Tom watched, fascinated, as the Baron took charge.

"My run-away wife, and a friend." His eyes flickered over Tom. "English, by the look of him," he said, his voice unbearably arrogant. "Decadant. Empire in decline." He smiled again. They were well-matched, he and Sasha, thought Tom. There was an extraordinary attraction about the older man, a force of character that could not be denied.

The Baron strolled over to the table and poured himself a sherry. Sasha was still at the window, looking out. Tom glanced at Zara. She stood trance-like, in shock, pale as a sheet, her terrified eyes fixed on the tall man with his back to her.

"Have you come back to me, my dear?" The Baron turned and looked at her mockingly.

"Don't be silly," Tom said coldly. "You know very well she has not."

The Baron raised his eyebrows. "I don't remember being introduced."

"Mr Tom Armitidge, so Portland said. I haven't really spoken to him, I'm afraid." Sasha's voice was sullen.

"Oh, my dear, you are going to be peeved about all this, aren't you?" the Baron said to Sasha, laughing, and Tom suddenly understood Zara's fears and nightmares of the past. This man was frightening. He enjoyed playing with people. He liked to hurt. The saturnine face was full of arrogance and malice. He looked as if he thought he owned the world.

The brother and sister, Tom saw, stared at him in fascinated horror. There was silence in the room, broken only by the sound of the rain. Sasha suddenly moved. He went to the Baron's side as if to align himself with Klaus Hoffen von Eldrich.

"Well, Zara? I'm still waiting for your answer."

She did not move but stood as if turned to stone, her eyes filled with fear.

"Come now. Lost your voice? You were always such a fierce little thing." He turned to Tom. "She used to fight so. Tried to kill me. Did she tell you?"

"Leave her alone," Tom said. It sounded feeble, he

realised, but no one paid any attention to him. Sasha and
Zara were both watching the Baron intently. He was smiling
at Zara, thoroughly enjoying himself.

"I looked for you but you covered your tracks very well.
Then when I found you, or rather had you followed, Sasha
came back to me. He advised me against trying to force you."

She drew in her breath. The man in the raincoat! His
watchful figure returned to her vividly.

It felt extraordinary to be standing once again in the same
room as the Baron. He seemed smaller to her. Over the years,
in her mind, he had grown in stature, become ogre-like. she
had forgotten he was actually handsome, remembering only
the violence, the brutality. She remembered her fear, the
terror she had lived with for years until that night when she
had walked into her brother's room and seen him in her
husband's arms.

She had jumped to the conclusion that Sasha had found the
Baron's advances as disgusting as she did. Had she been
wrong about that too? Was he, even then, enjoying the
experience? No, she thought, not then. His little face had
been so piteous. She stared at them both, mesmerised. No
wonder Sasha had not contacted her.

The Baron meanwhile was staring at her appraisingly.
"You have matured, my dear. You have become beautiful.
Come here," he commanded, his eyes narowing.

She nearly obeyed. Staring back at him as if hypnotised she
took a step. Unbelievably, she moved towards him.

But Tom put his hand on her arm. His clasp was firm and
warm and real. It stopped her, shook her from her mesmerised state.

"Stay here, Zara," he said firmly.

The Baron frowned at him. "Oh," he said drawing the
word out, "very proprietorial. But you have no place here.
She is my wife." He said it softly. He had cocked his head to
one side and Zara had the impression that his every nerve and
faculty was focussed on her.

315

"No she is not." Tom's voice was equally quiet.

"She is my wife and will stay here." The Baron said it firmly and coldly. "Did you, like your brother, get tired of poverty? Did you decide …"

"She is not your wife." Tom's voice was equally firm and cold, but it was lighter and sweetly reasonable.

The Baron looked at him a moment, then shrugged and went to the desk.

"This is a farce," he said. "Why is everything you do so melodramatic, Zara? I have the marriage certificate here. It's perfectly legal."

"She was underage," Tom said.

The Baron turned, holding the paper in his hand. "Not in Russia," he said, an edge to his voice. He was becoming angry.

Tom did not know whether it was true or not; whether in Russia she could have been married so young. But he could not let that stop him. He had to go on. He clutched at another straw. "Nevertheless, you tricked her into it."

"Is that what she says?" The German laughed confidently. "I have witnesses who will say she walked willingly up the aisle."

"You said I had to. To escape. You said …" Zara looked wildly at Tom, horror dawning in her eyes. "He can't make me, can he, Tom? He can't keep me." Her voice had risen to a scream.

"Leave her alone." Sasha's voice was loud but he sounded reluctant to speak. Klaus glanced at him.

"You did not tell me you knew where she was," he said to the boy lightly, but there was a threat in the tone. "Didn't you want to share me, my dear?"

"You bastard!" Tom cried, disgusted, then suddenly sprang at the Baron and tore the paper from his hand. He threw it on the fire. They all stared at the grate, at the scarlet tongues of flame licking the yellowing certificate.

Two spots of red appeared on the Baron's cheeks.

"That was foolish," he said, his coal-black eyes glittering. "Now you listen to me. She," he pointed to Zara, "is my wife. That foolish gesture availed you nothing. She stays here. That certificate can be re-ordered from the church."

"I doubt it," Tom said emphatically.

"And I say it can. The church is in the wilds. It has remained unscathed. I can have her arrested for attempted murder." The Baron's rage was beginning to show.

"Don't be foolish. You seem to forget that there has been a revolution in Russia and a world war in Europe. No one is that interested in what happened long ago and it would be almost impossible to prove."

"But I can and I will." The Baron was losing his self-possession. His rage was terrifying to see.

"I would advise against it," Tom said calmly. As the Baron's urbane pose slipped, Tom gained in quiet strength and assurance. Zara looked at him, grateful for the confidence that emanated from him. The belief grew in her that he might be stronger than the Baron, that he could save and protect her. She loved him more in that moment than she had ever done before. She was filled with pride that he was her champion, and amazement that he was so unconcerned by the man who had terrorised her. To her the Baron would always be the epitome of evil. Now, here in this imposing room, the devil was being routed by her god.

"Listen to me. I know a little of what is happening in Germany today," Tom's voice was conversational, pleasant even, and the Baron watched him in growing fury. "I can read between the lines, Baron. Of course, I am an outsider, but one thing I am tolerably sure of is that your relationship with Prince Vashenskov would cause a scandal if it were to become public knowledge here."

The Baron frowned as Tom continued, "Zara is *not* married to you, understand? She never has been. She never attempted to kill you, though I feel sure most judges would find her conduct understandable if she had tried to murder

317

you after what you had done to her! I want you to know that
if you try to contact her or cause her trouble of any sort, I
shall take you to court in any country you care to name.
Even here in Berlin. I'll dispute the marriage, I'll bring her
age and state of mind into it, and your lies about why she
had to marry you in the first place. Another thing – I trust
that the Prince would not go on to the stand and tell lies
about his sister?" He looked enquiringly at Sasha who shook
his head.

"I wouldn't go to court," he said, and smiled maliciously.
"Klaus, you seem to have met your match."

"If I have to, I'll plaster your behaviour across every
paper in Europe," Tom continued calmly. "I will speak
openly of your liaison with the Prince. I will ruin you.
Society will close its doors. And I guess that little man whom
you all think so highly of here will be disgusted. From what I
have heard he is not renowned for broadmindedness." He
turned to Sasha. "I apologise, Prince Vashenskov. I would
hate it to seem that I am blackmailing you.

"I do not presume to censure you. It is just that I will not
have Zara suffer any more, and I will use any method in my
power, quite ruthlessly, to prevent that."

"You are an English gentleman and you would not want
to be involved in scandal," the Baron said, but there was no
real conviction in his voice. "Mud sticks."

Tom looked at him, an amused smile on his face. "You
don't know me, Baron. I have been involved in quite a few
scandals. I am a black sheep, a gambler who cares little for
his reputation. You, sir, I can see, are formed from a
different mould. Appearances count with you. For your own
sake, don't take me on."

There was a pause. Rain spattered furiously against the
windows. The fire crackled in the grate. Sasha looked out
into the street. They could not see his face but his shoulders
drooped.

It must be difficult for him, Zara thought, her heart racing

318

with excitement and hope. She would never fear Klaus Hoffen von Eldrich again. She still hated him, could hardly bear to be in the same room with him, but she need never be afraid of him again.

Defeated, the Baron snarled at them in fury. "Get out of here. Get out!"

Tom took Zara's arm and they made for the door. Then she looked back over her shoulder at Sasha. There was something so forlorn about him she ran back and hugged him.

"If ever you need me, I'll be there," she whispered.

She did not know whether he had heard her. He made no move to detain or follow her and she was forced to leave him, a more or less willing captive of the nightmare figure who had robbed them both of their precious innocence.

"Get out and leave us," the Baron muttered, his face averted.

Zara took Tom's arm and they left the room, closing the door quietly behind them.

Chapter Eighteen

In the taxi on the way to the Adlon, Zara glanced at Tom. He was frowning.

"Are you angry?" she asked.

"Of course I am," he said, outraged. "How dare he behave like that? It's just not on."

The English understatement amused and delighted her. They did not speak again until they reached the hotel. When they got to their room he said, "I want a bath. I feel dirty."

Overwhelmed with gratitude she wanted to thank him but did not know how to express herself without irritating him.

She sat on the bed, thinking over what her brother had said. He had accused her of precisely that characteristic that Tom had found annoying in her: possessiveness. She realised that Sasha had taken away a lot of her new found confidence. Up till then, she had believed she had chosen an especially quirky lover; that he had an exceptionally free spirit that she had somehow to accommodate. Now she began to see that this might not be true, she did not know what to do or how exactly to behave.

Tom came out of the bathroom, towelling himself.

"Let's get out of here," he said, and going to the wardrobe began pulling out their clothes. "Come, Zara, pack this stuff, will you? Berlin is not a healthy place to be."

She smiled at him. "Oh, I agree. Let's go at once. Home to Nice."

He kissed her. "No. Paris, I think," he said softly. "Oh, I

can't resist you when you look so like a helpless little girl."
He kissed her again and laid his finger on her lips as she
opened them to speak. "Shush, darling. Don't say a word. I
don't need to be thanked. I understand how you feel.
Probably more than you realise. God, what a man! You did
not exaggerate, my dear. I want to keep you safe from him
and the best way to do that is to marry you. We'll get
married in Paris." He kissed her lightly on the forehead.
"Now hurry and pack. I'll throw on some clothes and fix up
things at the desk. Goddamn city! Can't wait to leave."

She could not believe her ears. He *had* said they'd marry,
hadn't he? Or was it a trick of hearing? Had she
misunderstood? No, he had said he was marrying her. She
could not imagine anything so unexpected, so bizarre. She
wanted to laugh and cry at the same time. She was afraid
something might happen to stem the tide of joy that flooded
through her. She was afraid he would change his mind.

Suddenly her world was bright, bright, bright, and she,
like Tom, wanted to leave this sinister city. She galvanized
herself into action and began to pack. Tom hurried through
the bedroom on his way to the desk.

"Be up in a moment," he said, and she had to hold her
impatience in check, pack the cases and wait as calmly as she
could. She looked out of the hotel window. A long phalanx
of red swastika-embellished flags lined the other side of the
street. Zara shivered. She saw in her mind's eye her brother,
pale and beautiful as a statue of Apollo and almost as cold
and unfeeling. She saw the Baron, swaggering, attractive
and evil and remembered the fear he had inculcated in her.
He had instilled in her the totally erroneous idea he was a
superman, powerful and indestructible. But Tom, her
darling Tom, had crossed swords with him and won, and
now they were to be married in Paris of the light, bright sky.
Paris of the romantic cafés. Paris where she had felt instantly
at home.   She did not worry about the psychology behind
Tom's proposal. It did not bother her that it might have been

said on an impulse that he might later regret. She only knew that quite unexpectedly her dream had come true.

Above all she would avoid being posessive she vowed. She had learned how that terrible weakness of hers could destroy love. She would hold Tom to her lightly, so lightly, with only the silken threads of those words: 'We'll get married in Paris'.

It did not even occur to her to regret the wedding she had dreamed of in the Russian Church in Nice with the Rostovs there, Nina as her bridesmaid and Uncle Vassily giving her away. She could not have everything and she already had so much more than had ever seemed possible.

When Tom came back she restrained herself from running straight to his arms.

"I've booked a sleeper on the 10 o'clock out of here," he said.

"It means we shall have to eat downstairs in the dining room, which means dressing. That all right?"

"Yes, my darling."

"I hate having to wait until then. This place oppresses me.

"We're going straight to Paris?" she asked tentatively. "And ... er ... we'll get married there?"

He glanced at her, smiling and nodding. "I know what you're thinking," he said, raising one eyebrow. "You're dying to ask why I changed my mind."

She shook her head. "No, my darling. It's enough that you have."

He sat beside her on the bed and took her hand between his own. "Listen, Zara, I don't know why I did." He smiled ruefully. "No one is more surprised than I am. But, dash it, you don't seem able to manage your life, do you? When I saw you facing that beast you looked so ... helpless. I thought of how you had suffered. I thought of how I love you. I knew I could not leave you out of my life ever again. It's that simple. Now let us get ready to go downstairs and eat. I'm starving and we have a long journey ahead of us."

She prepared carefully for dinner that night. She wore a new cream satin dress she had bought in Paris. It was the latest shape, clinging and cut on the bias. She wore pearls around her throat and the earrings that Sonya had given her long ago in Russia.

They were a striking pair when they entered the dining room later that evening. The hotel was full of military with their polished boots, their gold braid and medals. The food was excellent; the Adlon's guests dined well. There was an orchestra playing and the smoke of cigars and cigarettes drifted up in grey clouds towards the chandeliers. Zara drank a little too much champagne and felt tipsy. For a while she felt happier than she had ever been before, despite the shocks of the afternoon. Towards the end of dinner though she grabbed Tom's hand. Her naturally pale face had turned chalk-white, paler than the pearls at her throat.

"Look, Tom."

He followed her gaze towards the entrance. The Baron stood there in the full uniform of a Colonel. It was a glamorous uniform and it suited him. His height and the monocle he wore made him the most distinguished-looking man present. The air of superiority he had temporarily lost in his meeting with Tom had returned a hundredfold. Heads turned in his direction. Beside him stood Sasha, willowy and graceful, impeccably groomed, very beautiful in his evening clothes. He was languidly smoking a cigarette, the smoke curling into light blue eyes as remote as a dreamer's.

Tom patted her hand. "It's only the Baron and your half-brother. Do we want to greet them or not?" he asked her lightly.

She caught his mood. Her heart had stopped for a moment but now it quickly resumed its normal pace. The Baron was, after all, simply another diner at the Adlon.

He had seen them and stood stiffly, staring at their table.

"I think it would be polite, don't you?" she said, and giggled.

They bent their necks in unison, a graceful acknowledgement of the Baron's presence. He returned it. Sasha did not move. He seemed to be physically present, mentally elsewhere.

The waiter waved to the new arrivals, obviously having procured them a table, and they disappeared down the crowded dining room.

Zara was able to turn back to Tom, almost unconcerned by the distanced confrontation.

They finished their meal, drank their coffee and smoked a cigarette. Neither felt like talking. The day had been a long and tiring one, both mentally and physically. Zara was trying to assimilate her new feelings and Tom was mentally checking they had everything for the journey. Their silence was companionable. Looking at Zara, he suddenly leaned over and touched her face.

"I love you," he said, "you're beautiful. I don't think I could bear it if anything happened to you." Then, before she could react, he looked at his watch. "Come along, darling, we must leave."

He put his arm on her shoulder as they left the room. At the entrance he turned to tip the *maître d'* and Zara looked back, her eyes raking the room.

She saw them at a table in an alcove near the back. Sasha was standing. His face had lost its remote expression. She could see even at this distance that it was red and twisted, and he was shouting. His mouth was open, his expression ugly. The Baron was glancing to right and left, obviously embarrassed.

Tom touched her arm and they left. In the foyer he asked the bell boy to get him a taxi. Their luggage lay piled beside the desk. Tom stood behind her, draping her chinchilla wrap over her shoulders.

"We'll be sleeping on the train," he said. "You can change then."

He hugged her, kissing her hair lightly. She smiled,

glancing towards the door where the bell boy was signalling. "Your Taxi, Herr Armitidge."

As she smiled she saw Sasha come out of the dining room. He was almost running and did not seem to notice her.

"Sasha, Sasha! Are you all right?" She caught his arm. He turned and looked at her, his eyes glazed. Then he shook his head and his eyes cleared. She was shocked by the expression on his face. He was almost unrecognisable.

"Sasha. Oh, Sasha," she whispered, still holding his arm.

His face crumpled and suddenly he looked like her little brother again. He leaned his forehead on her fur-clad shoulder, sighed deeply then looked up at her. His eyes were focussed now, and despairing. He leaned over and kissed her cheek.

"It's better you forget you ever had a brother," he said, then to Tom: "Take care of her, eh?" And walked away.

She made as if to follow him but Tom restrained her. As Sasha reached the entrance, he turned and gave her a little half wave.

"I love you," she called after him. "If you ever need me ..." He nodded gravely, then he was gone.

"He'll catch cold. He'll get wet. He has no coat on," she said.

"That is not your business now," Tom said firmly. "Come along, my dear, we don't want to miss that train."

He glanced around the opulent foyer. "Personally I can't wait to leave Berlin."

They were married in Paris in a civil ceremony. They had their wedding breakfast in bed at the Ritz, stuffing themselves with caviar and drinking Dom Perignon. They teased one another, made love, and Zara felt closer to Tom than she ever had before. The visit to Berlin had forged a bond between them that hitherto had not existed.

"My past is over. Buried. No, not buried ... exorcised," she told him, standing before him in their room, arms over

326

her head, wearing peach *crêpe-de-chine* cami-knickers trimmed with fine ecru lace, with her tumbling hair and pale skin, Tom thought she looked like an Art Nouveau figurine. He reached out and pulled her to him, kissing her. She wrapped herself around him.

"I'm so happy," she cried, kissing him back. "So happy, my darling. Nothing can spoil this."

He gently detached her from him.

"Oh, Zara, don't try to – hell, how can I say it? Don't try to insure us against the downs we will have. Please don't. Don't try …"

"To possess you?" she asked, and before he could reply: "No, I won't, I promise."

"I was not going to say that," he said, his eyes narrowing. "I simply don't want you turning me into a hero. I'm not, you know. I'm just an ordinary chap who doesn't want to be looked on as …"

She threw herself across him, laughing, spilling champagne. "I won't. I promise I won't."

"You smell of fruit," he said, burying his face in her neck. "Ripe, sun-kissed fruit."

Zara had written to the Rostovs. When it was time to return to Nice, she was a little apprehensive. Would Sonya be angry with their secrecy?

She was not. She couldn't have been more understanding. "How wise of you both," she said, greeting them, holding them at arm's length. "It's put paid to all the gossip. You no longer have to explain or make excuses. Well, my dears, no need to ask you how marriage suits you. You look glowing." She kissed Tom on both cheeks then drew Zara into a warm embrace.

"Vassily, come and see. Tom and Zara are home."

He came hurrying from his study. "Zara, welcome. Congratulations! Oh, it is good to see you. We have missed you, my dear." There were tears in his eyes and she felt her

327

own fill as she kissed his cheeks. She noticed that his skin was clammy and his colour unhealthy.

'You have been smoking too many cigars, Uncle,' she gently reproved him.

"Good to have you back," he kept murmuring as he looked at her lovingly. "Come, let me kiss you again. This house, I say to Sonya, is not the same without our darling Zara."

"Come, you're in time for tea," she said.

They all went into the shuttered living room. It was cool and pleasant. Sonya looked beautiful that day, Zara thought, and Vassily made her laugh. He fussed around like a puppy trying to please its master. Occasionally Zara noticed that Sonya shushed him as a mother might a naughty child.

"Vassily, get Nina, there's a dear. Tell her Zara and Tom are home."

"Yes, my dear, at once. At once, my love." And he ran to do her bidding. As he hurried out of the room, Zara smiled contentedly. How wonderful to be 'Tom and Zara'. How blissful to be a couple, to be acknowledged as a pair.

"How wise you were to get married without fuss," Sonya said over tea. "Weddings can become circuses."

She sighed, tilting the samovar and holding the cup carefully beneath the spout to allow the hot liquid to fill it.

"We have news of our own, Zara," said Sonya as Vassily re-entered the room, nodding his head and rubbing his hands together gleefully.

"Oh, Aunt, what news?" Zara looked from one to the other.

"Nina and Chuck became officially engaged when you were in Paris."

"Oh, nothing could please me more. What lovely news!"

"As long as you don't all go off and leave us," Vassily said a little plaintively.

"I am trying to keep Nina's wedding plans within the

328

bounds of good taste but she and her father seem intent on putting on an almost vulgar show." Sonya cast her eyes up to the ceiling. "I keep trying to put the brakes on, but you know what Nice is like."

Tom laughed. "Indeed I do! They'll turn anything into a *festa*. It's the Italian in them."

"But when is it to be?" Zara asked.

Sonya sighed. "Spring," she said. "We have the whole winter before us, yet to talk to Nina you would think it was tomorrow." She sipped her tea and smoothed the folds of her cyclamen crêpe dress. "But let me look at you," She smiled at Tom who looked suddenly like a little boy, then at Zara. "You both seem very happy. I cannot tell you how pleased we are for you."

"And I thought you might be angry."

"God heavens, Zara, why? Of course we are not."

Nina rushed in like a tornado, displacing everything in her passage. Vassily skipped out of her way, a magazine fell to the floor, Zara and Tom rose and she hurled herself at them.

"Oh, Zara, Tom! Oh, how lovely – Mr and Mrs Armitidge. How happy I am for you both! Do you realize how lucky you both are?" They all began to laugh. Her exuberance was so like her father's, Zara thought; their emotions so near the surface, the desire to please so obvious. Except that there seemed to be an edge of pain in Vassily's every expression. She made a promise to herself to ask if he were in trouble; perhaps he had been gambling and was in too deep. She would check when she got the chance.

The conversation became desultory. In a momentary lull, Sonya asked, "And Sasha? What of your brother?"

"He's well," Tom said calmly, "and living in Berlin."

Sonya looked at him with brows raised. "I see," she said dryly. She would have left the subject there but Vassily intervened. "Why then did he not want to see Zara?"

Tom cleared his throat and Vassily glanced at Sonya to ensure he had not been indiscreet. She ignored him and said to her niece, "You can talk about that or not, as you please, but later. Anyone for more tea?"

Nina stood and collected the cups as required while Sonya refilled them. When the little ceremony was finished she looked at Tom. "Where will you live?" she asked.

Zara glanced at her husband uncertainly. They had not discussed this; at least she had not yet had the courage to broach the subject.

"Why, in the villa in Saint-Paul," Tom said as if it were an obvious choice. Zara's heart sank. Sonya glanced at her, saw her expression and the struggle not to protest.

"Nonsense," she said briskly. "I haven't seen it but I am sure it is not at all suitable for Zara."

An expression of annoyance creased Tom's forehead. "I'm sure it's perfectly suitable," he said coldly.

"And I'm sure it is not," Sonya was firm. "Start as you mean to go on, Zara. You cannot be stuck out in the backwoods. You must have a nice apartment here in Nice. All your wife's friends are here, Tom. You must not isolate her up there in the hills if you mean to keep her happy."

Tom seemed to be grudgingly acquiescent. Zara sat fearfully, hopeful that her aunt's calm logic would win the day. She said nothing.

"She'll be hanging on your every move, Tom, otherwise," Sonya said astutely. "I know I would. All alone up there. Why, you'd have to take her everywhere you went. You could not expect her to remain up there all by herself, especially in the evenings. And what about a servant?" she continued relentlessly. "Surely you don't expect her to do the housework? You'll never find anyone who is any good to work for you up there. And even if you did, they would be on top of you. No, it's impossible. Don't you think?"

Tom gave in with good grace, much to Zara's relief. He knew when he was beaten, he said. Zara, morbidly nervous of upsetting him, was very grateful to her aunt. Now that she was married to Tom she wanted to give him no cause for regret.

They all looked around as Dmitri arrived, clasped Zara in his arms and shook Tom's hand.

"Nice to have you back, cousin," he said, kissing her cheek. She felt the almost forgotten surge of love for this most precious cousin. She always would, she supposed. Not as she loved Tom, not possessively, not fiercely, but with the closeness of a common heritage, a shared past, of knowing he loved her no matter what she did or said. And the certain knowledge that he was her friend. "I took Lucinda home. Her mother wants her for some fitting or other." He glanced at Zara. "You girls! At least Tom here had the sense to contrive a quiet wedding. Wonderful, Tom, how did you manage it?"

"Dmitri, darling, have some tea."

"I'd love some, Mother." Then he turned to Zara. "Lucinda and I have fixed a date."

She smiled. In her happiness with Tom she had only the best wishes for her cousin.

"Yes, I'm stuck with Lady Abercrombie's plans. She is hell-bent on breaking the bank and mortgaging the family heirlooms to give Lucinda a 'splendid send-off', as she puts it. Mama, here, is determined that Nina will have the most elegant wedding the Riviera has ever seen." He lifted his hand as Sonya was about to interrupt. "Now don't bother to deny it, Mama. No one here will believe you. Here we both are, lambs to the slaughter. Or sacrificial, I suppose. How did you avoid it, Tom? That's what I want to know."

He simply laughed and did not reply. Dmitri carried on, "Mama, you'll have to pray that Chuck's parents and friends don't spoil it all for you by being too casual. Americans tend to be. They don't like to dress up like you, dearest. How did Chuck put it, let me see … 'I hope you understand, ma'am, my folks are simple people, not sophisticated at all.' Oh dear!"

"Dmitri, I told you not to speak about Chuck like that," Nina screamed. "I'll kill you. Your soppy little Lucinda has not a thought of her own in her empty head. It's all 'Mama this' and 'Mama that',"

"How dare you speak of the woman I love in that ..."

Sonya raised her hands. "Hush, you pair! What will Tom and Zara think of you? It's infantile to speak like that. Little Lucinda is a sweet girl. I can only hope, Nina, you make Chuck so delightful a wife. And as for Chuck's folks – I mean family – well, I'm not in the least worried. Except about the Russian Orthodox service which I hope they'll not object to."

"I'm sure they'll love it," Vassily said firmly. "They are fine people to have brought up a young man as pleasant and good as Chuck is."

"Papa, what a nice thing to say." Nina blew him a kiss.

"What were you discussing when I came in?" Dmitri asked Sonya.

"An apartment for Tom and Zara," she replied. "I'm determined they'll live here in Nice. I've got to persuade Tom to let her stay near us for we love her so." She smiled at him. "It's no use, Tom, I'm determined."

Sonya won and the next few days were spent looking for a suitable apartment. Nina was thrilled to have Zara home. She loved to share her thoughts and feelings with her cousin, whereas Zara seldom confided more than generalities to her. Zara knew that Nina was not a deep girl. She was uncomplicated. She loved Zara and looked upon her as her closest friend but she did not understand her in the least.

"How exciting it must have been, running away to Paris to get married."

"But we didn't ..."

"Of course you did! I don't blame you at all, Zara." Nina's plump and pretty face was pink with excitement. "I would invent all sorts of excuses to get Chuck to put a ring on my finger. Mama thought Tom was the perennial bachelor."

Zara nodded, smiling. Let her think what she pleased.

"Stil, I'm glad we don't have to run off. I want the biggest wedding Nice has ever seen. That will show them." Her mouth became a hard line.

"Show who?" Zara asked.

"Oh, those cats who say I'm too plump." Nina stuck out her bottom lip petulantly. "Those awful old harridans and gossips who say Chuck is marrying me for my title. To show off back in the USA. It's not true, Zara. It's just not true. He really loves me." She looked at her cousin, her blue eyes swimming.

"Of course he does, Nina. Anyone can see that. In any event, you surely don't believe those gossipy old bats. Jealous, all of them. More to be pitied than anything else. There now, dear, don't cry."

"Oh, Zara, sometimes I get so nervous about leaving Europe, even though Papa says there is going to be a war. I'll be so far away from everyone. But I love Chuck, I love him very much. So what can I do?"

Zara put her arms around her cousin, not answering, giving silent comfort in the warmth of her embrace.

After a moment when the storm had passed and Nina had blown her nose and wiped her tears away, Zara asked, puzzled, "Why will a big wedding 'show them'?"

Nina tossed back her hair.

"Because it will," she said defiantly. "It will show them."

Zara gave up.

A little later, regretfully, Nina and Zara came downstairs and Tom rose to go.

"You *must* stay for dinner," Sonya begged.

"Not tonight, Aunt, I'm really tired."

They said farewell until tomorrow and Tom drove through a still evening to the little villa in Saint-Paul. When they arrived even he had to admit that it would be impossible for them to live there. Cold and damp, bleak now in early winter and darkly surrounded by trees, it was essentially a summer house, too small to be convenient or comfortable.

Tom smiled at his wife ruefully. "Sonya is right," he said, sighing. "This will never do."

So they checked into the Negresco even though the Rostovs wanted them to stay at the Villa de la Rose. Tom did not want that. He preferred the hotel, he said, so they stayed there for one month and their lives continued, as in Paris, a round of pleasure: no household management was needed, and meals and laundry came at the press of a button.

They were welcomed back to the South of France by a host of parties. The Marquis d'Arrent gave a masked ball in their honour. Lady Frobisher, the Duke of Barbridges, the de Montaignes, all gave parties and soirées for them. They were fêted and congratulated, and by the end of the month had ceased to be in the spotlight and become ordinary members of society again.

They found an apartment on the Boulevard des Anglais, facing the sea. It was owned by an obscure French Countess whose husband had died and who had, to her own vast surprise, remarried. Her second husband was an American who wanted to return to his native Virginia and breed horses.

The apartment comprised the first and second floors of a large house. Spacious and roomy, high-ceilinged, it was nevertheless furnished in late Victorian style with heavy dark pieces and totally unsuitable soft furnishings. But it was beautifully proportioned and had enough space for them to be comfortable. Tom gratefully left the arrangements to his wife and her aunt. To Sonya and Nina's surprise, Zara proposed to leave the interior decoration as it was, choosing only to replace what the Countess was taking with her. Zara ordered linen and little else. She seemed uninterested in her surroundings, her mind filled with other considerations.

"Darling, it's frightfully important to fix up the apartment nicely for yourself and Tom," Sonya said in exasperation one day, having spent half a morning trying to get her niece to see reason.

"Why?" Zara asked sweetly.

"Because it will give you something interesting to do."

"But I'm looking after Tom. That's all I want to do," Zara replied.

"Oh, my dear, you must not make him feel you are totally dependent on him."

"But I don't. He's happy wherever he is."

"Even in that dark heavy place surrounded by that grotesque furniture? It's more suitable for a shooting lodge in Scotland than a house in the South of France."

"Oh, darling Aunt Sonya, I don't *care*. Don't you see? We are perfectly happy as we are. Besides, I wouldn't know how to begin. I'm an awful duffer at decorating. After all, I've never done it before."

Sonya found them a housekeeper and cook all rolled into one. Conchita was a dumpling of a woman and perfect for Zara, and she fitted into the household beautifully: it soon seemed as if she had always been there.

Chapter Nineteen

The first evening that Tom spent away from her plunged Zara into a depression. She knew she was being unreasonable. He had nonchalantly told her he was going to Monte Carlo for a game. She had bitten back her disappointment and anger and, smiling, kissed him goodbye without even asking him when he would be home.

Alone in the bedroom, irrationally angry, she hit her fists against the wall, developed a headache and went to bed without food at eight o'clock in the evening.

She tossed and turned, asking herself the unanswerable. 'Why didn't he take me with him?' 'How could he leave me here all alone?' 'Doesn't he love me?' 'If he loved me as I love him he would never leave me like this.' 'Perhaps he is tired of me?' 'I have begun to bore him.' 'Oh God help me.' And she curled up into a ball, hugging her knees, aware of how silly she was being, unable to stop herself. It was the first of many such evenings.

At first she did not let him know how she felt and whether or not he realised remained unclear. Sometimes, out of the blue, he would say something like, "I'm playing cards, darling. That's *all*." Or he would catch her eye in the mirror and smile: "At least you know where I am. At least you know I'm faithful."

Such remarks made her think he divined her feelings and was not going to do anything about them. He left her alone a lot and, it seemed to her he did so happily. He resumed his old life as if there had been no interruption, no wedding.

She had thought he would change but Sonya said, "Men don't change. With age they remain themselves, only more so. A mean man becomes meaner, a generous man more generous. A woman is a fool if she thinks she will change a man."

Zara knew she had wanted to change Tom. She wanted him to be like other husbands yet loved him because he was different.

It was all right in the daytime. She met Sonya and Nina. Her aunt had a very good idea of Zara's expectations and disappointments.

"My dear, you are very young in experience." She waved her long elegant fingers at Zara's protest. "Oh, I know you have had more trauma in your life than most have in a lifetime. It's not that. It's perhaps *because* of that that you are so ... intense."

"Possessive, yes." Zara's voice was regretful. I have been told that before. But I seem unable to help myself."

"Begin by trusting Tom," Sonya had said kindly.

Zara had confided their adventures in Amsterdam, Paris and Berlin to her aunt. It had been a relief to share the dramatic events and the burden of their import with Sonya who was the closest thing she had to a mother.

"I'm not surprised," her aunt had said of Sasha, "blood will out. He's his mother's child. Nothing of your father there."

"Oh, Aunt, don't say that. I love him so."

"Too much, it seems," was the stringent rejoinder.

Now once again her aunt was warning her that she might lose someone because of her fatal weakness of loving too much.

"You must release Tom, Zara, if you want to keep him," Sonya said. "Give him a child."

But Zara found out she could not have children. Somehow she was not surprised at the news. Since her liaison with Tom, wed and unwed, she had taken no precautions and hoped vaguely to become pregnant. But it had not happened.

The doctor explained that she was barren. He asked tactfully about her past.

"You have been badly damaged, internally, when you were young," he said. "So badly that conception is impossible."

He went on to give her the exact reasons why this was so but she did not understand the technicalities. He expected her to be upset, but she was not. His tone was sympathetic and he looked at her with pity but she was not at all sure that a baby would make her husband happy or keep him home more. Rather, she felt it would give him an excuse to be away more often. Tom was not at all domesticated. He seemed to be so self-contained that she feared the mayhem of family life might drive him further away.

His reaction to her news was in character.

"Sorry, my sweet, for your sake. If you're upset about it, I'll do all I can to help you feel better. But if you ask me, it's just as well. Can't see either of us settling down to domestic bliss and all that. We're not the types."

She was hurt by his remark for that was precisely what she had wanted to do; settle down with a husband and children, a dog, a cat, happy domesticity.

Thinking rationally she could not see her debonair Tom in the scenes she imagined. Would he be doing much more than putting in an appearance, handsome in his evening dress, kissing everyone goodnight? She doubted it. Dirk would have fitted into her fantasies perfectly. She could visualise him nodding before the fire, his soft mop of brown hair tinged with grey, his eyes gentle behind his spectacles, bouncing a baby on his knee, or sucking a pipe in the evening while he read the paper. Why had she not fallen in love with Dirk? Or Dmitri?

It was Tom that she loved, lean and intense over a card

table, smoke from a cigarette making him narrow his eyes, all his concentration on the task at hand. A baby would have brought her closer to a man like Dirk but it would probably have driven Tom away.

But it was pointless speculating. The damage had been done. And by the Baron. Ultimately it was his fault. Another reason to hate him.

For now Zara was back in the sun. Even in winter the sky was clear and the light bright. She determined to enjoy what she had, taking a leaf from Tom's book, concentrating on the moment.

She had time now to assess Chuck Kenelly. The American seemed genuinely in love with her cousin. He was as simple and uncomplicated as Nina. They would, Zara decided, probably suit each other perfectly. He was a good-looking, amiable fellow, but he had very firm ideas about marriage and women. He was certain that the fair sex belonged in a different world to men, that boys will be boys but that girls should be chaste. He was convinced that the 'little lady', as he called Nina, would be happiest staying at home where she belonged, bearing his children. His views were old-fashioned and set.

"Kids are great. A woman isn't a woman without them," he said after dinner, one evening at the Rostovs'. Nina looked at him fondly, Sonya with some disdain.

She had said to Zara a few days previously, "Why she chose such a caveman is beyond me!"

Now, seated about the fire, a cold moon shining through the French windows, Zara glanced at Sonya and Nina, then at Dmitri who sat on the arm of Lucinda's chair, playing idly with her red curls. The girl leaned against him in silent adoration, alternately closing her eyes and looking up at him as if he were the Archangel, Zara thought, annoyed. Then she chided herself. Just because Tom wasn't here she must not take it out on poor Lucinda. She was sure she looked at Tom in much the same adoring, if soppy, fashion when he

340

was with her. In fact, she knew she did. Dmitri looked up and caught her eye and gave her his most angelic smile.

"Suppose a woman didn't want children?" she said to Chuck, looking away from Dmitri. Chuck spluttered into his brandy.

"What? Oh, you're joshing me, Zara. Why, that would be unnatural."

"I don't see why," she said. "Why should women be tied to their houses and their children? Who decides that that is all they are suitable for? I'll tell you who – men."

There was a shocked silence. Zara did not know why she had said what she did. She felt very near to tears.

Sonya glanced at Chuck's apalled face, then laughed lightly. "It takes all sorts to make a world, Chuck. The only crime as I see it lies in not acknowledging that, in supposing that there is only one opinion – yours. Some women should not have children because they do not truly want them. But not Nina, so I wouldn't worry my head over it. It is not, as you Americans say, your problem."

A dazzling smile split Chuck's face and Nina leaned over and kissed him.

"I certainly want babies, dearest," she cooed, and Zara wondered if she really meant it.

Nina's wedding went off without a hitch. Chuck's parents thought the Russian Orthodox ceremony was beautiful if a trifle incomprehensible. His family were not, after all, backwoods folk but an amusing, well-educated, likeable couple. They came with a remarkably pretty daughter, Janet, who set all heads turning on the Riviera, and a formidable grandmother. This seventy year old ruled the family with a rod of iron. Her husband, now deceased, had arrived in America as a Scottish emigrant and made a million dollars manufacturing women's corsets. She quickly made friends with Vassily, entertaining him with stories of the pioneer days when her parents had crossed the Old

West, braving Indians, drought, battles with cow-men, outlaws and Sheriffs who hampered them, she said, all the way.

The cake arrived the morning of the wedding when Sonya had given up hope of it ever appearing from the special cake shop in St Tropez. Nina looked beautiful, ripe and blonde. The nervous rash that had threatened to spoil her looks had disappeared the night before the great day.

Zara was matron-of-honour. Tom was there at her side which made her childishly happy. She felt no regret about her own civil marriage, but suffered a pang of nostalgia when Father Ivan swung the censer and intoned in his deep Russian bass while the twin crowns were held over the heads of bride and groom. She was pierced with a longing that was fierce and sweet and sad, a longing for a lost innocence, a lost childhood, a lost national identity. The sounds of the Russian language brought back a few scattered memories that seemed infinitely precious.

Happiness, she decided sadly, was fragmentary. You had to snatch what you could of it while you had the chance, savour your allowance before it melted into pain of one sort or another.

Watching Father Ivan, seeing the crowns hovering over Nina and Chuck, hearing the deep swell of male voices filling the incense-heavy air, she thought of an ice-cold church in Northern Russia, and of the Baron. Shivering, she glanced at Tom who sat with his face closed in thought. I'll never nag him again, she promised silently, if only, dear Lord, you make him want to stay at home with me.

She immediately recognised the condition attached to her prayer. When will I learn to trust and be grateful? she wondered. Once I was happy he even noticed me. Then I was ecstatic because he made love to me and brought me back to life. After that I could only be happy if he married me, and he did. Now I want him with me, body and soul, all the time. I know I am wrong but I cannot seem to help it. I

342

know I will lose him if I go on like this yet I cannot stop myself.

Nina and Chuck went off on their honeymoon. As they drove away from the villa Zara, holding Tom's hand, heard the Princess d'Artelli say: "I'll give it two years at most. My bet is that Zara and the divine Tom will have split up in a year. The best bet in that family is Dmitri. He's the only one who is marrying his social equal."

Suddenly turning to Tom, Zara kissed him fiercely. "I love you," she whispered. "Don't let me spoil it, Tom. Promise?"

He smiled at her. "I promise," he said.

Summer came and Tom seemed to spend more and more time away from her. There were private sessions in small rooms at lunch-time; high-rolling games after the big sessions at night. Sometimes it seemed to Zara he was shut away from the world of sun and blue skies and all the riotous colours of the South of France for weeks on end. In the morning he would sit on the balcony, his face grey and exhausted, smoking his everlasting cigarettes, monosyllabic as Conchita brought them their breakfast. Whether he won or lost seemed to make little difference to him either way and the subject was taboo. All she knew was that she hated what he did.

The *mistral* came. As usual it arrived on the last weekend in July. It churned the sea, turning it into a turmoil of frothing foam, bringing the wind that sings in the head and makes men mad. It moaned through the apartment and Zara was filled with unease, a premonition of anxiety. Reason told her it was her imagination. Tom went out as usual, losing his easy grin as he left her, his face closing in as he reached the lift. A look of quiet awareness came over his face, replacing the gentle smile he wore in the presence of company, even her own.

He is never totally unguarded, even with me, she thought.

343

She had watched him once, standing at the door of the lift as he waited for the creaky old conveyance sighing and groaning its way up to him. She had seen the professional look take over and watched all thoughts of herself slip from him. She felt very lonely then.

When the *mistral* had blown itself out and calm returned in the form of a placid clear green sea under a yellow sun, Zara started a new round of parties, determined to shake off her *malaise*. She tried to take Sonya's advice. She made every effort to enjoy cocktail parties, bridge, dinners, balls and *soirées*, but was left bored and frustrated after every attempt.

Her days were broken up by meaningless entertainments: luncheon, tennis, swimming. She idled away her time, doing little, accomplishing nothing, constantly acting the acceptant wife for Tom's benefit. She felt herself more a victim of male dominance even than Nina. She was bound slave-like to Tom's dictates. If she did not behave as he wanted, she might lose him. It was as good as blackmail.

Sometimes they were invited aboard a friend's yacht and then Tom would accompany her, for a game was frequently in progress. As soon as they arrived and had greeted everyone, Tom would join the gamblers. A new arrival gave new life and impetus to jaded players who often had barely moved from the tables for months as the ship followed the sun.

But mainly Zara was alone, drifting from one villa to another, surrounded by people yet completely isolated from them by her mood. When Tom was not with her, she felt lonely.

She did not like gossip, and the people who surrounded her all loved it. What was important to them was to know who was sleeping with whom, the latest scandals and the sexual proclivities, real or imagined, of anyone who was anyone. They tore at reputations like vultures over a carcase. Zara was afraid of them, the scandalmongers. For what they said before her, the dirt they kicked up, the stories they embellished with innuendo, all shocked her spirit of fair play. Worse, she knew that what they said in front of her they also said behind her back, about her.

A lot of women in a similar position took a lover but Zara could not do that. Others gambled or drank.

The Marquesa d'Aurto Mendoza, who was still revelling in her Cockney lover's embraces, chided Zara one afternoon at a cocktail party.

"Take that sulky look off your face," she said sharply, "it's not becoming. If you object to being a gambling widow, then for God's sake take a lover. Poor Tom married you, didn't he? What more do you expect of him?"

"His company," Zara replied tartly.

"Well, you won't get it," the Marquesa returned equally tartly, "and you'll lose him if you try to corral him."

Her cheeks were heavily rouged but her eyes were kindly, "Listen to me. You are about half my age, no?" Zara nodded. "Well, people deride me, they make jokes behind my back. Oh, don't imagine I mind. They're merely taking out their envy in spiteful remarks. I pay them no heed. But they cannot understand how or why Fred and I are so happy.

"Shall I tell you? We take each other for what we are. He is honest with me and I with him. We don't expect too much."

The stupid thing was that Zara knew that her aunt and the Marquesa were right but she did not seem to be able to do as they advised. She clung fiercely to Tom, wanting only to become indispensable to him.

He found her once sitting on the sofa in the living-room, clutching a cushion to her breast, wearing a tweed jacket of his.

"Why are you wearing my clothes?" he asked coldly.

She glanced at him, disturbed by the edge in his voice.

"Oh darling, you're back early. Wonderful. We can have supper together. I'll call Conchita to …"

345

"No." He stopped her. "Why are you wearing my jacket?" he repeated.

"Because I am cold," she said sulkily. He shook his head. There was an expression on his face, of irritation and controlled anger, that she hated to see there.

"Don't be silly, Zara, it's hot in here." He stared at her. "Well?"

"I ... I ..." She hung her head like a guilty schoolgirl. "I was lonely," she said.

His head snapped back and he stared at the ceiling. He took a deep breath then looked at her again.

"Lonely," he said, "when I'm here every morning. We eat lunch together every day. I go out in the evenings, it's true, but it's my occupation. It's what I do. It's my business. And still I don't go out every evening as I could, as I should. I try to be fair. I stay with you two or three evenings a week ..." He broke off. "Oh God, why am I justifying myself to you? Are you trying to make me feel guilty? Well, you won't succeed."

He turned as if to abandon her but she ran to him and stood between him and the door.

"Tom, wait!" She realised how angry he must be, despairing that she could not seem to manage to play the game his way.

"You are like a spider, Zara, weaving a web around me. You sit here and wait for me. I can feel you even when I'm not here. The apartment is a waiting-room. I can be in Monto Carlo or Cannes and I can feel you waiting for me."

She cried out in protest but she knew that what he said was true.

"Listen to me," he took her roughly by the shoulders, "I can't cope with much more of this. Don't you understand? I thought you would get better with marriage. I thought that would give you more trust in me. But I was wrong. I'm not your property. You don't own me. We cannot live in each other's pockets."

"We did in Paris." She had said it before she could stop herself. He groaned and let his hands fall.

"We were travelling. It was different. If you cannot understand that ..." He sighed. "Oh Lord, I should never have married you. Never."

Her heart sank and she felt sick and panicky.

"Oh, don't say that, Tom. Please don't say that."

She would lose him. Oh God help her, she would lose him and if that happened she would die. The hard lump in her chest dissolved into a storm of desperate weeping.

"Oh, there now," he said awkwardly, and put his arms around her. She sobbed into his shoulder and when the storm had abated looked up at him and hiccupped, her tear-streaked face childishly appealing, her large eyes damp as violets in the rain.

"I'll be better. I promise, Tom. Dearest, dearest Tom."

She pressed herself against him and kissed him, a series of tiny kisses, punctuated by a repetition of, "Sorry, sorry, sorry." Her lips were soft and seductive, and drugged with honeyed kisses he sank into her embrace.

They made love. It was hectic and passionate, a powerful urge that both consumed and satisfied. Temporarily.

When it was over, Tom, having smoked a cigarette and lain a while in silence, got up and began to collect his clothes.

"What are you doing?" she asked drowsily.

"What does it look like?"

"You're not going out?"

"Yes, I am."

"But you came home early."

"Well, I'm going out again, Zara."

"But you said we'd dine together."

"No. *You* said that."

"Oh, Tom, don't go."

The bathroom door slammed to and there was silence. When he re-emerged he kissed her lightly, crossed the room and turned at the door.

"Please don't wear my jackets," he said in a kindly tone. "I just don't like it."

He was, in general, patient with her. He put up with the 'Don't go out', 'I'm sorry I didn't mean …' with fortitude and tried to understand, but his patience was not inexhaustible and he thought her childish and demanding. It went on and on. Every time she said those words she swore to herself she would never say them again, never think them or show by her attitude that she minded his way of life.

But then: "Why can't I come too? I'd be very quiet. You wouldn't even know I was there."

"God, Zara, give it a rest."

"No, Tom, I mean it. If I could be there, completely quiet, I'd be content. I'd never …"

"Please, Zara. It wouldn't work. You can't come with me." He fought to keep his voice calm. "My game would be affected … use your imagination. A lot of the places I play in are unsuitable for women of your sort. The men would not like it, and you'd be a distraction. I'd have to think about you."

"Meaning you don't now! Meaning you forget about me the moment you go out that door. I've seen you at the lift. Your whole face changes."

Why was she saying it? she asked herself. Why did the words rattle out, thoughts she did not want to utter suddenly and irretrievably spoken.

He turned and was gone without another word. So many times now he left without replying and she was alone, abandoned to her rage and to pacing up and down, up and down, the apartment in which she still had not changed anything and in which she still felt like a visitor.

He did not return that night. Zara slept fitfully and when she woke, which she did frequently, she groped for him and found the bed empty.

The next day he telephoned. When she heard his voice she began to cry.

348

"Oh, darling, darling, where are you?"

"Paris," the voice said. She was incredulous. "Paris? How? Why?"

"Darling, I need a break. I need to be by myself for a while."

"But you can't ... what will I do? I can't live ..."

The phone went dead.

Never in her life had she felt so desolate. She did not know where he was, had no way of contacting him. She became terrified, blamed herself and alternated fits of crying with furious bursts of anger against him. How dare he leave her like that without a word? How could he go to Paris, their beloved Paris, without her? Where was he? What was he doing? How dare he! If he returned she would give him a rapturous welcome, she decided. Ten minutes later she was equally convinced she would not have him back, no matter what he said.

Then she was sick with fear that he would not come back at all.

Tom stayed away for a month. Frightened and shocked, Zara told herself that it was all her own fault. She did not know what to do. She thought of phoning the Ritz but restrained herself. She prayed fervently, bombarding heaven with demands for his return, making wild unrealistic promises she could not fulfil if only he would come home, repentant.

Sonya was the only one who guessed that his absence was the result of a rift. Zara had told everyone that he was away on business.

"What are you playing at, child?" she asked the white-faced girl.

The weather was cool and her aunt had arrived unexpectedly at the apartment. Zara sat in the gloom, a cardigan around her shoulders, curled up in a chair. She looked as if she had not moved for weeks. Conchita had told Sonya that she was not eating anything.

"Oh, Aunt, I don't know. It's all my fault. I nag him and nag him. I don't seem to be able to help myself."

"Well, you had better or you'll lose your husband. You're afraid to trust, Zara, afraid to grow up. And it's time you did. I'm warning you now that if you don't you are guaranteeing a future for yourself without Tom."

Zara had never heard her aunt speak so firmly.

"If you want Tom then keep the independence you talked about to Chuck," she continued. "Listen, Zara, you must learn to love your husband *the way he is*. Otherwise you're done for. Unless you really accept him as he is you'll never be able to leave him alone. You are bright, beautiful. You have endless potential. You'd loathe to be restricted. If you were Tom you'd balk, exactly as he does. You'd run away. Don't you see?"

Zara had never thought of it that way before. She knew Sonya was right, that she would hate it if Tom tried to possess her.

"I'm so afraid of losing him, Aunt Sonya."

"Well, you're going about it the right way."

Zara shivered. "Help me."

Sonya shook her head. "No. You must help yourself. You have to do it alone. It's something that has to happen inside you. If you are willing, really willing, then that's half the battle."

Tom returned. He breezed into the flat one tea-time with a pal, Pete Whittaker. Zara had met him with Tom in Paris. A tall dark-haired Englishman, charming and diffident, his presence made it essential for Zara and Tom to behave casually.

Conchita prepared them a light supper and Zara behaved perfectly. She concealed her seething emotions and laughed with the men, asked all the right questions, and when after dinner they sat down to a game of backgammon, with exactly the right air of tranquil acceptance she kissed Tom and said she was off to bed. He seemed surprised but said nothing.

She lay in bed praying. He had come back to her. She had very nearly lost him but he had returned. She prayed for courage, for the ability to let things be.

"Oh God, why does everything matter so much to me?" she sighed.

When he at last came into the bedroom she found she was quite calm.

"Tom, is that you?" She could hear him moving about in the darkened room.

"Yes." She could hear the dread in his voice. He thinks I am going to make a scene, she thought.

"Come here. Sit by me a moment."

He sighed again and sat beside her.

"Listen," she said as he opened his mouth to speak. "I want to apologise."

He seemed surprised. "You?" he queried. "Apologise to me? Surely it should be the other way around?"

"No. Don't say anything more. Just hear me out. I've been behaving like a romantic fool. I've lived too long in the past, Tom. I have to learn to let it go, heal myself. I carried around my pain, my bewilderment, my confusion for so long, I couldn't bear to be parted from them. They became my crutch, my weapon. I refused to grow up and take responsibility for my life. I've made you suffer. Heaven knows you have been good to me. You have healed me. I've tried to cast you in the role of father when all you wanted was to be my lover, friend, husband. I've realised all this, Tom, and I want to change. I'm going to try. I want you to help me. Will you?"

She was surprised to see tears in his eyes.

"I've missed you so," he whispered. "God, how I've missed you." He drew her into his arms, holding her close. "Sweet, precious princess, dearest princess, you make me ashamed. If you are to blame, then so am I. I have to change too. Be more flexible. Oh, my darling, let's help each other." He began to kiss her hair, her face, and then there was no more conversation, only greeting and a reaffirmation of love.

Chapter Twenty

Zara gave up her fight, gave in, and in accepting found a depth of happiness she had not known before. She asked Sonya for advice and the Princess said briskly, "Decorate the apartment. It is in execrable taste. You could do so much better, Zara. It will occupy you and you have to make a proper home for Tom and yourself. You cannot continue to live as if you were in lodgings, with someone else's possessions all around you. You may as well start now. It will keep you interested. Remember what they say: the devil always finds work for idle hands to do."

Zara began in a mood of resigned acceptance, prompted by Sonya's nagging to create a home. To her surprise it really helped. To her mortification, the old cliché proved true. Occupied by something other than her husband, she became genuinely interested in her home and a whole new world was opened up for her.

She got great satisfaction from planning the redecoration, buying and ordering. She kept the colours light and bright, the walls unpapered, which was an innovation. The chairs and sofas were cream-coloured and the vast rooms she kept uncluttered, carpeted in cream, with just a hint of peach. Everything was lighter than light. She bought a lot of Art Nouveau statuettes and scattered them here and there on pale marble surfaces. And then there were the paintings. The Chagall, the Picasso, the Derain, most of all the Gauguin, glowed brilliantly on the walls.

When she was finished the main part of the work she realised that she was proud of what she had done. It was useful, too, in conversation with other women. No longer need she stand listening to malicious gossip. She found she could with impunity change the conversation to interior decoration and not feel a complete fool.

She was able for the first time to enjoy cocktail parties without Tom. She often went to social events merely to pass the evening. Sonya said it was better than sitting at home. One night they were on the balcony of the d'Arrents' villa, under a star-strewn sky. Zara asked who had lost at bridge last night. She was leaning on the balustrade puffing on her Balkan Soubranie, its grey smoke hanging on the still air.

Lady Frobisher said she had but that Georgio Lampelli was too drunk and played execrably. He had been her partner and she could not forgive him. He was sleeping with Oria del Angtain and everyone knew how that nymphomaniac wore out her lovers. Poor Georgio had no strength left for bridge. There was a lull in the conversation and Zara thought of Anya. Nymphomaniac. She knew the word now, she thought. Everything had a label. The little group on the balcony drifted inside. Someone said it was getting chilly.

Zara held out her glass for a refill she knew would come without her looking round. It did. She sighed. These conversations bored her. She moved to the French windows and stared out.

"There is a new ninety ton in Cannes. Have you noticed it?" the Marquis d'Arrent asked. "It is the most beautiful boat I have seen in a long time. German I think."

"Oh, do tell? Who's the lucky owner? Anyone we know?"

Zara smiled to herself. If whoever owned it was not up to scratch then all interest in the beautiful boat would soon be lost.

"It belongs to the Baron Klaus Hoffen von Eldrich." Maxwell Clover, who was American and knew these things before anyone else, delivered the information. Zara's hand tightened on the stem of her glass. No one knew of her relationship with the German.

"He is the oddest fellow," someone said, "handsome in an austere sort of way. Quite wicked-looking. David and Julio, those dinky little pansies, went on board. They were invited. They say the Baron swings both ways."

"What a waste!"

"A waste, my dear, is the young Prince the Baron has in tow. His *bon ami*. A Greek god, they said. Oh, Sylvana was with them but she is so boyish, so gamine, it doesn't count. Like Zara here."

She stood frozen at the open French windows, poised as if for flight. She did not turn for she did not want them to see her face until she had control of it. They were professionals at reading nuances like a sudden change of expression. She simply shrugged and made a non-committal noise. It came out high and nervous but the conversation was continuing.

"The Apollo was very doped, Julio said. Semi-comatose. What a shame. On opium. Or cocaine. There was some of it about and you know how nervous David gets when he's near anything like that. The last time he ..."

Zara did not hear the rest. Sasha here, in that white yacht she had noticed yesterday. Sasha in Berlin, eyes shuttered, the distant look she had noticed on his face. The scandal-mongering had explained so much. Of course drugs would dull the pain. But she had offered him a way out and he had rejected it. Why? She did not understand. Because he could not bear the poverty, he had said. But he had money of his own now so that was not a believable excuse. Because he needed drugs? Money enough to live in comfort and pay for a supply of dope. She could not bear to believe that he had stayed with the Baron from choice.

The next day after Tom had left in the heat of the afternoon she pulled on a pair of shorts and a striped navy and white cotton top and drove to Cannes. There was a smell of tar melting under the sun and the heat scorched the backs of her hands. The road before her swam in the fierce red-tinged light, molton crimson one moment, platinum the next. She winced behind her dark glasses and dabbed her forehead with her handkerchief. The hair beside her ears was wet.

When she reached the port she saw the boat immediately. It differed from the others in being the only one flying a swastika. She padded in her espadrilles down the quay until she came to its berth.

Rhinemaiden lay in the heat, still and beautiful, its sails trimmed. Zara walked up the gang-plank. As she jumped lightly into the boat the Baron appeared from below. If he was surprised by her sudden appearance, he did not show it.

"*Bonjour*, Zara," he said, then smiled his thin savage smile. "Wife. How nice of you to call. So, you haven't forgotten us?"

It was not a question and she did not answer him. He put out his hand to steady her for she stumbled a little, but she refused to take it. She sat aft on immaculate white and aquamarine cushions, her knees primly together, her hands clasped as if in prayer.

"I came to see Sasha," she said uncertainly. The Baron always made her feel awkward and childish, like a schoolgirl before a stern headmaster. Now that she was here she realised that she had not planned what to say or do. She was not even sure what she wanted. She supposed it was to see that her brother was all right.

"Sasha is sleeping," he said. There was a slight hesitation, something that told her all was not well with her brother. "I thought we had settled how he felt about seeing you in Berlin."

"You may have settled how *you* felt about it. I did not resolve anything about my own feelings. By the way," she added as firmly as she could, "I am not your wife. I am married to someone else."

God, it's like a scene from a silent movie, she thought.

356

Lilian Gish … no. Theda Bara being dramatic.

He shrugged, his face sardonic.

"No, Zara, there is no divorce in the Russian Orthodox Church. No matter what you or the Englishman say, our marriage is legal and binding." He looked at her archly. "I believe your marriage to the gambler was a civil one." So he had found that out for himself …

"Isn't one of us enough for you?" she asked. She was surprised to feel not a trace of the old fear returning. She hated him, thought him evil, but Tom had taken her fear away.

She looked at the powerful man before her with distaste. Everything her husband was found its opposite in Klaus Hoffen von Eldrich. Tom was gentle and considerate. She remembered the Baron's physical brutality. Tom was kind and good-humoured. This man's savage moods were destructive and she had never known him to laugh with joy. At people certainly, derisively, but with unaffected gaiety, never. Tom lived and would fight for fair play, honesty, the freedom of others. This man believed in the survival of the fittest; he was incapable of honesty and indifferent to another's pain.

He looked at her now and she remembered all those years ago in St Petersburg, thinking him handsome. She had characterised him in memory after his brutal behaviour to her as a monster. Now she realised that her first assessment of him was right. He was savagely good-looking and she shuddered for the power of evil and its attraction. She must accept that her brother, for whatever reason, was in his thrall while she would never be entirely at peace until the Baron was dead.

His eyes narrowed. "I liked it best when I had you both," he said, and moved nearer her. She could smell his skin and see the hair on his tanned chest. Overcome with revulsion, the memories of the plunder of her body, the humiliation she had suffered at his hands, she opened her purse. Taking

357

out a handkerchief she pressed it against her face. She breathed in its perfume, trying to block out his nearness, his words.

"I had you both, so young, completely in my power. Oh, it was wonderful. You were so sweet, Zara, in your innocence and youth. So exciting in your resistance. You know my body well, don't you? Do you never think of those days, *leibling*?"

"No. Or not without revulsion," she said as coldly as she could.

He laughed. "You hate me, don't you? Do you hate me more than you love Tom Armitidge? You see, hatred is the same as love. Deep down, *leibling*, I am a more powerful influence in your life than your gentlemanly boyfriend."

"There was never a moment when you gave me a second's pleasure, never a moment without loathing."

Still he smiled. "Listen to you! You are very passionate about me, are you not? I don't know a woman who does not enjoy being mastered. I like your hate, Zara. I thrive on it. It gives my life zest. It's challenging. And, you see, for me it was always good and that is what really counts."

He moved even closer and she could feel the heat from his body. Though she had her face turned from him she could sense everything he felt and how he looked. She thought that if he came any nearer she would jump over the side into the crystal cleansing water.

"What I wanted and still want; what I was done out of; what I dream about, is both of you sweet, sweet creatures together. You and Sasha. You don't know how it haunts me: how I visualise us, all of us in an ecstatic embrace ..."

She hit him. With her open palm and all her strength she struck him as hard as she could, her teeth clenched. She realised her mistake almost at once for he laughed and caught her wrist.

"That is more like the Zara I appreciate," he said, laughing. "You used to be so fierce. So, violence from the meek, eh? Aha, sweet Zara, for me there has never been another woman to touch you. Except Anya, the lioness Princess. The man-eater."

"Klaus? Klaus?"

They both turned. The Baron dropped her hand. Sasha stood on deck, blinking. He looked pale, his body emaciated in a pair of crumpled white shorts.

"Klaus?" he said again, then shading his eyes with his hand he caught sight of his sister. "Zara, what are you doing here?"

There was little interest in his voice. It might have been only yesterday that they had met instead of the years it had actually been. He looked at her dead-eyed and she ran to him and kissed his cheeks which were cold and faintly damp.

"Dearest Sasha, you are ill."

"Let me go to hell in my own way, Zaroushka," he said indifferently. She felt a stab of pain near her heart. He was the only one who called her that now.

"No, Sasha, listen. You don't have to stay here. I'll take you to the Rostovs. I'll build you a house, a magnificent one. I'll feed you and have you taken care of and I promise I won't be possessive, on my oath. I've learned with Tom how not to be. Oh, darling, darling brother, you don't have to stay with this ..."

She glanced at Klaus. His eyes were narrowed and smiling. He was watching them intently.

Sasha's face was working with annoyance. To him at that moment Zara was merely an unwelcome distraction, an obstacle between himself and the satisfaction of a craving which left him hollow and desperate. Later, in the quiet hours after Klaus had ministered to him, he would feel the familiar despair and regret but for now he could not afford to. He scowled at her.

"I don't want to be taken care of Zaroushka, don't you understand? Will you give me my fix on the hour, exactly

359

when I need it? Or will you try to cure me when I don't want to be cured? Don't you see – I don't care about anything but ..." He shuddered and looked at the Baron. "Please, Klaus, it's time." At his nod, Sasha went below.

Before the Baron descended he looked over his shoulder at her: "I'll get you back eventually. I always get my way, just as I did with Sasha. How he hated being poor! It took remarkably little persuasion to bring him back to me."

Disgust tightened her throat. She had not mistaken the significance of the shocking scene in the castle. Then and afterwards Sasha had been as much the Baron's prey as she herself had been. How terrible that his craving for the ease and luxury of Princess Anya's world had led him back into the lion's den.

"I am a humane man." The Baron's terrible smile belied the silken smoothness of his words. "I am also far-sighted. I realised that I must keep Sasha happy and tied to me."

She could barely breathe, sensing what was to come.

"He fought the first few times I ministered to him with a soothing injection, but in time he came to realise that the needle was his truest friend. Now, as you have seen, he positively welcomes it."

"But can't you see," she cried, agonised, "you are destroying him?"

"Oh, give me some credit, *liebling*. He is not what he was, it's true, but trust me to make sure he stays alive. It is in my best interests, after all."

She felt cold and sick. "I – I don't know what you mean."

His mocking smile had slipped to reveal the implacable resolve beneath. "I think you do. The detectives who found you in Amsterdam – I never called them off. All these years I've known exactly where you were, but I'm a patient man. I wanted *you* to come to *me*. And while I have Sasha, I know that one day you will."

"Never!"

"Oh yes, one way or another you'll come to me. We're

360

going to be very powerful, you know. We're going to be masters of the world."

Even in casual sailing clothes there was something soldierly about him. She remembered the swarming military of Berlin; the blood-red swastika adorned flags lining the Unter den Linden.

"I must go," she said, struggling to keep panic from her voice. "My husband will be wondering where I am."

"From what I've heard of him, I doubt that very much," taunted the Baron. "But if you must, for the moment ..."

"Klaus," a voice called feebly from below. "Come now. I need you."

He cocked one eyebrow. "You see? That will be you one day."

"Don't push me, Klaus! I almost succeeded in killing you once. Never underestimate the power of my hatred."

He laughed mirthlessly. "And never forget what I told you about hate."

Without a word of goodbye he turned and left her, shivering in the heat haze of a perfect Riviera day.

The *Rhinemaiden* left Cannes the next day. Zara checked. With deep regret she realised she had lost her brother again. However, she had learned by now that life went on. It was relentless. It ticked past and you could not stop it. Grief passed, joy passed, every emotion passed and changed into something else.

Dmitri's wedding was splendid. Zara embraced her cousin, wishing him all the joy in the world. Lucinda looked delightful and the only tension was created by Lady Abercrombie's unremitting efforts to see that everyone had a good time.

"Be happy with him," Zara said when she kissed the bride. Lucinda looked at her and there was a tight little note of anxiety in her voice.

"If you let him go. Please, Zara, let him go. You hold on so tight."

"But I have," Zara said, surprised. 'I really have."

"That's all right then," Lucinda said brightly. Too brightly, Zara thought.

They went to Lake Como on their honeymoon. When they were leaving Lucinda held her mother tightly as if she could not bear to part from her. There was a quiet desperation in the way she said goodbye. Zara felt a chill to see the bride clinging so to the plump Lady Abercrombie. But they left and Zara missed her cousin. They had never had to explain their feelings to each other, had never had any difficulty in communicating with each other; often words were unnecessary between them.

I take so much for granted, she thought. When they are here I don't cherish them as I should. Then they go and I realise how much I love them and miss them. The Côte d'Azur was not the same without Nina and Dmitri.

She found herself thrown back on her own resources more than ever before, and to her surprise began to appreciate her own company.

She bought a little Ford and drove herself around the south coast foraging for bits and pieces for the apartment. She liked the bright pottery she found and the handwoven rugs and mats. She discovered antiques in unexpected places and learned to haggle over the price. She had grown to know the coastline and the small villages around the south and Provence during the pre-marital years with Tom. During their 'love in the afternoon' years, as she called them. Now she looked back with a smile on those wonderful times, forgetting the pain she had suffered, allowing time to cast a cloak of nostalgia and change the pain to happiness.

She grew to love her jaunts alone, eating lunch on the pavement restaurants of seaside towns and mountain villages, basking in the sun. She found she could be content and relaxed in a way that eluded her at home. Driving along the bright coastline dotted with candy-pink and white houses that were garlanded with cerise bougainvillea, purple bindweed, bushes of crimson hibiscus and mauve wisteria, bargaining with a shopkeeper, merchant or antique dealer, she was suspended in the now. Tom had gone gambling and was not yet due to return. For the moment she was content just to drift along.

Dmitri returned from his honeymoon. He seemed normal to all who did not know him well. He talked a lot about what was happening in northern Europe. Zara asked what northern Europe had to do with them. He replied that Austria had disappeared, but Zara could not think it had much to do with their life in this Garden of Eden. She thought of Sasha and the Baron. Dirk and Gerda and Frau Kettner. Gerda came from Austria. She wondered how she felt about her country being absorbed by another. Then a bird sang, or the perfection of a flower caught her attention, and she forgot everything else.

There was something else about Dmitri that she could not put her finger on.

"There is something wrong there," Sonya said, echoing her niece's thought. "We'll have to find out what it is all about."

Dmitri looked strained and there was a false note in his banter. For the first time in their lives he avoided Zara's eyes. Lucinda was subdued and seemed, for a change, to contemplate the toes of her shoes instead of her new husband. Gone were the looks of melting adoration that had given Zara cause for jealousy.

Sonya had given a celebratory dinner for them a week after their return and, much to Zara's annoyance, Tom was not able to attend.

"I would have thought you could have come with me tonight," she said, waiting for him to zip up her flame-coloured silk frock. He was frowning as he tied his bow tie, biting his lip in concentration as he always did when so engaged.

"Darling, you know I can't. Three guys from the States

363

are passing through. Here only for tonight. High rollers by the sound of it. Can't pass it up."

"But it's a *family* occasion," Zara protested. "They'll expect you."

"Every day of the year would be a 'family occasion' if you had your way, my love," he said ruefully.

"That's not fair. I never pressurise you now," she said. "I used to but you have to admit I have got better, haven't I?"

He took her in his arms and kissed the curve of her neck, burying his face in her soft flesh.

"That's true, my love, and don't think I don't appreciate it. You have been very good. Didn't I tell you?"

The charming smile that melted her heart accompanied his words, and she nodded.

"Well then. As a reward ... just this once," she coaxed.

He let her go abruptly. "No, love. No." He said it lightly but firmly.

She missed having him beside her at the Rostovs'. Without him on such occasions she felt lonely. Without him the effort to respond to people eluded her.

It was a strangely subdued party. Prince Vassily tried to be his usual jolly self, entertaining and concerned, but he failed miserably. His face looked thin and grey to Zara and she reminded herself again to ask privately if he felt all right.

Zara herself did her best but realised how hollow her banter sounded. Lady Abercrombie bumbled on and on in meaningless unfinished drifts of conversation that no one listened to.

Dmitri was silent, moodily pushing his food about with his fork and eating little. And the blushing bride's mood could only be described as morose.

Everyone seemed relieved when they sauntered into the house for coffee and the formality of the dinner table had broken up. Zara went and sat beside Dmitri. Before their marriage Lucinda would have rushed to his side, but now she lingered near her mother, red-head bent, and glanced

364

only once at Zara with an expression of dislike as she passed by to sit next to her cousin.

"What on earth did you do to her?" Zara whispered in his ear as she sat down.

He blushed but smiled at her, she thought with relief.

"Oh, Zara, you make it all sound so silly."

"What?" she asked. "What's silly?"

"I can't talk to you here," he said, glancing at Lady Abercrombie who was staring at Zara, a hostile expression on her face.

"Why don't you meet me for lunch tomorrow?" Zara asked him. "I planned a visit to St Tropez. It's a peaceful little fishing village along the coast. Do you know it?"

Dmitri nodded. "Umm, I think so. That's where the *patisserie* is. The wedding cake, remember?"

She laughed, drawing another hostile glance from Lady Abercrombie. "Yes," she said softly, "I'm driving there. Starting about eleven o'clock tomorrow morning. I want to see a ceramics works, some tiles for our bathroom. I'd love it if you came with me."

He nodded. "Yes," he said. "We need to talk. Oh, Zara, what a long way we've come since the ball. You remember?"

She smiled at him. "It all seemed so simple then," she said. "So very simple. And it isn't Dmitri, is it?"

He sighed and shook his head. Zara looked up to see Lucinda's sea-green eyes fixed on her. Their expression could only be described as resentful.

Silly girl, thought Zara. If she feels that way, all she has to do is come and claim him.

But Lucinda remained beside her mother until they left.

Dmitri arrived at the apartment next morning as Tom was leaving. Freshly shaved and dressed, the latter exuded an air of vitality and *joie de vivre*.

"Greetings, dear boy, off on one of Zara's expeditions with her, eh?"

Dmitri nodded.

"I must fly." Tom raised his voice to the still invisible Zara. "Goodbye, my love. Enjoy your day. See you when I see you." And he was gone.

She came into the room, clasping on her earrings.

"It's wonderful what you've done to this place," Dmitri said, looking about the bright and airy room. "It's lovely and so are you. Oh, Zara dear."

He took her in his arms and held her fiercely for a moment.

"What is it, Dmitri? What's the trouble?"

He shook his head. "Later. If I start to tell you now, we'll never get started and I need desperately to get away from Nice.

"Then let's go."

Zara slung a lemon cashmere sweater over her shoulders. She wore biscuit-coloured linen slacks and a white linen sleeveless blouse.

The put the hood of the convertible down and drove in silence along the coast to St Tropez. To Dmitri's surprise she was a good driver and handled the car masterfully. There was something sure and competent about her that seemed to him amazingly attractive.

The sun sparkled on a dancing, royal-blue sea. They wore dark glasses against the glare, the resonant light that Zara loved. There were tiny boats bobbing on the horizon and the screams of children wafted from the shore. Clusters of striped bathing-boxes dotted the beaches, and everywhere flowers bloomed in multi-coloured profusion.

They did not speak until they reached St Tropez. They drove up a narrow cobbled street, coming to a halt outside the arch of a tiny shop. They got out and were greeted by a nut-brown old man who led them into the cave-like interior. There he tenderly displayed before them marvellous tiles of all colours and designs: autumnal yellows and ambers; umber and burnt sienna; gold; chestnut; brown; orange;

spring-like pinks and powder blues; delicate floral patterns in lemon and rose, pale leaf-green and lilac. Then there were those in the colours of the Côte d'Azur and these were the ones that Zara selected: the French-blue of a cockatoo's wing; hard citrus yellow; cerise from a hibiscus stamen; and clear sharp turquoise, a bright colour that Zara wanted to splash on to the stark white of the bathroom.

At last she had finished and they went down to the water front where a local restauranteur sized them up.

Under the straw-roofed overhang interlaced with ivy and wisteria they sat at a table with a checked cloth and ordered *calamari* and salad, *carré d'agneau* and the harsh red wine of the district.

They ate and drank in silence. When they were finished Zara looked at her cousin and asked, "Well, what is it? What's the matter?"

"I always feel so tranquil with you, Zara, so relaxed. I've never felt so close to anyone as I feel to you."

She had thrown some bread to the two hopeful pigeons at their feet and the birds were fighting over it, pushing each other out of the way whilst their beedy little eyes darted hither and thither on constant alert.

"Like Lady Abercrombie," Dmitri remarked, watching them. His voice sounded bitter.

"Don't be unkind," Zara reproved him. "She's really a harmless old thing, not malicious at all."

She gestured to where a green-eyed black tom cat crouched in the shade, tail twitching, watching a clutch of fat little nervous sparrows with malign intent.

"No? She's so harmless that she has protected her one and only from any carnal knowledge whatsoever."

"What?" Zara was taken aback. "You mean …?"

"I mean that her child, that ignorant little idiot, screamed the hotel down on our first night together! They think me a monster there. She was fine when I kissed her and fondled her, but when I tried to … you know." He glanced at Zara who nodded. "Well, she thought I was, quote, 'a dirty unnatural monster', a 'filthy beast', and had a fit of hysterics that brought members of the staff banging on our bedroom door, convinced I was trying to murder her."

He looked at Zara who was shaking. He realised that she was laughing and frowned crossly.

"Oh, it's all right for you to snigger," he said, and she burst into a loud unaffected guffaw. The mirth was contagious. So contagious that in a moment he had joined her in laughter and together they sputtered helplessly and held their bellies as tears coursed down their faces.

"Oh, it seems so silly now. What a farce." Dmitri pulled a face when his fit of mirth had abated.

Zara leaned over, suddenly serious. "No, it's not silly, dear Dmitri, it's serious. I'm sorry I laughed. It just seems extraordinary in this day and age. How awful for you."

"She has hardly spoken a word to me since. Oh, Zara, you should have seen us exchanging pleasantries as if we had just been introduced and were not in fact husband and wife. 'How are you today?' 'Well, thank you, dear.' 'Would you like some lunch?' 'What a good idea.' 'How lovely.' 'Too nice.' Oh God, Zara, it was awful." He could not keep the bitterness out of his voice.

"After that ghastly first night," he continued, "during which I must tell you I slept on the couch – a sort of bony *chaise-longue*, as uncomfortable a resting place as I've ever endured – well, after that night she would not let me come near her. Physically, I mean."

"Not at all?" Zara asked and he shook his head.

"No, not at all. Even to help her fasten her dress. If I came anywhere within a radius of about six inches, or even casually touched her, she flinched. As if I might strike her, for God's sake! I saw a porter at the Grand give me a very old-fashioned look when she jumped nervously as I helped her into a taxi. I began to feel contaminated." He smiled at her. "It's good to laugh about it. It makes me feel less of a pariah."

"Dmitri, I'm sorry. It's useless to say that, isn't it? And I can't help thinking my behaviour that time you kissed me couldn't have helped you?"

He blushed and shook his head.

"Oh, Dmitri, *I* could tell her what it's like to have reason to flinch. How could anyone from you, dear gentle you? But what on earth are you going to do? You can have the marriage dissolved, it has not been consummated."

He shook his head sadly. "I don't know, Zara." She could barely discern his eyes behind his dark glasses. They looked troubled, she thought, sadness stirring in their depths.

"On the train home," he continued, "after the farce of a holiday, we were alone in the carriage. I said, 'Well, what are we to do, Lucinda?' 'What do you mean?' she asked, innocent as a babe in arms.' About us?' I asked. 'I think it would be best if we had the marriage annulled.' She burst into tears. I'd never seen her cry before. She doesn't cry the way you do, Zara, as if the tears come from the bottom of a well of sadness. No. She *bawled*, yowled, howled. I thought someone would come to see what was wrong. I thought I would be arrested, and after the hotel it was too much ... too much."

A deep chuckle began in his chest and rose again to shake him. He burst out once more in a fit of merriment, the funny side of the situation striking him as he explained it to Zara.

She laughed but she sensed the tears behind his laughter, the hysteria. In a moment the laughter had died and a silence fell.

"And then?" she asked.

"Then she said ..." and the chuckle grew again as he caught her eye and this time he burst out into a fit of genuine, spontaneous mirth "she said, 'Mother will kill me.' Oh, Zara, can you believe it?" He clutched her hand as the tide of their hilarity rose and fell and he interjected the story between bouts of laughter.

"Mother ..."

"Dear Lady Abercrombie. God, Dmitri, how awful! She must have known. 'Mother will kill me'. God, Dmitri."

She wiped her eyes, then looked at him.

"What did you say?" she asked.

"I said, 'Never mind Mother, *I'll kill you.*' "

They stamped their feet, laughing, and the restauranteur looked at them warily as if they might be dangerous.

The wine was finished, the pigeons pecked at the last of their sun-staled bread, the cat slunk away thwarted. "We'll sort it out somehow," Dmitri said, running his finger up and down the pattern on the tablecloth. "I've told her to ask her mother ... Oh, Zara, heaven help her. Can you imagine that interview? But the awful thing is ..." He hesitated.

"You don't want her any more," Zara finished for him, nodding.

"Too right," he said, a little surprised that she divined his feelings so accurately. "The idea of making love to her at all repels me now." He shrugged his shoulders and spread his hands. "So, what can I do?"

"Dmitri, you're too soft-hearted," Zara said, briskly brushing down her trousers as she stood up.

Dmitri called for the bill then turned to her. "What do you mean?"

Zara retrieved her sweater from the back of the chair and slung it across her shoulders. She stretched her back and legs which were cramped from sitting so long. "She has to go, Dmitri dearest," she said. "You deserve better than that. And if you don't do something right away, you'll give in bit by bit and be stuck forever. Lucinda is a leech. Her mother too. They're not interested in happiness, only appearances."

"Oh ho," he hooted, "my but we *have* become worldly wise!"

She laughed, he paid the bill and they left. They walked, arms around each other's waist, to the car.

"But what will I do?" he asked, suddenly desolate. "I loved her, you see. You are the only other woman I have felt like

370

that about."

She smiled up at him. "There will be others," she said, and touched his cheek.

He leaned forward and kissed her very lightly on the lips. "Oh," he sighed, "what might have been."

She climbed into the car. He followed and they were silent on the drive back. When they reached Nice they parted without looking at each other.

It became routine for Dmitri to accompany Zara on her trips. It suited everyone. Tom felt she was being looked after while he went about his business. After a lucky period he had been losing quite heavily and was therefore playing more than before. Having a wife had changed his attitude to money. He was more cautious, and realised he was becoming careful in his accounting. Responsibility was creeping in willy-nilly. It had not helped his form so he was glad to see her cousin accompanying Zara on her expeditions. Dmitri also took her to parties and dinners in his stead and Tom was grateful to the Prince.

Lucinda kept herself out of the limelight. She appeared at Dmitri's side on family occasions and at the more public social gatherings, but often she was absent. Not often enough, however, to invite comment.

Dmitri took no direct action. The situation hovered in limbo.

"Lady Abercrombie spoke to Lucinda," he told Zara as they drove along the coast and up into the mountains to Cagnes. The sun was liquid gold, the mountains shimmered mirage-like in the heat, not a leaf on the trees stirred.

"She came to me very contrite, saying she had not understood what she was supposed to do but now Mama had told her what was expected of her. She talked with a martyr's face and an air of fearful resignation as if she were to face a firing squad. It turned my blood to water. I told her thank you, not just now, and she nearly fainted with relief."

"When did all this happen?" Zara asked. Her hands were firm on the wheel of the car, her wrists strong. He loved the way she drove. Her large eyes were hidden behind her sunglasses and her shining hair blew off her forehead in the wind. Her mouth was painted the colour of the scarlet poinsettias that splashed the hills.

"Why, oh why, Zara did you have to fall in love with Tom?" he asked involuntarily, leaving her question unanswered. She rounded a curve and drew the car to a halt. They were pinned there in the dazzling heat. The sea lay below, a million sequins of silver and gold dancing in the sun. All was silent in the vast landscape except a bird which sang its heart out overhead.

"But I did, Dmitri, madly," she said, and added thoughtfully, "I don't know why, God help me, but I did."

"He neglects you dreadfully," Dmitri said. "If I were married to you …"

"But you aren't," she said. She had taken off her glasses and he saw that there were tears in her eyes.

"I love you, Zara, I've loved you all my life. I cannot escape from you."

"Oh, please don't say that," she begged. He drew her into his arms. She felt powerless to stop him. She wanted to but the sun on her head, the beauty of the scene before them, the wine in her belly and his mouth on hers, banished common-sense and prudence. She felt neglected. Tom did not kiss her enough, did not appreciate her enough. Like a flower turning to the sun she turned to Dmitri and was overwhelmed by his dear familiarity, laced as it was with novelty and surprise. The mouth that explored and took charge of hers was much more seductive, the kisses headier, than she could have foreseen.

Melting in his arms, drowning in his kisses, she never knew how she pulled back from the brink of abandonment. But she did. Then shaking her head as if to clear it she said, "We must never play those games again, Dmitri. They are dangerous."

Shaken, he too nodded.

"I suppose. Although Tom ought to ..."

"That is not your business, Dmitri," she said. "I love him. Not by choice, I don't even know why, but it is a *fait accompli*."

She looked at him and the bird sang its high, sweet song above. "Oh, my dear, don't you see? Part of this is Lucinda's fault. If she had been a proper wife to you, none of this would have happened."

He nodded reluctantly but said nothing, shaken by his emotions, aching to hold her close, aware it was impossible. She put the car in gear and swung it round, driving them back to Nice in silence.

Chapter Twenty-One

Zara froze when she saw the handwriting on the letter and to whom it was addressed: The Baroness Hoffen von Eldrich. It could only be from one person for Sasha would never address her thus. With trembling fingers she tore open the envelope. The letter began:

Mein Leibe Zara,
I do not think badly of you because of the past and am only concerned for your happiness. It is with a sad heart therefore that I write to inform you that your brother is extremely ill.

She laid the letter on her lap and closed her eyes in pain. Sasha. Oh, Sasha. After a moment she picked it up again.

Please come if you can and see him for the doctors fear he will not last long.

It might be a trick but she doubted it. Klaus had said he wanted her to come to him of her own accord. If he was actually asking her, things must have gone badly wrong with Sasha.

Tom came into the living room. Wordlessly she handed him the letter.

"Come on, my love," he said when he had finished. "Let's go now. No time like the present. You look after the packing and I'll make the bookings."

"Oh, Tom, thank you. I didn't know how to ask." She had

not dared tell him of her visit to the yacht, fearing to provoke him into action against a dangerous opponent.

"Did you think I'd let you go alone to that man? Go on, Zara, do as I tell you. And remember it will be cold in Berlin."

It was freezing. Snow covered the streets only to turn to slush under the wheels of the cars. There were flags everywhere, together with the portrait of the little man with the moustache.

But Zara was not interested in her surroundings. As soon as they had checked into the Adlon they bathed and changed then left for the Hoffen von Eldrich residence, taking a taxi from the Unter den Linden.

They sat huddled together against the cold and Zara thought she would never be warm again.

Suddenly she felt Tom's hand tighten on hers. She looked at him and followed the direction of his horrified gaze. There was a van in front of them. The winged back doors were open and people were sitting huddled inside. There were soldiers all around it, wearing black uniforms and high boots. As far as Zara could see the soldiers were taking some people forcibly from the house outside which the van was parked and trying to push them into it.

An old lady had fallen and one of the soldiers was kicking her. A girl stood by, blood trickling down from a mouth open in a scream.

Zara cried out, "Oh God, what are they doing? Stop them. Stop them!"

The driver of the taxi said, "*Fer felucter keurl*," under his breath and put his foot on the accelerator. They turned a corner and the street before them was quiet and serene.

Zara wondered if she had imagined the terrible *tableau*: the soldiers, the old woman being brutally kicked, the girl with the blood on her mouth, that sinister van.

"What is it?" she asked Tom, with an edge of hysteria.

"Nothing. I'll tell you later." His voice was curt. "So it is true," he added to himself, his brow creased.

"What's true?" she asked impatiently but he did not answer.

They were silent until they reached the beautiful old house which now, Zara and Tom saw, was draped with a swastika flag that hung from the first-floor balcony, a huge banner that brushed against the top of Tom's head as he passed under it holding his wife's arm.

They were shown into the same wide, high room they had visited before. The same butler offered them sherry from the same decanter then left them.

Zara was outwardly calm, but her mind seethed with anxiety for her brother. When Klaus came into the room she was shocked at his appearance. His face was grey. For a moment there was a helpless look about the iron man who had only ever known complete control over events. As if sensing Zara's assessment of him his shoulders straightened and he assumed his old air of command. "The doctors are with him. You can go up when they're finished. Cigarette?"

Zara took one from the silver box he offered. Tom already had one. Klaus forgot to light it for her and she picked up the heavy lighter and lit it herself. There was silence in the room. Zara could see the snow drifting down outside and the swastika flag on the building opposite. It reminded her of blood in the snow, the wolves, her step-mother and father, Maminka and Piotr. Red and black and white. Fairy tales, always cruel. Snow White, Rose Red. Red and black and white.

Tom broke the silence.

"Are you sure there is nothing to be done?" he asked. "Can we not get him to an English doctor?"

"He has an English doctor. And a German." A grim smile twisted the Baron's lips. "And curiously they both agree."

"The doctors are in the hall, my lord." They had not heard the butler come in. The Baron looked up and stubbed out his cigarette.

"Do you want to see them?" he inquired. Tom looked at Zara who shook her head.

"No, I want to see Sasha. Perhaps tomorrow the doctors."

The Baron led them out of the room. The medical men stood in the hall in their morning suits. The butler was dismissing them. The Baron ignored the doctors and led Tom and Zara upstairs. The stairway was hung with portraits of people from past, dead ages, a frown or a smile frozen on every face, all with pride in their eyes.

Sasha was lying, pale as milk, in the middle of a huge carved ebony four-poster. He was not at the side where he could reach the table, a lamp, or water, anything he might want. It looked as if he had slipped into the middle of the bed and had not the strength to move out.

His eyes were glazed. He seemed at one moment calm, and the next agitated and disorientated; always fragile, breakable as glass.

"He's had his injection," the Baron said as Zara sat down in a chair by the bed. She felt shocked at the sight of her young beautiful brother, lying in bed plucking at the sheets, his face looking as old and shrivelled as if he were sixty. His teeth seemed prominent, as if his gums had shrunk, and the skin on his face, once smooth and soft as a girls, now hung from the bones, its elasticity lost.

"Sorry, Zaroushka dearest," he murmured. "But this was the only way."

She took his hand. It felt like a bunch of dry twigs between her fingers.

"No, no, *golubchick*. Sweet, sweet brother, no," she chanted in the soothing voice she had used to him when they were children and she was the big sister who petted him.

"Mother," he said softly.

"No, dearest, it's Zaroushka.." He seemed calmer now, his agitation gone. "Hush, it's all right. Everything will be all right."

"Zaroushka. Mama." His eyelids fluttered closed and he

378

slept or became unconscious. Which, she did not know.

"What exactly do they think is wrong with him?" she asked in an undertone to Klaus once she was certain Sasha could no longer hear. "Those filthy drugs you've been feeding him, I suppose?"

He had difficulty meeting her eyes. "Not directly. It's pneumonia they say."

Her eyes sparked angrily. "But because of the years of excess you drove him to, he has neither the strength nor the will to fight it! My God, I could kill you for this."

"You've already tried, and I am still here." The old arrogance was there but Sasha's illness had left its mark. His face was drained of colour, the skin tight with strain over the harsh angular lines of his face. Something was hitting him hard – either his imminent loss of Sasha or, more likely, the subsequent severing of his last link with her.

She nerved herself to stare into the obsidian depths of his glaze. "My husband and I would like to sit with my brother. I take it you have no objection?"

His eyes narrowed at her reference to Tom as her husband, but he inclined his head graciously. "None at all. I will see that the servants bring you something to eat. Please excuse me, I have a very important reception to attend. Inform the butler if there is any change in Sasha's condition – he will send for me."

Zara watched him go, incredulous. That he could think of going out while Sasha lay dying appalled her.

Knowing her distress, Tom picked up a chair and set it down beside hers. When a nurse appeared he sent her away and the two of them watched over the dying man together, hand in hand. Zara had never been so grateful for Tom's comfort and support as she was all through that long night.

As the first feeble light of morning struggled to penetrate the thick brocade curtains, Zara sensed a change in Sasha's breathing. The harsh labouring sound grew quiet and light. The heavy bedclothes covering Sasha's emaciated form barely moved. "I love you, Sasha," she whispered and took his hand in hers. She was still holding it an hour later when they heard the Baron's arrival downstairs.

Tom put his hand on her shoulder. "Shall I go down and tell him?"

She turned wide staring eyes on him.

"Tell him what?"

"He's gone, Zara."

He waited for the tears and angry denials. There were none. She had felt Sasha's hand grip hers, she thought with affection. Now Tom had to prize her hand out of his death clasp.

"Go and tell the Baron," she said finally. "I don't want to set eyes on him ever again."

"Will you be all right?" he asked, face creased with tiredness and concern.

She did not answer.

She sat in silence, head bowed, repeating the prayers for the recently dead. She thought of her little brother in Russia, so young, so loved, his plump hand resting in hers so trustingly, the sobs rose in her throat, threatening to choke her.

Tom led her weeping from the room. She remembered little of what followed. Tom's presence was strong and comforting, his arms around her reassuring. She could not understand how she could allow him to make love to her, her brother barely cold, but back in the Adlon she fell into his arms, aching for him, lusting for his body.

"You want to make sure you're alive," Tom told her when she asked him how she could do it. "When we are faced with the inevitability of death we rush towards life and embrace it passionately. Do not be ashamed, my darling. It is normal."

They remained for the funeral. On Tom's advice, but much against her will, Zara allowed the Baron to arrange it. "He knows the country, darling. It's all a matter of papers, documents. Klaus can handle all that. It will be easiest. It's not as if you could take Sasha back to Russia."

380

She took his advice, finally seeing the sense of his argument.

At the graveside she wept, averting her eyes from the Baron's silent and malign presence, watching the sods of frozen earth fall on her brother's coffin. It was snowing and the small group around the grave shivered, their breath hanging on the air in white clouds. As they turned to leave and before Tom could stop her, she broke away and ran to face the Baron one last time. He stared at her, tall and gaunt in his black cashmere coat.

"You killed him!" she screamed, hitting his chest with her gloved fists. "You killed him, you killed him."

He flinched, but stood statue-still under her rain of blows.

"Come along, darling," Tom said quietly, "let's get out of here. We're going home, my love."

Nina and Chuck arrived for a stay at the villa after their honeymoon. Unlike Dmitri and Lucinda, the pair glowed with content and fulfilment. Their faces and gestures revealed at every turn that all was well with them. Who could have thought I could be so wrong? Zara mused, watching Chuck wink at his wife. The wink, which took a fraction of a second, revealed all: passion satisfied, games played, fondness, familiarity, good humour and lust. They've got it all, she thought the more she observed them, and I'd have bet anything they'd fail and Dmitri and Lucinda would succeed.

Sonya had thought so too. She asked Zara about it over tea in her apartment.

"You pour." Zara asked Conchita to leave the samovar next to her aunt. She knew Sonya loved to preside, often making the tea at the table herself. She sat now, elegant in an apricot Schiaparelli dress, pouring the tea and adding the lemon, gazing at her niece through narrowed eyes. The girl was too thin. Now it was fashionable to have curves, Nina's figure was all the rage. Sonya thought that Zara could afford to add a few pounds to round her out a bit. The girl was thin as a whippet, the bones of her face clear, the eyes bigger than ever. But she was beautiful, Sonya thought.

The older woman had grown closer and closer to her niece. Her own daughter had not, in her mother's estimation, the sense or the objectivity to participate in an intelligent conversation, nor was she overendowed with wisdom or sensitivity. Zara, on the other hand, was very astute. Sonya relished their conversations and her niece's company, and found comfort in the thought that she would still have Zara when Nina went to America with Chuck.

When they had their tea, Sonya said, "What a lovely room this is, Zara. Each time I visit it looks prettier."

The sun shone through the open floor-length windows, and the cream carpet and walls, pale furniture all gave an atmosphere of lightness and airy space. The scarlet poinsettias in the corner and the paintings on the walls drew the eye and focused attention on them.

"Thank you, Aunt. Now what do you really want to ask me?" She smiled gently at Sonya and her aunt sighed.

"About Dmitri and Lucinda. What on earth is the matter there?"

When Zara tactfully explained Sonya, too, laughed, then sighed again and frowned.

"Oh, how very sad," she said. "Damn that girl! If I'd known, I'd have taken Lucinda quietly aside and told her all about the birds and bees. It's hard to credit in this day and age. And now I suppose she knows my poor son can no longer work up any interest?"

Zara nodded.

"Dear, dear, dear. You mean they've never ...?"

"Not that I know of. I think he would have told me."

"She'll have to be got rid of," Sonya was saying.

"That's what I told him, but you know Dmitri. He cannot bear conflict. He's done nothing so far and the longer he leaves it the more difficult it will be."

382

"Oh, Zara, I'd forgotten about Lady Abercrombie! She'll hang on as long and as hard as she can. Oh dear, oh dear."

Zara thought how handsome her aunt still looked. What a formidable person she was. She led the Russian colony in Nice, everyone loved and respected her. The last thing she wanted was a scandal.

"Aunt Sonya, I think you'd better talk to Dmitri. I don't think he wants a fuss any more than you do."

Nina was preparing for her move to America. All her apprehension at living such a distance from her family had vanished. Zara sometimes felt jealous at the happy intimacy displayed by the newlyweds, and their obvious enjoyment of each other's company. Their constantly being together made her sigh in envy. She told herself she was being foolish and that as soon as Chuck arrived in America he would be out all day working, just as Tom was.

But not at night, a little voice whispered in her ear. And Nina wants no more. She is not as greedy as I am. She put the thoughts aside.

At the end of the summer Nina and Chuck left for America. There were no tearful goodbyes. Nina was too happy. She had her husband now. There was nowhere she would rather be than at his side.

"Write," she said to Zara, "you'll always be my best friend."

In December they received news that she was pregnant. Momma Bee and Grandma Myrtle were looking after her and she was as happy as a June bug.

"Awful Americanisms," Sonya said.

Zara thought how lucky she was. She could imagine Nina the centre of attention in Virginia, fussed over and pregnant, those warm American women advising her and mothering her, and once more she envied her cousin.

Sonya said, "I'll be a grandmother. I don't know whether to rejoice or go into a decline."

Vassily looked anxiously at Zara. "I'll love it," he said,

"being a grandfather." He glanced uncertainly at his wife but she was reading the end of the letter.

"I wish she was nearer," he said. "I miss Nina. I miss her jolly laugh." He sounded wistful and Zara thought he looked very tired.

Chapter Twenty-Two

It was a bright March morning two years later when Sonya called, her voice hysterical, to tell Zara that Vassily had died the night before in his sleep. He had had a heart attack and passed peacefully away.

Zara was shocked. Tom, instantly sympathetic, drove her up to the Villa de la Rose.

Dmitri greeted them, subdued and pale-faced, looking suddenly very like his father. He took them to Sonya and Zara was shocked by the change in her aunt's appearance. She looked her age this morning, eyes haggard, cheeks sunken. She had literally shrivelled, Zara thought. She looked small and bent, as if in the night a burden had been laid upon her and she found it unbearably heavy. Zara had heard the phrase 'bowed down with grief', and that was what Sonya appeared to be.

She looked at Zara through stunned eyes.

"I never forgave him," she said. Zara motioned the others to leave them alone. Dmitri said, "I must phone Father Ivan. We should let him know." And Tom kissed her lightly, "I'll wait outside, dear," he said, squeezing Zara's hand. "There's no hurry."

When the door had closed behind them Sonya looked at Zara. "I never forgave him," she said again, "for Anya. For your siren step-mother. For that bitch."

Zara was surprised at the venom in Sonya's voice. Usually calm and equable, the fierceness of the hatred coming to the surface, still strong after all this time, shocked Zara. We all have hidden depths, she thought.

"I've kept him all these years waiting for my pardon. He's had to beg for my approval. I've doled out my kindness to him in tiny portions. I always *meant* totally to clean the slate but kept on putting it off until tomorrow. From the day he returned to me from her arms, rejected by her, cast aside on a whim, I made him feel guilty." She looked at Zara, dry-eyed now, an old woman. "There was no moment when I allowed him to feel natural and relaxed with me, and he was a man who most needed to feel uncriticised, to be accepted just as he was. His self-respect depended on my unconditional love and acceptance of him, and I did not allow him to feel them, ever again."

She sighed and looked out of the window. The sun fell on the Louis XV chaise. A petal dropped from a bowl of blue iris on a table under the window.

"The sun will fade the silk," Sonya said, and rose and closed the shutters. Her movements were stiff and slow where before she had always been brisk and energetic.

A sudden gloom descended as she closed the slatted shutters and a dusty light, more suited to death than the brilliant beams of sunshine, suffused the room. She walked slowly back to Zara. There was a knock on the door. Her voice sounded harsh as she said, "Come in." It was Dmitri.

"Mother, there are phone calls. No one knows yet. Princess d'Artelli wants to ask you to a cocktail do tonight. I said you could not go. Shall I tell her why?"

Sonya looked uncertain. "I don't know, Dmitri. Do what you think best, dear."

'I'll tell everyone who calls then and ask them not to disturb you."

The Princess nodded, uninterested. Dmitri left and Sonya turned to Zara again.

"I loved him, but I never let him see how much after that incident with Anya. Never. He had to earn every kiss, every embrace. He had to spend the rest of his life wondering how he could please me, win my approval. I always meant to forgive him. Say, 'Darling, it's all over now. Forgotten. Come into my arms. I love you as much as you love me.' I used to imagine how ecstatic he would be, how relieved, how we would laugh together again as we once used to. Now he is dead and I left it too late, Zara, I left it too late."

The cry she made as she said this tore through the room, shattering the peace. It held all the pain of a wish that would never now be fulfilled. Too late! Too late! Abandon hope for death has cheated you.

Zara held the shaking woman close as she sobbed uncontrollably. Years of pent up emotion slewed through the dam of her restraint. Her head bent, held between her hands, Zara's arms around her, she wept for her loss, the dear man she had loved but never fully forgiven.

Dmitri came in again, and left. Zara asked him to order some tea. Drushenka brought it, her eyes red with weeping.

We all adored him but we took him for granted, Zara thought, and when Dmitri returned and Sonya's sobs had abated she said, "We must let Nina know."

Dmitri jumped to his feet. It seemed to make him feel better to run errands, make calls.

"I'll telephone America," he said.

"But she must not try to come," Sonya cried.

"I don't think she'll try," Zara said, looking after Dmitri, her heart heavy. He had lost all his boyishness. His hair had thinned and he wore spectacles. His waist had thickened and he had an air of defeat about him. These losses gave him a strong resemblance to Vassily, yet the charm was still there. Zara sighed.

He had never done anything about Lucinda and his wife had taken to drinking rather too much. She drank secretly, refusing alcohol in public, but everyone knew. She frequently lost her balance at parties or mumbled incoherent rubbish to her dinner partner, and Dmitri had his hands full excusing or trying to extricate her with dignity from these embarrassing situations.

Zara had been staring after him when Tom appeared in the doorway. Her heart lifted as it always did when she saw him and she thought wryly how his charm had never deserted him. Her aunt saw him and instantly held out her hands.

"Tom, how good of you to come. I don't know how to cope with all that has to be done. You must help me, dear boy. Oh, why must the birds sing today?"

He took her hands in his, nodding to Zara that it was all right for her to go and making reassuring noises at Sonya.

Zara went into the hall. Her cousin was leaning against the cold marble Venus, his back turned, shoulders shaking. Zara went and leant her cheek against him.

"Is it very bad?" she asked.

She had seen little of him lately. Glimpses of him at candlelit tables at dinner parties, or leaving with a glassy-eyed Lucinda on his arm. He always seemed to be fully occupied with her and Zara did not like to interfere. Her position with her cousin was ambiguous.

"Very," he said now, his face averted. "I loved Papa, but I never told him. It's too late now."

Zara thought of Sonya and her despairing pride. Was there always too much love or too little? Was it avowed too often or not at all? What is the matter with us, she asked herself, that we cannot manage this business of love? She kept her cheek pressed to his jacket.

"Lucinda is impossible now," he said. "Rarely sober, and it's all my fault. You and Mama told me to get an annulment, but I did nothing. Nothing at all. I just left it. It's not poor Lucinda's fault. Once she knew, well, I think she hoped we could … But I can't stand her now. It gets worse every day. She's sloppy. Messy. I keep seeing you, so neat and beautiful. Exquisite. Everything in place. I'm haunted. Oh God, Zara, what am I going to do?"

He turned into her arms, bending his head on to her shoulder, sobbing in harsh, dry bouts that made him shudder. She held him, patting him like a baby, trying to steady him, but she was small and nearly toppled under his weight.

Drushenka crossed the huge hall carrying a tray with a silver jug on it. She glanced at Zara and Dmitri but seemed to see nothing out of the way. She disappeared into the drawing room, leaving the door open. Zara could hear Sonya saying, "Tell Dmitri and Zara that there is fresh tea, there's a dear boy," and Tom's face appeared in the hall. He looked at her, mouthing, "All right?" and she mouthed back over Dmitri's shoulder, "Brandy." He nodded and went back into the room to re-emerge with a glass of brandy in his hand. He deftly took the distraught Dmitri's weight away from Zara, saying, "Drink this, old fellow. It will make you fell better." And then he walked Dmitri back into the room, Zara following.

They sat about drinking tea and discussing arrangements. Every now and then someone would weep a little, making a soft sighing sound under the birdsong that came floating through the window on a soft breeze. Sonya's poise gradually returned. She still looked ten years older.

"The servants are all very upset," she said, "they were all so fond of him."

"Yes." Dmitri seemed to rouse himself. "He was very kind to them."

"To everyone," Tom said. "He was a dear friend. True blue."

Silence fell. The shutters, still closed, allowed little shafts of light through the main window that were full of tiny motes, infinitesimal particles, aimlessly dancing in the golden rays. Just like us, Zara mused, just like us. On a summer day in Nice. Aimlessly dancing about. Our lives so purposeless. Or is there a pattern we cannot see?

Loud voices in the hall caused them all to look at the door.

"I will see him. He's my husband." Lucinda came weaving in and stood swaying uncertainly in the darkened room. Her hair and clothes were dishevelled, her speech slurred. She looked around at them all, half closing one eye.

"Creepy," she remarked. "Cree-py. Wha' cha doing? Seance? God, what a boring lot you are! Bloody Russians."

Dmitri stood and she turned and pointed an accusing finger at him.

"My husband. My bloody husband. Came to ask you, loverboy, are you impotent? Someone said today, men who can't – y'know … You always say it's my fault but," she tapped the side of her nose with her finger, "I think it's yours. Im-po-tent. Came to this creepy place to find out …"

Lucinda's voice petered out and Tom crossed the room to her. He took her elbow firmly and spoke to her in a kindly but authoritative voice, keeping up a steady stream of conversation as he led her out of the room.

"Lucinda, my dear, come along. Let me take you to your car. This way. It's been a long time since I've seen you. How have you been? And how is your dear mother? I haven't seen her in Monte Carlo in an age. Let me take you to her. This way. Careful."

He left the room, turning only to wave at Zara. The others watched him leave. Dmitri bowed his head low as if in shame. "Oh God," he murmured. "God."

Sonya's face had slackened and fallen once more into lines of despair. Zara watched the rays of light, the dance of the golden motes, and listened to the loud ticking of the clock.

It was a time for regrets, for all the times Zara had been to the Villa de la Rose and treated her uncle casually. They had all taken him for granted much as one would grow accustomed to a comfortable piece of furniture. Now they missed him every time they looked around for his warm sympathetic smile, Sonya most of all. She behaved as if she expected him to come back and enable her to set the record straight.

Zara also missed Nina. This surprised her for she had never felt emotionally close to her cousin. The Villa de la Rose seemed empty without the two more buoyant members of the family.

As time passed Sonya and Zara grew very close. Sonya had lost her air of natural command and become hesitant and uncertain. Things she had once effortlessly controlled she now wavered over. Plans were changed and changed again, and she found it hard to make decisions.

Zara loved her aunt and helped her all she could. It gave her own life new purpose and commitment.

"I'm glad you're so much with Sonya," Tom said. "It's good for both of you."

He came home one night, or rather morning, at three a.m. Zara felt him slide into the bed beside her and turned to him, groping for him in the dark. "Awake, love?" he asked softly, drawing her warm body to him. She curled her legs around his and tucked her face under his chin.

She bit back a dozen remarks that were on the tip of her tongue. 'I was hoping you'd come home early' or 'I missed you' or 'I was waiting' would be dangerous. So she merely said, "umm."

He drew away from her and lit a cigarette.

"Was it ... successful tonight?" He did not seem to have heard her. After a moment or two of silence he said. "There's a war, love. There's a war in Europe. It's gathering momentum and it won't be stopped easily. Do you remember the old woman in Germany, and the girl?"

She shivered. "Yes, darling."

"That sums it up. That picture, German soldiers kicking the weak and helpless, is what it's all about. We've had our heads buried in the sand here."

"But what can we do?" asked Zara. She raised herself on one elbow and looked at him closely. "I'll never forget what we saw in Berlin."

"Well, Hitler is taking over."

She thought again of the girl with the bloody mouth and the soldier kicking the old woman on the pavement.

"I'll have to go to England," he said after a pause.

Her heart sank. "But, darling, England's not at war."

"It will be very soon, and I want to be there. I want to be ready."

"Oh, Tom." She could not think of anything more to say or any questions to ask. All she could think of was that she did not want him to leave her, how a war would upset her life, ruin her hard won peace of mind. She realised she was being selfish. Tom was right, she knew, but she wanted to cry out in protest: 'I don't want you to go. You will not go.'

She made up her mind that if and when he went, she would go too. The slim satin strap of her nightdress slipped down her arm. She straightened it then took the cigarette from Tom's mouth and inhaled.

"Don't let's go just yet," she said, exhaling. "You don't know for sure. Maybe something will avert it."

But he shook his head. "It's already started. There's no way out. England will be in and I want to help out. I want to join the RAF."

She sat up abruptly, and stared at him.

"Fight? You mean actually fight?"

"He laughed at her consternation. "Yes. What did you think I meant?"

She shook her head bemused. "I don't know, but not fight. Oh no, darling, I couldn't bear it."

"Zara, let's not have a scene."

"But you don't understand – it's madness. I've seen war. I've seen how one moment someone I love is there living, breathing, heart beating. And the next moment – nothing. Don't ask me to go through that."

She stared at him as he frowned. He had not changed since their marriage. There were no grey hairs; no signs of ageing. He looked younger now than Dmitri, as debonair and good-looking as the day she had met him. She loved his face, was content to spend time just looking at him, tracing his eyebrows with her finger, the curve of his mouth, the line of his jaw. Now she laid her hand on his chest, feeling the fuzz of hair beneath her fingers.

"Please," she whispered.

He looked at her tenderly, turning on his side to face her.

"Sweet girl," he murmured, "perhaps it would be better if you stayed here with the Princess. I doubt if the Germans will come here to the south or hurt you if they do. Or you could go to Nina in the States. She'd love to have you, and you would be safe there and forget to worry about me."

She nearly cried out. She very nearly seized him by the shoulders and yelled her fury at his suggestions. But practice had perfected her ability to think before she spoke and she swallowed her anger.

"Dearest, no. I want to be with you," she said quietly, trying to inject a note of calm matter-of-factness into her voice. "I'd worry much more if we were apart." Thinking: I would die, beloved. I would die.

As usual he accepted what she said at face value. He was so uncomplicated. He pulled her into the circle of his arms and held her close, sniffing the scent of her hair.

"Nice," he murmured drowsily, "so nice," and fell deeply asleep.

She lay awake for a long time, trying to still her fears. War, the devourer of men! She did not care if the whole civilized world was destroyed, went up in flames, if only she could be in her husband's arms somewhere safe. But, she supposed, that was the very thing war would prevent.

Some weeks later Tom was in the bath and Zara on the phone, arranging with her aunt to meet for lunch in the Negresco, when they heard the doorbell ring.

"I've got to go, Aunt Sonya. There's someone at the door and Conchita is not answering. I'll see you at one o'clock. Yes, I've booked a table at the Chanticleer for tomorrow night, dear, so don't worry. 'Bye." She put down the phone and hurried to the door.

When she opened it, a man nearly fell into her hall, closely followed by a woman. It took her a few startled moments to recover enough to recognise Dirk, though his companion was unknown to her.

"Dirk! Oh, it's good to see you. You must be ..."

She could not remember the name of the girl Dirk had said he was marrying.

"Gerda, *bitte*." The woman had a round face very like her husband's. She had a mop of soft brown curls, a small berry-red mouth, bright pink cheeks, a button nose and bright blue eyes that peered anxiously through hornrimmed spectacles. Her face was innocent of makeup.

"Do come into the living room!" Zara felt awkward. Social chit-chat seemed out of place in the atmosphere of panic and alarm they brought with them.

Just then Tom emerged from the bedroom. "Who was it, Zara?" He saw the strangers and stopped.

"Darling, this is Dirk and Gerda Van Holstein. You've never met. They are friends from Amsterdam."

"I remember. You spoke of them," Tom said, giving them his charming smile and shaking hands.

"But what has happened? You seem agitated. Let me ring for some coffee. That would be a good idea, Zara, don't you think."

They ordered the coffee and looked enquiringly at their guests. They were obviously travel-stained and weary.

Dirk addressed Tom. "You must forgive us," he said, "we could think of nowhere else to go."

Tears welled up in his eyes. He pulled off his glasses and flung his arm across his face as if to conceal his emotion. His body betrayed him, shaking with silent sobs. His wife crossed to him. Tenderly, she drew him on to the sofa and cradled him in her arms.

"You must forgive us," she echoed her husband, "we

have been travelling for a long time as if the devil were at our heels."

Her voice quavered, but the air of strength about her was unmistakable.

"What happened?" Tom asked, taking Zara's hand and sitting down opposite Dirk and his wife. "Although I think I can guess. First, though you must have some coffee."

Dirk gulped his, spluttering as he swallowed greedily, then held out his cup for more.

"We haven't eaten. We've had no money," Gerda explained.

"Then we must get you some food immediately."

"We'd like to tell you first."

"Tell us what?" asked Zara, perplexed.

"The SS," Dirk said, and his wife shuddered. "They burned the books," Dirk explained. "Burned the knowledge of nearly two thousand years. Set fire to wisdom, tolerance, love and truth. Tried to obliterate them."

"Don't upset yourself, *leibling*," Gerda said. She looked at Zara and Tom. "It's always the same with him. The destruction of the books was, for him, a sacrilege. But there was worse even than that." She pushed the soft thatch of curls off her forehead. "For me," she said, "it was the humiliation. They make fun of you. They deride you in the streets. They come into your home. Jews are treated differently there. That was why we got into trouble." She bowed her head and there was silence.

Zara had begun to have an inkling what this was about. Her hand felt dead in Tom's tight grasp. Soon she would have pins and needles.

Dirk glanced at her, half afraid.

"I am a Jew," he said.

"Are you? I don't think it ever occurred to me. So what? What does it matter?"

"It matters in Germany. Outside no one knows, no one believes. It does not seem possible when you are here."

395

He looked out at the clear Madonna-blue sky. He could hear the swish of the sea and through the open window catch a glimpse of the palm trees on the Boulevard des Anglais. The sun drenched everything in a warm golden haze.

"What exactly happened?" Zara asked.

Dirk shuddered. It was his wife who replied in her halting English.

"The Jews are being hounded," she said quietly. "Let us not mince our words. You see, I am not a Jew, but I am guilty because I married one, because I love one. The Jews, Mrs Armitidge, are being persecuted at every turn. In Germany today, it is not safe to be a Jew."

"How do you mean?" Zara asked, struggling to understand. Dirk took over.

"Our business, our jobs, our money, our homes, are being taken from us because we are 'sub-humans'. No job is too low for us. We are left with nothing. People in polite drawing rooms like this one cannot believe their ears when we try to tell them what is going on. It disconcerts them. They do not wish to hear of anything so distressing and dangerous."

His voice was cold and hard and angry.

"The last we heard you were in Amsterdam," said Zara.

"We sent you an invitation to our wedding," Gerda said.

"I'm so sorry," Zara looked contrite. "We could not go. Oh dear, I'm so sorry."

"It did not matter. But Dirk would have liked you there. He loves you."

There was no jealousy in Gerda's voice.

"Why did you go to Germany?" said Tom.

"Well," Dirk continued, with difficulty, "Frau Kettner wanted to see her homeland again. You remember, Zara? She had heard wonderful things. Germany was once more a great power, a nation to be reckoned with. The Germans were suddenly the children of the Gods and she desperately wanted to go and see Berlin for herself. I know – " he corrected himself – "knew nothing of politics then. I was not interested. I am an academic after all. What had politics got to do with me? Or so I thought in my innocence.

"I told her if she felt so strongly and wanted so badly to go we would take her. She had been like a mother to me. You know that, Zara." She nodded. "I had always promised, and Gerda wanted to go too. Oh, how I wish we had never been so foolish!"

"We thought it would be interesting," Gerda said. "How näive we were! The three of us got cheap lodgings in Berlin with a Frau Buttenmeyer. The house had 'Jude' scrawled all over it but we thought nothing of it at the time. The work of stupid vandals. Dirk and I did not care for the city when we saw more of it. The flags and banners, the marching soldiers kicking their legs high." Zara nodded. She had not liked it either. "But Frau Kettner loved it. She said she felt proud to be German."

"We had said we would stay until September. We did not want to but we had promised." Dirk wrinkled his brow, took off his glasses and wiped them. "We met some friends from the University. The man was a Professor, an intellectual. It was he who told us that Jews were not popular in Berlin. Neither were Communists. Every day, in the locality where we were living, which he told us was a ghetto, we could see the hounding going on. Meanwhile, Berlin celebrated. There was an unholy excitement everywhere. But the Jews were being arrested for minor offences, some betrayed by jealous rivals and neighbours. The Professor told us that Hitler believed that Jews were inferior. He also said that the Communists met in our house which was why there had been a convenient room vacant. No one wanted to live there, it was too dangerous."

"We did not believe him. We thought he had gone soft or become alarmist in his old age. It surprised me for he was a truly enlightened man. However, he proved right." He cleared his throat. "The cause of what happened next is still a mystery, but it happened all right. In Berlin, such incidents are becoming an everyday occurence. Some uniformed thugs came and terrorised Frau Kettner. They reduced her to a gibbering idiot. Silly, stupid woman!"

"No, Dirk," Gerda interrupted. She turned to Zara. "She is silly, yes, but they are gangsters and would frighten a brave man. They are not human beings, they are ..."

"They saw her passport, then they asked her about meetings in the building. They suspected some Jews were assembling there. She denied all knowledge of it. Gerda and I were out at the time. They were just about to leave when one of them saw a letter addressed to us in the hall. They pounced on it and started questioning her about us. She said yes, we were visitors and lived with her. They asked had we been to the University. She said yes. They said subversive influences were holding meetings in Berlin and some outside agitators had arrived. Maybe we were among them? Frau Kettner agreed, maybe we were. God, how could she?"

Gerda leaned towards him. "Hush, *leibling*," she said, "she was terrified. She meant no harm."

"Oh, but how could she?" Dirk shook his head in disbelief. "The man who lodged upstairs, Herr Darrendorf, heard all this. They know to listen in those houses. By this time the thugs were up in our room, ripping open our cases. Mistakes are made all the time in that city. You have no idea. Such confusion. And there was a black van waiting in the street."

Zara cried, "Oh no!" Tom's hand tightened on hers. It was a vice-like grip now and his face was tight and tense.

"Herr Darrendorf went out of the house to watch for us and saw us coming down the street. I thought he was mad, standing there, staring at us and waving. We waved back, thinking he was greeting us. We came to the house. Frau Kettner leaned out of the window and shouted, 'It is them. They are the ones you want!' "

"Frau Kettner did that?" Zara cried in disbelief.

Gerda nodded. "You must not blame her. Fear makes idiots of us, Mrs Armitidge. The political climate in Germany feeds on fear."

"We ran. The thugs in uniform ran after us. I have never been so surprised." Dirk looked at Tom. "You must know we are very peaceable people. To find outselves running – you cannot imagine."

"I can," Tom said firmly.

"Well, we ran. We were very lucky because we were near the corner of the street and it led on to a main thoroughfare. By the time we reached the end and had slipped into the crowd, the thugs following us could not see us. There was a military parade and I think that made them give up.

"It had been raining and we had both been wearing mackintoshes. We stopped running, not wanting to draw attention to ourselves. The sun came out and we took off the raincoats which changed our appearance somewhat."

"We sat down at a pavement ale-house," Gerda interposed. "These glassy-eyed troops goose-stepped past. While we sat watching Herr Darrendorf came and sat at our table. He told us what had happened. He said we would be mad to return to Frau Kettner and that house. It would most likely be watched, and somehow or other they were convinced we were members of a Communist group. He said he knew a greengrocer who would be sympathetic. What he really meant was 'greedy'. This man said he would hide us in his van until he reached his destination in the south. After that it was up to us.

"We did not know what to do. We did not know how serious it all was but suddenly the Professor's warnings did not seem so extreme. I wanted to return to Amsterdam, but what could I do? What choice had we? We had no way to get home. There was no way out. We took the offer."

For the first time Gerda laughed. "We were buried in onions and leeks and other vegetables. It was terrible! Very uncomfortable. Herr Darrendorf said the greengrocer would deny all knowledge of us if we were caught but he still expected to be paid plenty. Herr Darrendorf got our money and our papers from Frau Kettner. The greengrocer took most of our funds. We were in no position to argue."

"He did give us a little money back," Gerda interrupted, scrupulous as ever.

"Hardly any at all. Enough to get the train here. We did not know what else to do, where else to go. We knew no one in these parts."

"We feel so stupid, so foolish," Gerda said. "I'm sure we behaved in a very naïve manner. Innocents abroad."

"We were shocked by the experience. Very shocked. More by what it indicated, if what we hear about the Führer is true. Oh Lord, I just don't know what to believe." Dirk sounded exasperated. "I don't know at all. So we came to you."

"You did the right thing," Tom said firmly. "You can stay here as long as you like. Treat this apartment as your home. I am returning to England to join the RAF. I know what's been happening in Germany for a long time now. I've heard many stories, much worse than yours. Chamberlain is a fool. Oh, why waste time talking about it?"

"We'll be glad to rest here a few days, a week at most. But we must get back to Amsterdam," Gerda said. "We have to fight this thing too."

"You're mad if you do that! Why not come with us to England, or go to the States?" Zara asked.

Gerda looked at Tom. Heedless, Zara continued, "Rest for a while, then make up your minds. There's plenty of time to decide."

"That's just the problem," Tom said sadly. "We've all thought there was plenty of time. We've all procrastinated. But Zara is right. For the moment you must rest. I think you should put off lunch in the Negresco, darling, and ask Sonya to come here."

"Of course," Zara answered swiftly.

There were protests from the Van Holsteins but Tom and Zara were adamant. Zara asked Conchita to prepare some Vichyssoise, a sea-food salad, and a *tarte framboise*. She then took Dirk and Gerda to the guest room, provided them with fresh towels, soap and a change of clothes. All they had was what was on their backs but Tom lent Dirk a pair of slacks that had to be rolled up at the ankles, and a shirt and tie and sweater. Zara, meanwhile, found an elasticated dirndl peasant skirt with a blouse and shawl to match that not only fitted Gerda but suited her delightfully.

After they had bathed and changed and had a short rest they joined Tom and Zara in the living room.

Sonya had arrived, excited and curious about their guests. It was obvious that from the first she took to the Van Holsteins. Dirk was a changed man. He relaxed and expanded happily in the welcoming atmosphere. And Gerda, they discovered, was a happy person with a contagious laugh.

"You have no idea how relieved we were when we found your house this morning. Oh, Zara, you were always lovely. Now you are beautiful," Dirk said.

"Well, you were kind to me when I was alone in Amsterdam," she replied briskly.

"I was in love with you then," he said, eyes twinkling behind his spectacles.

Gerda laughed. "Yes, he was," she said, "terribly. You have no idea how hard I had to work to convince him that flesh and blood is more satisfactory than a ghost."

There was no bitterness in her voice and with the smile she gave her husband she revealed the bond of love and trust that they shared.

Sonya took them under her wing. She warmed especially to Gerda whose bright manner, honesty and amiable personality endeared her to the older woman. There was nothing pretentious in the little Austrian and Sonya decided she needed looking after.

401

"We'll go shopping tomorrow, get you clothes you can wear," she said. "I remember Zara arriving in Nice with barely a stitch to her name, too." She smiled fondly at her niece. "Remember our first shopping spree, Zara?"

She nodded, happy in the company of so many people that she loved.

"We can't go shopping," Gerda said, "we have no money."

"But if there is a way we can get some from Amsterdam ..." Dirk began.

Tom interrupted. "I'll arrange it for you, and we can float you until it arrives. But, I beg of you, don't worry about something as paltry as money."

"No, you must not fret," Sonya added her advice. "Have a quiet week and then worry about the awkward things like money and plans."

"Now come along," Zara said. "You must tell us all the details again. Sonya hasn't heard the whole story."

She led them to the dining room, a small room with a balcony. French windows stood open and the curtains stirred in the cooling breeze from the Mediterranean. They could see sports-clad people below, and the white sails of boats bobbing on the deep blue sea. War seemed very remote indeed, from the peace and joyousness of the scene.

The table was covered in a white damask cloth. Pale green and white dishes and wafer-thin glasses, silver cutlery, apple-green and white napkins and a silver bowl of pale pink cabbage roses in the centre decorated the table.

They sat, sun slanting over them, and Conchita put the Vichyssoise before them in little green bowls on beds of ice in larger silver dishes. They shook their napkins and placed them across their knees, smiling at the thought of the good food they were about to share. Sonya smiled at Zara, Dirk and Gerda exchanged a glance of relief and gratitude and Tom poured the wine.

They did not realise it would be the last meal they would eat in a world at peace.

Part IV
England

Chapter Twenty-Three

The next day, September the 3rd 1939, hostilities between England and Germany were declared. A flurry of activity hit the South of France. Hitherto impervious to the upheavals that had been taking place in Europe, now that England had declared war on Germany the Riviera dwellers became suddenly mobile. The English left for London, the Germans for Berlin. Some head-in-sand types waited to see what would happen, firmly convinced that their particular Eden would not be disturbed.

Tom told Zara that he was going home immediately and she and Sonya insisted on going too. Dirk and Gerda decided to return to Amsterdam and refused to be talked out of it. People who had heard about the war and who had rationalised it, were suddenly relieved that it was decided, that at last it was in the open. The uncertainty was over.

Zara hated London. The smoke, the rush and bustle and noise, appalled her after the slow, sleepy, sun-filled life she had led on the Riviera. She was terrified of the underground and had an acute attack of panic on her first excursion on the Northern Line. Sonya, however, adored her new life. She fell in love with the murky old city and its cheerful people. She became an expert on the public transport systems and Zara insisted on her aunt accompanying her whenever and wherever they travelled.

She and Tom joined up. Tom enlisted in the RAF and Sonya for a nursing course. She decided she was not suitable

405

for the Land Army or work in a munitions factory. She informed the authorities of this, much to their amusement, and decided she would be most useful as a nurse.

"No matter what age one is, one can always nurse, and there's always work to do," she said. "Actually it's a glorified First Aid course I'm on," she added apologetically, "but it makes me feel useful and that's all that matters."

She got a flat in Oakwood Court and there she remained, refusing to budge when Tom was sent to train at RAF Lentmead and Zara accompanied him. Her aunt urged Zara to join her in some volunteer work but she refused. All she wanted was to be with Tom.

"I must be there for him, Aunt Sonya," she said, "always there when he needs me."

They left her behind reluctantly but had to admit they had not seen her so confident and busy since Vassily died. Zara stayed in a local pub-cum-hotel, and Tom joined her when he could get away, which wasn't often.

Autumn came, then winter. It was nearly as cold as Russia, Zara thought, and damp. So damp. She wondered what would happen when they could not get coal and she could not have a fire in her room. She wondered what would happen when food got short as the locals in gloom-laden voices promised each other it would over a pint of ale of an evening.

She listened to the news. She sat enthralled at Churchill's speeches. He gave you the feeling that this was a great moment in history, that you personally were important. But she thought him crazy. No one would stop the little man, she was sure. Austria was gone, Czechoslovakia was absorbed. Denmark invaded, Norway over-run, Holland fallen (Oh Dirk, oh Gerda!) then Belgium. Dear beloved France ... Dmitri, where are you? Zara knew about the war now. She had maps on the wall and little arrow pins in red and black. Red for England and the Allies. Black for Germany. Along with everyone else in England, she followed the progress of the Nazi advance with a sinking heart. She heard Churchill call England the 'sole champions' of world freedom and admired his gallantry while fearing he would fail. The curse of Hitler would not be taken from the face of Europe by this tiny nation, these brave fools who, David-like, had taken on a giant. And her husband was one of the brave fools.

Despite her forebodings, it was a glorious time for Zara; when she looked back on it, the happiest of her life. It made her feel guilty that she could be so happy in the midst of death and destruction, but she had one very good reason: Tom had changed completely. He was now everything she had dreamed he might be. She could say what she liked to him now. He needed demonstrations of love, revelled in her excesses.

When he began going on bombing raids over Germany he would come back to her hungry for her passion, greedy for her protests of love, welcoming her possessiveness. He was the exact opposite of what he had been in the South of France and she thrived on his need for her.

It was a time of energy and excitement. There was a buzz in the air. They went to dances. They drank, smoked and laughed. Strangers warmed to each other and an atmosphere of 'we're all in this together' lent an air of close comradeship to casual relationships.

Tom's great friend was Squadron Leader Peter Whittaker, whom Zara had met in Paris and Nice. She grew very fond of the tall and attractive RAF man and they often made a threesome to go out drinking and dancing. It was a hectic, heightened time of devouring passion and long agonising watches in the darkness of the night.

Flight Lieutenant Tom Armitidge took to Air Force life like a duck to water, bolstered by his wife's support. He was proud of her beauty, amused when Peter fell in love with her. She was the toast of the Squadron. "Kiss Zara for luck," the boys would say, pecking her chastely on the cheek. She had never been more beautiful.

She rented a cottage near Lentmead. It was thatched and set in woodland. The garden was full of bramblings and warblers, chaffinches and cuckoos. Wild flowers grew in abundance, so delicate compared to the blazing opulence of the flowers on the Côte d'Azur: lily-of-the-valley and hollyhocks, yellow archangel and wood sorrel, snowberry, azaleas, and yew and elder trees. The garden was full of butterflies, purple emperor and holly blue, white admiral and yellow brimstone, and watered by its own stream.

Zara loved the cottage. Its chintz curtains patterned with salmon-coloured cabbage roses. its herb garden, its little crooked path and swinging gate, its big log fires and awkward kitchen, were completely different from the spare economic elegance of their apartment in Nice, yet Zara found it a welcoming and cosy place to be.

She observed the blackout cheerfully, accepting rationing not so cheerfully, was careful with fuel and waited for Tom to come home.

When he did she was always ready for him. He never came home, day or night, and found the cottage empty. She was always there.

Sometimes he brought Peter with him and they drank too much, and Peter slept on the sofa or the floor and mumbled embarrassed apologies the next morning. Zara laughed and forgave him prettily.

The news became a little better. The Germans had been winning, their southern offensive was effective. But they made a mistake. Some *Luftwaffe* pilots bombed London against Hitler's orders. It gave Churchill the perfect excuse to bomb Berlin, the dictator's centre of operations.

"We've begun to make progress, Pete," Tom said rubbing his hands.

"Yes, the tide has changed, old boy," Peter said, sipping his whisky. Zara listened.

Tom needed her, needed her love. He told her so often.

She did not allow herself to think of danger. When he was

gone she simply prepared for his return, and waited. When he arrived home at last he was hungry for her, could not keep his hands off her, and she relished his greedy lovemaking, their joint passion. She did not care that the weather was wet, misty, damp and cold. She did not care that there was not enough to eat and a sad lack of choice in food. She did not care, at least not consciously, that Tom was dicing with death. All she could think about was how he loved her, needed her, desired her, and that for the first time in their marriage she was essential to him as he had always been to her.

Peter said, "You give him his strength, Zara. Without you he would be lost."

"He'll never have to do without me."

She was content, her life rich. She adopted twin-sets and tweed skirts. She wore flat brogues and a scarf over her hair. Sonya said she had become dowdy and had lost her chic, and Zara laughed and said she didn't care. Tom loved her just as she was, and she looked like all the other RAF wives. Sonya still managed to look fashionable although Zara was not sure how she did it.

"Black market, dear," her aunt said. "I don't suppose you have it down in Lentmead, but here in London the spivs abound."

They often visited her in London and she phoned them when she could. She always sounded brisk and happy and said she was very content in her role as helper in the Red Cross.

London was being bombed. The Blitz, she called it, and refused to allow Zara to worry about her.

"Look, my dear, if I'm killed – no, don't shriek, *if* I am – it will be for a worthy cause. I don't want any weeping and wailing over me. I've had a rich, full life and really, my dear, I feel quite privileged to do my bit at this advanced stage of my life. I'm actually enjoying myself.

Dmitri, they heard, had joined the Free French Army.

Lucinda had died tragically. They had found her one morning, asphyxiated on her own vomit after a particularly heavy nights drinking.

Lady Abercrombie came home to England after the funeral and bumped into Sonya in a Lyons Corner House. The two had tea together, renewed their friendship, grandly agreed to overlook the mistakes of their children and became the best of friends. Lady Abercrombie, who had a neglected and crumbling old manor house in Lambourne, moved into the flat in Oakwood Court with Sonya. The arrangement suited them both and, Tom said, laughing with Zara one evening over dubious sausages and mash, the two ladies had taken a new lease of life and were thoroughly enjoying themselves helping out in the war-torn capital.

Nina wrote, urging them all to go to the States.

You are mad to stay, Chuck says. He dotes on little Chuck Junior. We all call him just 'Junior'. He is chattering now and has big blue eyes just like his Mommy. Aunt Mary-Anne Pollock and Aunt Sarah-Jane Wilson send you lots of love. I'm doing the kitchen over in blue. We have a refrigerator and ice on tap *all the time*. Can you believe? And a dishwasher. *And* central-heating! Junior is a genius, I promise you. He'll be a ball-player, his Poppa says.

It was so tragic that I lost the baby. We are trying for another so pray for me. It was sad but the doctor says we are both strong and that there is no reason why I should not have more children.

I go to the beauty parlour once a week. Chuck insists. He is *so* good to me. He was incredibly kind when I lost the baby.

When the silly old war ends I hope that you'll all come over here. But if you can, come *now*. Oh, how happy I would be to see you! I long to kiss you all again, Mama and Zara and Dmitri. Tom, too. I pray for Papa every day. I just wish I had told him how much I loved him. If you want to come, just let me know. You are welcome anytime.

God bless you all. Chuck sends regards and Junior a sloppy kiss.

Much love, Nina.

"Imagine having a grandson called Junior," Sonya remarked. "It was hard enough getting used to having a son-in-law called Chuck."

They did not even discuss going to America. Neither of them wanted to leave.

The war raged in Europe. Nightly, Zara watched the searchlights, and could hear the muffled boom of guns and the sound of German planes overhead. She thought of Klaus and realised that he would be in his element in this vast sea of violence.

They went to London when Tom had leave and they could beg a lift from someone who had urgent business, usually government, and a couple of seats to spare, or else they took a train and saved their petrol coupons until they had enough to drive all the way.

They stayed with Sonya in Oakwood Court. She kept them up to date with whatever family news she had received.

London was chaotic. "There is so much to do," she told them. "The homeless – they are so very brave and cheerful – the wounded, too. Whole streets reduced to rubble." She glanced at Zara. "Still, it's good to feel useful."

She changed the conversation and talked of other things. Londoners were dedicated to putting on cheerful faces, she said. Their courage was inspiring.

One night Sonya and Zara got caught in a raid. Tom and Peter had been called back to base and Tom had suggested that Zara stay on and get the train the next morning. There was a party and they sang, 'Run Rabbit, Run Rabbit, Run,

411

Run, Run' and got high on whiskey. On the way back to Oakwood Court the wail of the air-raid warning split the night. They made for the nearest underground and held each other close until it was over.

On other leaves Tom, Zara and Peter went to night clubs in Mayfair, saw shows in the Windmill which, despite the Blitz, boasted 'We Never Close'. Peter had an endless number of Wrens, Waafs, Wacs, nurses, land girls – girls of every description – at his beck and call. When he and Tom hit town he would go immediately to the telephone. Sometimes that was the last they saw of him during their stay. Sometimes he joined them bringing a girl, and sometimes he came alone. Sonya adored him and flirted outrageously with him.

She was worried sick about Dmitri. France had fallen and there was no word of him. Nina's news remained cheerful and positive. She was pregnant again. A little girl arrived. They called her Mitzi.

"It's a dog's name surely?" Sonya asked incredulously. "Chuck Junior I can just about come to terms with, but Mitzi! Oh lord." She shrugged good-humouredly. "I suppose I'll have to get used to it. The war has its uses after all. If Nina saw my face, she'd know how I felt. As it is I'll be accustomed to those names by the time I do see her. She'll never know how I really feel. Oh, Tom, do you really think the Americans will come in?"

"Sure to."

"Oh dear, I'm not sure I want them to. At least part of my little family is safe over there."

"We need them badly, Sonya. We desperately need their help."

He realised what he had said and bit his lip. He glanced across at Zara and smiled reassuringly and, as usual when it became serious, he changed the conversation.

"Let's go to the Savoy for a drink before we eat. I told Peter we'd pick him up there, Gerry permitting."

"Well, after last night I sincerely hope he does," Sonya said. She had been caught the previous evening in Battersea in the ambulance and had spent the night very uncomfortably.

"I do miss my Balkan Sobranies," Zara said.

"We're lucky to have Gold Flake," Tom said, smiling at her and kissing her cheek.

There was the usual piano tinkling and Peter waited for them in the cocktail bar of the Savoy. He was nursing a martini and greeted them with a little less than his usual enthusiasm.

"What is it, old chap?" Tom asked instantly concerned.

"Nothing."

They did not pursue the conversation. They had learned it was better not to. But later, after dinner when Tom was dancing with Sonya, very reluctantly and rather awkwardly, Zara leaned over and took Peter's hand in hers.

"Someone died?" she said, then shook her head. "What a stupid thing to say. Millions are dying. What I mean is …"

"I know what you mean, Princess," Peter said. He always called her that. "Yes, your instinct was right. You're very intuitive. A mate got his last night. Tom, as you know, was off."

There was silence for a moment. The piano was playing 'Roll Out The Barrel'.

The majority of men in the room were in uniform. Zara glanced into her compact mirror, and dabbed some powder on her nose. A piece of the swansdown stuck to her nose and she blew upwards to dislodge it. Peter laughed and removed it for her. She laughed with him and closed the compact with a snap, then rewound the chiffon square around the puff, replacing them in her bag. She took out a Gold Flake which Peter lit for her. She looked at him through the smoke. They smiled at each other, an intimate but friendly smile, and both looked across the floor to where Tom and Sonya were bobbing up and down to 'Sing Boom Ta-ra-ra'. Peter laughed.

413

"Sonya is certainly enjoying herself," he said, "but Tom isn't."

"No, he hates dancing," Zara said and Peter nodded. Her eyes glittered in the smoky atmosphere.

'Take care of him for me, Peter," she whispered, "he is my life."

He nodded again. "I know," he said gravely. "I will."

The band struck up. 'We'll Meet Again', and Sonya and Tom returned to the table. They all joined hands, including a little sailor whom none of them had ever seen before and who was more than a little drunk and tearfully sentimental with it. Tears streamed down his face as he joined with the others and the unmusical but full-throated chorus rose to the rafters,

Keep smiling through just like you always do,
Till the dark clouds turn the dark night into day,
Won't you please say hello to the folks that I know,
Tell them …"

Zara put her arms about Tom and Peter. The drunken sailor tried to encompass them all in an embrace. She held the two men tightly to her slight form, nearly toppling under their weight. They stood holding each other, the three of them, until the music stopped.

The band broke into a romantic rendition of 'Goodnight, Sweetheart' just as the air-raid sirens once more broke into the evening, bringing it to a dramatic close.

It was an ordinary day some weeks later. There were, Zara found, many unremarkable days in England: days when the cool sun neither shone nor didn't shine but hid behind wispy clouds, peeping out every so often before shyly drawing back again. On those days it often rained softly.

Tom had been in a strange mood the previous day. It too had been grey and they had sat on the sofa sipping tea.

"Sonya is quite wonderful," Tom had remarked. "She

does the work of three people up there in London, and is as full of energy as an eighteen year old."

"She's so cheerful in the face of death," Zara agreed. "They all are."

Tom went to the window and looked out at the misty scene. " 'The Soul Sleeps'," he said.

"What was that, darling?"

"It's a poem by Spenser.

Is not short pain well bourne that brings long ease
And lays the soul to sleep in quiet grave,
Sleep after toil, port after stormy seas,
Ease after war, death after life, does gently please."

There was silence in the cosy little room when he had finished. Zara shivered. She disliked talk of death. It was all around but usually not mentioned.

"I love this country, Zara. Oh, I know the weather is abysmal and the food atrocious. Jam roly-poly, rice pudding and semolina!" He laughed. "But I love and respect all it stands for: democracy and freedom, courage in adversity, and a fundamental decency. If I don't make it, darling ..."

She rose swiftly and hurried to his side, laying her cheek on his shoulder. "Don't talk like that. It frightens me," she whispered.

"No, you mustn't be frightened, ever again. It's letting them win, the Nazi scum." His brow wrinkled. "I always remember the Baron. It seems to me that he epitomises everything I despise, everything I'm fighting. Domination of the weak. Arrogance. Insensitivity to others' pain and frailty. Brutality. A worship of strength for its own sake.

"So darling, if I'm for the chop, please, I beg you, remember I chose it. I chose freedom."

She blinked, refusing to assimilate what he was saying.

"I've loved you since the first time I saw you, Zara. I will always remember how you looked that evening at the Negresco, your face touched by the light of a hundred

415

candles. So beautiful. I loved you when you were impossible, and when you were sad and frightened and needed me; when you were glowing with joy, radiant with love, and when you were stubborn as a donkey. I love your passion and your courage. And, my dear, I love you most of all now, here in dull old dreary England, faithfully by my side.

"When I touch you, I never want to let you go. You always give so much of yourself. I'm sorry for the times I wasn't big enough, wise enough, for your love. We are so frail, at the mercy of such passions and storms. I tried sometimes to avoid them, avoid life you could say. For that alone I'm sorry."

She cried, "Hush, hush! I love you, Tom. I've always loved you. Even then."

"I know," he said. "We've been very lucky. Thank you."

It was a lovely mellow moment and in such a mood they made love. She held him close before he left that night, kissing his closed eyes.

"I love you, Tom, my dearest," she whispered, her love for him flooding a body soft from spent passion.

"I know you do. Sweet woman, I love you too."

That night he had a mission to fly.

The next morning she was full of languid content as she drank her weak tea. They would not receive their next ration for another two days.

She reflected ironically that never had life been so uncomfortable, yet never so fulfilling. She had never before been so happy, so content, so tranquil.

She had, over the years, come to terms with her brother's death. She realised that he had been a doomed person and that he had courted disaster. He had a self-destructive personality. As a child she had always thought Anya tough but now, in retrospect, was not so sure. The strong bend with the storm. They were like Tom, she thought fondly. Dear beloved husband.

When she saw Peter walking up the little pathway to the cottage door she knew what had happened. Instantly, in half a heart-beat, she knew. Yet she refused the knowledge, rejected it. She put on a social smile for him when she opened the door.

"Good morning, Peter, have a cup of tea?" she said brightly.

She did not ask him why he was alone. He had never come to the cottage alone before when Tom was not there, but she did not comment on it now, keeping up a bright and brittle chatter all the time, as if he were a stranger at a cocktail party.

"I think we have enough tea left to make you a cup. I try to save it, make it last. I'm very frugal with my ration but it's difficult. Still, only one more day to go, or is it two?"

They stood in the small living room. It was cold. She had been sitting in the kitchen where it was warm. There were the dead ashes of last night's fire in the grate.

"Don't, Zara," Peter said quietly. "Please don't."

"I found a little man," she continued relentlessly. "Tom and I met him in the local. He's what I think Sonya calls a 'spiv'. Anyhow, he can get one almost anything for a price. Human nature never changes, does it? There are the survivors and ... and ..."

"Please, Zara, don't make it hard for me."

There were tears in his eyes but she rattled on, as if by preventing him from imparting his news she might keep things as they were. Once the words were uttered it would be a fact, a fact she could not bear.

"He got me the sexiest nylons, and he even managed a packet of Balkan Sobranies, but it must have been an old packet because the tobacco tasted vile. They can't make them any more, I'm sure. All the boys are fighting. Even in Russia. The Communists. They are on our side, Peter. That's odd, isn't it? They are saving the lives of a lot of what they call 'White Russians'. Life is certainly strange. I don't think they are ..."

417

"Zara, he's dead. Tom's dead."

There was silence. She looked at him piteously, a pleading expression in her eyes.

"No," she moaned, turning her head from side to side. "Please, Peter, no. Please, no."

"The party was nearly over when he got it. I said, 'Look, Tom, you've got a 109 on your tail.' It was too late. He didn't hear me. I saw him crash. There's no hope. But I got the blighter that did it. Tom died a hero's death, Zara."

She turned on him, eyes blazing. "Do you think I care about that? Do you think I gave a damn about anything except him?"

"Zara, it's what he would have wanted."

"I don't believe that. Not at all. He didn't want to die. None of you do. You just mouth platitudes like that, not meaning a word. It helps you to feel better about the carnage. Tom was in love with life, I know that. You didn't hold him and feel the life-force within him. So don't tell me he wanted this. It's not true."

"Zara, I only knew him as a friend. He was your lover and husband. He told me to take care of you ..."

All the anger and defiance went out of her face. She sank back into her chair.

"Oh, Peter, what will I do without him? How shall I live?"

"I can't imagine. I only know you will. You will live, you will survive, because Tom expected it of you."

She shook her head wearily. "I don't know how, without him. I don't know how." A shuddering, aching sigh shook her body.

"Have a brandy, Zara."

She shook her head but he gave her a glass with a large measure of the fiery liquid and stood over her till she drank it.

She was fortified by brandy for the next few weeks. Even before the funeral service, rigid with grief, she gulped down a generous measure in a vain attempt to numb her feelings.

Peter tried his best to be supportive but was aware of the fact that she was unconscious of his presence at her side. Like a wounded animal she shrank from contact with others, shuttering herself up behind the wall of her grief. She held people off with tablets and drink.

Sonya wrangled some time off and came down to her. Tom had won every medal for bravery in the book: DSO, VC, MC, DFC. It meant nothing to Zara.

"Wait, my dear, it will take time," her aunt said. "When you can see more clearly you'll come to realise, as I do, that Tom's death was a wonderfully generous action. And a necessary one. You had such love together. Enough and more to keep you warm. That was how your husband wanted to go."

"Peter said that too, but I want him here with me ..."

She looked at her aunt, the streaks of tears across her ravaged face. "I miss him so, Aunt Sonya. I miss him with every bone in my body; every minute, every second. You cannot believe the pain I feel."

"Well, it is better to have that kind of pain than the kind I suffered," Sonya said sadly. "You loved him. You told him so. You proved it to him every minute, as you say, every second. You have nothing to reproach yourself with. Whereas I ..."

"Oh, Aunt, I'm sorry, so sorry. Sometimes I'm so selfish."

"And you should be, at this time. You have every right to be selfish. But, dear child, you were generous with Tom Armitidge. I was niggardly with Vassily until it was too late."

The gas fire was burning low. The women sat hunched over it, their cardigans clutched tightly around themselves, hands under arms to keep warm.

The next morning the look of overwhelming sadness had lifted from Zara. Her aunt was returning to London that day and at breakfast was thankful to see the change.

419

"Thank goodness," she said. "You've acepted it at last. I don't mind telling you I was worried."

Zara shook her head. "No, dearest Aunt. Sit down. I want to tell you something." She took Sonya's hand. "You must not think I'm mad or imagining things," she said earnestly, "but something wonderful happened last night. I saw Tom."

"What?"

"No, listen, he was not as he was when he was here with us. Alive. He was different – I can't explain – more grown up without being old. I know it's difficult, Aunt, but I can only tell you what I saw. He said, 'It's all right, Zara. Everything is all right. We'll meet again.' Then he was not there anymore."

She looked at her aunt who had opened her mouth to protest. "I don't want to discuss it," she said. "*I* know it was Tom. I know he was reassuring me. I don't care whether you believe me or not ..."

"Of course I do," Sonya mumbled, but Zara hushed her.

"It's really not important, Aunt. The important thing is that I saw him, and I know I'll see him again. Some day."

Epilogue

When, twenty years later, Zara told me of how she had seen Tom so clearly in her mind after he had died, I did not know what to say.

"It's all right, Janine, I know. You're young and it sounds crazy to you. But believe me, my dear, just that time after his death I saw Tom and it brought me great strength and comfort. Perhaps he knew I was to need it all before those bitter years of war would finally be over.

"In 1942 we learned that Dmitri, working undercover in the French Resistance, had been captured by the Nazis, tortured and shot. My poor cousin," she sighed, "I still miss him so." And for a moment the light went out of her magnificent dark eyes.

She shook her head as if to clear her thoughts. She was smoking the cigarettes which made me cough. "I say it now so calmly, as if it was an ordinary thing. 'He was captured, tortured and shot.' What do you know of these things today? Then it was an ordinary occurrence. In German concentration camps, in interrogation centres, in Japanese prisoner-of-war camps. But the agony of living with the knowledge of it happening to your loved ones is something else. It is lodged here." She thumped her heart fiercely. Her lips trembled and the large dark eyes were pools of pain.

"After the war we were all looking for relatives and friends. Finding out the almost always tragic fate of loved ones. Oh God, it was a sad time, a shameful time. The concentration camps disgorged skeletal horrors. The world was appalled. Too late. Too late. I was left quite alone. I lost everyone I had loved and known except Nina. But she was American by then. She had not known war. My one visit to her proved a failure. I could not begin to be interested in the things that preoccupied her: motherhood; housewifery; bargains; the latest fashions. We had been apart too long, our lives had taken such different directions.

"Ah, Janine, it was a terrible time, knowing I had lost all my loved ones. Gerda and Dirk died in Auschwitz. They were arrested in Holland and transported there. Frau Kettner was killed in Berlin in the Allied bombing. Sonya, dearly beloved Sonya ..." Her breath caught in her throat and for the first time I saw her cry." She died so close to the end of the fighting. A doodle-bug, I think they called them ... something that sounded like a child's toy blew her to dust.

"I came here after the war. This was Sonya's flat. I was so sick of Europe. It was mostly rubble anyway, and the sight of the Côte d'Azur brought back memories so unbearably, sweetly painful that I could not live there. Besides, I admire the British. This was, after all, Tom's country. I felt life would be ..." she sought for a word ... "undemanding here. Here people respect your privacy. They leave you alone." Again the glorious smile that chased away age and revealed exactly how beautiful she must have been in her youth. "I did not mean you, my darling. You are my friend. *Ma chère amie*. But I miss the sun so much. The sun changes everything. Ah, well."

I thought I would not hear from her until the Monday. I had a lazy, hair-washing, man-forgetting evening at home watching 'Danger Man' on the TV, a towel around my head, and went to bed around ten o'clock.

The phone rang at 10.30. Wondering who it could be, I picked up the receiver.

It was an overwrought Zara. Would I come over? she kept

asking repeatedly. I agreed, of course, and pulled on jeans and a sweater.

The door to her flat stood open when I got there. I knocked and when there was no answer stepped inside, looking around for her. She did not answer my greeting and I grew alarmed. She was not in the sitting room or the little kitchen. I pushed open the door to her bedroom, unfamiliar territory, and recoiled at the sight which met my eyes. Zara was sitting on her bed, her upturned hands hanging beside her. They and her dress, the lovely silver silk, were splashed with blood. She looked at me, her large eyes shining with a weird excited light.

"This time I made sure," she said.

I did not know what she meant at first. I could not think. Then realisation dawned as I remembered the shooting in the castle in the snow.

I was in turmoil not knowing what to do, how to react. This was not war-torn Europe. This was England and there were laws and policemen to enforce them. This was murder. But she was my friend. "Oh God, what have you done," I cried.

But she was somewhere else. There was a far-away look in her eyes. "Viscountess Bunsell was so kind," she said. "I hate to repay her generosity like this." She spoke as if she were talking of being late for a date.

I had known about the Viscountess Bunsell from Zara. She was a good friend who had been an acquaintance on the Riviera in the old days. She always asked Zara to her parties and Zara enjoyed them. The Viscountess lived in a large mansion in Richmond and entertained on a grand scale. Zara plucked at my arm.

"She told me she had a surprise visitor who was an old friend. Can you believe that? He said he was an old friend? Perhaps he thought of himself as that, I don't know. I long ago ceased to try to figure out his behaviour. She said this old friend was looking forward to meeting me again."

She paused and opened the case on the table beside her. As she lit a cigarette I noticed the blood had dried on her hands. She did not seem to notice.

"Can you imagine how I felt when I saw him – the Baron – after all these years? No, silly question, of course you can't!

"I walked into her large drawing room. It's very overcrowded, rather Victorian. Not my taste at all, Janine, wine damask and big game trophies. I stood in the doorway."

I knew that habit well. Zara always did love making an entrance.

"There was a buzz of conversation that became muted as they all looked round and began welcoming me. There were a lot of people there but I would have known him anywhere. He stood there, smiling at me. I had been greeting people, happy to see them, but as I saw him I froze."

She had been talking to me on a wave of excitement, like a young girl telling you of her first party or a ball where she has met someone special. But now she seemd to droop. Her shoulders sank and the lines of her face turned down. There was a dumb animal bewilderment in her eyes. I sat beside her and held her hand. She did not seem to notice.

"He had not changed much," she said. "He looked well. Sleek. His hair was white, his face tanned. He shook my hand and I said, 'You are brown,' and he said, 'Yes. I have been skiing.'

"I couldn't believe it, Janine! I was talking to him there in the reception room. I hated him so much, all my life had been poisoned by this devil, and here I was exchanging pleasantries with him. I thought of Sasha, that lovely innocent. Perhaps of his own accord he might have become a homosexual, I don't know. Perhaps he might have become a drug addict. But not that way. Not so soon. Not the way it happened. And I stood there telling that monster he was tanned!"

She looked at me, then glanced away. "If that had been

424

all … I have never been reconciled for the loss of my brother. But seeing me there, taken offguard, he couldn't resist taunting me with his own cleverness."

" 'I was delighted to hear that you came through the war safely, my dear. But then, you always were a survivor, with a little help from me, of course.'

" 'I can't imagine what you mean by that, Klaus,' I said. 'I haven't laid eyes on you since 1939.' I could well imagine how he had occupied himself under the Reich, but he always was adept at covering up unpalatable facts. To look at him there, tanned and smiling genially, you would have thought him the picture of respectability.

"I wanted to run. I swear to you, Janine, if it had been possible I would have fled from the place at that moment and none of the rest would have happened …"

The cigarette had burned unheeded almost to the level of her bloodstained fingers. I guessed what 'the rest' entailed but let her go on, uninterrupted.

"He was too quick for me. He took my hand between both of his, imprisoning it, crushing my fingers cruelly when to a casual observer he would seem no more than a handsome old man behaving gallantly. And all the time that foul insinuating voice …

" 'From the moment I saw you at the Rostov's ball, I knew you were the one. I had to have you, but I'd dug a hole for myself, taking Anya as a mistress. Your father knew about it, of course, and I hardly think he'd have held it against me. After all, half of Moscow and St Petersburg had had her, including his own brother-in-law!

" 'No, oddly enough it was your step-mother who tried to warn me off. For an unscrupulous, totally degenerate whore she had a streak of moral rectitude when it came to you.'

"Oh, Janine, his smile when he said that! He was evil incarnate and no one else in the whole crowded room had any idea what was among us.

" 'When she realised what I had in mind for you, she

threatened to speak to Andrei,' he told me. 'I thought it best that both of them should meet with an accident, and with things the way they were at the time, nothing could have been simpler to arrange. Your poor fool of a father played straight into my hands, allowing me to make the arrangements for his family's flight from Russia.

" 'A band of deserters was located for me by a servant. I gave them a little money and just enough vodka to put fire in their stomachs until they had carried out my instructions.'

"I felt my head begin to swim. My knees started to give way. I would have fainted on the spot if the grip of his hands on mine hadn't been so painful.

" 'You led my family to destruction!' I wanted to scream. I thought of broken bodies, staining the snow around with their life's blood. 'You murdered our faithful servants and poor brave Princess Anya and my dear papa,' I whispered, my lips stiff.

I sat there in that civilised gathering and I knew he had to die. Alwyas he had been a black shadow, an evil darkness spreading over my life. He had harmed all the people I had loved best. He had destroyed my brother, killed my father. I knew I blamed him, indirectly for Tom's death; he was, in my mind the epitomization of Nazism. All the energy I had was gathered together inside me and it impelled me towards his destruction. And I believe Janine, fate directed me too. Why else should I have come prepared? Why else?

" 'It's very hot,' I said to him. 'Why don't we go outside for a moment?'

"I had dropped my bag when he took my hand. He allowed me to pull free of him, and pick up the bag with bruised and shaking fingers.

" 'Excuse me,' I said to the Viscountess who had come to join us. She was surprised. 'Where are you going?' 'Something I have to say to Klaus in private.' He smiled as if I had suggested an assignation. So stupid! I had attacked him once before, I had threatened him since, yet he was quite

426

unconcerned. Maybe he would not have been if he'd realised that among Dmitri's effects, returned after the war, was a revolver. A strange memento, perhaps, but one of the few things of his I possess. I take it everywhere.

"He followed me into the hall. There is a Persian carpet there, priceless, silver and blue, grey and magenta, a thousand years old. He stood on it, smiling at me. I turned and took the gun out of my bag. He looked at it and laughed. It struck him only as funny.

"The Viscountess had followed us a little way behind. I was a few feet away from Klaus, about the distance I am from that table." She pointed at the table half-way across the room. "I think she was puzzled by my behaviour, and a little curious. She stood at the door and I heard her gasp when she saw the pistol.

"Then he said, 'Oh, don't be silly, Zara. Put that away.'" The Viscountess said, and I nearly laughed, 'Don't spoil the carpet!' I kept my eyes on him. He said, still unconcerned, 'The time for recrimination is past.' He told me that 'We can be friends,' he said. 'We have shared so much.' He walked towards me, just like the last time." She paused and sighed, "I shot him five times.

" 'This is for the rapes.'" And I shot him.

" 'This is for the corruption of Sasha.' And I shot him.

" 'This is for his death.' And I shot him.

" 'This is for the babies I could not have.' And I shot him.

" 'This is for my father and for Anya.'

"After the first shot he kept walking, just like the first time. After the second he stopped. He looked at me in astonishment, listening. He said, 'Yes, yes,' then sank to his knees and I shot him again and again and again.

"Suddenly there was blood everywhere, spurting from his nose, his mouth, his body. I knelt and felt his heart and the pulse in his throat. Nothing. The Viscountess just stood transfixed. "I am sorry about the carpet," I said. I walked to the cupboard and got my coat then calmly left the place. The taxi was there. 'I want to go home,' I said, and the driver obediently took me, and here I am. Quite soon all hell will break loose. But I wanted to tell you the end of the story. I want you to know the truth. Hold my hand, Janine."

She looked exhausted. There were dark circles under her eyes. She lay down on the bed.

"I'm at peace now," she said, "at last I'm at peace. It's all over. Get me some water, please. And as I went I heard her remark. "It's amazing how if you tell people to do something firmly enough, most of them will obey you instantly."

I did not notice until later that there was a carafe and glass on her bedside table. And an empty pill bottle. It was all over by the time I did see them. I'm not at all sure it would have made any difference if I had noticed straight away. She would never change her story, bend the truth a little for a plea. She would tell them she had deliberately shot and killed in cold blood Baron Klaus Hoffen von Eldrich, and she would tell them she had felt no remorse. One way or another Zara was doomed.

I brought back the water and saw she lay almost as I had left her. I raised her up and she sipped it. I put the glass on the table beside the carafe but still did not see it. I was too concerned about her.

"I'll see Tom," she said.

I did not understand.

"I'm going to see Tom," she repeated to me.

It was then I had the first stirrings of suspicion. I became more and more certain as the minutes passed that she had taken something. I thought about it and decided, under the circumstances, not to do anything. What good would it do to force her to live on in a world she was tired of and that she knew would try her for murder?

It was very dark in the room. She motioned to me and I leant nearer.

"Get me the 'Chypre'," she said. I brought her the bottle from the dressing table.

She could hardly focus now and her words were slurred.

"It was his favourite," she said, and put some behind her ears. "I want to smell nice for him," she whispered.

"Oh, Tom, my darling, I will see you soon," she said.

They were the last words she spoke. Soon afterwards she fell into a coma. I sat with her, one blood-stained hand held loosely between my own.

By the time the bell rang and there were footsteps, boots pounding up the stairs and the loud voices of police calling me to 'open up', her hand was quite cold, her pulse had been still for some time. She had gone. To Tom.

DARK ROSALEEN

Genevieve Lyons

She was a gypsy woman, as wild as she was beautiful. They called her Rosaleen. Dark Rosaleen – after Ireland . . .

Some might say their love had been destined. He came to the old ruins one pale-gold day, drawn there by the sweetness of her song. He came and he stayed. But he was Creagh Jeffries, aristocrat and son of Ireland, and he could not stay for long – could love no woman as much as he loved his country and its cause. Not even her, Dark Rosaleen, the mother of his child. But the legacy of their love would set into motion a chain of events that would change both their worlds forever.

From the opulence of Usher Castle to the slums of Dublin, from the lush countryside of Wicklow to the dazzling decadence of Paris in the 1860s, here is a story peopled with unforgettable characters, filled with life and love. Here is a story that only Ireland could have inspired

'Engaging'   *Irish Times*

FUTURA PUBLICATIONS
FICTION
0 7088 4218 6

THE GREEN YEARS

Genevieve Lyons

In the lush, idyllic countryside of County Wicklow, two friends share their childhood years . . .

Aisling, rich and beautiful, looks forward to a charmed life. But disappointment and tragedy are to shadow her as her career as an actress is shattered and love eludes her.

Camilla, impoverished but fiercely proud, learns early to expect nothing for free and it is in Dublin that she finally finds the success and fame for which she has fought for so long.

As Aisling's life deteriorates into the self-destruction of alcoholism it is Camilla who stands by her, who reminds her of the precious green years of their youth and who shows her how to realise those far-off dreams of happiness and love.

From the beauty of Ireland and the quiet charm of Tuscany to the sensuality of South America, THE GREEN YEARS is the passionate, vivid story of two women and the friendship that shapes their lives.

Also by Genevieve Lyons from Futura:

SLIEVELEA
'Fantastic . . . totally absorbing'
Daily Mirror

FUTURA PUBLICATIONS
FICTION
0 7088 3677 1

All Futura Books are available at your bookshop or newsagent, or can be ordered from the following address:

Futura Books,
Cash Sales Department,
P.O. Box 11,
Falmouth,
Cornwall TR10 9EN.

Alternatively you may fax your order to the above address. Fax No. 0326 76423.

Payments can be made as follows: Cheque, postal order (payable to Macdonald & Co (Publishers) Ltd) or by credit cards, Visa/Access. Do not send cash or currency. UK customers: please send a cheque or postal order (no currency) and allow 80p for postage and packing for the first book plus 20p for each additional book up to a maximum charge of £2.00.

B.F.P.O. customers please allow 80p for the first book plus 20p for each additional book.

Overseas customers including Ireland, please allow £1.50 for postage and packing for the first book, £1.00 for the second book, and 30p for each additional book.

NAME (Block Letters) ....

ADDRESS ....

....

☐ I enclose my remittance for _____

☐ I wish to pay by Access/Visa Card

Number ☐☐☐☐☐☐☐☐☐☐☐☐☐☐☐☐

Card Expiry Date ☐☐☐☐